APHRODITE'S
STAND

SANDRA SCOTT

APHRODITE'S STAND

iUniverse books may be ordered through booksellers or by contacting:

iUniverse
1663 Liberty Drive
Bloomington, IN 47403
www.iuniverse.com
1-800-Authors (1-800-288-4677)

ISBN: 978-1-5320-3464-0 (sc)
ISBN: 978-1-5320-3466-4 (hc)
ISBN: 978-1-5320-3465-7 (e)

Library of Congress Control Number: 2017917744

Print information available on the last page.

iUniverse rev. date: 11/30/2017

This book is dedicated to Mike and Andra.
Mike inspired me to learn more about Greek culture,
and he introduced me to his lovely wife, who gave
me permission to use her beautiful name.

A special acknowledgment to
Jonelle, LaSchelle, LaTrice, Sonya, Vallerie, and Kenisha,
the classy women who suffered through my first rough draft
of this book, willingly sacrificed their time and withstood
abuse of their sagacious senses to be my beta readers,
and gave me valuable input for the finished product.

Last but certainly not least, I dedicate this book to my
heavenly Father; his son, Jesus Christ; and the Holy
Spirit, to whom all the honor and glory is given.

In remembrance of
Herman Scott, Nathan Scott, and Johnny Felder Jr.
Gone but never forgotten.

Also for Sharron,
a busy wife, mother, and caregiver who is also
one of my editors, a spiritual sister, and the
dearest friend anyone could ever have.
I cherish you.

What is that which most seek yet are
unwilling to embrace once it is found?
The truth.

Jesus responded, "All who love the truth
recognize that what I say is true."
"What is truth?" Pilate asked.

—John 18:37–38

PROLOGUE

They say the first step on any journey ultimately leads to one's doom.

Did "they" actually say that, or is it something you just conjured up? Andra Williams chewed her bottom lip and then caught herself before she wreaked havoc on her perfectly applied lip gloss. *Shoot, I don't know.*

She looked around. *Are you sure about this?*

The question piggybacked on other nagging thoughts, and with each passing second, her uncertainty increased. Desperate, she searched her mind's tumultuous depths, trying to find anything that resembled a reasonable answer. To her dismay, she couldn't.

She swallowed the nervous hiccup that followed on the heels of her accelerated breathing. *It's not too late. You can turn around and—*

"Andra, did you hear me?"

The female spoke quietly yet delivered her words with icicle sharpness. Each pierced Andra's ear canal like a shard of glass. Racine, her younger sister, leaned in closer, her rigid mouth projecting a fine mist that sprinkled Andra's earlobe.

"Sis, are you sure about this?"

Racine's question startled her—not so much because of its claustrophobic proximity but because it echoed her own thoughts.

Andra hated when Racine read her mind.

Am I? she thought. *Am I sure?*

The truth was—no, she wasn't sure.

Andra's pulse sped up, competing with her rapid breathing,

the combination pushing her toward hyperventilation. Frantic, she performed a nosedive into the miniature white roses she held and breathed deeply. She then went the extra mile by mouthing a prayer, hoping the combination would anesthetize her nerves.

It didn't.

"Please think about this, Andra," Racine pleaded, her previous ire replaced by a quiet desperation. "Hey, daydreamer, are you listening to me?"

The roses trembled. Light perspiration popped across her forehead, but she dared not wipe it, for fear of messing up her makeup.

Andra swallowed a whimper, while stifling the urge to bite into perfectly manicured fingernails. Beside her, Racine shifted on impatient feet, waiting for an answer to a question that, quite frankly, Andra considered a rhetorical one. She was determined to assert her right as the older sister, so she chose not to respond.

This was her day; she wasn't about to let the brat ruin it.

Laying imaginary odds on a bet she knew she'd win, Andra anticipated more doomsday whispers from her sister. *Nope, not gonna have it!* Discreetly, she applied an elbow to Racine's ribs. Her nervousness temporarily forgotten, she choked back a giggle at Racine's "Oomph!"

"Boy, you'd better be glad ..." Racine grumbled, nursing her bruised side.

Glad about what? Andra wondered. *I could only imagine!*

Flashing a victory smile Racine's way, she looked to her right.

Jayson.

A classical face displayed a high, aristocratic forehead and cream-colored skin that glowed beneath a headful of thick black hair. Jayson's eyes—*Oh, his eyes!*—were arresting. They were the color of rich, swirling chocolate, ready to spill into the blackest of midnight.

Jayson's looks, manner, and stature were reminiscent of his country's legendary Greek gods—and he was only moments away from being all hers.

That's a good thing, right?

His dark irises shone brightly with a hunger that left Andra breathless. Soon her anxiety gave way to an animalistic desire, and she glanced away. However, seconds later, her eyes magnetically returned. Shivering with delight, she surrendered to his captive stare.

"You look beautiful," he mouthed.

His stare intensified. A different rhythm now drove her heartbeat, its tempo flowing into her ear and throat canals to simulate a deaf-and-dumb state.

From what seemed a great distance, she heard Jayson's response to the question asked of him.

"Yes," he said. "I do."

This is such a major step, girl, Andra thought.

A humongous one. Andra imagined telepathic agreement from Racine, who now stood perfectly rigid. *This is nuts! You have no right to do this to the family.*

Yes, Andra knew it was crazy—the craziest thing she'd ever done in her characteristically sane, if not monotonous, life. Yet because it was so crazy, maybe it couldn't be anything but right?

At the sound of her name, her eyes locked onto the officiating minister's kind face.

"Do you take this man, Jayson Theonopilus, as your lawfully wedded husband?"

"You mean *awfully wedded*, don't you?" Racine mocked for Andra's ears alone.

Andra Williams, what do you know about love? Do you really want to do this?

"Yes," she said with 95 percent surety. "I do."

Separating her fingers, Andra presented her hand to Jayson. His face sober, he reached forth with his own—so pale in contrast to hers—and tenderly slipped on a diamond-arrayed platinum wedding band. He maneuvered it halfway up and stopped. With an exaggerated frown, he struggled to push it past her knuckle.

"Quit playing," she said, attempting to keep a straight face.

Grinning, he winked and finished shifting the ring into place.

She next placed a matching band on his left ring finger.

Beside her, Racine sighed heavily.

The minister concluded the intimate ceremony by pronouncing them husband and wife.

She finally exhaled; her lips parting as she waited for Jayson to claim them.

I'm a twenty-six-year-old virgin, Andra thought. *After tonight, I can retire that title for good.*

His well-sculptured hands pulled her in. As their lips touched, she sighed in both ecstasy and agony.

Jayson was Greek. Andra was black.

What have we gotten ourselves into?

As their kiss deepened, the force behind it pushed aside her sister's vehement objections while hardly leaving any breathing room for her own doubts.

She could hear giggly oohs and aahs across the sanctuary.

"Jeez!" Racine rattled her bridesmaid bouquet as if ready to pitch it at them. "Get a room, why don't you?"

"Oh, we will," Andra said against her husband, causing him to pull back with laughter. "Gladly."

"Family and friends, let us celebrate." The minister smiled, prompting Andra and Jayson to face those gathered inside the small chapel. "I'd like to introduce to you for the rest of their lives Mr. and Dr. Jayson Theonopilus."

Was she sure?

Glancing at her wedding rings, Andra looked up to stare at a room filled with grinning faces. Bravely, she reciprocated with a shaky smile.

She guessed that question didn't matter much anymore.

1

"Ladies and gentlemen, welcome aboard overseas flight 2638 to Athens, Greece. This will be a full flight, so please store your items in the overhead bins, and then take your seats as quickly as possible. We suggest you try to position your carry-ons efficiently in order to accommodate all passengers. Once again, I repeat: this will be a full flight. Thank you for your cooperation."

The intercom voice continued its drone, commending everyone for choosing that particular airline and assuring the boarding passengers they would have a wonderful and safe flight.

Obediently, Andra lifted her black medical bag and, with fumbling hands, attempted to efficiently maneuver the case into the overhead compartment.

"Pardon me, miss."

A male passenger pivoted sideways in the aisle to avoid coming into contact with her bottom but still managed to brush against it anyway. She threw a sizzling glare over her shoulder, and as the man intercepted it, he produced a lopsided grin as an apology. Then, as if tipping an imaginary hat in gratitude for the impromptu contact, he continued his stroll toward the restroom a few rows down.

Her hands curling into fists, Andra thought, *Jackass.* Then she willed her fingers to uncurl. *Peasant girl, put that on a slow burn.*

Exhaling, she mentally made way for genteel Lady Andra; it was she who refused to get off her queenly throne, chase the prick down the aisle, and belt him one. Still, before she had a chance to settle into true sovereign mode, jostling from another passenger forced Her Ladyship to abdicate the throne and gladly return it to peasant Andra.

She swore under her breath. Not caring anymore if her black bag took up more room than necessary, she shoved it into the bin's corner and plopped herself down in her window seat. Suddenly, a boarding passenger wearing a white shirt tickled Andra's peripheral vision. Its appearance pushed her anger to the side, making way for guilt. Thoughts of future patients traipsing with familiar regularity through her hospital's ER, knowing she would be absent, made her feel like a mother hen who had deliberately abandoned her baby chicks.

Sighing heavily, Andra reclined. Closing her eyes, she recalled her trek to the chief of medicine's office to request a leave of absence. The hospital's well-scrubbed corridors gleamed almost too brightly as she meandered along them, her hands stuffed inside her white smock's pockets, her head down. It took more than the usual travel time to make it there, and upon her arrival, she shifted on nervous feet before the chief's massive desk, feeling like a high-schooler called into the principal's office.

That day, Dr. Sherman graciously gave his approval for an indefinite leave of absence. Despite his agreement, she sensed the elder gentleman's disappointment at her request, which forced her to accept his consent with an awkward thank-you and a quick exodus from his office.

She sighed. Her memory of that visit piled on even more guilt than before.

"Excuse me, miss. Is there anything I can do for you before we take off?" The man's voice, slightly effeminate, was delightfully agreeable. "Anything at all?"

Blinking, Andra took in a friendly face lit with pale anticipation. His sandy hair, although cut neatly enough, fell over his light brown eyes. Liking him instantly, she read his name tag.

"Thank you, Keven. I'm fine."

Returning her smile, his eyes immediately rose to the open overhead bin. Excited, he pointed to her black medical bag.

"Is that yours? Are you a real honest-to-goodness doctor?"

Andra laughed. Using her pointer finger, she drew on her chest. "Cross my heart."

"And hope to die," Keven said, finishing with a childlike flourish. He then glanced around and leaned forward to whisper, "But not on our airline, of course."

"Of course," Andra said, laughing.

He straightened, resting a pale hand on the headrest belonging to Jayson's empty seat. "Doctor, if you don't mind, I'd like to tell the other attendants about you. We're always on the lookout for, for instance, physicians, policemen, or even pilots who're traveling with us. You never know when we might need one."

"Okay by me."

"Good," Keven said, nodding professionally. "Now, if there's anything you need, just let me know."

"Thank you," she said. "I will."

As the eager-to-please attendant moved on to greet other passengers, Andra diverted her attention to the small, round window and the activity on the tarmac beyond.

A slow-moving tram pulled to a jerky stop just as three baggage personnel jumped off. With a brisk efficiency manufactured by routine, they unloaded luggage from the flat cargo bed, transferring each into the airplane's belly as if racing against an invisible stopwatch. Studying the quickness with which they worked, she made a game of searching for her matching maroon cases.

Unable to spot them, Andra gave up and faced forward. A coldness deep inside made her frame shiver as her mind involuntarily traveled back to the day Jayson had placed the dreaded international call that had introduced her to his Greek family.

She harbored mixed feelings about the overseas conversation. Her lips produced a smile at the memory of speaking with Jayson's father, Georigios Theonopilus; his tone had proven friendly, sporting a warm, charming accent.

Her smile disappeared.

Then there was Stefano Theonopilus.

In contrast to his winsome father, Jayson's older brother was cold and reticent.

Andra shuddered as she replayed her conversation with him. While Jayson had stood close by, his face glowing with unaware delight, she'd forced Lady Andra onto center stage to put on a performance that would've rivaled any Oscar-winning act. She believed Lady A had done a fantastic job, despite Stefano's bouts of unfriendly silence.

Once the excruciating call had ended, she'd wanted to put the whole thing into rational perspective, but she found it difficult. From the day she and Jayson had tied the knot, an embryo of dread had planted itself inside her emotional womb, where it slowly grew, until finally, she'd given birth to out-and-out terror the moment she'd hung up from speaking with Stefano Theonopilus.

The word *seat belt* filtered in from somewhere overhead. Obediently, Andra clasped hers together and pulled tight.

Since then, that frosty phone conversation had revisited her many times. Like a bully, it picked on her, forcing the occasional nightmare she'd had prior to their nuptials to reoccur with alarming frequency.

Her vision cleared. The front cabin came into sharp view, along with the slowing trickle of remaining boarders. Andra bit her lip.

"What a time to grab a sports magazine," she whispered. "If Jayson misses this flight, I'll kill him."

Yes, he'll be dead—and you'll be flying off to Greece alone.

A tiny smile broke out at Lady Andra's response. She imagined her husband would rather throw himself under the aircraft's crushing wheels than let her fly off to Athens without him. Deliberately, she depressed her panic button and put her total focus on him.

Despite the fact that he was only three years her senior and sometimes goofy as hell, at twenty-nine, Jayson's maturity went beyond his age. He was what her elderly family members called an old soul, and it was that particular character trait that had convinced an independent woman like herself to come to love him.

Immediately, her mind revisited the last forty-eight hours. Intense lovemaking had consumed that first night as husband and wife.

"The plane ride's going to be more than eighteen hours," Jayson had whispered in her ear after the third time, somewhere around two o'clock in the morning. "I want to make sure I have my fill of you before then."

Her laughter answered him, its sound somewhere between a chuckle and a purr. His strong hands lifted her onto his outstretched body. Straddling him, Andra arched her back as their bodies fused to become one again.

"Still," he'd said, his busy hands capturing her breasts, "there's always the airplane's restroom."

They'd slept away the next twenty-four hours.

"A penny for your thoughts, Doc."

At the inviting voice, she grinned mischievously. Slowly, her eyes opened. Standing over her was the stuff sensual dreams were made of—well, at least hers. If her dark pigmentation had allowed it, a blush would've burned both cheeks until they were fiery red.

Jayson's eyes studied her parted lips and then lowered to her silk blouse, which covered the pebbly effects of her lustful musings.

His lips curled in an animal-like manner.

"Or maybe I should give you a hundred dollars for your thoughts. They seem to be expensively juicy."

"Whatever!" Andra said dryly. "I wouldn't take a million for them. They're all mine." She waited for her husband's eyes to return to hers. She then shook her head. "Now, Mr. Theonopilus, I don't believe ministers-in-training are supposed to ogle females in such a lewd, suggestive way."

He lifted his left hand, wiggling the finger that sported his wedding band. "When it comes to you, baby, I've got permission—from the Big Guy." His roaming eyes scanned her face and returned to her blouse. His soft growl was both a warning and a promise. "So, Doc, even the things we're going to do in that bathroom will be ordained by God himself."

Jayson's seductive threat gut-punched Andra. Delicious images of their coupling inside the plane's enclosed lavatory flooded her brain. The first-class cabin shrank until they were the only people aboard.

"Well—"

"Welcome aboard."

The cabin widened to its normal dimensions when a blonde flight attendant appeared at Jayson's side. Her lightly tanned skin glowed as she watched him, and her sparkling blue eyes displayed a mix of professionalism and desire.

"Sir," she said, her tone familiar, "we're just about ready to take off. Is there anything I can do for you? Anything at all?"

Andra compared the female flight attendant to Keven, her male counterpart. Although both had recited the same customary words, assuring a passenger that great customer service was just one request away, the delivery had been world's different.

At the woman's brashness, she stirred angrily, causing the attendant's blue eyes to dart her way. After studying Andra for all of half a second, the leggy attendant immediately dismissed her.

"Come, sir; let me assist you to your seat."

The flight attendant's voice flowed like molten gold, her words dripping in honeyed persuasion.

Jayson paused to wink at Andra, only to rearrange his expression into pleasant indifference. He faced the enamored woman. "No bother," he said. After lowering himself into his seat, in one fluid motion he clasped together the silver buckles of his seat belt and took Andra's hand. "Here's my seat—next to my wife."

The woman's disapproving eyes shifted back to Andra, taking more time to scrutinize natural shoulder-length locks, dark skin, and matching brown eyes. In a microsecond, the flight attendant's baby blues turned, changing from simmering warmth to glacial heat once they dropped further to the brown and cream-colored fingers intimately entwined.

"Of course, sir," she said, stiffening. Her quick expression displayed a threat of future neglect and avoidance. "Of course!"

Throwing her nose in the air, the flight attendant stalked off to assist other passengers.

Andra clamped her mouth around her giggle. She shrugged. "Well, hubby, I guess the bathroom rendezvous is out," she whispered. "If we get caught by her, she might just have us arrested for indecent exposure in a public place."

"Let her."

Casually looking about, Jayson reached over to undo Andra's top button. When his fingers slipped to the next button, she swatted at him. He chuckled, pushing her hand aside. "Are you wearing anything under there?" he asked. Lifting her blouse, he peeked inside. His lips lifted in devilish delight. "Oh yeah."

Displaying more firmness, she slapped his hand. "Stop it." She giggled. "It's none of your business what's under there, sir!"

"Uh-huh—you're wrong, Doc," Jayson said, settling back into his chair. He closed his eyes. "Everything about you is my business."

Wetting her lips, Andra returned her attention to the round window, noting that the luggage tram and its loaders were gone. As if on cue, the intercom aired three musical chimes that should have evoked excitement in traveling to a new place, but to Andra sounded much like a warning to turn back. It was followed by the captain's voice. Nestled inside his cozy airplane cockpit, he welcomed his passengers with reassuring words that floated throughout the cabin, their sole purpose to mentally prepare his human cargo for takeoff.

Behind her, someone coughed, a newspaper rustled, and passengers spoke quietly. Beside her, Jayson shifted for comfort and sighed. Suppressing her own sigh, she mentally said goodbye to her peace and greeted a more ominous feeling.

She chewed on her previously moistened lips, which were now arid from worry.

The overhead intercom went quiet. Its silence indicated her

trip into the future would soon begin—an unknown future that she dreaded more than anything she'd ever experienced.

Tapping into what was left of her inner strength, Andra attempted to vanquish her fears about landing in Athens the next day and meeting Jayson's foreign family face-to-face.

She coughed at the sudden blockage in her throat once she found out her strength reserves were empty.

2

A ndra woke, gasping for air.
Her abrupt climb from the depths of a rapidly fading
nightmare made her dizzy. As her eyes darted about, her mind
refused to register its surroundings. When she saw Jayson
silhouetted against the dimly lit airplane cabin, her memory
abruptly returned.

"We're on our way to Greece," she mumbled. Straightening,
she leaned forward, rubbing her grainy eyes. Jason's blurry
form came into better focus. "What time is it?" she croaked.

"It's going on one o'clock in the morning. Babe, you okay?"
Frowning, Jayson dropped his sports magazine into his lap
and reached up to switch on her individual light. "You have
another nightmare?"

Blinking beneath the overhead beam, Andra allowed her
eyes to fully adjust to the waking world. Embarrassed, she
nodded, turning toward the plane's window. Within its circle,
she glimpsed her reflection against the night sky's blackness,
noting the worry etched on her doppelganger's face as it stared
back. Turning from the troubling expression, she fell against
Jayson's chest just as he reached for her.

She sighed, marveling that he'd chosen to love her despite
crossing paths with countless beautiful women of his own
color and heritage.

The love they shared was a miraculous thing, yet it was
also terrifying. She truly believed God had gifted Jayson to
her; still, she also understood that falling in love with him

came with a price that grew more expensive the longer they remained together.

Andra had to believe she was up to the challenge.

Upon hearing his sigh, she bravely looked up.

"Same nightmare, Doc?" Jayson asked. At her nod, concern shaped his next words; they came out slowly, causing his Grecian accent to become more pronounced. "The truth is, your nightmares started day one of our marriage. They've become more frequent."

Feeling she'd just been pronounced guilty of an unknown crime and not wanting to admit to him that her nightmares had started before they were married, Andra remained silent.

"Can't you remember—"

She shook her head, cutting him off. Pulling away, she exhaled unevenly. "Jay, I tell you, it's vague, only darkness around me. The air is swirling, stormy," she whispered. "The only thing for sure is that whatever this is, it's not good. Something bad is coming."

"Is there a problem here?"

At the voice, Andra jumped. Beyond Jayson's head, steely blue eyes came into view. *Maybe that something bad has just arrived.*

The flight attendant's soft tone failed to hide her inner conflict, which seemed to house a tug-of-war between performing her required duties and her personal distaste for the couple. Her sapphire eyes pierced the night, their glacial hardness showing contempt at Jayson's embrace of Andra.

Refusing to flinch beneath the weight of the attendant's stare, Andra instead placed the woman underneath her personal microscope for a closer look. Under the right circumstances, the flight attendant would have been considered a beauty; her sparkling blue eyes and generous lips, if allowed, had the ability to curl into a winsome smile.

However, at the moment, her lips were drawn in a straight, unforgiving line across her face.

Jayson glanced toward the attendant. "We're okay," he said. He placed a kiss atop Andra's mussed hair. "My wife's had a bad dream. That's all."

Upon hearing the word *wife*, the flight attendant stiffened. The tips of her pencil-thin lips pulled downward. "Well, please keep it down," she hissed. "You're disturbing the other passengers who are trying to sleep."

With a short rustle behind Andra's seat, a silver mane popped into view, causing all three to turn toward it. A tall and sturdily built gentleman who looked to be in his mid-fifties rose as high as the airplane's ceiling would allow.

"You know," he said, yawning through his heavy Texan accent, "you're right."

His pale blue eyes stared intently at the flight attendant, who, at his words, glared at Andra and Jayson with an "I told you so" smirk on her face. The older gent cleared his throat to regain the woman's attention.

"You're right on target. You do need to keep it down. These young'uns ain't disturbing nobody. You're the one stirring up all the commotion. Now, skedaddle and go about doing whatever it is you do."

The flight attendant bristled at his command. "Who do you think you are?" she said, only to clamp her mouth shut.

Having to provide excellent customer service has gotta bite at times, Andra thought wryly.

The man perused the flight attendant's rigid form fit within her starched white blouse and straight blue skirt. "Who am I? Someone who could buy you a hundred times over." He dismissed her with a jerk of his head. "Now, scat."

The blonde woman's previous condescending sneer disappeared, replaced with a tight-lipped glare. Mute, she pivoted within the aisle, only to trip in clumsy haste. Her face reddening, she calmly righted herself. With a haughty lift of her chin, she stalked off toward the rear area, where the other off-duty flight attendants now gathered.

Andra gawked at the silver-haired gentleman until his eyes lowered to meet hers, his smile devilish under her mute scrutiny. A second later, he chuckled outright.

"The little filly's had that coming for quite a while now," he said. Sliding over a bit, he folded his arms, one on top of the other, across both headrests. "I've seen the way she's been treating you since we first took off."

For a contemplative moment, the man's silver brows wrinkled. He lowered his head, allowing his chin to rest upon his stacked arms. "It's jealousy, plain and simple." He paused, seemingly delving deeper in thought. "She's like those wild Texas stallions—you know, the ones you guys probably see on TV. I see them on the regular. Well, what she needs is a strong fella to ride her like one until she breaks."

Andra choked back a laugh, while Jayson freely let go of his. The man's head lifted at the jovial sound.

"Figuratively speaking, of course," he added gruffly. He returned Jayson's smile. "However, literally couldn't hurt either. I wouldn't mind takin' on such a chore, you know?"

At the couple's bemused silence, the man winked suggestively and lowered one hand over the seat, shaking first Jayson's and then Andra's hand.

"Anyway, the name's Harlan Orlando Grainger. They call me Hog for short. I'm in Texas cattle," he said, his voice confident that they knew what he meant. Andra did know—he meant money. "And please spare me the jokes—I've heard them all before, especially 'You're a hog in cattle?'" He snorted ruefully. "Man alive! Can't those morons come up with something new?" When a new giggle erupted from Andra, Harlan good-naturedly cleared his throat again. "Got off the subject, didn't I? Well, anyway, I'm considering broadening my investment portfolio—jumping outside the cattle box." He chuckled at his own joke. "So what're your names, youngsters?"

Jayson produced a delighted chuckle as well, most likely at being called a youngster. "Jayson and Andra Theonopilus."

"Ah," said the older man, nodding. "And what line of work you guys in?"

"Well, Mr. Grainger—"

"Hog, young man," the older man said, breaking in.

"Well, Hog, I'm going to school for my PhD in theological studies," Jayson said. His tone then went from humble to pride-filled. "My wife, Andra, is a resident in internal medicine at Good Samaritan Medical Center in West Palm Beach, Florida."

The Texan stared at Andra with one eyebrow lifted in surprise. "Doctor, huh?" He pondered the information for a moment. "Never would've guessed it."

Andra straightened. "Why? Because I'm black?" she asked.

"Well, she does talk!" Hog said good-naturedly.

Sharply, she pivoted in her seat to face him directly, just in time to see him swat the air between them.

"Oh, settle down! No, not only because you're black but because you're black and a woman," he declared. At her heightened astonishment, Hog chuckled. "Sorry, but that's the way of the world, darlin'."

"But," Andra sputtered, her mind searching for an appropriate answer that was both respectful and rebuking. "But what you're speaking is Ice Age philosophy. That's cold—"

He cut her off with another swat. "Cold?" Hog's other bushy brow lifted. "Let me explain something to you, little lady. You can't set a thermometer to gauge imaginary degrees of the truth. Hot or cold, the truth's the truth. Anyway, the statistics don't lie."

Silently mulling over his words, Andra had to admit the older man was right. She'd come across a report somewhere with dismal findings that backed up the Texan's observation: although more African American women applied to and got into medical school than their male counterparts, the total average for her race and gender was still below the averages for other prominent racial groups.

Still, did he have to say it out loud?

Begrudgingly, she met his eyes, conceding to his point.

"Besides, seems to me you have a colder issue to deal with." Hog jerked his head back toward the narrow doorway the flight attendant had disappeared through. "Or should I say, you two have to deal with."

"Look, Mr. Grainger." At the older man's corrective glance, Jayson amended the name again. "Hog, we're very much in love, and—"

He too was cut short as the Texan straightened. When the

older man disappeared from their sight, Jayson rose to peer over the headrest.

Settling into his roomy seat, Hog wiggled his broad shoulders to get more comfortable. "Yeah, you do have love goin' for you, I must say. Still," he continued, plucking his Stetson from the empty seat next to him and placing it on his head, "truth be told, sometimes it's not enough. But sometimes it is. I guess we'll just have to see." Hog shifted the hat forward to cover his eyes.

Jayson gave a slight cough at being dismissed by the shifting of the Texan's expensive hat and sat down. His glance was apologetic, prompting Andra to return it with a sympathetic smile. Then, in sync, they both twisted toward the crack between their seats at Hog's throat clearing.

He let out a long yawn for good measure. "Maybe now's a good time you young'uns take a bathroom break. While it's available."

Her cheeks warming, Andra glanced at Jayson, speaking softly. "You think he overheard us talk about—"

A low reply came from the other side: "I didn't hear nothing."

Andra's eyes and mouth opened wider. "He did hear us," she whispered even lower. "He knows what we were going to—"

"Nope. Didn't hear that either."

As Jayson held in his laughter, his compressed smile morphed into one that could've been spawned by Lucifer himself. Stuffing his magazine into the slot on the seat before him, he stood and stretched his long, muscular limbs.

At the sight, Andra suppressed a moan.

Her husband fixed his gaze upon her. "I'll be back," he said. "I'm going to use the facilities."

Andra remained seated, painfully aware of the man behind her who called himself Hog. Although it was invisible, she felt his powerful presence. Involuntarily, her eyes moved with Jayson until he reached the narrow restroom door. Popping it open, he paused to stare across the cabin at her. The intensity in his eyes took her breath away, setting fire to her loins.

An instant later, he disappeared from sight.

Prickly eternal seconds passed at her dilemma. She wanted to go after her husband yet was too embarrassed to follow. Shortly, the problem was solved for her.

From behind, she heard a snore—one that sounded a bit exaggerated.

Resigned, she sharply sucked in air. If that was her cue, she'd take it.

Exhaling in one puff, she arose on shaky limbs and stepped into the aisle. Strolling forward, her frame moved as if magnetized toward the closed restroom door.

Halfway between her seat and the lavatory, Andra could've sworn she heard Hog's low guffaw follow her.

3

Their bodies intimately joined, Andra wiggled on Jayson's lap, her knees parted and her spine pressed against his chest. Reaching around her, he used magical fingers to play a sensual tune with her feminine core, strumming a heavenly melody only she could hear.

Physically charged, she closed her eyes against the erotic haziness that distorted her vision, vaguely marveling at the limited space the aircraft afforded its tiny john—and at how her husband used every cramped inch of it for her sole pleasure.

An abrupt tapping sounded off like firecrackers.

"Hello?" A female's heavily accented voice filtered in from the other side of the narrow door, giving the muffled words a distant quality. "Do you know how long you will be?"

Jayson's probing fingers ceased, causing Andra to release an uneven sigh. "Time's up, baby," she said over her shoulder with some difficulty. "We'd better—"

Jayson shook his head. "This bathroom's occupied!" he called out. Pushing aside Andra's thick locks, vampire-like, he clamped down on her neck, chewing as he talked around the delicate flesh. "Please use the other facility, ma'am."

There was a pause, as if the woman struggled to decipher the noises from the other side. Seconds passed before they heard subdued retreating footsteps.

"She's gone, babe." Jayson's palm blazed a warm trail upward, slipping inside her unbuttoned blouse, while its twin stayed at her core. "But we should finish, okay?"

A gasp broke free from Andra's lips as his hands simultaneously fondled her breast and her feminine core. From behind, his body pushed with greater force against hers.

"Okay," she said with even more difficulty. "I love you so ..."

Andra's remaining words dissolved as her mind and body burst into a kaleidoscope of pulsating sensations. She welcomed their sensual emancipation with a violent shudder, and Jayson's frame followed with an intense tremor of its own.

His breathing amplified against her ear, and their eyes met in the oblong wall mirror before them.

"I love you too, Doc," his reflection said.

Barely holding his stare, Andra weakly smacked the arm that encircled her waist. "Took you long enough to say it."

"My bad."

"Your bad?" She laughed. "You sound cute talking street lingo, especially with that gorgeous accent of yours."

He grinned. "Well, I've managed to pick up a few things from my peeps."

Smiling, she fixated on the reflected eyes that captured hers. Gradually, her mouth relaxed as she studied their faces as a whole, taking note of the extreme outward contrasts between them.

Chewing her bottom lip, Andra wondered if her husband's thoughts mirrored her own at that moment.

"My beautiful wife, I can guess what you're thinking."

Feeling like a wild child caught doing something naughty, she swallowed hard. "You can? What?"

"That what we did just now can be crossed off both our bucket lists," he said. Palming her waist, he helped her onto unsteady feet. "In fact, it was actually number one on mine."

Grateful her man wasn't a mentalist and able to read her mind, she nodded guiltily. "Yeah, you got me. That's exactly what I was thinking."

Jayson gently paddled her behind, coaxing her to move to one side. As he stood, their eyes clashed again inside the looking glass. He grew quiet, watching her.

Uncomfortable, she exhaled sharply. "What?"

"We belong together, Doc," he finally said. "No matter

our differences, you were made for me. I was made for you. Understand?"

"Yes," she said quickly. "Sure."

Ducking her head, Andra tugged paper towels from the dispenser. She turned on the water, wet her hands, and added liquid soap. With more vigor than she'd intended, she cleansed herself. A moment later, Jayson joined her, bumping her playfully in the process.

Their carefree laughter amplified within the small space as they collided with one another in a race to get clean.

"Well, look what I've found," Jayson said, holding something up high. "I wonder whose these could be."

"Hey, I need those." Stifling a giggling fit, Andra grabbed for the panties he kept out of her reach. "Buddy, sometimes you play too much."

After finally seizing the silky drawers, she laughed as she stepped into them and jerked them up at a sudden pounding.

Jayson zipped his jeans with a hard yank. "Occupied!" he called out. Looking around Andra toward the closed door, he raked a hand through his hair. "Go to the other—"

"Sir? Is your wife in there with you?"

Smoothing her clothes with one hand, Andra reached out with the other to restrain Jayson from lunging toward the voice.

"Baby, calm yourself," she whispered. "Please, Jay?"

"I've had enough of their persecution," he said, shoving her hand away. "Move, Andra!"

Jayson pushed past her, forcing her to grab the compact stainless-steel face bowl for support. With two angry steps, he reached the door. "Yes, she's in here with me," he said, yanking the panel open. Jayson glared at the flight attendant framed within the doorway. "What's with you people? Andra is my wife, so why must you persecute ..." Jayson's words trailed off at the flight attendant's anxious expression and trembling hands.

Her face transforming into frantic relief at the open door, the brunette captured a wayward strand of hair and unevenly tucked it behind one ear with one hand while simultaneously beckoning with the other.

"Please. Keven said your wife's a doctor. We need her right now." The flight attendant, named Martie, pivoted on quick feet and headed toward the back of the plane, giving Andra and Jayson no choice but to follow. "Hurry! She may be dying!"

Passing their overhead bin, Andra stopped to spring open the latch and quickly pulled out her medical bag. Her doctor senses fully tuned to the potential crisis at hand, she ignored Hog's sleep-drowsed question "Hey, what's happenin'?" to catch up with Jayson and the harried flight attendant.

"Who is it?" Andra asked, barely noticing the other passengers who stirred in their seats. "Who's dying?"

"One of our flight attendants—Sapphire," Martie said over her shoulder.

As Andra crossed the lounge's threshold behind the stewardess and Jayson, her attention was immediately drawn to the cabin's floor and the blonde-haired, blue-eyed flight attendant stretched out on it.

With grasping hands, the steely-eyed, rude flight attendant clutched at her throat, her face turning a sickly shade of green.

4

Stefano Theonopilus glanced up from the paperwork in perfect disarray atop his massive mahogany desk.

Taking a break, he allowed his gaze to travel across its surface to the wall-length picture window on the other side of it, which displayed a stunning view of the back acreage of his family's villa. His mind now split between the paperwork that needed handling and the outdoor scenery before him, he scanned the familiar sun-kissed fields that led to the olive groves miles beyond. Vaguely, he observed a fat fly bump against the glass in a vain attempt to enter the office study.

A sound much like the one his father had produced when Stefano was a boy—a noise birthed by frustration, anger, or a combination of both—traveled up his esophagus to slip past his tense lips.

Surprised that at age thirty-five, he could make the noise, which signaled he too was getting older, Stefano soothed his furrowed brow with an unsteady hand. Try as he might, he couldn't prevent the same daily thoughts from revisiting him, their loud returning footsteps traipsing across his brain like an unwelcome parade.

Nor could he stop himself from repeating the noise.

The paperwork before him revealed something he had dreaded yet already known: the olive harvest that year would be smaller than last's year—much like the year before. Each harvesting season brought in a lesser crop and, therefore, a lesser value, and he feared that pretty soon the multiple rows of planted trees would refuse to yield any crop at all.

It was unlikely yet not impossible.

Once he'd taken over the family business, to his discouragement, it had continued to be a constant uphill battle just to maintain a thriving grove. It had gotten to the point where he now considered outside resources to keep the Theonopilus family enterprise afloat. *Investors.*

"Why now?" he muttered. "Why me?"

He had come to the conclusion he must be cursed.

Staring down at his unsteady hands, at that moment, what he wanted most was a strong drink. Stefano shook his head, ignoring the impulse to drown his mental and physical woes in alcohol, and considered his next worry.

His next sigh broke forth with such ferocity that it produced a faint headache. After dropping his pen atop the scattered paperwork, he used his cool fingertips to rub circles into his temples.

His father, Georigios—George, as he liked to call himself—had been an invincible rock during Stefano's youthful years, a formidable tower built from strength and vitality. Yet right before his eyes, his papa was growing older, more tired and less attentive with each passing year.

His father's mental and physical decline had forced Stefano, as the oldest son, to prematurely step into the elder's shoes as the patriarch of the family and its business. More and more lately, his father talked of nothing but his wife, Cecilia—Cecil, as Papa lovingly called her. He longed to go where she now resided.

A grave among the ancestral burial grounds in the northeastern section of their property had been her permanent home for the past twelve years.

Sometimes George would head out early in the morning, walking with his tired old-man gait toward the cemetery, and he refused to return until late in the evening—or until someone went out in search of him.

When the latter was the case, his father could usually be found on his knees in the soft grass, hunched over his beloved Cecil's grave, as if willing her to reach beyond it and pull his body in with hers.

On the occasion it fell to him to search for his papa, Stefano automatically averted his gaze once he discovered the older man. He refused to stare directly into haunted eyes that in many ways mirrored his own.

Stefano grumbled. He'd politely considered and ultimately dismissed suggestions from meddling relatives about placing his father in an elderly care facility. At fifty-eight, his papa was far too young for such a depressing fate, he believed; therefore, he refused to do it.

Still, the more his papa lingered in his grief, the older he appeared—it was as if the life were slowly draining from him, ultimately revealing the shriveled shell of a man he now appeared to be.

However, Stefano believed George's deteriorating condition was due not only to his mother's passing but also to something else just as devastating.

Upon taking over the helm years before, Stefano learned from George of a tragic event surrounding a consumer's death, which was attributed to a batch of their family's custom-made olive oil. It had resulted in a hush-hush lawsuit and subsequent rush for a punitive-damage settlement.

When George told him of the horrible event, he swore Stefano to secrecy. Attempting to probe more information from his father had proven futile because Stefano soon realized George actually knew little. The older man, distraught over the tragedy, had refused to learn anything about the deceased consumer.

In blind anguish, he'd simply turned the entire matter over to his lawyers and allowed them to handle the out-of-court settlement. And that was that.

Now, feeling the need to mentally move on, Stefano allowed his tumultuous thoughts to shift in a new direction, and he produced the noise a third time.

Swiveling in his chair, he turned his back to the window and faced the open office door. Too exhausted to fight them, he surrendered to the newest encroaching thoughts, allowing the mental gate he'd willfully constructed against them to open.

Obtaining their freedom, they stampeded forth with vicious determination.

Shutting his eyes, Stefano leaned back in his chair to rest his elbows on the armrests. He clasped shaking hands against his stomach.

A facial tic jumped above his left eye.

His baby brother Jayson, the so-called rebel of the family, would return home that day after living for years in America. Unfortunately, he wouldn't be alone; he would be carting behind him someone he should've left behind in the States: his black bride.

Indignant, Stefano snorted. His cheeks grew hotter with each tick of the office wall clock, until his face sizzled. Initially, he refused to identify those burning emotions, but it wasn't long before he couldn't help but acknowledge them: humiliation and embarrassment mixed in equal parts with anger.

"My second curse," he said. Behind the darkness of closed lids, Stefano shifted. His clasped hands pressed tighter against his abdomen.

Jayson couldn't simply have married someone from their own heritage—no, that would've been too simple, too right.

There were many beautiful Grecian women in and around town—little Sylvia Menkos being one. Why could he not be satisfied to marry any one of them? Why did he have to become some religious rebel without a cause, run off to America, forget who and what he was, and join himself to—of all women—an inferior black female?

Or would it be politically correct to say an African American? he thought. He shook his head. *I don't know. Who cares?*

He knew that no matter the title, the woman was beneath his family.

To Stefano's irritation, his mind handed him the memory of Jayson's first text informing him that he'd fallen in love while in the States. Stefano had to admit his initial happiness at the sudden news was fueled by selfishness: he had hoped the engagement would pave the way for Jayson's return to

Greece. He would bring back a bride, settle down there, and help Stefano run the business.

However, his joy had turned to immediate disgust once Jayson had texted him a picture of a fiancée who—although beautiful, he grudgingly had to admit—was black.

The following week, the horrid introductory phone call had occurred.

Stefano grimaced as he recalled the over-the-top bliss in Jayson's overseas greeting. Seconds later, he'd put the woman on the phone. The next few moments had been excruciatingly painful as her attempt at polite conversation fell short. Relieved that Papa had picked up the study's extension, Stefano's hostility-driven hypocrisy had forced him to hang up his end.

He exhaled at the memory.

Finally, the dreaded call had come in from the States to inform the family Jayson had married her. Stefano recalled staring at the receiver in his hand; the urge to do his sibling bodily harm had swept over him with such ferocity it nearly paralyzed him.

His mind emerging from the turbulent past, Stefano experienced a foreign pressure behind his eye sockets. He willed his male pride to subdue it before that pressure turned into actual tears.

He sniffled anyway.

He hated the fact that both she and Jayson were arriving that afternoon to show their faces among the village and publically disgrace the entire family with their unnatural union.

There had been another incident a few years back, when his distant cousin Meego had run off and married Sarah Smyth, a white Protestant from New York. It had taken a long time for both close and distant relatives to get over that particular act of family terrorism.

"Maybe this is all Meego's fault," Stefano said to the air, verbally testing the weight of his words. "He must have set a precedent with his rebellious, thoughtless behavior."

The thumbs of his clasped hands twitched. To counteract their spasms, Stefano twirled them around each other.

No, he refused to compare Meego's rash matrimonial actions to Jayson's blatant rebellion—the situations were different, worlds apart.

How could his stupid little brother act in such a way? Had he lost his *philotimo*?

Honor, integrity, dignity, sacrifice. Stefano snorted, knowing Jayson had none of those—the selfish brat.

A rustle brought Stefano's mental tirade to an abrupt end. He opened his eyes.

His father stood inside the doorway.

As usual, Stefano couldn't bring himself to stare directly at the older man's haunted eyes; instead, he focused on his attire. A familiar mental alarm sounded upon his scrutiny of George's white polo shirt and light khaki pants, which only a few years ago would have fit him perfectly but now hung several sizes too big for his stooped frame.

"Son, I'm going to visit your mother," he said, his voice wearier than usual.

At George's slow turn, Stefano leaped from his seat and entered the hallway. He gently placed a hand on the older man's sleeve, stopping him.

"But, Papa, Jayson is coming home today." Nausea hit Stefano's stomach at the spark of life ignited inside his father's eyes at the reminder. He swallowed hard at the bile that soon rose. "You want to be here when he returns, yes?"

Papa's worn eyes filled with joyful, shimmering tears that threatened to spill. Stefano hoped they wouldn't; he doubted Jayson deserved as much.

"Jayson," his father said quietly. He nodded once and turned in the opposite direction to shuffle along the corridor that led back to his bedroom. "Yes, I forgot about Jayson."

Stefano stood there with his fists on his hips, fighting to hold back a tidal wave of fury so great he wanted to release it on somebody. Momentarily, he too performed an about-face and returned to his chair. As if through osmosis, his body seemed to have absorbed his father's fatigue, and as he lowered onto the cushy leather seat that used to bring him comfort, he felt only exhaustion.

A building rage soon pushed aside his weariness, compelling him to strike the mahogany desk's surface. Loose papers fluttered at the disturbance.

He took a deep breath and slowly exhaled.

"Calm yourself," he muttered in self-admonishment. "Think!"

Needing to regroup, Stefano once again gazed beyond the big picture window that handsomely framed the villa's backyard.

Stefano rationalized that Jayson's return home could be a good thing. With his baby brother near, he could talk some sense into him man-to-man and make him see reason. He'd convince Jayson to dump his present disgrace for a more suitable local Greek woman.

Stefano's brow crinkled in the midst of his introspection. Another benefit to Jayson's arrival was that maybe his presence would keep Papa from visiting their mother's grave site so often.

He shivered, his thoughts producing an inward fear that one day his father would walk out the door never to return, his heavy mourning overtaking him to the point that he would be discovered slumped over the grave, his spirit finally crushed beneath the weight of his sorrow.

Stefano shook his head to clear it of the dismal image. Wearily, he gazed at his hands, which were becoming more unsteady by the second, again wishing he held a brandy and ice in one of them.

Curses usually come in threes.

Unexpectedly, the urge to cough engulfed him. Quickly, he reached inside his pocket to retrieve a handkerchief. He slapped it over his nose and mouth.

Pain gripped his frame once the hacking commenced, the tremendous force of it bending his body forward, rendering him helpless. The coughing seemed to stretch on for an eternity—*Please, please stop*, he thought—yet he knew once it finally ceased, the spasm would've lasted less than a minute.

As his cough tapered off, he leaned back in his chair. His actions meticulous, he used the cloth to remove any residual spittle left on his lips, and then, as if he couldn't help himself, he pulled the snow-white fabric away to examine it.

To his confirmation, a large section was stained bright red.

Stefano folded the soiled cloth and placed it back in his pocket.

This time, his sigh was bathed in resignation.

Then, of course, there was that.

5

"Would you please calm yourself, child?" Al Williams asked.

Racine's mother stopped her sewing. Concern painted her mature face as deep brown eyes followed Racine's progress of imprinting a permanent trail into the den's carpet.

"You'll give yourself a stroke—and you're too young for one." Patting the cushion next to her, Al smiled. "Come sit down."

Despite the gentle command, Racine continued to pace. Every once in a while, she stole a glance at the stunning older woman, whose birth name was Alexandria, though she preferred the nickname Al. Eventually, Racine exhaled dramatically and graced her mother with a look comprised of both impatience and love.

"Mama, you don't understand. Andra's made a terrible mistake—one she's gonna regret for a long time!"

Her mother's sharp teeth bit into the blue thread she was using to mend a torn blouse, breaking the string in half. Carefully, she pushed the freed needle into a tomato-shaped pincushion, dropping the newly repaired garment in her lap.

"Well, it's been over six months now, and I don't see any signs of the marriage crashing and burning into a heap of failure," she teased. Again, she patted the cushion. "Take a load off, baby girl—you're making me dizzy."

Finally taking her mother's advice, Racine produced an exaggerated sigh and defiantly crossed her arms, plopping onto the sofa. Her jostling caused the round decorative throw pillow to her left to slip out of place. She snatched it and positioned it exactly inside the couch's ninety-degree corner. Critically eyeing the pillow, she rotated it a degree counterclockwise until it met her standards.

Sensing her mother's curious stare, she stiffened. The room's silence stretched out as if climbing a hilly mountain until it reached its uncomfortable summit. Racine whipped around.

"What, Mama?"

"Sweetie, why are you taking this so personally?"

"I'm not, Mama! This is not about me. It's about her and how she's ruining our—I mean her—life."

"Seems to me you're making this about you."

"Well, I'm not, I tell you!" Hot tears bubbled up, and Racine angrily brushed them aside. She glared accusingly at her mother. "Besides, I don't understand why you're not more concerned! She's on a plane right now, flying off to a foreign country where she has no family and no friends for support. She's all alone over there with only him and his family!"

Al chuckled softly. "I'm kinda jealous, if you ask me." Her eyes dreamily stared into space. "So romantic, flying off to Greece with the one you love."

"Mama!"

The older woman grinned mischievously. "Stop yelling. I'm right here. Of course I'm worried about her flying abroad— the same as if it were you." She paused to fold the repaired cerulean blouse and placed it inside the laundry basket at her feet. "However, like I told you before, this is Andra's life, and it's her decision. Besides, she's marrying a man who's going into the ministry."

Frustrated, Racine threw up her hands. "Oh yeah, I forgot. Him being in ministry makes everything okay!" Trying another attempt at persuasion, Racine evened out her tone. "Look, Mama, Andra's too young to get married. We never got a chance to do all the things we said we were going to do together."

"So this *is* about you," her mother said. At Racine's tightly compressed lips, she continued. "Listen, honey, Andra didn't abandon you—she simply got married. End of story."

"Yeah, and she made one big, fat mistake in the process."

At Racine's stubborn expression, Al pressed on. "She's a grown woman—a doctor, for goodness sakes."

Racine couldn't grasp the reasoning behind her mother's rationality—if someone were a doctor, he or she must have good sense. As far as she was concerned, when it came to Andra and her recent choices, that perception had to be a misnomer.

"But, Mama," she said, striving to inject logic into their debate, "don't you get it? Marrying someone outside not only her race but also her culture and religion—everything—is asking for trouble. It doesn't make sense."

The room grew quiet as Al selected her next sewing project: a sock with a hole in its toe. After threading her needle with the right color, she commenced darning. The silence finally broke when she said, "Love rarely makes sense, darlin'."

Exhaling in disgust, Racine sprang to her feet only to resume pacing. "Don't have time for your outdated clichés, Mother."

The next silence was dense and compressed, amplifying small noises not usually noticed in the routine activity of daily life: the ticking of the wall clock's second hand, the tweet of a backyard bird, and the vague sound of a car horn one street over.

Racine bit her bottom lip. She realized immediately she'd stepped over the invisible line of parental respect. Covertly, she peeked at her mother, only to observe her full dark lips pursed, carefully arched eyebrows lifted, and unusually beautiful brown eyes squinting in reproach.

Racine swallowed. Stopping in her tracks, she slowly faced Al's displeasure. "Sorry," she said sincerely. Racine retraced her steps back to the couch, this time lowering onto it wearily. She glanced over at the throw pillow to make sure it hadn't slipped again. "I don't know what's with me."

Putting aside her darning, Al slid over to Racine and draped her arms around her. Sighing deeply, Racine lowered her head onto her mother's shoulder, breathing in her musk perfume and hating the fact that Andra's marital fiasco had burdened her body to near exhaustion. Racine closed her eyes against the stroking of her short, perfectly styled hair.

"Andra's going to be all right; she's carrying around loads of good common sense," Al said. She gently kissed Racine's crown. "I believe I know why you're afraid—and this is not that situation."

Tense, Racine pulled away from her mother's embrace. "What do you mean 'this is not that situation'?"

Al dropped one hand to cover Racine's tightly clasped fist. She squeezed, looking deep into Racine's eyes. "You know, baby, what happened." Shock kept Racine rooted to the spot as Al quietly continued. "Please don't unintentionally punish your sister because of it."

Shame-filled rage propelled Racine off the couch again. Her momentum drove her toward the den's exit, and she refused to look back to see if the pillow had shifted out of place again. *Damn the pillow!* Her back to her mother, Racine finally allowed her tears to break free.

"Please, baby girl, wait."

Ignoring Al's plea, Racine bolted from the room to escape words that, if allowed to be spoken, would be too painful to hear.

6

"Please give her room."

Pushing past a fidgeting Keven, Andra dropped to the floor across from Martie, who was already on her knees by Sapphire's head. Placing her medical bag on the floor, Andra stifled her alarm for the patient when her body suddenly went limp.

"Can anyone tell me what happened?" Andra asked calmly, pressing fingers against Sapphire's carotid artery to locate a pulse.

The room filled with nervous silence.

Quickly rummaging through her black bag, Andra retrieved her penlight. Andra parted one eye and then the other, flashing the beam across Sapphire's orbs. "I believe she's gone into some kind of shock," Andra said.

The hovering attendants gasped.

"I'll do whatever I can to help her," she assured them. "Quick—is she allergic to anything you know of?"

Keven wrung his hands. "It beats me. Martie?"

First shooting him an annoyed glance, she nodded at Andra. "Yes, she's allergic to tree nuts." She sat back on her heels, her face contorted with worry. "In the past, she's gone to the emergency room for accidentally eating a peanut."

"Uh-oh!" Keven slapped a hand across his mouth.

Jumping to her feet, Martie glared at him. "Uh-oh what?"

"Sapphire came back here all angry, snatched my granola bar outta my hand, and tore into it," he said. Keven shrugged helplessly. "She didn't give me a chance to even tell her what she was eating! How was I supposed to know she was allergic?"

"Didn't you ever read her bracelet, dummy?"

Keven's expression was pathetically comical. "Well, Martie, I thought her bracelet was for show, not medical!"

Spotting the medical bracelet on Sapphire's left wrist, Andra twisted it around and read the small words confirming the woman's nut allergy. She shuffled through her medical bag again, this time pulling out a fresh EpiPen filled with a single dose of epinephrine. After ripping the package apart, she shoved the unconscious woman's skirt further up her thigh. Positioning the needle over her upper left thigh, Andra plunged it into the exposed skin and injected.

Sapphire's chest stopped rising.

"She's going," Andra said, withdrawing the needle. She swiftly dropped it into her black bag. "Jay, can you help me? Hurry, baby!"

Jayson jumped into action. "Sure thing, Doc!"

Lowering to his knees, he positioned himself alongside Sapphire's chest. Time seemed to pause; the room went deathly quiet as husband and wife performed their tasks. Andra used sharp breaths to blow into the woman's mouth, while Jayson sharply compressed the chest area with one-two-three synchronized movements.

"It's not working," Keven whispered hoarsely. With each passing second, his brown eyes grew wider, darting between Andra and Jayson. "Why isn't it working?"

"Shh! Don't panic!" Martie said, her rising voice projecting her own fear. "She's a doctor—she knows what she's doing!"

Dread weighed heavily in the atmosphere; the only sounds inside the small cabin came from Andra's puffs of air and Jayson's grunts as he worked.

"Look!" Keven shouted, pointing.

Sapphire's left wrist produced a faint spasm.

After blowing more air into her patient's lungs for good measure, Andra jerked back just as Sapphire's body abruptly twitched to life. Sapphire's pale lips opened to alternately cough and gasp for air; her closed eyes fluttered open. Her sky-blue orbs, at first dazed, suddenly cleared, transforming Sapphire's expression from confusion to disgust as her eyes focused on Andra's hovering face.

"Hey, get your hands off me!" Indignant, Sapphire pushed at Andra and struggled to sit up. "What do you think you're doing?"

"Saving your life—that's what she's doing," said a gruff voice. Everyone's attention went to the narrow threshold opening. Sturdily built Hog filled it. "And you'd better be grateful."

Her adrenaline rush plummeting, Andra laughed with tired relief. "Hog, what are you doing back here? You're supposed to stay in your seat."

The Texan shifted to lean against the doorframe, his silvery head cocked to one side. Calmly, his sight traveled past everyone to settle upon Sapphire's hiked skirt and shapely thighs. Nodding appreciatively at them, he shifted his stare to Andra.

"I hardly ever do what I'm told, young lady—except when it comes to someone tellin' me how to make more money. Besides, I wanted in on what the ruckus was about," he said. One bushy white eyebrow went up. "So, I guess you *are* a doctor, Doctor. And from what I can tell, a damn good one too."

Andra caught a glimmer akin to admiration—as well as an indecipherable glimmer—in Hog's eyes. Self-conscious, she rose to her feet, mutely thanking him with an uncertain smile.

Hog's stare intensified as it briefly touched on Andra's breasts before returning to Sapphire's exposed limbs.

Seeming to blush at Hog's scrutiny, Sapphire used unsteady hands to tug at her skirt's hem, pulling it to her knees. With her coworkers' help, she labored to stand on unsteady feet and then stumbled her way toward one of the narrow cots tucked away in the cabin's corner. Unevenly, she sat down. "I don't understand," she croaked, the sound prompting Martie to fetch her some water. Sapphire gripped the proffered bottle only to pause. Her skin's paleness blossomed into faint crimson as she stared Andra's way. "You saved my life?"

"You experienced an allergic reaction from the granola bar you consumed, Sapphire," Andra told her. The flight attendant appeared to go into temporary shock at her name being spoken, but Andra ignored it. "It was dumb luck I had some epinephrine in my medical bag to counteract the attack."

"Not luck, baby," Jason said, cutting in. "It was God's providence, along with your preparedness."

Beaming at her husband, Andra received his silent kiss. She then watched as he strolled over to Hog, and the men immediately talked in hushed, friendly whispers. Her peripheral view caught Sapphire studying her with an unreadable look, yet she decided she was too tired to decipher it.

Wanting to get in on the praise fest Jayson had created, Keven waved a carefree hand at Andra. "And don't forget you and Mr. Doctor had to perform CPR on her," he said. Hovering over Sapphire like a fluttering sparrow, he gently rubbed her arm. "Girl, my granola bar was chock full of peanut butter and nuts. It could've murdered you!"

Her nod disbelieving, Sapphire coughed nervously as she fumbled to open her water bottle. When Andra placed a hindering hand upon hers, the woman stared at brown skin overlapping white.

"Due to the fact we're forty thousand feet in the air and I can't pump your stomach, you might want to consider taking some syrup of ipecac before drinking that water. It will force your body to evacuate the remaining granola bar."

At Sapphire's continued silence, Andra pulled back. "Of course, I'm not your doctor. It's just a suggestion." She smiled as pleasantly as she could. "However, you don't have to take it. It's your call."

"Yes, she'll take it," Martie said, staring hard at Sapphire. "It's good advice."

"Hey, don't we have a bottle of that nasty stuff in the med cabinet? Man, I'm glad I don't have to take it." Making a face as if he'd just swallowed a spoonful of it, Keven quickly headed for the medicine cabinet on the opposite wall. "I'm on it!"

With noisy determination, he yanked open the doors and, with much zeal, rummaged through the pharmaceutical supplies. The dramatic scene was not complete until Martie lifted her hands in exasperation.

"Stop, Keven—you're making a mess in there! Let me find it." Pushing him aside, she proceeded to conduct her own less noisy search. She then graced him with a supervisor's look. "Why don't you walk the aisles to see if any of the passengers are awake and needing assistance?"

Mumbling that nobody ever let him do anything, Keven reversed direction and, with pouting lips, walked between Jayson and Hog to disappear into the passengers' area.

Forcing back a laugh, Andra glanced toward her short-term patient and was surprised to find Sapphire sporting a smile as well. It transformed her previously hard expression into a soft, more comely one.

"My team—they're always so melodramatic." Sapphire's nervous chuckle mingled with the various noises within the cabin, Jayson and Hog's conversation, and the search for upchuck meds. Her chin lifted. "Sorry about before, and thank you, Doctor."

Andra nodded. "I accept, and you're welcome."

A gruff chuckle filled the small cabin. "Well, it didn't take an actual stud," Hog said, glancing between Andra and Jayson. "But she's been ridden and broken—don't cha think?"

Sapphire and Martie stared at the older man, puzzlement transforming their pretty faces comically; however, when Jayson lifted a knowing eyebrow Andra's way, they both laughed in delighted understanding.

7

Her mother's words chasing her, Racine slammed the door in an attempt to shut them out. Hotly, she resumed her pacing inside the privacy of her bedroom.

Try as she might, she couldn't stop the past from crashing in on her. She whimpered. Routine senses switched to overload; sight, sound, smell, and touch intensified as unwanted pictures slid across her brain like a fast-moving slideshow. Just as she knew it would, a woman's scream commenced, causing her to cry out in anguish. She shoved her fists against her ears to block out the woman's squeals.

Akin to an alcoholic's delirium tremens, her frame vibrated from her struggle to prevent more disturbing images from downloading. Yet for her, the true terror lay within the silence once the woman's cries ceased, because Racine knew what happened during that ominous hush—unspeakable things a person could never fully convey with words, no matter how much coaxing and encouragement was received from well-meaning others.

Personally, she never wanted to talk about it—she wanted to forget.

Her cell phone rang. On autopilot, Racine reached inside her jeans pocket and pulled it free. "Hello?"

A bubbly female voice poured into her ear, the volume competing with the frightened screams inside her head. Racine flinched at the disparity between it and the caller's gaiety.

"Hey, girlfriend! You ready to do some insane shopping?

My dad gave me his credit card, and the sky's the limit! Woo-hoo!"

Racine was speechless at her friend's happiness, which poured forth like golden rays of blinding sunshine. Racine's building envy of her friend's carefreeness pushed her into a dark place. "Tracey, I can't talk right now. I've gotta go."

"But—"

Tracey's voice, hurt and confused, was terminated. Racine tossed the cell onto her pristinely made bed.

In a fog, Racine circled the room, her hands itching for busywork. With a critical eye, she picked apart each section. The area as a whole was immaculate; no clothes required hanging, no shoes needed to be paired and then stored away, and there was no dusting to take care of or trash to throw out.

Inside her bedroom world, everything was nice and orderly, in its perfect place.

On wobbly legs, she headed for her dresser. After first staring at its well-organized, previously dusted surface, she proceeded to lift her anguished eyes to the dresser's mirror, staring at the person framed within it.

Why can't you simply forget? Racine silently asked herself.

Her double stared back at her, lacking an expression, as if waiting for Racine to give her the appropriate one. Desperately, she searched the other's features, taking in styled short-cropped hair, smooth caramel-colored skin radiantly free from cosmetics, a generous mouth, and dark brown eyes the spitting image of Al's.

You're so pretty, yet why do I feel so ugly?

Blinking, the other remained mute.

"What do you want from me?" she screamed.

Snarling, Racine snatched at a perfectly aligned perfume bottle and proceeded to pitch it at the glass, wanting to shatter the beautiful, apathetic image into a billion pieces.

Mid-throw, her imagination dished up a futuristic montage: broken glass everywhere, pieces of shimmering slivers flying into places she didn't have the strength to crawl into, followed by a complete mental meltdown at the mess she'd just created, and Racine having to clean it all up in the end anyway.

Why would you want to do that to yourself? her reflection calmly asked.

Racine froze. Why couldn't she forget that poor girl's terrified screams? She now loathed the existence of the pathetic female, whose attackers had known she was a virgin and sought her out for that reason. It had been a night long ago yet could've been only yesterday; the girl had walked into the college frat party in a complete state of naïveté, painfully unaware she'd already been claimed, hunted, and tagged like a safari animal months prior, only to be ultimately used as a fraternity initiation sacrifice.

Why couldn't I help her? What could I've done to prevent it?

Blinding tears broke forth, blurring her mirror image. Slowly, she replaced the perfume bottle with painstaking perfection and then swiped at her bloodshot eyes.

"Andra, where are you?" She sniffled hard. "Oh yeah, right! The Virgin Bride's traveling abroad!"

The image in the mirror now frowned in disapproval, causing Racine to bristle defensively. "I know, I know! I have no right to be mad at Andra. It's not her fault; she has her own life to live with her white husband."

She couldn't push aside the thought that Andra had betrayed her by marrying Jayson. Abruptly, another distorted picture of that night at the frat party flashed inside her head, diverting her attention from her older sister.

She trembled more violently than before.

Why can't I forget?

Unable to stomach a staring contest with the image that now glared at Racine accusingly, she dropped her head into her hands and sobbed. *Why?*

Racine knew why.

She couldn't escape the fact that she and the girl who'd been raped that fateful night were one and the same.

8

Fidgeting with sunglasses in hand, Andra stood a few feet from the luggage conveyor belt, surveying the moderate-sized, crowded overseas airport.

At the thought of meeting her husband's family, she swallowed painfully. Taking a deep breath, she deliberately switched her brain from panic mode to inquisitive mode.

Studying the people who moved about with pleasurable leisure, she enviously noted that their measured pace was foreign to her frantic, Americanized way of life.

"Wow," she said.

The packed airport projected an old-world quaintness, and people strolled along with ease. Yet at the same time, they transmitted an invisible energy that suggested each person lived and breathed in the now. It was unlike the hustle and bustle of US airports, where people appeared to be in a race to get to their future destinations as fast as their frantic feet could carry them.

Despite her anxiety, Andra broke into a smile upon observing a twenty-something couple stand in rapt anticipation as an older gentleman shuffled along the boarding ramp toward them. Their bodies sprang to life even before he reached them, their enthusiasm enveloping his frailty within a loving circle of youthful vitality.

Straightaway, her mind conjured up a guessing game to determine the older gentleman's identity: *A grandfather? A great-uncle? Maybe a longtime friend of the family? A beloved teacher or aged mentor?*

Slipping on her sunglasses, she watched the young couple sandwich the older man and his single piece of luggage between them. Faint laughter filtered through the crowd, reaching out to her as she watched them link arms. Walking in one accord, the trio headed toward the airport's exit, their images disappearing and reappearing among the crowd until they vanished completely through the airport's automatic sliding doors into a bright, sunny day.

The touching scene prompted Andra to silently pray that what she'd witnessed with them was a sign of what was to come for her once meeting the in-laws.

"Here's hoping," she said.

"What are you hoping for?"

An arm reached from behind and slid around her waist. Instantly, she was pulled back into a hearty embrace, perfectly timed to a low chuckle against her ear, signaling Jayson's return from the men's restroom.

"Nothing," she said. She strove to eliminate any tremors in her voice by injecting it with forced levity. "My mouth was thinking out loud."

"And such a beautiful mouth," Jayson whispered. He proceeded to nibble on her earlobe. "Doc, I can literally read your thoughts. Your mind is filled with worry and all kinds of crazy stuff. But I'm telling you—please don't. They're going to fall in love with you the same as I did."

The words *delusional* and *naive* floated inside Andra's head. Instead of voicing them, she simply nodded.

She leaned against Jayson's steady frame, endeavoring to gather strength from his presence. However, like a tape recorder, her mind rewound what he'd just said to her. Now she wasn't sure if his voice had carried a false bravado, or was it her imagination?

"I'm not afraid," she said, which was almost the truth. Lifting her dark sunglasses into her thick curls, she looked over her shoulder. "Buddy, as long as you're with me, I can face anything."

Jayson's palm caressed her cheek, his eyes magnetically holding hers. "You know, Doc, making love to a sexy woman in my childhood bed is another thing I'll be able to cross off my bucket list—thanks to you," he said, his voice husky. "I can't wait to turn in tonight."

Andra laughed. "You're insatiable, dude. You know that?"

Nodding agreeably, Jayson produced a grin akin to *Alice in Wonderland*'s Cheshire Cat.

Staring forward again, Andra felt her body tingle as fleeting images from their recent lovemaking session in the airplane's restroom trekked across her brain. Thanking God for her husband's virility and overwhelming desire for her, Andra took a moment to leisurely scan the area, until her sights landed upon a beautiful young woman across the airport, her head pivoting from side to side as if in search of someone. Long, flowing tresses bounced seductively about her head and shoulders; below, she donned a flower-print sundress that molded to her shapely frame perfectly.

Frowning at the lovely creature, Andra couldn't prevent a small measure of jealousy from creeping in. She'd come to terms early in the relationship—at least she thought she had—with the fact other women, maybe even someone similar to the female across the way, had known Jayson in the biblical sense prior to their meeting and falling in love.

However, she tried to reassure herself that at least she was his final lover, so technically, she'd won over all the others—Jayson was her husband. However, she also realized that sometimes dominating a quarter in a football game didn't necessarily mean that the team currently in the lead would ultimately win the game. She'd witnessed too many football skirmishes in which one team was initially ahead only to turn the game over due to clumsy fumbles during the last quarter.

Your marriage is not a football game. You're not going to lose Jayson. You're a doctor, for heaven's sake—suck it up, Andra!

She firmly dismissed the attractive young woman across the terminal.

Taking her own advice, Andra smiled as she pivoted inside Jayson's embrace. Tilting her head back, she cocked it to one side to stare adoringly at him. "You're such a liar. You've probably deflowered many hot babes in your bedroom. I mean, long before you met me."

Jayson smiled ambiguously and then shook his head in what could've been denial or agreement. She matched his grin and parted her lips, waiting for the delicious impact of his slowly descending mouth.

"I see you still have the magic, J. J.—she doesn't stand a chance."

At the lilting voice, Jayson abruptly pulled back to gaze over Andra's head. "Sly!" he exclaimed.

To Andra's disappointment, the security of Jayson's arms withdrew, followed by his body, as he stepped around her to enthusiastically greet the newcomer.

For a second, Andra stood motionless. Her heart quickened at coming face-to-face with the unknown. Yet she already knew Fate gleefully waited for her to turn around in order to force-feed Andra a serving of irony. Pivoting slowly, she sobered upon seeing Jayson and the mysterious woman embrace.

She held back a sigh of defeat.

Her gorgeous husband was now hugging the same beautiful young woman Andra had spied across the airport terminal only moments ago.

"Sly, what are you doing here?" he asked. Wrapping one arm around the girl's neck, he proceeded to muss the crown of her head with scrubbing knuckles. "What's up, kid?"

"Stop it, J. J." Sly laughed, her charming accent exquisitely framing each word. "Do you know how long it took me to get my hair like this? Hours and hours!" She brushed wayward black strands from her face and playfully pushed at him, although to Andra's disgust, the beauty managed to stay within Jayson's one-armed embrace.

"Aw, come on, Sly. Since when have you cared about your hair?"

The woman named Sly displayed a pouty expression, forcing her dark-eyelash-fringed emerald eyes to widen.

Andra felt ready to upchuck at the revoltingly breathtaking sight.

"Ever since I turned twenty-two this year," Sly retorted. "Evidently, you did not notice just how much I've grown since you last saw me at sixteen years old!"

"No, don't get me wrong—I noticed!" Jayson took Sly by both hands, stepped back, and spread her arms wide, scanning her from head to toe. He nodded. "You've probably got every man in the village trailing behind you like a panting dog."

"Not everyone," she said. Grinning flirtatiously, she cocked her head. "And I have noticed your Americanized speech. Very cool!"

"Cool?" he asked, laughing at her attempt at American slang.

Andra's body bristled at the friendly and flirty exchange. Boiling, she marched the few feet to stand between her husband and the woman named Sly. Her back to Jayson, she crossed indignant arms to confront the brazen hussy whose lovely face now displayed wide-eyed surprise.

"Hey!" Andra's eyes steamrolled the other's fit body. "You think you can disrespect me by pretending I'm not here?"

The younger woman eyed her with bored contempt. She abruptly poked a finger into Andra's chest. "You need to step back from me, Miss Lady," she said, her accented voice infused with both anger and grace. "I have known J. J. a long time. He is like family to me."

Andra's left arm wind-milled, knocking her finger away. "And he's like a husband to me, so it's you who needs to step off!"

Andra saw the punch coming and ducked, and the woman's fist missed her crown by a mere inch. Straightening, she immediately threw a counterpunch. A sickening crunch sounded as Andra's fist connected with the woman's perfect nose.

Andra smiled with satisfaction as her victim lay sprawled on the airport floor. Blood spurted from her victim's nostrils, gushing forth like an open faucet and splattering her form-fitting sundress bodice.

Andra blinked, her focus tumbling back to reality at the sound of more laughter from Jayson and Sly.

Andra cleared her throat to recapture her husband's attention. She formed a polite smile. "Aren't you going to introduce me to your little friend?"

At her words, Sly politely withdrew and lowered eyelids over unreadable eyes just as Jayson turned toward Andra with an expression that was both contrite and tense. Moving to her side, he casually draped an arm across Andra's stiff shoulders.

"Surely, baby. This is Sly—Sylvia Menkos. We grew up together. Sly's family home borders my family's eastern acreage." Jayson's arm tightened—in loving support and not tense-filled guilt, she hoped. "Sly, this is Dr. Andra Theonopilus, my wife."

Sly's expression revealed big orbs painted in deep green, her eyes silent and studying. Andra bristled beneath the woman's curious inspection, wondering if she had been assessed, weighed, and measured only to fall short.

Still, begrudgingly, Andra couldn't help but think if she were a man, she'd already be in love with such a gorgeous creature, which made her further contemplate what affect Sly was having on her man.

Now smiling as if Andra posed no competition, Sly held out her hand. "Yes, I heard you were a beautiful African queen," she said politely. One eyebrow rose prettily. "I hope my words are politically correct, as you Americans say."

Andra shook Sly's hand with all the confidence she could muster. "Even if it's not, sounds good to me." Andra released the handshake and attempted a matching breezy tone. "And you are, what, a Greek goddess?"

Sly's youthful, bubbly laughter filled the area, causing a few male passersby to glance appreciatively her way. "It sounds good to me too, yes?"

Their laughter mingled; the sound was hesitant at first and then rang out with sincerity as time stretched on.

"So, Sly, why do you call him J. J.? Jayson's not a junior." Andra glanced briefly at her husband. "Is he?"

Sly laughed with delight, as if Andra were a dim-witted kid who'd finally said something intelligent. "No, no. His name is Jayson Jonas." Her eyes bounced off Jayson's now uncomfortable expression back to Andra. "Did you not know that?"

The words *as his wife* were left hanging in the air, unspoken.

Too embarrassed to admit to Sly that she hadn't known, yet refusing to lie in order to save face, Andra gave her a noncommittal smile.

"Hey, Sly, why are you here?" Jayson interjected quickly, nervously glancing over at the baggage conveyer as it came to life. He turned, his feet performing a weaving dance through the terminal crowd, leading Andra and Sly on either side of him. Reaching the moving belt, he spotted familiar luggage and quickly retrieved it. "Where's Stefano? He decided not to come, so he sent you to pick us up?"

"No," Sly began.

"Certainly not, baby brother. I'm right here."

Andra and the others turned toward the deep voice. Upon first encountering her brother-in-law, she had to hold back a gasp.

Staring at Jayson's older sibling, she was first aware he was extremely good looking. Like Jayson's, his slightly older face gave the impression it had been etched from the likeness of ancient Greek gods. However, whereas Jayson's face was open, honest, lively, and inviting, Stefano looked as if his face had been carved from actual stone—it was dark, closed, brooding, and sporting.

He radiated an undeniable hardness.

She moved closer to Jayson; however, a second later, her husband was gone.

"Big brother!" he called out, rushing into Stefano's arms and crushing him in a bear hug. Moments later, Jayson took a step back from an embrace that was both welcoming and restrained. Tilting his head, he beamed at Stefano, who stood a couple inches taller. "You're looking good, my man!"

Upon witnessing Stefano's frown at being called "my man," Andra looked at Jayson. To her surprise, he seemed not to notice Stefano's negative reaction.

"You are looking surprisingly well, little brother." Stefano's accented tone sounded as stiff as his posture. "I'm glad for your safe return."

"Thanks. And now," he said, and fearfully, Andra watched Jayson turn toward her, his hand rotating Stefano's frame with him. "I would like you to meet your sister-in-law—my wife, Andra."

Her peripheral vision afforded her a glance at Sly, who watched the scene with a bemused smirk. Although uncomfortable under her scrutiny, Andra dismissed the female Grecian's unspoken critique to focus on her new brother-in-law.

"It's nice to finally meet you in person," she said, hating the tremor that fueled her tone. Undecided regarding whether she too should hug Stefano, she held back, waiting for his signal. "I've heard so much about you from Jay."

Stefano produced another frown at her nickname for Jayson. She decided not to hold her breath waiting for a welcoming embrace from him, when Stefano launched an impromptu stiff bow her way.

"It is meaningful to make your personal acquaintance." As he straightened to his full height, his brooding dark eyes raked her body. "Unfortunately, my brother has not told me quite enough about you."

Meaningful? What does he mean by that? Does the word 'meaningful' even go with that sentence? She shivered despite the warmth of the airport. *Don't take what he says personally. This is a foreign country. Their manner of conversation differs from the States.*

Again, Andra experienced Stefano steamrolling her body. She stiffened further when Sly sidled beside her.

"Well," Sly said, looking at Stefano and back again. "How you like, African Queen?"

Andra wasn't going to touch that question with a ten-foot Grecian pole.

Gracing the annoying woman with her most charming smile, she returned her gaze to the brothers, who were now deep in conversation. Since his attention was diverted elsewhere, she bravely took a closer gander at her in-law.

Stefano stood proudly, his demeanor taciturn, projecting an aura of displeasure at the whole situation—meaning he was displeased with her. A fleeting picture of the young couple and the older gentleman walking arm in arm through the airport exit flashed before Andra's eyes only to dissipate into a puff of smoke.

Andra had to resign herself to the fact that the lighthearted scenario she'd hoped would be hers too had vanished into dismal nothingness.

9

D inner was to be promptly at six o'clock.
Arriving early at five forty-five, Andra hesitated inside the doorway of the villa's formal dining area, holding tightly to Jayson's hand. The room was vast and tastefully ornamented. The decorator had made excellent use of space and light, creating both intimacy and opulence.

"Wow."

Andra realized that since her arrival in Greece, she'd been unable to stop saying that word.

Her wide eyes traveled the elegantly decorated rectangular room. Looking upward, she stared in awe at the crystalline chandelier hanging in all its elegance over the long dining room table. To her delight, the sound from multiple dangling teardrop-shaped crystals tickled her ears as they gently swayed in an invisible breeze, tapping one another to create a faint melodic tinkle.

She imagined that her own eyes reflected the same sparkling flecks produced by each piece that caught the ebbing afternoon sun.

Although the flickering lights contributed to the brightly lit dining area, the main illumination came from the opposite end of the room, courtesy of two white French doors thrown open wide to reveal a cobblestone-covered veranda beyond.

"Hey, buddy," Andra said, awed, "I knew you said your family was holding, but you failed to mention just how much!"

Jayson laughed. "It's only home," he said, squeezing her hand. "No big deal."

"Yeah, right!"

She blew a single breath upward, the puff causing a lock of curly hair to lift off her forehead. Shifting downward, her eyes critically appraised her black blouse, form-fitting blue jeans, and black low-heeled leather boots.

"You like?" Jayson whispered into her ear.

"Yes," she whispered, turning to him. "Your home—this room—is beautiful, but what I'm wearing doesn't go. Maybe I should head back up and—"

"No," he said, lowering his head toward her. "You're beautiful—just as you are."

Andra lifted her chin, anticipating a kiss suddenly aborted by a biting tone.

"If you don't mind, you are blocking the entrance for others."

Andra automatically stepped back, allowing a regal Stefano to stroll between them. George entered the room behind him, taking advantage of the opening as well. Upon passing through, he murmured a polite "Excuse me" in his heavily accented voice.

She managed a friendly smile for her father-in-law; however, she threw Jayson a displeased glare concerning Stefano's rudeness. To her annoyance, he ignored the small incident, looking relieved when his cell phone rang. Pulling it from his pocket, he hesitated and shrugged at her with a silent message: *Don't mind him—that's just Stefano.*

"Whatever, dude," she muttered at his retreating back.

As Jayson headed to the other side of room for better phone reception, Andra's mind revisited the uncomfortable ride from the airport.

An unobtrusive Stefano had chauffeured while the lovely Sly rode beside him. Turned sideways toward the backseat, she'd filled the car with lighthearted prattle and charming local gossip. Meanwhile, sitting next to Andra, Jayson had struggled to contribute polite responses to Sly's chitchat. However, the effort eventually exceeded his male capabilities and he ended up staring out his window at passing scenery, leaving Sly to continue with an awkward one-sided dialogue.

Her mother's saying "Even fools seem intelligent when silent" had bounced around inside her head. She'd kept quiet.

Coming back to the present, Andra fought to contain tears at the situation she now found herself in. She sniffled once, again opting for silence, hoping to appear to the others as the wisest woman there.

Trying to avoid Stefano's gloomy presence, she scanned her in-laws' stately dining room and the subtle wealth it conveyed. Suddenly, not wanting her mute idleness at the dining room's entrance misconstrued as imbecilic, Andra purposefully strolled over to the long dining table. Undecided on where to sit, she decided to outwait the men in taking a seat.

Specifically, she wanted to see where her brother-in-law would park himself—in order to choose the chair farthest from him.

Her antsy mood heightened when no one appeared in a hurry to claim a spot at the table. Making better use of her fidgeting hands, she lightly touched the artfully arranged silverware set before her while keeping a covert eye on Stefano. He seemed reluctant to be anywhere but next to the dining room's self-serving bar.

Notwithstanding her distaste for him, she watched in fascination as his large hands lifted a brandy glass, threw a few ice cubes into it, and slowly poured dark brown liquid over them.

"Great," Jayson said, breaking the silence as he stuffed his cell phone back into his pants pocket. "I have a meeting with the church's padre next week. I'm eager to see what's happening over there."

Next week? Andra's mouth dropped open only to quickly shut. *We're going to be here that long?*

Jayson chuckled, his face bemused as he too watched Stefano. "I've noticed you're still putting ice in your brandy, big brother," he said. "Isn't expensive brandy supposed to be sipped at room temperature?"

"I like it cold," Stefano said.

Just like you. Immediate guilt washed over Andra at the

unkind thought, causing her to silently repent. Still, she couldn't help but mentally lament why they couldn't just have dinner and be done with family hour. *This is madness.*

As if reading her thoughts, Stefano stopped pouring. "We all should have a drink while waiting for the others to arrive."

Others? Forcing herself not to wring her hands in despair, Andra sighed heavily. *Great!*

Filling his snifter to its preferred limit, Stefano glanced toward the veranda doors, where George stood. "Father?"

"A small one, please," his father replied, breaking free from the approaching sunset to glance over his shoulder. "No ice."

Stefano then raised the brandy container—and one sarcastic eyebrow—Jayson's way. "Reverend, care for one?"

Jayson's good-natured expression switched off. "No, thank you," he said. His face grim, he strolled across the room to stand next to Andra and placed a possessive arm about her waist. "And you know I'm not a reverend—simply a seminary student."

Stefano took time for a microscopic shrug. His averted face was filled with hard angles and rigid planes as he poured liquor in a second glass for their father.

"Stefano," Jayson said, his arm around Andra's waist tightening, "you didn't ask my wife if she wanted a drink. It's rude, big brother."

The silent air in the room grew more stifling while Stefano calmly delivered George his drink. Only after he'd returned to the bar to retrieve his own brandy and taken a leisurely sip did he respond.

"I'm sorry. I figured since you are now matrimonially one mind and one flesh, I assumed she, like you, would not care for one." His dark eyes resembled twin stalagmite rocks. "However, I stand corrected. Would your nurse care for a drink?"

Andra gasped indignantly. "Why you—" She stopped short when Jayson released her waist.

"First, my wife's name is Andra," Jayson said firmly. "Second, you know she's a fully licensed doctor, not a nurse."

"My mistake, little brother," Stefano said. He turned to

face Andra directly. "And my sincere apologies, madam. Would you care for a drink—or would you prefer Jayson answer the question for you? It appears that for a physician, you lack proper communication skills—or has a cat claimed your tongue?"

In her anger, Andra lifted a hand to silence Jayson and almost backhanded him with it. "Thank you, babe. But I've got this one." She stared intently at her husband's brother, whose appearance was made of stone. "It's Dr. Theonopilus to you, sir. And for the record, the expression's 'Cat got your tongue?'—to which I can reply no, it hasn't. I'm just determined not to respond to asinine gibberish that pours from the mouths of self-centered, self-absorbed blowhards like you."

"Andra," Jayson warned.

"Enough," George said from across the room. Straightening, he rotated toward the others. "That is quite enough."

Thoroughly rebuked, Andra bowed her head and faced the music her father-in-law was about to play. Yet to her surprise, the older man's stern expression turned not to her but to Stefano.

"Son, there is never a time for rudeness. Please apologize to your sister-in-law this instant."

The room's attention shifted toward the silent Stefano. Andra held back a smirk. It now appeared a pesky feline had latched onto his tongue.

Stefano's defiant pause lengthened. Embarrassed, George looked to Andra. "My daughter, I must apologize for my son's behavior—something I have not had to do since he was, what, ten years old?" The older man sighed as distress, anger, and sadness mixed to paint his face. Disapprovingly, he shook his head at his oldest son. "Your mother and I did not raise the man you are right now."

Stefano's frame swayed slightly at the parental rebuke. He downed his drink in one gulp and performed an exaggerated bow Andra's way.

"Again, my sincere apologies, Dr. Theonopilus," he said, emphasizing her title.

Andra stifled a snort, knowing that despite his father's chastening, Stefano mocked her anyway. As the room's attention refocused upon her, the waiting silence bullied her into being civil in return.

"Apology accepted," she said. Then, in an attempt to outdo his politeness, she begrudgingly added, "And it's Andra."

Once again, Stefano bowed slightly, and in her estimation, he dismissed her with the gesture.

"Looks like one big, happy family," a lilting voice called out from the doorway. "Are we late?"

Upon hearing the female accent, Andra bit back a retort. *Oh, great! More toxins to fill the air.*

Her ire at Stefano was downgraded to simple annoyance once her focus rerouted to the doorway. Standing there was Sly, looking more beautiful than ever. Her long, thick hair was swept high upon her head. Curly tendrils and big gold-hooped earrings framed her heart-shaped face, while her toned body sported a simple white silk blouse over black slacks. Her radiant loveliness nearly overshadowed the handsome male who stood next to her.

"Sly, Paulo, your timing's impeccable," Stefano muttered as he turned to refill his glass with more ice cubes and brandy. He raised his replenished drink in salute, speaking with a louder monotone. "Yes, just one big, happy family gathering, as you can see."

At the word *family*, he looked succinctly at Andra, his cold stare implying she needn't consider herself included.

"Papa Georigios!" Sly cried, her accented voice causing her exclamation to sound melodic. She raced to his side and hugged the older man with great enthusiasm. "You are looking extremely handsome this evening. What—you got yourself a girlfriend? I'm jealous."

Ha-ha! Andra thought, wanting to roll her eyes. *Kiss-up.*

George's carefree laughter filled the air. "Thank you, Sylvia," he answered, beaming with a newfound happiness. "And you become more and more like your lovely mother—may she rest in peace." His eyes bounced from Sly to Andra and back again. "No new love interests, but the beauty in this room can revive even the loneliest of hearts. And speaking of beauty, have you met my daughter-in-law, Andra?"

"Yes, I've met the ravishing Dr. Theonopilus." Sly smiled at George, peeked over at Andra, and then turned her brother's way. "Paulo, this is her. What did I tell you?"

I can only imagine, Andra thought wryly.

Paulo's long stride quickly covered the distance between him and Jayson, and he stretched out his hand in a friendly fashion, prompting Jayson to grab it with an ardent handshake. "J. J., so nice to see you again!"

"It's been a long time, Paulo." Jayson pulled away, grinning. Simultaneously, they turned to Andra, and Jayson said, "This, my friend, is my lovely wife, Andra. Andra, this is my childhood friend Paulo Menkos."

An appreciative gleam entered Paulo's eyes, his smile escalating charismatically. "The word *lovely* does not quite fit, my friend, nor does my sister's description." He leaned over and lifted Andra's hand. His lips barely touched her skin, making the gesture more or less erotic. "*Stunning, breathtaking,* and maybe *magnificent,* yet still, those words are not quite enough. It's so nice to make your acquaintance, my *omorfi* Andra."

"Down boy," Sly said, her tone playfully suggestive. "Be respectful. Do not forget she is a doctor."

"Stunning," Paulo said, searching Andra's overwhelmed expression. "And intelligent."

Under his opulent praise, Andra lifted her free hand to her cheek and smiled in shy embarrassment. "Thank you. It's a pleasure to meet you, Paulo." She paused to gather her scattered thoughts. "I'm not sure what *omorfi* means, so I guess you'd better just call me Andra."

"It means 'exceedingly beautiful,'" Paulo said, bowing even lower over her hand, wiggling his eyebrows in a playful manner.

"By all means, call me omorfi!"

Laughter broke out in the room. She raised her head, taking in the sight beyond Paulo's bowed frame just as the antique clock upon the wall struck 6:00 p.m.

Across the room, the disapproving snarl on Stefano's face froze her smile.

Like during the car ride from the airport, maybe even more so, Andra fervently wished the situation she found herself in was already over.

10

At brunch, Al studied her youngest daughter as she chewed in silence, knowing Racine deliberately ignored her watchful stare.

Sighing in an exaggerated manner, the girl used her fork to worry her scrambled eggs. Concentrating hard, Racine picked up her triangularly cut wheat toast. She smelled it before taking a small bite only to then return it to her plate at an exact ninety-degree angle. She munched the bread mechanically and finished by washing it down with a long swallow of orange juice.

Her second sigh deeply soulful, she placed her glass on the table at a precise distance from her plate, rotating it once to her specifications. She forked her eggs once more. Seconds later, she dropped the utensil with a clatter, her voice contrastingly quiet.

"You don't want to hear it, Mother."

With agitated importance, Racine retrieved the downed fork, meticulously folded her napkin, and placed the utensil on it.

Al observed her daughter's precise actions before wiping her mouth. However, unlike her daughter, she tossed her napkin haphazardly over her half-eaten brunch. "So tell me anyway," she said.

The third sigh escaped with a blast, its sound a combination of resignation, anger, and worry. Her eyes swung in Al's direction. "I've texted Andra three times since she left, and I've yet to get an answer back."

Wanting to keep her demeanor void of the same worry she currently witnessed in her daughter, Al plastered a serene expression upon her face. "Well," she said slowly, "maybe she hasn't had time to respond to your texts."

Racine scooted back in her chair, throwing one arm carelessly over its back. "Look, I texted her twice during their flight over there." Racine's dangling hand lifted when Al was ready to interrupt her. "I know, I know—she probably turned her phone off for the flight. But that shouldn't have stopped her from calling the minute she landed."

"And when was the third time?"

"Right before I came to the table."

Al glanced at her wristwatch. "It's around dinnertime over there, so maybe ..." Al's head lifted at her daughter abruptly rising. Warily, she watched Racine round her chair to stand behind it, her hands straining as they gripped its headrest.

"Mama, there's no excuse. Either Andra's too selfish to give us a heads-up she made it to Athens—"

Al shook her head. "No, Andra would never make us worry."

"Okay. So the only other alternative is that she couldn't contact us."

Al sat forward in mute contemplation, studying her daughter's rigid posture. As if unable to stomach the silence, Racine pushed her chair under the table, stopping it a near-perfect two inches from the table. Without another word, she pivoted on her heels and headed for the exit.

"Wait, Race. What are you trying to say?"

Racine stopped. Calmly, she faced Al again, her expression now determined. "What I'm saying is, I'll give her a few more days to get in touch."

Across the room, Al's chair scraped loudly against the polished linoleum when she too rose. "Or else what?" Stepping around the table, she moved toward Racine. "What are you planning to do, child?"

"Mother, I'm going to get my passport in order," Racine said. She turned to leave. "And I'm heading for Greece."

Al swiftly closed the distance between them and grabbed

her daughter's arm, spinning her around. "Racine, you can't just go over there unannounced!"

"Watch me."

Under her grip, Racine's limb was hard and unmovable, and her facial features were just as inflexible. Al withdrew and crossed her arms. Leaning back on her heels, she stared unblinking at her obstinate daughter. "And once you get over there, where do you plan on staying, hmm? With them, I suppose?" She produced a mocking laugh. "The so-called enemy?"

Racine's chin lifted defiantly. "Maybe," she said. A second later, she grinned wickedly. "They are family now that she and Jayson are married, right?"

Saying nothing, Al blinked twice.

"See ya, Mama. I gotta go dust off my passport." Racine paused. She looked toward Al's chair, which was all askew. "Don't forget to push in your seat."

It was Al's turn to sigh heavily as she watched Racine spin on her heels and disappear through the door.

Returning to the table, she straightened her seat and wearily deposited her body in it.

Her eyes immediately traveled across the cozy room to the north wall.

"Our little girl's so much like you, Raymond," she said, looking toward a silver-framed picture atop the fireplace mantel. A striking dark-skinned man proudly wearing a tailor-made Marine Corps uniform stared out at her. "Obstinate and headstrong, trying my last nerve."

She smiled fondly at her husband's stately image, mentally hearing the answer he would've spoken if he'd stood before her alive and well.

"Okay, okay," Al said, rolling her eyes in exasperation toward the ceiling. "I guess I'd better dust off my passport too."

11

The dining room remained politely quiet.

Helena, hired help from a nearby village, served their first course: Mediterranean salad greens appetizingly topped with onions, creamy feta chunks, and plump black olives, drizzled with a light olive oil. The table, recently loaded with a variety of savory-smelling dishes sporting exotic-sounding names, such as moussaka, baklava, and halva, was set in a way that allowed everyone to self-serve at any time during the salad consumption.

Waiting until the last salad plate was placed on the table, George gave Helena a smile, relaying brief instructions in Greek. Dressed in a simple dress overlapped with a big white apron, she nodded pleasantly and disappeared after closing the dining room door.

At that moment, Sly lifted her wineglass and waited for everyone at the table to duplicate her action.

"Stin iyia sas!" she exclaimed.

Andra noticed everyone, with the exception of a reticent Stefano, boisterously repeated the Greek toast.

Tentatively, Andra took a sip from her wineglass and immediately delighted in the wine's sweet, subtle bouquet. After taking one more approving swallow, she returned her stemware to the table and looked across at Sly.

"I'm not quite sure what we toasted to," she said, a little embarrassed. "My Greek is not where it should be. What does *'Stin iyia sas'* mean?"

Sly giggled with delight, and Andra hoped she was not

laughing with her, not at her naïveté. She still hadn't quite gotten a handle on the attractive younger woman.

"It means 'To your health.' It's an old custom," she said. A twinkle appeared in her green eyes as they shifted to Stefano, who was sitting at Andra's right. "It's so ancient that it's even older than Stefano. Am I right, Stefano?"

Andra turned to casually glance Stefano's way. To her trepidation, she somehow had managed to be seated next to him, even though it had been her intention to do the opposite. To her amazement, a faint, indulgent smile appeared upon his face; it was so quick that Andra thought she might've imagined it.

"Yes, Sly," Stefano replied, "and that is old."

Grinning happily, Jayson reached for a thick porcelain platter filled with a delectable eggplant concoction smelling of spices and roasted onions called *imam baildi*. Using the accompanying silver spoon ladle, he scooped a hefty portion of it from the platter and, with gusto, deposited it onto his plate.

"I have to agree; Stefano is pretty ancient," he said. He handed the large platter off to his left, where George took it. "I believe he's even older than our father. Right, Papa?"

George chuckled as he carefully spooned the stuffed eggplant onto his empty plate. "It does sometimes appear as though Stefano was born aged." He passed the dish to Stefano, who immediately took it. "Yes, yes, my son is well beyond his young thirty-five years."

Stefano grunted noncommittally. After ladling a much smaller helping than the previous men had, he shifted the dish Andra's way. Reaching for it, she grew mortified when Stefano placed it on the table next to her flatware. Trying to repress her resentment at the subtle yet deliberate snub, Andra quickly glanced around to see if the others had caught the action.

Fortunately, the other men were engaged in conversation while attempting to choose from the remaining dishes located at the table's center.

Unfortunately, Sly focused upon her with a closed expression. Blanching inwardly, Andra knew the girl had witnessed Stefano's slight. Eternal seconds ticked by under the other's scrutiny, and her body sagged in relief once Sly's attention eventually turned to Jayson, who was sitting on her left.

Andra mentally massaged her stomach's queasiness, again wishing she was anywhere but there. *Dorothy, you're surely not in Kansas anymore!*

Yet unlike the beloved heroine associated with *Wizard of Oz* fame, she couldn't simply slap on jewel-encrusted shoes, click their heels, and magically appear inside her bedroom back in Florida.

Forcing aside her anger at the useless make-believe, she calmly used the serving spoon to ladle up a small helping of the imam baildi. The eggplant delicacy, which initially had smelled like heaven on earth when Helena placed it on the table, had somehow lost its savor. Its aroma instead caused her already diminished appetite to shrink further.

Why had she been forced to sit next to this insufferable man?

She shifted the platter Paulo's way, and he charmingly smiled his thanks. After easily loading his plate, he handed the dish off to Sly, who scooped a hefty ration onto her plate, more than twice Andra's. Gracefully, she returned the platter to the table's center and then immediately dug into her food with delight.

"Mmm," she moaned, her chewing wrapped in a smile. She swallowed slowly. "This is my favorite dish. I love coming here for the delicious meals."

Stefano took the time to sip his wine. After picking up his knife and fork with long fingers, he cut into perfectly grilled sea bass stuffed with garlic and herbs. His glance traveled across the table to touch upon Sly's face. "Yes, I know. I asked Helena to prepare it especially for you."

Again, Andra tried not to flinch at his statement, yet she experienced a sharp stab in her gut all the same. At first, she didn't understand why Stefano's words stung so much that time around.

Eventually, it came to her: she was the guest there; the dinner should've been prepared in her honor, not Sly's.

The churning in her stomach increased a notch in its intensity. As a physician, Andra knew if she didn't control her toxic emotions and stop allowing her infuriating brother-in-law to upset her, by the time she and Jayson returned to the States, she'd be in possession of a full-blown ulcer.

Determined, she willed herself to an emotionally serene place. However, she had to take a sip of wine, straighten her napkin on her lap, and lastly force-feed herself some imam baildi in order to get there. A short time later, an invisible force tugged at her senses, alerting Andra to the fact that Jayson now studied her. Glancing over at him sporting a frown, she squashed the desire to stick her tongue out when he mouthed, "Are you okay?"

Instead, Andra nodded diplomatically. Forced to plaster on a neutral expression, she ducked her head to study her half-empty plate. Casually, she played with her food until she chose to spear a black olive from her salad and slip it inside her mouth.

"Andra, my dear, would you like to partake in an entree other than the imam baildi? Some grilled bass or pasta salad perhaps?" George asked. "There is plenty here. I hope it is to your liking."

Startled at being addressed, Andra almost choked on her food. Coughing once, she stole a moment to sip her wine to wash down the half-chewed olive. Pushing aside her self-consciousness, she smiled at her father-in-law. "Uh, no, thank you, Georigios." She willed her smile to brighten for his benefit alone. "I'm not too hungry this evening. You know, jet lag and all."

George nodded, his expression sympathetic. "I understand." He paused for a moment before continuing. "Andra, it would please me much if you called me Papa George. We are family now."

Andra glanced over at Jayson, who gave her a winning "See? I told you they'd like you" grin. Personally, she wanted to slap it off his face. She curtly dismissed him, returning her attention to her father-in-law.

"Yes, of course," she said, her smile sincere. "I would be honored, Papa George."

Sitting directly across from her, a taciturn Sly speared a feta cube with her fork and slipped the morsel between her lips. She chewed carefully, her eyes intense upon Andra. Suddenly, her expression turned innocent as she looked upon Stefano. Her green orbs studied him for a moment before they eventually slid back to Andra. "So how are you adjusting to the Grecian life, *Yatros*?"

Having just placed some salad in her mouth, Andra paused at the question. Instinctively, she knew Sly had waited for her to put food in her mouth before deciding to ask her a question. Calmly, she took time to chew and then swallow. Glancing over the flawlessly arranged flower centerpiece at Sly, Andra put on an affable smile. "*Yatros*?" she asked. "What does the word mean?"

"Let me provide the answer for you, omorfi lady," Paulo said eagerly. He smiled generously. "*Yatros* is Greek for 'doctor.'"

Annoyance lit up Sly's face as she threw Paulo a "Mind your own business" glare. To counteract it, Andra smiled gratefully at him before directing her less-than-congenial attention back to Sly. "Well, I'm adjusting as well as can be expected, I suppose. Everyone's been so cordial."

She experienced the temperature drop another degree beside her. In her peripheral vision, she witnessed Stefano stiffen. He made a strange, throaty noise she somehow knew came from his irritation.

Good. "However, Sly, it is only my first night here."

Again, Sly's attention landed upon Stefano, who rarely lifted his head from his plate, and then she scanned the entire table. "Yes, we all must make sure Yatros feels right at home," she said irritably and to no one in particular. "How do Americans say? Show her the ropes?" She graced Andra with a subtle, hardened glance. "I say it correctly, yes?"

Puzzled, Andra noted Sly's cheerful demeanor had dropped a notch since she'd first entered the dining room. "Sure," Andra said, unconsciously massaging her neck. It appeared Sly not only desired to show her the ropes but also wanted Andra to hang on them.

The question was, why?

Jayson winked suggestively across the table at Andra. "You'd better believe I'll make sure she feels at home—after we retire," Jayson said, wiggling one eyebrow her way.

To Andra's left, Paulo laughed robustly. "And if you need some help tonight, my friend, please ask."

Jayson produced a mock frown. "Paulo, why would I need help with my own wife?"

"Children," George said, smiling indulgently, "we must display some decorum at the dinner table, yes?"

Throwing his napkin over his plate, Stefano abruptly stood. The blunt action caused Andra to jump in her seat. All heads jerked in his direction.

"If you would excuse me, I'll be a little under the weather this evening." Embarrassment touched his face. "I am a little under the weather," he said, correcting himself, nodding in general at the table. "My apologies, family." He bowed slightly in Andra's direction. "Madam. Good evening."

The entire room remained quiet at Stefano's curt departure. Andra, now stiff with humiliation, strained to suppress the fiery tears that pressed with intensity behind her eye sockets.

The last snub separating her from what Stefano considered family was not lost on her.

From the smug expression on Sly's face, Andra realized it wasn't lost on her either.

12

The mattress dipped gently and immediately sprang back. Yawning, Andra woke. Blinking against the early morning sunlight streaming both invitingly and intrusively through the balcony's twin doors to their bedroom, she rolled over to see Jayson lazily stretch. Andra's sight roamed over bare muscles that bunched and released across his bare back, and as usual, his nakedness stirred a primal response deep inside.

Andra experienced her own abdominal muscles clench at his nearly perfect physique.

However, her overwhelming desire for him couldn't stop her internal alarm from chiming; the warning bell rang with an urgency that forced her into a sitting position. Simultaneously, last evening's dining fiasco downloaded into her brain, bringing to mind the tension that had thickened with each passing minute, her horrible fate of having to sit next to Stefano, his deliberate snubs, and, finally, his abrupt departure from the dinner table, which she knew had everything to do with her.

"Hey, mister, where're you going?" she asked. Dread infiltrated her brain, causing her mouth to dry. "What?"

As if caught doing something illegal, Jayson slowly turned. His eyes immediately lowered to her exposed breasts, where the sheet had slid unnoticed to her waist. His eyes glazed over before he lifted them. Taking note of the look on her face, he frowned. "Doc." He sighed heavily. "I've got to meet Stefano before breakfast to discuss family business. I told you last night."

He glanced away to read the nightstand clock, although Andra thought he did so guiltily.

I can only imagine who the family business is about, she thought miserably.

She fidgeted with the top sheet, which lay soft and cool across her lap, experiencing her once unfamiliar yet now constant companion: jealousy-driven insecurity. "And will Sly be there also? Evidently, your brother considers her part of the family too."

Andra's tone, combined with the name she threw out with it, caused Jayson to quell her with an irritated look. "Why don't you give it a rest, Andra?" he said. Placing one hand on his hip, he used the other to comb through his tousled hair. "I don't get where this is coming from, but there's nothing going on with her—and nothing ever will. I love you."

"Ha!" she said.

As far as Andra was concerned, Jayson's declaration of love sounded more like an accusation than an affirmation, yet she believed she had to take partial blame. She knew she was wrong the moment she mentioned the Grecian femme fatale, but she was unable to stop the hated woman's name from sliding off her tongue anyway.

Tearing up, she reached over to his side and flipped aside the cover, exposing the rumpled sheets underneath. "So, if you honestly love me, you'll come back to bed."

Jayson's eyes bounced between the empty mattress and her expectant face. "You know I love you. I don't need to get back in bed to prove it."

A thick, hurtful fog filled her head. Enraged, she reached over, snatched his pillow, and aimed for his head. He easily ducked the feather-filled projectile, which landed with a soft thud somewhere on the floor behind him.

"No, you don't love me—I can see clearly now!" Frustrated the pillow had missed its target, she proceeded to pound both fists into the mattress on either side of her body. "Ever since we stepped into your family's house, you've been distancing yourself from me, finding all kinds of excuses for keeping away from me. You wouldn't even sit next to me at dinner! Am I not good enough for you anymore?"

Jayson remained mute, as if her question were too stupid to answer. His prolonged silence turned her angry expression into a spiteful smirk: "Or do you need your brother Stefano, to answer the question for you?"

Impatiently, Jayson's eyes returned to the clock.

Now ashamed, Andra tried to squash her anger since she knew she was acting like a spoiled brat. Still, she wasn't ready to admit that to him. However, Jayson's next words all but confirmed he too believed she was acting like one.

"Why don't you grow up?" he asked. He shook his head in astonishment. "You're twenty-six years old and supposed to be a doctor!"

At his mentioning her age, she bristled. "What's that supposed to mean? I'm too young for you?"

"Maybe," he said. "Look at the way you're acting!"

His confirmation concerning her immature, bratty behavior further mortified her. Panicked at his leaving without resolving their argument, she tried to salvage what was left of their morning by attempting a coquettish attitude.

She only managed to convey the demeanor of a frightened child. "Please. Don't leave me alone."

He studied her for a moment, allowing his face to soften at her plea. "Hey, where's the highly intelligent, independent, sexy woman I married?" he asked. Through watery unshed tears, Andra watched him round the bed to sit beside her. "Baby, there's no reason to be afraid—is there?"

Is there?

As if to soothe her fears, he massaged one breast, forcing Andra to recline against her pillow. She closed her eyes against his stimulating touch; however, the apprehension she experienced remained.

"I know, but just stay with me," she murmured, arching her back as he took the massaged flesh into his mouth, his lips forming a powerful suction cup over it.

Moaning softly at the sensation, she found herself exhaling

in frustration when he withdrew, his recently busy hands now pulling the sheet firmly over her heaving mounds.

Opening her eyes, she witnessed her husband rise, his lips slightly compressed. An inward shiver pierced her at Jayson's accusing stare, which circumspectly replaced his previous lustful gleam.

"Andra, I have to go."

Once again, Jayson's agitation caused him to comb his fingers through his tousled hair, and with the repeated gesture, Andra knew he was frustrated with her.

"I'm not leaving you—I'm just meeting with my brother." He paused to stare at her. "Can you at least let me do that, please?"

It was their first fight, and of course, inside its cyclonic center sat Stefano.

Shutting her eyes, Andra turned away from him to press her burning face into the pillow. She relished the coolness of the soft material against her skin, for she needed something to chill her gathering hot tears.

She sensed Jayson standing over her, his motionlessness conveying unspoken words of appeasement. Yet the silence between them filled the seconds—until she felt the atmosphere shift upon his pivot.

Jayson's footsteps hardly made a sound as he made his way to their private bathroom.

When its door closed, the quiet click placed an emotional divide between them that was vastly thicker than the wooden panel itself. Andra let out an unconscious breath to allow her feminine pride to kick in, powerful in its attempt to prevent her sobs from escaping. She buried her face deeper into her pillow.

However, she couldn't stop her hand from trembling when she pulled the sheets over her head.

13

Emerging from her latest nightmare, Andra shot straight up, gasping for air.

Throwing aside the claustrophobic sheets, she quickly scanned the unfamiliar room. Upon closer examination, she took in antique framed pictures featuring generations of Greeks hanging proudly against clean whitewashed walls. For a moment, she actually believed she was in a simpler time past, when big Greek families gathered together, laughing, talking, and eating with people synonymous in ancestry, color, and ethnicity.

A bell-like tone came from the nightstand next to the bed, alerting her of a text message. The distinct sound forced an abrupt return from an imagined homogenous past when everyone was similar to the unsettling diversity of the present.

She sat still, listening. No light or sound came from the slightly ajar bathroom door; the bedroom conveyed an atmosphere of abandonment. She realized she must've fallen asleep while Jayson performed his morning ablutions; then, in order to keep his meeting with his brother, he had quietly slipped from the room so as not to wake her.

Coward, she thought begrudgingly. Her mind produced an image of Jayson stealing from the room on mute stockinged tiptoes, his shoes gripped tightly in each hand. A second later, she banished the image, realizing that if her imagined scenario were true, she had to assume equal share of the blame in creating it.

Her cell dinged again. Reaching over, she snatched it off

the stand, knowing even before she read the message exactly who had texted.

"Hey, U up? R U okay? I've texted you a million times. What R U doing?"

A million times? Andra smirked in irritation. *More like six.*

Somehow, Racine managed to pick the wrong moment to contact her. Glancing at her nightstand, she read the face on the silver-rimmed clock. Its wide hands revealed the time to be 10:07 a.m. Mentally, she performed a quick calculation, figuring it had to be around 3:00 a.m. in her sister's neck of the woods.

What is that girl doing up that time of the morning?

Sighing irritably, she allowed her fingers to fly across the cell phone's small keyboard: "Doing fine. On my way to shower. Text U later. Go to sleep!"

Sighing heavily over the lie she'd just transmitted—no, she wasn't doing fine, and no, she wasn't going to text Racine later—Andra rose from the bed and made her way to the bathroom to take care of business.

After flushing the stool, she pulled on a shower cap and stepped into the antique white bathtub, pulling the white-and-blue shower curtain shut. Sighing with weary pleasure, she allowed hot water to run over her tense muscles. Inevitably, she lost all track of time until the water ran cold.

After turning off the knobs, she pushed aside the shower curtain, stepped from the tub, and wrapped herself in a clean, fluffy towel.

Somewhat energized—yet not enough to leave her bathroom's sanctuary—Andra headed for the sink and its oval mirror. Tugging free her shower cap, she vigorously shook her head to remove any excess water from her hair.

Preoccupied, she used her towel to scrunch the ends dry.

She contemplated a self-imposed exile. Her purse contained a bag of airline nuts and one granola bar, and with the unlimited supply of bathroom tap water, she could barricade herself inside the bedroom for the remainder of the day.

Andra made a "Yuck" face at her reflection. She knew if

she carried out her plan of isolation, she'd undeniably walk the rocky road of cowardice.

Despite that unsettling thought, her anxiety blossomed at the thought of venturing out beyond the bedroom and possibly running into Jayson, whose face might display residue of his disappointment concerning her earlier childish behavior, or, even worse, crossing paths with a stone-faced Stefano.

As her brain summoned up his likeness, a fear she'd never known swept through her. "No." She shook her head, forcing away his image. "Go away, you."

She pulled out a large-bristled hairbrush and maneuvered it through a major kink as she pondered her newfound timidity. She'd never been a scaredy-cat when it came to most situations before marrying Jayson, so why was she afraid to face life's challenges now?

Was it that in the past, she'd viewed her trials not as stumbling blocks of doom but as challenges to overcome? And if that used to be the case, why did she now believe being with Jayson was a battle she could never win?

She knew why.

The solution wasn't as simple as overcoming her own issues and problems. Her situation with Jayson came with outside influences from strangers and family alike. It was their prejudices, judgments, and scrutiny she couldn't control—they plagued her as the true adversaries.

She lowered her hairbrush as hot tears gathered. Through a watery haze, she studied her image in the mirror. *Are you sure? Are you sure about this?*

She heard a soft, muffled sound. The noise filtered in through the closed door, as if someone had quietly entered the bedroom. Lowering the hairbrush to the sink's edge, Andra listened intently, her heart pounding.

"Jay?" she called out. At the answering silence, she spoke louder. "Baby, is that you?"

When no response came, her heart rate slowed.

She understood the villa, although elegantly grand, had been passed down from one generation to the next, and like most aged structures, it tended to settle at times. Unlike

Jayson, who had fallen asleep soon after they made love last night, she'd been unable to succumb to a quick slumber. Her mind had refused to switch off due to the dinner debacle, and she'd tossed and turned into the wee morning hours. During that sleepless time, she'd struggled to become familiar with the consistent creaking of the structure as it whispered long into daybreak.

Andra let out a sigh, knowing that was one more thing she had to deal with.

She caught a glimpse of herself in the full-length mirror secured to the bathroom door. Facing it directly, she cocked her head to study the curvy image. *Looking kinda good, my friend.*

At twenty-six, she believed she was in the best shape of her life; she was young, sexy, and full of fire, especially when cocooned inside her husband's embrace. She leaned forward to whisper at the mirror. "Jay's lucky to have you."

Deliberating on that declaration, Andra rolled her eyes at the reflection.

No, she was lucky to have him.

Without warning, Stefano's stern expression faded in from somewhere inside the mirror, his steely eyes roaming her body with a disapproving scowl. She gasped. Embarrassed, she turned away from the unsettling illusion and threw on her bathrobe.

Shaken, Andra loosely tied the terrycloth belt at her waist. For the life of her, she didn't understand why he'd come to mind just then.

Then again, she knew why.

Jayson's older brother was never far from her thoughts; for reasons stranger than she could comprehend, she experienced a tiny thread of unexplainable, illogical attraction for the scornful man. His cold attitude toward her repelled her, yet also drew her to his dark side.

Mouth open, she shook her head. Did she imagine herself to be a heroine in a Jane Austen book, in which she played a plucky Elizabeth Bennet to Stefano's brooding Mr. Darcy? Maybe she had landed in an Emily Brontë novel in which she played a dark-skinned Catherine drawn to Stefano's white-bred, emotionally cruel Heathcliff.

Andra jerked her head hard. Was she going stark raving mad?

Pushing aside thoughts that precariously balanced on a scale of insanity, she opened the bathroom door and entered the bedroom.

Straightaway, a subtle movement caught her peripheral attention. She swung in its direction only to choke back a frightened cry. With a shaking hand, she pulled her bathrobe's collar tighter against her throat.

Stefano was in her room.

14

Jayson poked his head inside Stefano's office and glanced around.

Upon realizing it was empty, he exhaled his relief. Although he was scheduled to meet with Stefano after breakfast, he was a little thankful he couldn't locate his big brother just the same. Jayson knew one major issue he needed to address with Stefano was his unspoken dislike for Andra, yet at the same time, he didn't want to deal with the subject at all.

Denial was a state of refuge most men chose to reside in; he wasn't ashamed to admit (at least to himself) he didn't have a problem visiting it from time to time, especially when it came to the subject of his marriage.

He pondered briefly his anger aboard the airplane coming over; he'd been ready to fight with the flight attendant who banged on the restroom door, believing she'd unfairly persecuted him and Andra because they were an interracial couple.

Yet as bold as he was with strangers, he couldn't seem to stand up to Stefano, despite knowing that was exactly what he was doing.

Jayson moved farther into the room, heading straight for Stefano's massive desk. As he stood over it, his eyes scanned the paperwork, folders, and different office supplies scattered on top. Angrily, he exhaled. All he wanted to do was discuss the family business with Stefano—and how he didn't want any part in it.

At once, Andra's naked body surfaced inside Jayson's

brain, forcing him to lose his train of thought. Lifting his head, he stared with unseeing eyes beyond the big picture window only to experience his crotch tighten in pleasurable discomfort. He not only lusted after his intriguing wife but also loved her deeply—more than he'd ever thought he could love any woman.

Replaying their argument, he raked one hand through his hair. How could he convince not only Stefano but also Andra of that irrevocable truth?

He jumped and then closed his eyes when a pair of feminine arms circled his waist. His crotch tightened further upon feeling the sensation of supple breasts pressed intimately against his back.

Jayson's finger blindly blazed a path along one silky arm. "Ah," he said, his face breaking into a devilish grin, "I was just this minute thinking about you, gorgeous."

"And I you," a feminine voice said. "Stefano told me I would find you here."

Jayson's eyes popped open as he quickly disentangled himself from Sly's embrace. Pivoting, he immediately stepped away from her, yet to his dismay, she matched his retreat with a steady advancement.

"Come on, Sly! What do you think you're doing?"

Her answer was a coquettish smile. He frowned, grunting impatiently as his backside came in contact with Stefano's desk. Sly took the opportunity to hem him in, moving closer still. Throwing a glance at the open door, he placed restrictive hands on either side of her waist.

"Someone might see us," he said. "Stop it, Sly—this isn't funny."

She laughed. Unbuttoning her top buttons, she gave Jayson a glimpse of her firm, perky breasts. "No, it's not funny." She giggled, the delighted sound contrary to her words. "This is very serious."

His darting eyes revisiting the empty doorway, Jayson cleared his throat. Sly was more than a few years younger than he, yet why did he feel like a clumsy schoolboy being propositioned by an older, more worldly woman?

"Sly," he said, attempting to straighten her out with a patient older-brother voice, "get real. You know I'm married to Andra."

"Yes, yet still, you're as nervous as a cat around me," she said. Her smile deepened as her spiderlike fingers crawled up his arms, stopping at his ears. Playfully, she tugged both lobes. "And I've always been fond of cats, you know."

Not wanting to drop his restraining hold, Jayson jerked his ears out of her reach. "I thought dogs were your specialty," he quipped.

Her laugh was light and breezy yet somehow deep and seductive. "Yes." She smiled, her eyes roaming Jayson's face. "Those too."

Despite his effort to the contrary, Sly wiggled past his hands to press against his body. Her resulting sigh slipped out in breathless contentment.

"Sly, why are you doing—"

"Ever since I was a little girl, I've looked up to you," she said saucily, interrupting. Her hands slid around Jayson's neck, where her fingers locked together. "I've wanted you since you first stepped off the airplane."

Pelvis to pelvis, Sly rubbed against him only to pull back, her eyes lowering to his crotch. Her full, glossy lips produced a pout. "But evidently, you do not want me in such a way."

"Of course I don't want you. I'm in love with my wife." Jayson reached behind his neck and unclasped her hands, jerking them to her sides. "Besides, from what I remember, you've always had a crush on Stefano, not me."

Sly grinned. Shrugging in defeat, she turned on her heel and strolled to a nearby settee. Gracefully lowering herself in it, she waited until Jayson reciprocated with Stefano's chair. Her dainty hands smoothed a nonexistent wrinkle on her skirt. "So, my friend, you've got me," she confessed. "I've been in love with Stefano as far back as I can remember. I still am."

Jayson raised an eyebrow in surprise. "So," he said, pointing in a circle to include him and her, "what's this all about?"

Again, Sly shrugged prettily, her well-sculpted body shifting to adjust to Jayson's question. "I did this for him."

"For who?"

"Stefano, silly. He put me up to this." Sly took a moment to refasten her blouse. Patting the buttons primly, she leaned forward. "The plan is to seduce you away from Dr. Andra."

15

"Stefano!" Andra gasped. "What are you doing in here?"

He sat across the room, looking both at home and formidable in the small settee nestled in the corner beside the balcony windows.

The late-morning sunlight spilled partially across his skull, giving the illusion the light made up half his face, the other half created from the shadows. His long legs stretched forth to cross at the ankles, while his outstretched arms traveled the length of the chair's armrests.

Upon her appearance, his hands gripped the armrests' ends, causing his knuckles to turn white. He studied her intently, as if she were a foreign specimen to be examined, dissected, and then discarded into an experimental junk pile for instantaneous removal.

Nervous, she darted her dry tongue over her dry lips.

He looked lethal and powerful and projected the aura of a man most would dare not cross. His lean frame was as taut as that of an uncaged beast ready to spring on her at any second, and there he was, unrestrained, inside her room, and they were alone.

She was afraid.

The earlier scene in which she'd begged Jayson not to leave flashed inside her head; it shamed yet simultaneously toughened her. Her husband's frowning face lingered inside her thoughts, and she bravely straightened from the defensive stance she'd curled into upon discovering Stefano.

She lifted her chin. "Stefano, I asked you—what are you doing here?"

At his withering glance, she cleared her throat to speak with greater authority. "What do you want? I thought you were meeting with Jayson this morning."

Unhurriedly, he uncrossed his legs and rose to his full height, saying nothing. His dark eyes moved, roaming her entire length, his expression a mask of disgusted interest. At his assessment, she nearly lost her courage and took a step backward; instead, she drew herself up further, returning his steely look.

"I'll ask you once more. Why are you here?"

"I should ask the same of you," Stefano finally replied. "Why are you here, hmm?"

At his deep, carefully pronounced accent, a tremor streaked through Andra's core. His voice reminded her of something dark and mysterious, a deadly unknown, yet it was powerfully alluring, as if a targeted object had no choice but to draw nearer and find out whether it was heading for certain death or, upon contact, would experience a sensation so pleasurable it would die anyway from the sheer ecstasy of encountering it.

To her trepidation, Stefano descended upon her.

"I don't know what you mean," she said, watching his approach. She refused to give in to her fear and stood her ground. "You understand perfectly why I'm here—I'm your brother's wife. He wants me with him."

Andra's voice trailed off when he stopped to glare at her from what seemed a great height. She tilted her head to stare directly at his stony visage and realized her mistake. Her eyes were immediately lost in his.

She had to admit that her hateful brother-in-law was one sexy specimen.

She cried out when he suddenly grabbed her upper arm and pulled her close, causing her nose to collide with his chest. She found herself breathing deeply, her nostrils taking in the subtle scent of his morning aftershave beyond his polo shirt. Irrespective of his aggression, she wanted to run her itchy fingers through the springy hairs that peeked out from his open collar.

"So you're my brother's wife?" he asked, his tone deceptively serene.

Stefano dipped his head toward hers, their lips close yet not touching. His bodily aroma was immediately replaced with the cool hint of minty toothpaste.

For a brief second, she thought Stefano might cover the miniscule gap between them and kiss her; the notion made her both repulsed and weak with expectation.

"We shall soon see."

His words sounded like a threat.

Her blood boiled. Its heat succeeded in pushing her fear of him away—and she tried to do the same with his body. To her frustration, his grip tightened. She was unable to wrench her arm loose, and her alarm levels rose until she found herself in a shoving frenzy.

"Let me go!"

Too late, she realized her struggles had loosened her robe, giving him more than a glimpse of her nakedness underneath.

Stefano's breathing became shallow. He grabbed her wrists and, with a powerful jerk, twisted her arms behind her, pinning her hands to the small of her back. He forced her captured body forward.

"I said let me go!" she wheezed. "You ..."

Words failed her. Through her fury, Andra realized her nakedness now meshed against her brother-in-law's hard body.

16

At Sly's words, Jayson bolted from his chair. In shock, he stormed across the room and loomed over her. Appearing not at all intimidated, she stared up at him. Unconsciously, he switched from English to Greek.

"What do you mean Stefano asked you to seduce me?" At Sly's silent shrug, Jayson shook his head in disbelief. "No. I know my brother acts as if he doesn't care for Andra, but he wouldn't dare do anything—"

"Oh, wouldn't he?" Sly interrupted, also transitioning smoothly to their native language. She stood, walked around Jayson, and peeked out the office door. After glancing both ways, she pulled back and gently closed them in. As she twirled to face him, her skirt billowed sexily about her legs. "So why am I here? I believe you know I'm telling the truth."

Speechless, Jayson returned to Stefano's desk, but he chose to remain standing, his eyes once again staring across its surface and through the window. This time, he didn't flinch when Sly's arms encircled him, for her embrace was more of a sister's than a seductress's.

"Look," she said. "Your brother can be extremely persuasive and demanding. He believes he will get his way if he works on you from different angles—me and him. I don't believe in what he's trying to do—yet I understand where he is coming from." Sly squeezed his waist briefly before letting go. She returned to her chair. "This is what Stefano wants."

Jayson sighed angrily. "But this is not what I want." He scanned important paperwork that signified his family's legacy in the olive oil industry. He resisted the impulse to take a huge stack and, in a temper tantrum, tear the papers to shreds. "This is my life. I have a right to live it any way I want to. To marry whomever I want!"

"I agree. However." Sly paused until Jayson reluctantly faced her. "You are acquainted with your brother, aren't you? He will stop at nothing until he wins—whether it's keeping you here or breaking apart your marriage. If he had to choose, I believe he would prefer the latter."

"Why?" Jayson said, mostly to himself. "Why can't he accept Andra? Why doesn't he like her?"

The younger woman stared across the room; her hesitance to answer was clear, yet even clearer was her expression of pity. Momentarily, she graced him with a wistful smile. "Because sometimes we hate that which we cannot have."

"Huh?" Jayson asked. "What do you mean?"

Ambiguously, Sly shook her head. She then rose from her chair. "Jayson, you must not tell your brother what I just told you."

"And why not?" Jayson fumed. In an instant, he realized denial was now much too dangerous a place in which to stay put. "Stefano and I need to have this out—the sooner the better."

"What are you—a teenager?" she asked with a smirk. Her expression grew serious as she retraced her steps back to him. Placing a palm against his chest, she used one finger to lightly tap its center. "You must reason clearly as an adult. You're reasoning with the emotions of your heart, not the logic inside your head."

Knowing she was right, Jayson took a calming moment to breathe in and out. Once he focused back on her, his expression turned dubious. "Okay, Sly, so what do you suggest?"

"The only way to truly win this battle against Stefano is to not let him believe you are on to him. Let him think you're ignorant to his schemes," she said. Thoughtfully, she fingered a strand of shiny hair. "You must figure out a way to undermine them, understand? Do a Trojan-horse thing on him."

Jayson had to admit what Sly suggested made sense. Folding his arms, he leaned back against the desk and took a closer look at her. "I'm wondering—how did you get to be so smart at your age?"

She grinned. "My training has been years of experience hanging around your brother; I followed him around like a little puppy dog, hoping to get a few crumbs of his affection."

Jayson nearly returned her grin. Then the thought of his brother's plot, and the part Sly nearly played in it, prevented his smile. He frowned. "What's in this for you? Why are you helping me to defeat the love of your life?"

Abruptly, Sly's youthful face took on a hard edge. "In order for me to win, you must win—and Stefano must lose."

Sly spun and headed for the door. Before turning the knob, her hand rested upon it. "And in order for you and me to win, J. J., we must separate him from the thing he now wants most."

Jayson lowered his hands to clutch the desk's edge, his knuckles turning white from the power behind his grip. "And what would that be? The destruction of my marriage?"

"No," she said. After opening the door, she paused to give him a shrewd green-eyed stare. "You are still using juvenile logic and not thinking with your brain. It is bigger than you're willing to imagine. Much bigger."

Jayson watched Sly silently close the door in his face.

For the first time in a long time, maybe since he was a small kid, he was afraid.

17

Hearing the knock at his hotel suite's door, Hog set his drink on the bar's counter and strolled toward the door. Once he swung it open, his mouth stretched wide into a welcoming grin. In appreciation, he skimmed the shapely physique attached to the lovely face framed outside the doorway.

"Well, good morning! Come on in." He stepped aside and waited as the blonde hesitated before crossing over. She jumped when he closed the door and quickly encircled her waist with a one-armed embrace, pulling her farther into the room. "I'm so glad you took me up on my invitation to meet outside the airport. A single man can get pretty lonely traveling abroad."

Clutching a white strapless purse to her chest, Sapphire pulled away to distance herself. Her eyes darted about the suite in nervous curiosity, her wary expression gradually transforming into admiration at her surroundings.

Seconds ticked by as he watched her wide-eyed stare.

"You like?" he asked once she'd scanned the entire area. "Are you impressed?"

She gave him a tiny smile. "Very. I knew you were well off, but ..."

Hog chuckled modestly and headed for the sitting room, which doubled as his personal bar area. Behind him, he heard no movement. Casually, he sidled to the counter and reached for the scotch bottle. Curious as to whether he'd succeeded in projecting a nonthreatening air, he leaned backward to look past the threshold that separated them.

"Drink, darlin'?"

Her feet hesitantly carried her forward to stop a few feet away. "Okay," she replied.

Her answer satisfied his curiosity. Nodding his approval, he threw ice cubes into his glass and saturated them with equal parts liquor and water.

"Scotch and water's what I'm having, but I can fix you something else if you like."

"Seven and Seven, if you have it." After pausing, she added, "Light on the alcohol, please."

Motioning her toward the couch, he brought over their drinks. Sapphire took the cold glass with a nervous hand and straightaway took a sip.

Standing over her, Hog studied her tan loveliness. His eyes drank in her sapphire-blue eyes, long golden hair, and ears adorned with large hoop earrings. His eyes lowered to inspect her body, which was now minus her work uniform. She sported a white silk blouse printed with bright flowers of red, yellow, green, and a blue that matched her eyes perfectly. Sunshine hip-hugger slacks and white sandals completed her outfit.

Although what she wore was fetching, Hog would've welcomed the sight of her flight uniform. Maybe they could do a little role-playing—the sexy flight attendant and the rich rustler. His eyes returned to her blouse to examine breasts slightly smaller than he preferred.

But they would do.

She coughed nervously under his scrutiny.

"So," he said, sitting down on the couch next to her, "is Sapphire your real name, or did someone hang it on you because of those gorgeous eyes?"

Unevenly, she took another sip. "You got it," she said, looking edgy and wistful at the same time. "My father gave me that nickname. You see, he was in the diamond business before he retired. Whenever he came across an exceptional gem at work, he would come home and say, 'I found another sapphire almost as beautiful as my Sapphire's eyes.'" She blinked back building tears. "My Christian name's Carie Anne."

Hog scooted over a bit closer. "Well, Carie Anne, I was hoping it was just a nickname. Couldn't imagine you being a stripper on the side." One eyebrow wriggled. "But then again ..."

Her eyes studied him with a side glance only to widen when he moved in closer, but to Hog's delight, she chose not to perform a countermove, probably out of courtesy so as not to offend him.

He liked good manners.

"I totally agree with your pappy. Looking into them eyes of yours is like opening a treasure chest and discovering rare gems." He reached over and firmly plucked her drink and then her purse from her nerveless hands and placed them on the low coffee table. He boldly eliminated what little space remained between them and slid directly against her side. "Can I open your treasure chest and take a peek inside, Sapphire?"

As he placed an arm across the sofa behind her, her blue eyes ignited with red-hot fear. "Mr. Grainger, when you approached me at the terminal, I thought you said we were getting together so you could show me the sights of Greece."

Hog smiled. "Call me Hog, my lovely one." He reached over to entwine a thick strand of blonde hair around one finger and smelled it. It had a fresh, citrusy scent. "We'll get to sightseeing later if we have time. But right now, I feel like doin' a little bronco busting."

Her confused sapphire-colored eyes stared into his. "Bronco busting? You mean riding a horse?" At his silent nod, she finally shifted her body away from him. "Where are you going to get a horse?"

"Come with me—I'll show you." Easily, Hog stood, turned, and grabbed Sapphire's nearest hand, pulling her to her feet as well. With a firm grip, he led her a few feet to a closed door. "In here."

Reaching out, he pushed the door open to display a king-sized bed, still unmade from his earlier rising.

Whimpering once, she tugged her hand within his tight grip, her body leaning away from him in an attempt to pull free. Easily, he jerked her body in front of his. Wrapping her waist in a steel-like embrace, her spine now snug against his chest, he forced her to face her destiny.

"No," she whispered. She shook her head at the rumbled bed. "I believed you were a gentleman. Please."

Hog grinned gratuitously as her words turned into a pitiful moan. He'd come to expect it from them all, but more importantly, he'd come to relish it.

A woman's defeated whimper always infused him with power.

"I told that beautiful doctor on the airplane—remember, the one who saved your life?—that you, my little filly, needed a man to break you like a stallion." He nuzzled her ear. "And I've had plenty of experience."

"Breaking horses?" she asked, her voice hopeful.

He chuckled ambiguously into her ear.

"No," she pleaded, almost choking on the word. "I thought you were a decent man. I only agreed to go sightseeing with you."

"So you shall, little lady. So you shall. As a gentleman, I'll show you the sights right here." His self-assurance grew when her frame went slack only to give way to violent spasms. Pushing her body forward, he kicked backward, shutting the door. "And if you're good and quiet, I'll make sure this breakin' in will be worth your while."

Behind the closed bedroom door, the first muffled slap sounded, cutting off Sapphire's sobbing response.

18

"Don't, Stefano," Andra whispered, wishing she could free herself from his tight hold, slap his face, and retie her bathrobe. "Let me go now, and I won't tell Jayson about this."

Stefano's eyes watched Andra's mouth, they leisurely trailed across her lips that had gone completely arid. A strong impulse to wet them with a nervous tongue compelled her, and she nearly obeyed. Yet she resisted the urge, believing it might set off a chain reaction that would bring their mouths together.

His dark orbs delved back into hers. "You won't tell him," he said softly. "Your eyes speak it."

"Yes, I will," she said weakly, knowing he was right. Her simply being in Stefano's arms would have hurt Jayson beyond anything else she could ever do to him. Still, she uttered her lie with false resolve. "I will. I promise."

His slight smile refuted such a promise.

To her dismay, he chose to wet his lips, and afterward, she resisted her own temptation to rise on her tiptoes and kiss the glistening flesh. Instead, she pulled away from the captivating sight to return to his gaze. She immediately flinched under his fiery scrutiny as his eyes lowered to her breasts crushed intimately against him.

A low, hungry growl broke free between his curled lips. "Yet I believe this much. You've somehow put a spell on my brother, leading him around by the nose." He sniffed her.

"Mentally blocking his senses with your scent, face, and body so he cannot reason, cannot see you do not belong with him."

Abruptly, he released her hands. Wrapping one arm around her waist to keep them joined, he used the other to reach around to the nape of her neck, digging deep into her thick hair, holding her head in a power lock. His tongue blazed another trail across his lips, as if he hungrily contemplated a succulent meal.

"But you will never bewitch me like you did Jayson or even Paulo. I'm not afraid of you, Aphrodite."

Time skidded to a brief halt as Andra took in his words.

"What did you call me?" she finally asked, her eyes fastened like glue to his hovering lips. "Who?"

"Aphrodite."

He drew the word out as if he uttered it while in a hypnotic trance.

Andra remained motionless. Their intimate embrace paralyzed her, draining her body of strength. She knew she couldn't pull away, even if Jayson were to come into the room and discover them in such a compromising position.

"You make a man's blood boil," he continued. Contradictory to his words, the inflection in his voice remained monotonous. "You call to them with your bewitching face and perfect body and lure them to their deaths. Jayson is too naive. He does not have the capability to handle the likes of you. You should work your wiles on someone stronger, someone who can handle you."

"Who?" she whispered. "You?"

A crackling silence met her question.

Andra stiffened as his hand slowly pushed her head forward, moving her closer, and she found herself lost inside his eyes as his mouth descended upon hers.

Abruptly, Stefano ducked his head and coughed. He released her, pushing her away with such force that she staggered backward on surprised feet. While she fought to regain her footing, her alarm heightened as she watched his body spasm in a violent coughing fit. He covered his mouth, the seizure pushing his lips deep into his open palm.

His face turning an off shade of red, he turned from her and doubled over. His coughing continued as he stumbled toward the bedroom door.

Immediately, her inner doctor pushed forth, and she reached out to him. "Stefano, wait!"

Before she could stop him, he flung open the bedroom door and threw himself out into the hall. Stunned, Andra heard Stefano's feet trip along the corridor, taking him farther away; his coughing grew fainter until it finally faded in the distance.

It took a paralyzing moment to unfreeze from the electrified encounter with her brother-in-law and their even stranger parting. Shaken to the core, Andra quickly crossed over to the door and leaned out, searching the deserted hallway. Slowly, she backed up and kicked the door shut.

With a shaking hand, she locked it.

Struggling to regain her composure, she tried to make sense of what had just happened. She placed one hand over her mouth, recalling the unwanted physical pull her brother-in-law had over her. Gradually, her shame amplified upon her realization that she hadn't thought about Jayson during those final seconds locked inside Stefano's arms.

Lowering her hand, Andra used learned yoga breathing techniques to pull her physical and emotional state together. Just then, the cool midmorning air gently touched her bare breasts, causing her shame to reignite at her state of half dress. Her guilt-laden eyes lowered to her robe as she rewrapped it over her exposed flesh.

It was then she noticed the splatters, their crimson color heightened against the snow-white backdrop of the cloth—bloodstains that hadn't been there prior to Stefano's visit.

19

Strolling with precise movements across the hotel suite, Hog hastily tucked in his shirt and adjusted the waistband of his pants. He lastly combed his fingers through his thick silvery hair, making sure he was presentable for his next meeting.

The second series of knocks commenced before he reached the door. After taking a moment to plaster a welcoming grin upon his face, he pulled it open and automatically extended his hand toward the nervous person who stood on the other side. "Well, well, well, glad you decided to visit!"

"Good afternoon, Mr. Grainger." The young man paused to study the hand before reaching forth to complete the handshake. "I hope I have not kept you waiting."

"Course not; you're right on time. I like promptness in a business partner," Hog said. Severing their grip, he heartily slapped his visitor on the back, the force of it causing his visitor to stumble across the threshold. "Git on in here, boy! Don't be dawdling in the halls like some cagey, nervous cat."

He waited for his guest to take a step farther inside the room before he glanced out into the hall, looking both ways. Closing the door, Hog turned toward him with a wide grin. "You sure you wasn't followed, boy?"

The young man looked both confused and uneasy. "Certainly not, Mr. Grainger. Why would I be?"

Hog's laughter was rambunctious. "Just a little humor to break the ice, son! Don't you Athenians joke in this neck of the woods?"

The reticent man shifted from one foot to the other. With his nervousness, his accent grew thicker and his voice softer. "Yes, of course, Mr. Grainger. However, I did not believe this was the time for such levity."

"There's always time for such," Hog pronounced. He walked around his guest to head for the sitting room, where the bar and mini-fridge were located. "And the name's Hog, young man. Care to wet your whistle?"

The man chose not to follow and remained rooted to the spot. Hog glanced back toward the living room, and upon detecting the other's air of confusion, he once again hooted with laughter. "That means a drink, son! Do you care for one?"

From the distance of the other room, the man shook his head.

"Well, I hope you don't mind if I do." Hog slipped behind the bar, pulled out a small bottle containing scotch, and poured it into a glass filled with ice. Taking a small sip, he smacked his lips in approval. "I just love you Greeks and your expensive hotels. Finest liquors around."

Still standing by the exit, the younger man appeared at a loss regarding how to respond, so he simply nodded. "Mr. Grainger—"

"Hog," he said.

The man's face wrinkled in distaste. He then cleared his throat. "May we conduct our meeting? I'm expected back soon."

"Sure, sure," Hog said. He strolled from behind the bar, choosing the sofa to sit upon. "You're dawdling again. Come on in here. Let's do this."

After hesitating a moment longer, the man moved forward to enter the sitting room. He lowered himself onto the single-back settee directly across from Hog, his frame straight and proper, but hurriedly rose to his feet again when the bedroom door slowly creaked opened.

Hearing the sound, Hog twisted in his seat and frowned. Sapphire cautiously emerged, her makeup smudged, long blonde hair wildly tousled, and clothing askew. As if expecting someone to jump her at any moment, she tentatively inched her way across the threshold only to stop short at seeing Hog and the newcomer to her left. Flinching, she cradled one swollen wrist against her chest while wrapping the other protectively about her waist.

Hog plastered a welcoming smile on his mug. "Well, come on out, darlin'—don't just stand there simmering like a pig at a roast." Hog winked at his gentleman visitor and finally stood, scooping her large white clutch off the coffee table in the process. As he walked toward her, she reversed a step until her backside collided with the bedroom doorpost. "Now, darlin'," he said, overlooking her clumsiness to hold out her purse, "I know you want me to come back in and keep you company, but I'm conducting a business meeting right now."

Her face stiff with fear, she stretched out her uninjured hand and snatched the purse from his, clasping it to her bosom like a protective shield. Hog reached out, and at his touch, she bit her swollen bottom lip. Tears overflowed to splash on her torn blouse.

"Now, I've placed generous compensation for your time inside your purse."

Sapphire closed her puffy eyes as if trying to block out his voice.

He laughed. "When we're through, you go buy yourself some real expensive bauble, ya hear? Maybe get some medical attention for that wrist of yours; there's plenty enough for it as well. I don't have a problem paying for your clumsiness."

Her body trembling, Sapphire shook her head. "No, you did ..." Her voice trailed off when Hog stepped up to her, effectively blocking her from his other guest. "I'll tell what you did to—"

"Now, you hush up. You hear me?" He leaned in to whisper, so close that his lips touched her outer earlobe. "Say another word in front of my business partner, and I'll have a chat with your airline. I could tell them how you came to my hotel and propositioned me right here in Athens."

Unable to speak, she again shook her head.

"Yes," Hog threatened. He took his finger and gently ran it down the side of her face. "I even know enough of your higher-ups to get you fired and maybe get you sent to jail on prostitution charges."

"No," she moaned, more tears sliding down her cheeks. "They won't believe you."

"Maybe and maybe not. But I'll tell you this much," he said. His lips shifted until they almost kissed. "By the time I'm finished with you, your reputation won't be worth a counterfeit nickel, will it?"

The double threat of his voice and words silenced her for good.

"So kindly get back in that room and wait for me." Raising his volume for his guest to hear, Hog laughed good-naturedly. "Go on, darlin'. My friend here will understand that you prefer to stay in the bedroom—right, young man?"

His mouth open, the young man followed Sapphire with his eyes as she inched her way back into the bedroom and slammed the door. When Hog pivoted to face him, the visitor's face displayed his disapproval.

"Is the young lady alright? She does not seem well."

Hog waved away his alarm. "Don't worry about her—she's fine. She's just one of those skittish types that's not used to strange countries. Besides, I generously gifted her with enough money to chase away all her fears." Hog returned to his couch and reclined. "And I can do as much for you too."

Once the other settled uneasily in his chair, Hog reclaimed his scotch and took a long swig, draining it. He burped before plopping the empty glass on the coffee table between them. "Excuse me," he said, pointing to it. He hiccupped while trying to suppress a second burp. "Alright. First, I would like to apologize for not takin' a meeting with you when I first landed. I wrangled a few days for myself to sightsee. You understand?"

The man sniffed diffidently. "Of course. Our countryside has a lot to offer." His worried eyes took a moment to return to the closed bedroom door and then back to Hog. "So how may I be of assistance to you?"

"Well, as I told you in my earlier communique, I'm looking to expand my investing," Hog said, his voice lowering in its seriousness. "I understand from certain sources you might be able to help me with this particular investment."

The man shifted anxiously. "How?"

"Well." Hog yawned, stretching his arms out to his sides before letting them drop. "I know you're pretty close with the owners, and I could make it worth your while if you help me make it happen."

The man leaned forward. "To whom are you referring?"

"The Theonopilus clan."

The man grew still, his facial expression a nonplus. "You mean Mr. Georigios, Stefano, and Jayson?"

"Uh huh," Hog said with a short nod.

"Make what happen?" The younger man's eyes narrowed. "If you are investing, would it not be easy to accomplish this on your own by simply asking them?"

Remaining silent for a moment, Hog slowly rose to head for the sliding glass door that led out to the balcony. Slipping his hands into his pockets, he gazed into the clear blue-and-white skies the land of Greece offered. Gruffly, he cleared his throat. "Well, if it were merely to invest, yes." His back still to his guest, Hog cleared his throat again. "But if it were a complete takeover, now, that would be a totally different situation."

"A takeover?" The man's confusion abruptly cleared. He jumped to his feet. "You mean rob the owners of their business?"

Hog pivoted to face the agitated man. "Now, look here, son. You and I both know they're struggling to maintain themselves." Hog shrugged. "Wouldn't it be kinder to simply buy them out and take over the business? Would be kinda cruel to watch the owners lose everything and become destitute as the business folds on its own. Don't ya think?"

Uncertainty crossed the man's face. "But how are you to manage a—how you say—takeover? And what would you need with me?"

Hearing the reluctant acquiescence in the younger man's voice, Hog returned to his chair and settled in. Much more relaxed, he waited for the other man to do the same. "Son, you just leave the logistics to me. But I need you as my eyes and ears on the inside; report any strategies or plans being made concerning the business. It could mean a lot of money in your pocket for your services." Hog snatched up his glass for a refill; however, he put off revisiting the bar to stare intently at the other. "This could be a lot of money for everyone concerned, especially the owners. I'll make sure to take real good care of them."

Hog's visitor shifted his eyes uncertainly, looking everywhere in the room but at him. "I don't know."

Hog abruptly slammed his empty glass on the coffee table, deliberately missing its protective coaster in the process. The man witnessed the reckless action and jumped in surprise, his eyes registering fear once they swung back to meet Hog's.

"Listen, son, you're either in or out. I met one of the owners while flying over here. I've already spotted his weakness. Once I get a hold of the older brother's weakness too, I'm in like Flint. I may not even need you." Hog settled back in his chair, his smile returning. "With or without your help, this is gonna happen. My boy, you need to stop playing possum—decide whether you want your piece of the pie before it's gobbled up." Hog stood. "I'll walk you out."

After rising slowly from his chair, the man doggedly trailed behind Hog, and his much thinner frame halted just as Hog reached the door.

Upon hearing the other's footsteps cease, Hog turned to him. "Well, youngster?"

The man bristled. "Mr. Grainger, I'm not a youth."

"Oh, for goodness sakes, settle down! It's just a figure of speech," Hog replied. He reached out and straightened the youngster's shirt lapel. "One day, son, when you're much older like me, you'll learn to love such words."

When the other remained silent, Hog sighed impatiently. "So you in?"

The dark olive tone of the younger man's skin appeared ashen, as if he could throw up at any moment, but he managed a nod.

Good-naturedly, Hog slapped him on the back. "Cheer up, son—this is gonna work out just fine for everyone involved."

He opened the door to let his visitor out. "By the way, do you have a nickname?"

His young business partner swallowed hard, as if still attempting to suppress rising bile. He shook his head.

"No? Okay then," Hog said, nodding pleasantly. "Now, this goes without saying, but you can't let on about our plan to the Theonopilus clan. It wouldn't do anyone any good."

The warning was subtle, cloaked under the false ruse of friendliness, yet at the young man's mute nod, Hog knew his young cohort had translated the words into their true meaning.

Hog gave him a friendly push out the door. Once in the hallway, the ejected visitor turned to stare mutely at Hog.

"Well, it's been a pleasure doing business with you, youngster. We'll be in touch." Satisfied, he closed the door on Paulo Menkos sickened expression, turned, and headed for his bedroom.

Now he just needed to tie up some loose ends.

20

With Sly's parting words echoing inside his head, Jayson paced the floor inside Stefano's office.

His attempt to wrap his mind around the things she'd revealed was a slippery, mind-boggling thing. The plot to destroy his marriage was hard enough to swallow, but Stefano's attempt to include Sly in its sabotage was simply unbelievable.

Still, he couldn't figure out what she'd meant by Stefano wanting something bigger than destroying his marriage to Andra.

With a small gasp, he stopped pacing when a childhood memory rushed at him.

His neighborhood friend Hermes had inherited a pony around the time they all turned ten years old. The brown-and-white-spotted animal had been given the name Eliá in honor of Athens's local olive trade. Upon meeting the pet, he and Paulo had immediately fallen in love with it; even better, Hermes had unselfishly taken turns with them, where they learned to ride her throughout the countryside. However, after a few weeks, Paulo's fascination for the animal had waned and shifted to other boyhood pleasures, while his enthrallment had grown until he'd jealously desired the prized pet for himself.

In childlike desperation, he'd asked Papa for a pony of his own, but Papa had denied his request for some reason he couldn't recall. After his Papa had said no to his having a horse of his own, whenever he'd encountered Eliá, he grew angrier and angrier.

Subsequently, Jayson's boyish love for Hermes's pony had grown into hatred.

Now he knew why: because he couldn't have her.

Ruefully, Jayson frowned as the mind-boggling revelation buried him under a cascading ton of bricks only to force from his lips a humorless laugh. Sly was wrong; he'd actually had to go back to his juvenile past in order to decipher the events that now took place in his adulthood.

A coveted horse and Andra.

Obviously, he would never compare his sexy, intelligent wife to an animal. Yet he now realized his childhood memory was an analogy for his brother's present behavior.

Stefano desired Andra.

Yet it appeared Stefano's prejudices against his wife evidently hid that reality from Stefano himself. The thought caused Jason to slam a fist into his open palm, and he barely noticed the pain.

Stefano has some nerve treating Andra with disdain yet all the while desiring her.

Jayson's mental processes paused to insert another thought.

Maybe it was a good thing that his brother's feelings were smoke-screened by his stupid prejudices against his wife. At least his aversion to her would keep him at bay, therefore preventing Stefano from pursuing his true feelings for Andra.

Realizing his conclusion was a negative positive, Jayson shook his head. Sooner or later, his brother's psyche would force him to acknowledge his feelings for Andra.

Then what would his big brother do once those feelings were unlocked?

Preferring not to figure out the answer, he decided to shelve the matter for later contemplation.

Again, Jayson paused to stare out the window toward the villa's backyard acreage. To most, the green scenery had a serene appeal, the sun-drenched fields appearing open, free, and fresh.

To him, it was a grass-carpeted prison.

He sighed heavily, again scanning the business papers

in collective disarray upon Stefano's desk. Even those represented a ball and chain made to tether him there.

Why had he ever talked Andra into returning home with him?

He resumed pacing.

For as long as he could remember, he'd always wanted to dedicate his life to the church. For him, ministry represented personal freedom as well as a way to express his walk with the Lord spiritually. His calling was a personal thing, deeply private, yet at the same time, he felt led to openly share it with others.

He wanted to do this for himself apart from the family. His desire to pursue his calling solo had led him to travel abroad to America in order to attend seminary school there.

At least he had initially believed so. Now he knew he'd followed God's providential will to the States to meet and fall in love with Dr. Andra Williams.

Jayson stopped before an old family photograph. The picture, taken when he was about fourteen years old and Stefano was around twenty, had begun to fade around the edges. Nostalgically, he studied it, vaguely recalling the events surrounding its taking. Stefano had just returned home on college spring break, and his expression displayed a grin both smug and easygoing—the epitome of most college students' demeanors. His eyes shifted to his father, who stood tall and erect within the center of his family. He studied his papa's distracted expression. Jayson often had pondered over the years what had happened behind the scenes to make him appear so melancholy.

After hesitating, his eyes eventually gravitated toward his mother, who at first glance projected a beautiful, youthful radiance. However, if a person looked closely enough, behind her beauty, she too masked a deep-seated sadness.

He shifted the frame a little straighter on the wall, still gazing at his mother.

Although Andra and his mother were different in their physical appearance, Andra was the spitting image of his mother spiritually: beautiful, witty, intelligent, and similar in the special way she carried herself.

"Mama, you would've loved Andra—she's a lot like you," he whispered, tenderly fingering her one-dimensional likeness. "I miss you so much. Why did you have to leave?"

His watery gaze eventually visited his teen self. His face was slightly turned to stare up at his grinning older sibling; he recalled being engulfed with genuine euphoria at being Stefano's little brother at the time.

Smiling wistfully, he left his youthful image to study Stefano's once more. He couldn't help but compare the happy-go-lucky college student in the photo to the stoic man he was today. Right after his mother had abruptly succumbed to a rare form of breast cancer, Jayson had noticed a subtle change in his father—a despairing listlessness and soul-numbing lethargy.

However, her death had vastly affected Stefano as well. Unlike the days in the photo, when Jayson couldn't recall ever seeing Stefano without a grin, nowadays his big brother had a dark disposition and rarely smiled at all.

Jayson believed his mother's untimely death had been the beginning of Stefano's surly trend, as well as a contributing factor in why he'd never married.

Well, he silently told his brother's image, *at least you had our mother longer than I did.*

Upon hearing a noise behind him, Jayson swung around. Stefano abruptly materialized inside the room, his face clean-shaven. Looking at his older brother, Jayson swiftly thought about Andra alone in their bedroom, lying naked across the bed, the bedroom door slowly opening ...

"You're late," Jayson said, taking in Stefano's crisp light blue shirt, which was different from the white polo he'd worn at breakfast. "Where have you been?"

Stefano walked past Jayson, his eyes averted, to stare at the clutter on his desk. He stopped, picked a sheet from among many, and studied it. "I spilled coffee on myself and went to change," he said. He cleared his throat. "I'm sorry to keep you waiting."

Jayson observed his brother's underlying discomfort and immediately thought about the conversation he'd had with Sly. Anger clouded his thoughts as he switched gears to think about Andra, of her wanting to hide out in their bedroom like a criminal—due mainly to Stefano. His hands shook.

Studying his brother closely, Jayson jammed his hands into his pockets. "Stefano, we need to talk."

"Oh?" Stefano said, sitting down. He paused to take out his handkerchief and cough into it. After glancing at it, he quickly folded the cloth and returned it to his pocket. "What about?"

You know what! Jayson silently fumed. *My wife, Andra!* Then he heard Sly's voice in his mind: *Do a Trojan-horse thing on him!* He angrily raked a hand through his hair as he watched Stefano shuffle papers into some manageable order.

"You will go bald if you keep that up, little brother."

Jayson suppressed a frustrated, throaty sound; his fist shook with the desire to connect squarely with Stefano's averted jaw. Instead, he headed for the chair Sly had earlier vacated; however, in his agitation, he remained standing.

The stifling silence inside the office hung thick and heavy.

"You want to talk about what, little brother?" he repeated.

I want you to stay away from my wife. She's mine.

"The family business," Jayson finally said, feeling like a coward despite the Trojan-horse plan.

Briefly, papers rustled. "What about the family business?"

"Stop pretending you haven't a clue," Jayson said, shifting on restless feet. "I want no part of it."

More silence followed. Finally, Stefano swiveled in his chair. "May I ask why not?" A facial tic appeared above Stefano's left eye, its throbbing pulse faint yet perceptible. "Because of her?"

"Her who?" Jayson demanded. His eyes narrowed at the telltale brow spasm. "Her being my wife, Andra? That's her name, as you well know."

Stefano swiveled back to resume tidying his desk.

Again, Jayson found himself staring at the back of his older sibling's head. He let out a mirthless laugh. "You can't even say her name—can you, big brother?" As much as he didn't want it to, Jayson's volume rose. "Why is that?"

Maybe you might discover just how much you like the taste of it on your tongue?

As if he'd heard Jayson's thoughts, Stefano placed both palms upon the desk and slowly rose, his spine as stiff as a rod. Not bothering to turn around, he inhaled deeply only to let air out gradually and methodically. His eyes stared out the huge picture window before him.

Jayson took a moment to glance toward the glass too, trying to envision what Stefano saw, knowing he probably couldn't see anything beyond the blockage of fury his mind now constructed.

"Why don't you grow up, little brother?" Stefano finally said. Persisting in his refusal to face Jayson, he performed a 180-degree turn and headed for the exit. "Why can't you see past your own selfish needs when it comes to this family?"

Jayson winced at Stefano's suggestion he grow up—those were the same words he'd thrown at Andra earlier, before escaping into their bathroom. The embarrassment of being fed his own words nearly made him gag.

His eyes followed Stefano's robotic frame as it disappeared beyond the doorway. He was pissed off at his abrupt departure, yet deep inside, he was glad to see him go.

21

Across the way, her mother stepped out into the hall just as Racine did. They both reached behind themselves and, at the same time, pulled their bedroom doors shut.

Believing her mother should be the first to speak, Racine waited.

Their silent contest lasted a good thirty seconds—an eternity in dog years, Racine determined, knowing that if a dog had been sitting in the hallway between them, it would've gotten up and left two seconds into the game.

"I just spoke to a travel agent," Al finally said.

Intrigued, one of her eyebrows lifted. "Oh?" Racine casually asked. "What about?"

Her mother's eyebrows lifted as well.

"Mama?" she said, urging her to continue.

Sighing heavily, Al produced a wry smile. "I've booked us open-ended first-class tickets to Greece."

Excited, Racine clapped. Although she possessed a virgin passport, Racine never had any money to purchase an airplane ticket anywhere, let alone overseas, in order to break it in. But for Andra, come hell or high water, she would've found the resources, even if it meant selling the cherished coin collection she and Daddy had built together when she was little.

Daddy wasn't there to stop her anyway.

"Are you serious, Mama? Really?"

"Yes, really." Her mother stood in silence until she finally exhaled in defeat. "I knew I wouldn't be able to stop you.

Despite your past threats of glorious international trekking, this time, I believe you'd hop your butt on a plane. At least by my buying the tickets and tagging along, I can keep an eye on you."

Eyes brimming with grateful tears, Racine crossed the hall to give Al a hug, only to stop halfway at seeing her mother's irritated face. Evidently, she wasn't currently in the forgiving mood for being manipulated into international trekking in order to run after Andra.

Shoving her hands in her jeans pockets, Racine stared at her feet, kicking an imaginary rock. Seconds crawled by at a snail's pace before she was able to bravely glance up, entreating Al with her frequently used impersonation of a round-eyed Little Orphan Annie.

"Thank you so much, Mama. You're so sweet," she said. Her voice took on a hero-worship tone. "You know, you're the greatest! I'm always telling my best bud, Tracey, that my mother's Superwoman and how—"

"Cut the crap, Racine," Al said. To Racine's relief, her mother's expression softened a degree. "Your daddy used to try to handle me the same way, so I'm familiar with the procedure."

"And it worked, right?" Racine asked hopefully.

The hallway fell silent once more. In the end, Al relented. "Every time."

Together they laughed, the sound carefree and unrestrained.

"When's our flight, Mom?"

Her mother checked her watch, causing Racine to do the same. Sheepishly, Racine clucked her tongue when Al bestowed her with a "Gotcha!" look and giggled with delight, sounding like a young girl herself.

"Sometimes you make it too easy, Race." The older woman wiped away a merry tear. "Anyway, it'll be three days from today. We're flying out at six fifteen sharp, tomorrow morning. That'll give us plenty of time to pack and get our affairs in order before traipsing off internationally after Andra and her husband."

Not caring if her mother was still irritated, Racine closed the distance between them and threw herself at Al. Her mother sighed as if extremely put upon, yet in the end, she hugged Racine tightly.

"I'm only doing this for two reasons," she said. Racine pulled back, putting just enough distance between them to stare into eyes so similar to hers. "First, I sense this trip would be good for you, baby girl. Let you take in some different scenery and get away from ... things."

At those words, Racine stiffened inside Al's arms, waiting for the same old turbulent emotions to wash over her. Yet to her surprise, she discovered that her overwhelming excitement about traveling abroad to see Andra left little room for a painful invasion of the past. "And the second?" she asked, breathless in her joy at the discovery.

Al took a moment to kiss Racine's cheek and then pulled her close. "I've always wanted to see Greece."

"Me too," Racine said, feeling a tear slide down her cheek.

22

A soft knock sounded, faint yet insistent.

What now?

Straightening in her chair, Andra placed her medical book on the table beside her. Seconds lapsed as she worried her silver crucifix, her eyes fixated on the locked bedroom door. She couldn't decide whether to answer the beckoning knock or simply pretend she was in a deep blind, deaf, and dumb sleep.

She bit her lip in contemplation, knowing it couldn't be Jayson on the other side. He wouldn't have knocked; he would've just entered.

Maybe it's Stefano.

She shivered remembering his arresting face, her thoughts rolling back to her encounter with him. She prayed it wasn't his return; one electrically charged run-in with her husband's brother was enough.

Then again, she doubted it could be Stefano either. He too would've barged arrogantly into the room without so much as an invitation, as if he owned the joint.

Well, she thought, *technically, he does.*

She heard another soft tap, followed by the sound of a female voice calling her name.

Sly.

Andra sighed loudly. Was a visit from her any better?

Momentary confusion furrowed her brow. In a way, she was surprised at Sly's unexpected visit—even more so than a dreaded reappearance of Stefano.

At least *he* belonged in the house.

Andra rose, crossed the room, and threw off the lock. She opened the door.

Hating herself for doing so, she immediately compared her attire—a worn and shapeless yet comfortable sundress and flat white sandals—to the younger woman's green sleeveless buttoned blouse, flared floral peasant skirt, and matching olive-colored strappy sandals.

Her first instinct was to slam the door in Sly's face, call out that she'd be only a moment, and change into an outfit she believed would accentuate her figure flawlessly.

Andra pushed aside the fantasy, knowing she couldn't pull it off without appearing totally nuts.

"Hello, Sly. What are you doing here?" At Sly's raised eyebrow that implied Andra was being rude, she bit back words concerning the rudeness of uninvited guests. Andra stepped aside, opening the door wider. "My apologies; please come in."

"Thank you," Sly said, glancing about the room as if looking for someone else. "I almost thought ..."

The younger woman's words trailed off accusingly as she breezed by, wrapped within a subtle fragrance of lilac and lavender. Andra closed her eyes. Silently counting to ten, she took a cleansing breath. Shutting the bedroom door a little harder than she'd intended, Andra turned to face her accidental nemesis.

"So," she said, feeling as if her face would break under her manufactured smile, "to what do I owe this pleasure?"

Sly chose not to answer right away; instead, she stopped before the chair Andra had vacated, pivoted, and gracefully lowered herself onto it. She stretched out the silence further by reaching for Andra's discarded book.

Her Grecian smile was vague as she studied its title, *The Art of Medicine*, only to grimace prettily and return it to the table with a flourish.

Unblinking, Andra stood by the door, waiting.

Sly's smile turned cagey as her eyes shifted about the bedroom. "By your tone, I cannot determine if it truly is a pleasure on your part."

Again, Andra waited. Beyond the open balcony doors, two birds called to one another in cheery salutation.

"I've come by to check on you," Sly said. Soon enough, she gave Andra her undivided attention. "I haven't seen you since our family dinner on your first night here. You arrived, what, four days ago?"

Warily, Andra nodded.

"So have you—what is the word?—acclimated to our Greek lifestyle?"

Although impressed Sly knew the word *acclimate* and even more so that she'd used it correctly in a sentence, Andra shrugged. "I suppose."

"Mmm," Sly said with a toss of her shiny hair. "One wouldn't imagine so. You have not been to dinner since. You were most absent at breakfast this morning." Innocently, Sly peered at her. "Are you in hiding?"

Andra suppressed her own grimace, because hiding out was exactly what she'd been doing. However, she wasn't about to admit that to the brat who sat watching her like a demented hawk.

So you're aware I've taken all my meals in this room since my arrival and wasn't at breakfast today. Don't you have a home to go to? What's on your agenda, Ms. Thang? My husband maybe?

Taking a cue from Sly, Andra withheld a verbal response and instead strolled over to the made bed and the small pile of clothes strewn atop it. She picked up an item and carefully folded it.

"It's ten o'clock, and the sun is shining outside." Sly, like a feline stealthily watching a mouse, studied Andra's movements. "Are you ever going to leave this room, Yatros?"

What's it to you?

When no answer came, Sly shifted in her seat, looking at her perfectly groomed nails. "Papa Georigios is in notice of your absence, yes? Might even be put off by it, as you Americans say."

Andra forced her demeanor to remain calm and kept

folding. Coolly, she glanced toward the direction of her discomfort. "What can I do for you, Sly?"

Sly giggled, evidently amused at Andra's dodge of her questions. "Oh, I just want some girl talk. I was unlucky not to have a sister while growing up."

"But lucky for her," Andra muttered.

"*Signomi*? What did you say?"

"Nothing."

With a slight smile, Sly crossed her legs and adjusted her skirt accordingly. Tilting her head, she again watched Andra perform her activity through fathomless green eyes. She sighed dramatically. "Does Jayson know?"

Something in Sly's tone caused Andra to involuntarily stiffen as her brain simultaneously flashed an image of her half-covered body crushed inside Stefano's embrace. She let out a steady breath, proud of the fact that she kept her hands from outwardly trembling at the memory. "I don't understand what you mean," she said, selecting a lacy bra. With deliberate movements, she folded it the best she could. "Does Jayson know what?"

Feeling like an American field mouse closely watched by a Grecian hawk, she moved to the dresser and put the neatly folded clothing in its assigned drawers. She then straightened various knickknacks on the dresser's surface. She kept her face averted, making sure to focus on the task at hand.

"Come now, Yatros," Sly said, leaning forward. "You and Stefano."

Andra's head jerked up, only to catch her reflection in the mirror. It pronounced her guilty.

"Me and Stefano?" Her words trailed off at the memory of his glistening mouth hovering so close to hers—and the overwhelming desire and anticipation of a kiss that never came. She coughed and then put on her best haughty expression. "I cannot comprehend what you're talking about— and I assume neither can you."

Sly sat back and clapped with glee, although the merriment she displayed didn't quite reach her eyes. "Maybe the lady protests too much. It is the correct saying, yes?"

No! Andra silently objected, although she knew the girl had quoted it accurately enough. She reminded herself a good defense was a greater offense.

"Sly." She spoke slowly, attempting to make her words painstakingly clear. "You were there at the dinner table. I'm pretty sure you witnessed how rude Stefano was to me."

"Yes. I saw something."

Andra's shoulders lifted with a "There you have it" shrug. *Her naked breasts pressed against Stefano's solid chest.*

The room remained silent. Momentarily, Sly's gaze traveled south to Andra's chest, which was thinly covered by her well-worn sundress. Her Grecian eyes zeroed in on hard and pointy nipples. Smiling knowingly, Sly returned to Andra's face. "There's no need to get excited, Yatros Andra," she teased with glossy red lips. "Stefano is not here, only me!"

Andra silently counted to ten again. "Sly." Self-conscious, she hid her breasts behind crossed arms and took another deep breath. "I don't know where you're getting this stuff from, but what you're doing is how rumors get started. There's nothing going on between Jayson's brother and me. Absolutely nothing."

Their lower bodies pressed intimately together.

As if reading Andra's mind, Sly giggled again.

Andra felt forced to attempt more reasoning. "I love Jayson—he's my husband!"

Stefano's hot breath slipping between her parted lips.

Andra forced aside that mental image, as well as Sly's head bob—a nod Andra believed was in denial of, rather than agreement with, her declaration of love for Jayson.

"You should stay away from Stefano," Sly said, her voice hopeful. "Avoid him altogether. So it can be no one will ever know."

Her mouth open, Andra stared in paralyzed disbelief at the younger woman. A second later, she unfroze. "I've had enough." She marched over to the door and yanked it open. "Sly, I won't stand for your innuendos and snide comments. I didn't want to be rude, but I guess I've got to. Please leave now."

After peering one last time at the medical book, as if it

would provide her the answers Andra refused to give, Sly once again dismissed it. She rose in all her loveliness and gracefully strolled toward Andra and the open door. "You are wrong. I believe you do want to be rude. But yes, I will leave."

At the threshold, Sly turned to look directly at Andra. "However, let me ask you this—if I can see what is happening here, do you think maybe J. J. can see it too?"

Sly's hawk-like stare regarded Andra's ring finger, and her green eyes appeared to smolder as they took in the large solitaire and the accompanying diamond-studded band, which sparkled with genuine brilliance. Abruptly, she grabbed Andra's hand, bringing the expensive wedding set in for a closer inspection. "Very nice." She smiled sweetly as Andra jerked free. "You want to be careful not to lose such a valuable possession."

Feeling childish, Andra stuck her left hand behind her back. "I can assure you the rings are insured if I lose them."

The younger woman's eyes widened slightly. "Oh, your wedding rings." Her lips curled into a wicked smile. "Of course—those too."

Andra never wanted to belt someone so much in her entire life.

Sly tilted back her head, laughing with extreme merriment. She immediately composed herself, throwing Andra a sideways look. "Your return to the States—is it soon, yes?"

Staring at the insufferable woman, Andra had to stop herself from making an unsavory face. "I can only hope."

Sly clicked her tongue, her expression pure innocence. "With or without J. J.?"

"What's that supposed to mean?"

"Oh, nothing."

"Get out." Grabbing hold of the doorknob again, Andra yanked the door open wider, yet to her irritation, her unwanted guest pretended not to notice.

"Well, I am off to shopping. Would you care to join me?" At Andra's glare, Sly's face beamed with pleasure at the silent refusal. "Maybe Jayson would like to go. I'll ask. Have a good day, Yatros."

Wanting to be done with their meeting, she forcefully shoved the lingering Sly into the hallway. "Yeah, you too."

When shutting the bedroom door, Andra didn't realize just how hard she slammed it until the noise behind it caused her to jump.

23

Stepping inside the family library located off the formal dining room, Andra blanched once greeted with a blast of balmy air.

As the sweltering noonday heat rolled over her body, Andra stopped to unfasten her sundress's top buttons and immediately piled her thick mane on top of her crown. With her free hand, she wiped the beading sweat from the back of her neck.

She blew upward, the puff momentarily lifting curly ringlets off her moist forehead. Although other rooms throughout the huge villa allowed for circulation via their oversized doors and windows, their coolness didn't quite reach the library area, which had much smaller windows.

Letting her hair tumble back into place, she paused to poke her head through the door to survey the library's outer perimeter. It was deserted. Pulling back, she decided to shut herself in, choosing to bake inside a hot room than have anyone—whether friend or foe—catching her unaware via the open door.

At the thought of the word *foe*, Sly's mocking expression rapidly invaded Andra's thoughts. She pondered if the Grecian brat was currently with Jayson—or had her threat to occupy her husband's time been a bunch of crap? Determined, she shook her head to clear it; she had no intention of expending any more brain neurons on the silly girl and her sly insinuations.

Drawn deeper into the room, Andra stopped alongside a round mahogany table located at its center. She took a moment to admire the heavy wood's exquisitely formed dropped edges around the circular tabletop; the craftsmanship used to carve each vine, leaf, and flower implied its uniqueness and worth. Resting on its recently polished veneer was a Grecian-style wide-bottom vase that held a fragrant, colorful bouquet of freshly cut anemones, wild irises, and multicolored daisies that cheerfully rivaled the painted flower images on the container.

Each freshly cut flower was distinctive in its own right, yet together, as a whole, they formed a perfect sphere of beauty.

The beautiful flower arrangement caused Andra to think of her bridal bouquet, and the memory of its much smaller spherical perfection on her wedding day produced a sharp tug at her heart. She yearned to return to that carefree, albeit brief, period in her life.

Six months. I've only been allotted six months of happiness with Jayson, and now ...

Swallowing the lump in her throat, Andra forced her thoughts beyond her wedding day and glanced about her. Her watery eyes magically dried as they circled the room, ultimately landing on the ceiling-high bookcase that climbed majestically up the entire north wall. She marveled at the number of books shelved within the multiple bookcases— enough to keep a person occupied until the next millennium. The overwhelming need to pull random books off the shelf and run back to the safety of her bedroom all but consumed her.

Are you in hiding? Sly's voice asked inside her head.

"Shut up, you! What I want is to get back to the coolness of my room."

Andra frowned at the outspoken lie, knowing her reason for a hasty retreat had little to do with the heat.

A handsome face, all angry hard lines, mentally replaced Sly's question.

Piss off! You go away too!

Her brother-in-law's image now chased into mental oblivion, she scanned the massive bookshelf. Each ascending shelf dared her to climb the bookcase's literary bounty until she reached the top. Accepting the challenge, she approached the sliding ladder, reached out, and positioned it a few inches to her right.

She paused, her hand resting on the eye-level rung. Due to the heat, she wore only briefs underneath her sundress; she realized that once atop the ladder, she would be vulnerable to anyone passing below.

Maybe I should've put on a bra and shorts too before I left the room.

Andra chewed her bottom lip over her dilemma only to dismiss her fear of flashing people below her. Only Helena presently occupied the villa besides her. After her earlier encounter with Sly, she'd purposely dismissed the silly girl's claim on Jayson's time, remembering that he, Stefano, and their father had planned an all-day inspection of the southern vineyards—at Stefano's request.

She snorted. *Of course, at Stefano's request. Figures! The man always has to have his way in everything.*

Deciding to leave her negative thoughts concerning her brother-in-law at the foot of the ladder, Andra allowed her spirit of adventure to take over and carefully ascended the bookcase. At the top, she sighed with dizzy contentment. She reached out to run light fingers over expensive leather-bound spines, halting every few seconds when a title caught her interest.

After deliberating for a few minutes, she finally pulled three books of authors she recognized.

Humming the song "Man in the Mirror," she hooked one arm through the ladder's rung, tucked two of the classics under her free arm, and proceeded to flip open the third book. Her lips curled with delight as she mouthed the first few lines on page one, her anticipation mounting at getting lost inside the book's rich plot once she returned to the bedroom.

The ladder jerked to one side.

Startled, Andra nearly dropped her books. Tightening her looped arm against the rung, she glanced past her feet to the ground below.

His head tilted, Stefano stood gazing from the bottom rung, his large hands now holding the sides of the ladder.

His eyes were as sharp as a hawk's and just as predatory. His sudden appearance, along with his intense expression, caused her body to tremble.

He stood perfectly still, his lips saying nothing, his dark eyes simply watching, waiting. A fire ignited within her cheeks in sync with the hammering of her heart. As if a faucet had turned on, Andra felt her sweating increase; however, she knew her body's reaction had little to do with the closed-off heat inside the room, because her body had gotten used to it.

The inferno she now experienced rolled upward from him.

Andra closed her eyes and groaned, knowing her prophecy had come true. She was in a compromising position, perched on high, while the person she least wanted to be doing so was looking up her sundress.

Her eyes popped open. Silently, she cursed him for putting her in the predicament she now found herself. However, she overcame her blistering emotions to project an air of indifference by tossing her sticky hair.

"You look all of fifteen years old when you do that," he said, his accented voice deceptively charming. "What are you doing up there?"

"What does it look like? I'm pulling books to read." Despite her bravado, her knees locked, paralyzing her. She exhaled sharply. "Would you please stop staring up my dress?"

Calmly, as if she'd just asked him to pass her the morning paper, Stefano complied and turned his head. However, his grip on the ladder remained.

"What do you want?" she asked, resentful that he'd disturbed her peace. "Why are you here?"

He appeared unfazed by her hateful tone. "This is my home, no?"

Andra allowed her silence to answer for her.

"Come down before you hurt yourself, Doctor. I'll steady the ladder for you."

At his suggestion, which actually sounded more like a command, she hesitated. As the seconds ticked by, she grew more uncomfortable at his refusal to relinquish the ladder and step away. Still, she couldn't stay perched atop that ladder forever; she didn't want to appear as an impetuous brat who refused his gentlemanly gesture.

She'd already been tried, sentenced, and condemned as infantile in Jayson's eyes. She refused to go through the same with his older brother.

Shifting her books to one arm, she inched her way along the ladder in a slow one-handed descent. Moving closer to him, she mentally crossed her fingers, praying he'd have the decency to step back and give her space by the time she hit the last rung.

He didn't appear to have the same mind-set.

Andra sighed impatiently upon reaching the ladder's midpoint. "Again, why are you here? I thought everyone left the villa to survey the groves."

She was now a few rungs from the floor. He still hadn't budged.

"I am a grown man," he said patiently. "May I come and go as I please without permission?"

When Andra's rear paralleled his averted head, his arms dropped, and he stepped back. Although she didn't respond to his question, he continued as if she had.

"Yes, we are at this moment inspecting the groves. However, I returned home to take care of a matter."

What matter? She almost asked aloud, only to bite the words back. She didn't care—well, not really.

Once her feet touched the last rung, she lightly hopped from the ladder to land on nervous feet. Rotating his way, she was grateful his sight remained averted, because her body grew agitated at his presence, which was still uncomfortably close.

"But why are you here?" she demanded. "I mean, in this room?"

Andra's breath caught once he finally faced her way. As always, his handsomeness took her by surprise, because when he wasn't around, her mind produced an obscure picture of the devil himself.

However, she had to remind herself the Bible revealed that

at one time, Lucifer was the most beautiful creature created—before he became Satan.

"I have come for the same reason you are here," the devil's counterpart answered, his Grecian accent deliciously decadent. "I needed to retrieve a book."

"Well, have at it."

As Andra moved to step around him, Stefano reached out a large hand and placed it on the rung behind her head, stopping her. Her breath caught, only to come forth in shallow puffs when he moved closer, forcing her backside to connect with the ladder.

Stefano's head dipped, his mouth stopping mere inches from hers. His lips mute, he hovered, as if waiting for a signal to cover hers.

"What are you doing?" she asked.

Her body vibrated with fear and another emotion she refused to identify. Sly's earlier accusations concerning their relationship floated inside her subconscious only to dissipate with Stefano's sigh.

"You are a lovely, mystical creature," he said, his voice low and seductive. "Siren. Temptress. I sometimes wonder if you are real."

After their last encounter, when Stefano had called her Aphrodite, she'd used her cell to troll the internet, searching for information on the Greek goddess. *Lovely, siren, temptress,* and *enchantress* were some words used to describe the mythical female, among other sensual, and sometimes lewd, definitions.

Again, Sly's smirking face filtered into Andra's brain.

Defiant, she lifted her chin. She then slapped him, the force of it causing his head to jerk to one side. "If you're referring to Aphrodite, I'm not that imaginary creature." She wanted to shout yet only managed to push her words forth as a whisper. "You're ..."

The words *delusional, deranged,* and *cuckoo* came to mind.

Slowly, he turned back to her, his gaze even more intense.

Seemingly unfazed by her violent action, he used his thumb and forefinger to lightly touch her chin.

"Stefano, please." To Andra's horror, her voice sounded breathless and throaty. "What do you want from me?"

His answering sigh was heavy. "What do I want?" he asked. A subtle hardness changed his tone. "I want you to leave my brother. Divorce him. Do what is right."

She wanted to slap him again but held back. The second time would feel too primal—too sensual.

Andra found she couldn't break free from his penetrating gaze.

"Leave him."

She shivered at the nearly perfect inflection of his voice; it came across deadly, yet not in the sense that she feared for her physical life.

The danger was how it messed with her feminine emotions, causing her to mistrust her ability to resist his magnetic pull.

"No, I won't do what you say. You can't make me," she said, wishing she didn't sound like a willful child. His eyes lowered to her mouth, causing her to moisten her lips. "I'll never give Jayson a divorce. I love him, and he loves me. Get over it."

"How?" he asked. His mouth was positioned so close yet appeared a million miles away. "How do I get over it?"

Confused, Andra grew quiet. His question didn't seem compatible with what they now talked about.

His head lowered.

Fighting the urge to meet his lips, Andra ducked underneath Stefano's arm and scurried for the exit. A warning shiver immediately shot up her spine, alerting her that he chased in hot pursuit.

Panic billowed from her gut to explode inside her chest, making it hard to breathe. She knew if Stefano caught her, he would sweep her into his embrace, and the forbidden opportunity she'd avoided just a few seconds ago would be an inevitable, undeniable fact.

Her fear flowed downward to virtually cripple her, making her knees wobbly and her sandaled feet slippery. She knew she wouldn't make it to the closed door before he captured her.

Feeling a slight tug and subsequent release of her skirt from behind, Andra realized Stefano had barely missed seizing the material within his grasp.

She darted to her right.

Racing for the room's center, she reached the circular mahogany table with the flower centerpiece mere seconds before he did. Her shaking hands grasped the curved edge of the furniture as she quickly rounded it to place the heavy barrier between her and her pursuer. She nearly coughed up her heart when she observed Stefano stop on the other side.

Slowly, his body circled the heavy furniture, his dangerous eyes aglow with passion.

Huffing as if she'd just run a grueling marathon, Andra felt her chest unwittingly tighten beneath Stefano's probing gaze. During her flight, her top had separated to display her twin crests, each drenched in beads of nervous sweat that slid down her neck to gather at the cleavage between them.

Stefano's dark eyes thirstily followed the watery trails leading to her unbound breasts clearly outlined against her damp bodice.

Shaking her head, she circled the table, timing her shifting in direct correlation to his. "Get thee behind me, Satan," she whispered.

Stefano's brow lifted quizzically, painting for Andra a sardonic face that proved irresistible in its presentation. She held back a groan at the seductive sight.

"Why? Why can't you just leave me alone?" Attempting to slow her breathing, Andra drew in deep, ragged breaths. "Look, I'm your sister-in-law. You shouldn't be doing this."

Stefano stopped in his tracks, forcing her to halt as well. His eyes took a moment to disconnect from her heaving chest to rise and meet hers. "What am I doing?" he asked quietly. He produced a slightly arrogant shrug. "I am attempting to speak with you. However, you continue to run from me."

"You're trying to come between Jay and me—that's what you're doing," she said. "And I'm not running from you! I'm just ..." *Scared.*

"Come to me."

The three words slipped off his tongue as a soft command, producing an irresistible summons to her ears. The command disabled her reasoning processes until they were completely deactivated; her legs, which were as unsteady as a newborn calf's, now grew strength.

Mesmerized, Andra took a step around the table toward Stefano.

Behind her, she heard a perfunctory knock, and the library door swung open, breaking the magnetic spell.

She whipped around in time to see Helena fill the door's threshold, a surprised look upon her face.

Ashamed at her near compliance to Stefano, Andra shifted her books to her chest, crossing both arms over them to hide his effect on her.

"Signomi, Mr. Stefano," she said hesitantly. Moving farther into the room, she then looked at Andra. "Excuse me, Dr. Andra."

In Andra's peripheral vision, Stefano's frame came into view.

"It's all right, Helena. My sister-in-law and I were in a discussion," he said. He shifted closer to Andra. "What is it?"

"It is the telephone for you, Mr. Stefano," she said in broken English, which Andra suspected she used out of courtesy for her. "I was told to search everywhere."

"Helena, could you tell whoever it is I will return the phone call as soon as I am through here?"

Andra snatched her opportunity for an escape. Clutching her books tighter, she sprinted toward Helena—and the freedom provided by the open door directly behind her.

"No, no—it's okay. You take your call, brother," she said. Breezing by the plump woman, Andra lightly touched her arm. "If you come across Jayson, tell him I'll be locked inside our bedroom to get some reading done. I'll see him when he gets back."

"*Nai*, Dr. Andra," Helena responded, her voice puzzled. "I will do."

"Sister, we will finish our conversation at a later time," Stefano called out after her. "I promise you."

"Not ever!" Andra said her shoulder.

As if the devil himself hunted her, she increased her speed to hit the main stairs running, taking them two at a time. She made it in record time to her second-level bedroom, where she slammed the door and locked it, not bothering to care how loud a noise it made downstairs.

24

The morning broke to hues that were bleak and dreary. The Athenian sun hid behind overcast clouds whose gloom made the bedroom darker than normal at seven o'clock.

After Andra's mind crawled into consciousness, she opened her eyes and squinted against the austere day only to shut them again. The dismal-looking sunrise was a sure sign the day could only get worse, so she decided once again to become a willing prisoner inside her and Jayson's bedroom.

Behind closed lids, Andra heard Jayson's padded footsteps round the foot of the bed and felt the atmosphere shift once he arrived on her side.

Exhaling wearily, she turned and faced the other way, pulling the cover to her ear. Her eyes fluttered open again, taking in Jayson's empty pillow and ruffled sheets, before shutting them against the now routine sight.

"So, Doc, you're just going to ignore me?"

She burrowed deeper into her bedding. "Isn't that what you've been doing to me since we've got here?" she asked, her voice muffled against the pillow. "Go away."

She heard him sigh. With her mind's eye, she imagined his frustrated stance, with his left hand resting on one hip and his right hand running agitated fingers through his hair.

"Keep it up," she said. "You're going to go bald."

"How did you know?" He sighed again. "Baby, please look at me. We need to talk."

"Since when?"

"Since when what?"

Andra threw off her covers, struggled into a sitting position, and glared at him. With precise, jerky movements, she untwisted her pajama top and then adjusted her bottoms for comfort. "Since when have you wanted to talk?"

Jayson exhaled impatiently, his eyes raking over her sleeping attire. "Since when have you ever worn clothes to bed?" At her silence, he said loudly, "Until recently, never!"

"Maybe I didn't feel the need until now—you ever thought about that, husband?"

Exasperation driving his expression, Jayson paced beside the bed only to stop and look over at her. "Can't you at least come downstairs this evening to dine with the family?"

A mental picture of Stefano scrutinizing her from across the dinner table with a hungry yet disdainful expression, not to mention Sly's eyes bouncing between the two of them as if she watched a forbidden Ping-Pong match, made Andra's stomach queasy. "No."

Losing steam, Jayson's feet slowed until he eventually stopped. His face weary, he returned to Andra's bedside. "Look, I'm sorry I haven't been around lately, but I'm trying to do something here for the family." Lowering to sit on the mattress, he gently took her hand. "I owe them as much. I already feel like a third-class heel for trying to disentangle myself from the business so that we can return to Florida." His hand tightened upon hers. "But, Doc, you've got to be patient!" At her frown, he chuckled lightly. "Sorry—no pun intended."

She didn't return his smile.

"Andra." He exhaled. "Listen, it's not so easy to simply walk away anymore, especially now, when the family's dealing with this investor situation."

Her first impulse was to snatch her hand from his. Yet they'd not caressed each other practically since the day they'd arrived, and she craved his touch. Nevertheless, the hurt that had been on a steady incline over the last few days due to his neglect overshadowed her desire for him.

She pulled away. Still, despite her emotional wounds, Andra's curiosity was piqued. "What investor situation?"

"The real reason Stefano asked me to return home."

Andra snorted. *You mean summoned you home, don't you?*

He ignored her snort, and his expression swiftly deepened with worry. "Stefano believes if the groves keep going the way they have, there won't be enough future crops to sustain the family business and keep the workers on. He has a plan to allow the grove's soil to rest for a time while we infuse it with a product manufactured specifically for this type of agricultural problem." He sighed forlornly and then continued. "But it will cost money, not only to allow the fields to rest for a season or two but also to purchase enough of the product to cover the entire acreage for at least another three seasons. This is where the investors' money comes in."

"So where's the problem if investors are the solution?"

Jayson stood to restart his pacing. "I guess there shouldn't be a problem. However ..."

"However what?" she asked, exhaling impatiently. "Although at this point, I don't even know if I care."

"Andra, don't be like that." At her silence, he sadly shook his head. "Stefano believes taking on investors could be a slippery slope. Unfortunately, when any business chooses such a path, there's always the chance of a possible takeover once outsiders are allowed in."

"But if it's the solution, why—"

"This is our family's livelihood, Andra," he said. "This business has been in our family for generations. Stefano's under a heavy burden; he feels a strong obligation not to allow a setback to happen while he's at the helm. And he's asking for my help. Even Paulo has volunteered to come on board to assist wherever he's needed."

Jayson's expression pleaded for Andra's understanding. Returning to the bed, he waited anxiously for her response. When none came, he gently covered the hand she had retracted earlier. "Baby, there are also the villagers, the people who rely upon our groves to provide for their families. If we go under, they go under as well."

Ouch! Low blow! An attempt to evoke sympathy with the "We're about to lose the farm, and the hired hands won't have enough food to feed their families" scenario. Wasn't that playing on the late show the other night?

With a heavy heart, she mentally recapped her present situation.

The manipulative Stefano wants his brother—minus her, his black wife—to stay put in Athens to help him run the business. Furthermore, if Paulo was involved, then his sister, Sly, couldn't be far behind with her "assistance."

Any way she looked at it, she fit nowhere in this Theonopilus plan.

Andra felt a retching despair at being systematically pushed from Jayson's life; the reality of the situation bubbled its way past her esophagus to nearly choke her. She swallowed painfully in an attempt to force the sensation back.

"You know what I think, J. J.?" she said, imitating Sly's accented voice upon saying his nickname. "You don't want to go back to the States. I believe since you've returned, you kinda miss it here and want to stay. You're just too chicken to say it to my face."

Jayson turned away but not before she captured the confirmation on his face. Inside, her beating heart deflated.

Seconds later, he faced her again. He shook his head. "Doc, my home is where my heart is, and my heart is with you," he said, and Andra's own heart twisted as Jayson's glistening eyes displayed his conflicting emotions. "I can live anywhere—as long as it's with you."

Andra's mind reached forth to wrap itself around Jayson's lie in an attempt to hold on to it, wanting desperately to believe his declaration of faithfulness to her was the truth.

Slowly, he moved toward her, and as he did so, her tears fell. "Andra, the question is," he said gently, "can you?"

One by one, Jayson undid the buttons on her top, and when the last one was freed, Jayson slid the garment from her body. His dark eyes held hers captive as he pushed her onto the bed, her back arching when he captured her breasts. Her surroundings magically faded into obscurity once he removed her bottoms.

Vulnerable, she lay before him feeling like a naked sacrifice.

Sensually, he worked her body with his mouth and hands, forcing it to climb to greater unworldly heights of pleasure until her writhing frame burst into a billion orgasmic particles. Once she was fully satisfied, he arose from the bed to remove his own bottoms and then blanketed Andra with all his gloriousness.

Jayson joined with her, and she wrapped her limbs around him, pushing him deep inside. Silent tears ran like tiny rivulets along her face and into her hair; her lips, open and straining, let out a powerful utterance birthed from both sexual gratification and grief-stricken sorrow.

"I love you, Doc," he whispered against her damp earlobe.

Mute, Andra received his words with a bittersweet grain of salt. She too loved her husband, more than life itself, yet she also knew she had to find the strength to leave him behind in Athens and somehow find a path to a new life back in Florida without him.

25

Gazing at her blank stationery, Andra was unable to hold a single thought in her head, except the thought that she planned to leave Jayson.

The ticking clock was the only evidence that time continued to pass, but she wasn't sure how much had slipped by when she heard the knock on her bedroom door.

Warily, she regarded the locked door, the unwritten letter to her family concerning her plans to return home quickly forgotten. An image of Stefano standing just on the other side mentally emerged, his sensual, full mouth curled into a ravenous smirk and his dark eyes turbulent and hungry. The thought made the ballpoint inside her grip tremble.

She slowly rose, allowing the pen to slip through her nerveless fingers onto the blank stationery. She couldn't find the strength to propel her legs forward. Wiping sweaty palms on her shorts, she coughed to clear her throat of the obstruction that now clogged it. "Who is it?"

The person on the other side paused, heightening her anxiety.

"It's I, Doctor Andra—Helena."

Sighing with relief, Andra made her way to the door and disengaged the lock. She swung it open to reveal the amply built woman quickly straightening from her bent position. Andra forced back laughter at the inquisitive servant who looked only mildly embarrassed at being caught peeping into the keyhole.

"Good afternoon, Helena," she said, enunciating her words

carefully to make sure the Grecian woman understood her English. "How can I help you?"

Helena gave the resemblance of a small curtsy. "Good day, Dr. Andra." Her voice too decelerated to perfect her return greeting. Holding one corner of her apron, she grinned excitedly. "Visitors are here. They come for you."

They come for you? Sounds like a mob with pitchforks and torches ready to subdue the monster and take it away, safe and sound from the villagers. She swallowed hard. "Visitors? For me?"

Helena nodded. "Yes, Doctor Andra. Family!"

"Family?" she asked, confused. "What?"

Helena turned to leave, beckoning Andra with a soft, meaty hand. "Yes, come. They are in sitting room," she said. Andra watched her wide girth hurry down the length of the hall. She was extremely quick, much too fast for someone her age and weight. "I start all refreshments!"

"But, Helena ..." Andra's words fell upon an empty hallway as the woman disappeared around the corner leading toward the curved staircase and the first floor.

Standing alone inside the doorframe, she exhaled in frustration.

It was one thing to meet Jayson's family with him by her side, but it was quite another to meet-and-greet them all by herself. Turning toward the dresser's mirror, she gaped in horror at the prison garb she'd hastily thrown on upon rising with the understanding she wouldn't venture outside that room. Knowing it was too late to change, she smoothed over her sleeveless light blue tunic and white shorts, and on sandaled feet, she left the room.

Like a condemned prisoner walking the last green mile to her execution, Andra traveled the long hall toward the second-level staircase.

Andra, girl, you can do this! You're a doctor, for goodness sake.

She imagined entering the formal sitting area, her arm extended in welcome, and flashing a confident smile to her unknown in-laws only to get a sandal caught on the edge of an expensive throw rug, trip, and fall on her belly, her prone body sliding with the rug across the floor to unsuspecting, shocked feet.

"Stop it," she said, admonishing herself. "You are a strong, confident black woman. Deal with it!"

Arriving at the staircase, she took a cue from Lady Andra and held her head high, took a deep breath, and ascended the stairs, heading left across the Spanish-tiled circular foyer toward closed double doors painted in brilliant white.

The brass doorknobs were cool to the touch, and she welcomed their cold against her warm, moist palms. Simultaneously, she grabbed both knobs and squeezed them tightly, pausing again to suck in another fortifying breath. Her hands trembled; however, she chose to ignore them and pulled open both doors. Regally, she stepped inside.

"Hello. I'm Andra."

She gasped. Across the room, two women rose from facing couches and turned her way.

"I know your name. I've said it since I could talk." Racine grinned mischievously, while Al stared with tears in her eyes, one hand covering her mouth.

"Mama! Racine!"

At her exclamation, all three took off running and crashed into each other at the sitting room's midpoint, hugging, kissing, and slobbering over one another after the collision.

"I can't believe it's you!" Andra stepped back to wipe tears and snot from her face. "What are you guys doing here? It's been so long since I've seen you two."

"Yeah, we know," Racine said. Her voice took on a scolding quality. "The last time we got a real good look at you was at your wedding. Since then, you, being a doctor and married and all, haven't had the time—"

"Enough, Racine," Al said. She took a moment to smile at Andra, placing a loving palm against her wet cheek. "This is a time to celebrate, not bicker."

Racine reconstructed her expression into reluctant remorsefulness. "You're right—I'm sorry, Mama." Racine grabbed Andra's hand in a tight grip. "I'm sorry, Sis. It's just—well, I've missed you, even though you've managed to cut us out of your life."

Another quelling glance from their mother shut Racine down.

Andra laughed with delight, which caused both women to stare at her in astonishment. In the past, Racine's immature tirades hadn't been met with such forgiving gaiety.

"I'm so glad you two are here, Mama," she said, grinning at their surprised expressions. She then grinned harder, looking directly at Racine. "Yes, even despite our baby girl's thoughtless rebukes."

"Um hum, that proves it," Racine said. Her eyes studied Andra for a moment before turning to Al. "Mama, I told you she needed us here. Something's definitely wrong in Grecian Candy Land."

Andra shifted uncomfortably as the waiting blank stationery upstairs came to mind. "Who said anything was wrong?" she demanded despite the mental image. "Who?"

It took every ounce of inner strength for Andra to maintain eye contact with her family. She mentally chased away her guilt at her deception while swatting the air at her sister.

"A little defensive, aren't we?"

"Oh, be quiet, you," Andra said, admonishing Racine. "Besides, if you thought something was so wrong with me, why didn't you simply call—and not spend hard-earned money to travel overseas?"

Racine snorted. "Please! You never responded to my texts or voice mails." She shrugged conclusively. "So I figured if Muhammad won't come to the mountain—"

"Then the mountain should've just stayed put!" Andra said.

Effectively blocking out Racine's put-upon expression along with her indignant "Humph," Al stepped forward to look into Andra's eyes. "Baby, we're here for you. But if you don't need us, we have open tickets. If you want, our butts will be on the first plane back to the States."

Andra beheld her mother's face, one of calm and concern. Hers was a kindly face that she'd looked to for support many times while growing up. The thought of her leaving was frightening. "No, I want you to stay!" She threw her arms around her mother and hugged her tightly. Looking over Al's shoulder to Racine, Andra forced gathering tears not to fall. "It's just, well, I wish I would've known, you know, to prepare Jayson and his family."

"But it's okay, because now that you're married, we're family too," Racine said, her face defiantly smug. "Right?"

"You are correct." The male voice crossed the room with bold confidence yet managed to be coldly subdued.

In sync, the women turned toward the parted study doors. Stefano, tall and straight, stood inside its threshold, his face unreadable. Only the tic over his eye alerted Andra of his inner struggle to maintain a calm, objective demeanor.

The room remained silent as he strolled toward them, stopped a few feet away, and presented them with a stiff, abbreviated bow. "The young lady is correct. Any family of the doctor's is ours as well. You are most welcome to stay."

Andra swallowed. She hated the fact that she was the only one who knew he was lying through his perfectly straight white teeth.

26

"**O**h really," Racine said, her eyes narrowing as she watched Stefano. "You don't mind that we've invaded your mansion unannounced and without prior permission?"

"No, of course not," he said coolly. "As I stated before—"

"Save it," Racine said. With a smirk, she returned to her place on the couch. Leaning back, she plopped her feet atop the coffee table and clasped both hands behind her head, leisurely locking them in place. "See, y'all?" she spat. "Massah's given us permission to stay on his property. Call off the hounds."

Andra knew if she'd been sipping on a drink, it would've sprayed in a wide arc past astonished lips.

"Racine!" Her mother gasped.

A fleeting smirk appeared on Stefano's face. "I do not understand your meaning," he said, one eyebrow lifting arrogantly.

Lowering her arms, Racine shifted to sit ramrod straight. "Oh, I doubt that. You appear to be a worldly man with a fair amount of intelligence and business sense, I suppose." At Al's continued glare, Racine reluctantly pulled her feet off the coffee table. "I'm pretty sure you get the reference."

Unable to intervene without feeling she had to take one side or the other, Andra remained in awestruck muteness.

Leisurely, Stefano made his way to the elegant bar area on the other side of the room. After reaching for a brandy container sitting on the countertop, he turned and lifted it in offering.

Andra and Al shook their heads; Racine simply scowled at him.

"Yes, unfortunately, I did get your reference," he said. He dropped ice pieces into his brandy glass and poured a hefty amount of liquor over them. "However, I felt it would be more polite to simply feign ignorance at such a comment."

Racine jumped to her feet. "Why, you arrogant piece of—"

"Hello, everyone!" Jayson breezed in, strolled over to Andra, and gave her a brief kiss. His grin broadened as he walked past her to quickly envelop Al in an enthusiastic hug. "Helena gave me the news my in-laws were here. What a wonderful surprise!"

"Jayson," Al said, smiling. "So nice to see you again, boy."

"Hello, Mama!" he said, placing a wet one on Al's cheek. "It's good to see you too. You're looking as breathtaking as ever. Lucky me!"

Inadvertently, Andra's sights swung across the room to Stefano. His back now to them, he faced the bar, his spine so rigid it appeared as if it would snap in two from the strain.

She deduced that Jayson referring to Al as Mama had to be a contributing factor. Not knowing whether to be gleeful or wary at his undue anger, Andra dismissed him to return to her husband and family.

"Jay, you flatterer," Al said, her face radiant as she beamed up at him. "So tell me—how's my beauty lucky for you?"

"It bodes well for me, given Andra has exceptional genes to follow later on down the road."

"Oh, you!" Al tapped him playfully on the arm. She smiled at Andra. "Looks like you've been taking excellent care of my girl."

"Yes, ma'am, I'm trying my best!" Jayson gave Al another squeeze, grinning harder. "But I can't take all the credit. Like I said, those genes."

"I don't know, Mama—looks like she's lost a few pounds to me. And her face appears peaked."

At Racine's words, Jayson looked over Al's head. "And there you are!"

He hurried over to his irate sister-in-law, picked her up off the ground, and twirled her around. A second later, she burst into breathless, restrained laughter.

"Still both beautiful and obstinate," he sang, lifting her higher. "I hope you know that's a sexy combination to most men!"

Dividing her attention between both sides of the room, Andra could've sworn she heard a disagreeing snort come from her brother-in-law's mouth.

Or maybe she'd only imagined it.

"Boy, put me down!" Racine giggled, rebuking him at the same time. "You are shoveling so much crap I'm gonna need rubber boots to walk through it all!"

Setting her on her feet, Jayson chuckled. He placed a solid kiss on her forehead. "One day, my dear little sister, someone's going to capture your heart, and you're going to be as docile as a kitten with him."

Jayson's smile quickly vanished when Racine abruptly jerked from his embrace and said, "No way! I'm gonna give any man that kind of control over my life! Not ever!"

Al immediately appeared at Racine's side. "Please calm yourself, child! Jayson didn't mean anything."

His face bewildered, he shook his head as mother calmly embraced her livid daughter. "I'm sorry," Jayson said, taking a step back. "I was attempting a joke, nothing more."

Feeling sorry for him, Andra moved to his side, linking a supportive arm through his. "Jay, it's okay," she whispered. "What's happening is not about you, so please don't take Racine's outburst personally."

Jayson nodded uncertainly. "Racine, I meant no harm. We're all family here."

The sound of throat clearing echoed loudly throughout the room, causing all eyes to swing in its direction. Stefano, his face lit with a sarcastic smile, lifted his glass. "To family."

Andra's glare traveled across the room to Stefano's. Yanking free from Jayson's arm, she marched over to her brother-in-law. She stood before him, her all-consuming anger stoking an inner fire, and all she could do was glower at him.

Behind her, the room exploded into silence.

Her fury shot to the next level when Stefano's sardonic lips widened into a mocking grin, taunting her.

She snatched the brandy goblet from his hand and threw the fiery liquid and ice cubes in his face. Upon the liquid's contact, he gasped with surprise, stunned into immobility. She gladly took advantage of his paralysis to rear back her other hand and slap him hard across the face.

Her satisfaction rose as a hand-shaped welt materialized across his cheek.

Suddenly growling in rage, Stefano grabbed Andra's hand and bent it backward, forcing the glass from her hand. With a small cry, she released it to him and watched in horror as he flung it against the wall, shattering the crystal into several pieces.

Her lips agape, she tore her disbelieving eyes away from the shimmering mess running the length of the wall to stare wide-eyed at Stefano. His previous growl deepened, becoming more sensuous as he forced both her wrists behind her back.

"You have been asking for this since the day we met," he whispered.

With her imprisoned hands, he pushed her lower body forward to mesh with his, and without preamble, he quickly descended upon her mouth, his lips drinking deeply from hers.

Her involuntary moan must have covered the gasps from those inside the room, because she heard nothing except the explosive pounding inside her head.

"Doc! Doc?" Jayson's voice traveled from a great distance until it gradually echoed loud and clear. "Baby, take your own advice, and don't let Stefano bother you. He too has his issues."

Andra blinked. Across the room, Stefano's stony face zoomed into view. Unable to tear her eyes away from the man who stood as if on the opposite side of a great chasm, she absentmindedly murmured in indecipherable accord with Jayson.

Just then, Stefano graced her with a knowing look, forcing

her to believe he too had envisioned the scenario she'd just created concerning him.

Only when Stefano turned his back did she feel she'd been given a much-needed reprieve from the imprisonment of his magnetic glare.

27

"So I take it you've met my brother, Stefano?" Jayson asked. Looking at Andra, he wrapped his arm about her waist, pulling her close. "Do we need formal introductions?"

"Well," she said.

"Yeah, right," Racine spat. She stared hard across the room at Stefano. "Whatever."

Jayson's left eyebrow lifted in worry, causing Andra to quietly shake her head.

"Okay, babe, allow me. Al, Racine, this is my brother, Stefano Theonopilus." Jayson waited for his brother to look their way. "Stefano, this is Andra's mother, Alexandria Williams, and Andra's sister, Racine."

Al bobbed to Stefano's short, stiff bow. Saying nothing, Racine looked on.

The sudden silence grew uncomfortable until several approaching footsteps echoed beyond the door. In a noisy flurry, George, Sly, and Paulo entered the sitting room.

With an energetic gait, the older Theonopilus moved toward the group gathered at the room's center. "Welcome!" he said, smiling. He deliberately bypassed Andra and Jayson, his sights on Al. "Andra, I was just informed your lovely family had arrived."

"Yes, sir" was all Andra said.

Gallantly, George procured her mother's hand and bent over it, bringing it close to his face. "I am Jayson's father, Georigios Theonopilus. But it honors me if you would call me

George." He pressed gentle lips against Al's flesh. "And you must be Andra's sister?"

Al laughed delightedly, while Racine rolled her eyes and muttered, "Oh brother!" under her breath.

"You're too kind, George," Al said. She removed her hand from his and placed it on her chest. "But as you can guess, I am Andra's mother, Alexandria Williams—Al for short."

Grinning, George made a quick bow, acquiescing to her friendly rebuke. "A mistake I am sure is made quite frequently." Upon receiving Al's affable smile, George turned to Racine. "And you must be—"

"Andra's mother, I guess." Racine allowed polite chuckles to die off before she reluctantly stretched her hand toward George. "The name's Racine, and please don't do that kissy thing to me. My mother may like it, but it's a little too medieval for my taste."

At Andra and Al's gasps, George smiled. He then enveloped Racine's smaller hand within his larger one. "Yes, yes, I understand!" George quickly aborted the handshake and nodded. "Today's youth is a marvel. I totally understand."

Racine's expression went from defensiveness to contrite wariness. She shifted nervously in place. "Well, uh, okay. Thanks."

Clearing her throat, Sly gracefully stepped to center stage. Her colorful bodice drew attention to her upper frame, while her bouncy skirt swished prettily about her tan legs. "Good afternoon, everyone," she said, her tone airy. "Welcome!"

Andra's neck muscles tensed upon hearing the voice; she wanted to copycat Racine's eye roll and "Oh brother!" at Sly's "I'm the mistress of this house" presentation. Instantly unclenching her jaw, she rearranged her expression into a more neutral one; however, before she completed her task, she sensed a weighty stare upon her.

Not wanting to look but doing so anyway, she glanced over at Racine. Annoyed, she took in her little sister's inquisitive gaze.

As she rebuked herself for showing her true emotions, guilt forced her eyes across the room, where they clashed with

Stefano's. Now feeling claustrophobic at being sandwiched between Racine's and Stefano's penetrating stares, she thought it safer to focus her attention back on the annoying Sly.

"*Yassou*. It means 'hello' in my language. I am Sylvia." She gave a short, happy giggle. Gracefully, she stepped to Al. "Sly for short, as you say, Dr. Andra's mother. It is pleasant to finally meet family."

Al smiled as she shook hands with Sly. "Yassou, young lady. It's nice to meet you."

"The pleasure is yet all mine." She hesitated before pivoting toward Racine. "Yassou. I am Sylvia—Sly for short."

"I heard you before." Racine's eyes gave Sly the once-over before they crash-landed on her face. "So who are you?"

Sly frowned as her green eyes briefly circled the room. A question mark now imbedded within them, they returned to Racine. "Signomi?"

"Gesundheit," Racine said.

Smiling, Paulo eagerly stepped forward. "No, no, beautiful lady. My sister did not sneeze. *Signomi* means 'Excuse me' in our language."

"Whatever," Racine said, her shrug dismissing him. Her blazing mocha-colored eyes locked in on Sly. "Excuse you for what?"

Sly's emerald eyes narrowed. "I do not understand why you ask who I am. I said my name is—"

"I know what your name is," Racine said impatiently. She jerked her head Jayson and George's way. "I want to know who you are. To them—my in-laws."

"Oh, Racine." Andra sighed. "Come on!"

With a nervous laugh, Jayson quickly stepped forward. "Race, Sly grew up with us—she and her brother, Paulo, are like family."

"Really?" Racine did another vertical scan of the Grecian woman who now stood in stiff agitation before her. "Hmm."

Tossing her long black hair, Sly jammed her balled fists onto her curvy hips. "No! We are not *like* family! Paulo and I *is* family!"

"*Are* family," Racine said.

"Racine!" Al said. "Behave yourself, please!"

George spoke up. "Sly, please present good manners upon entering this house."

"Sure, whatever," Racine said to her mother.

"Yes, Papa Georigios. I mean Papa George," Sly said.

Silently, the two younger women continued to size each other up.

"Forgive me. I almost forgot to introduce my best friend, Paulo," Jayson blurted out too quickly and, in Andra's opinion, too loudly. "Paulo, this is Andra's mother, Mrs. Williams, and Andra's sister, Racine."

After Paulo bowed quickly over Al's hand, his face lit up with appreciation as he approached Racine, ready to claim her hand.

Shaking her head, she snatched it behind her back. "Didn't you just hear me tell Mr. George over there I'm not into that stuff? So you need to back off, buddy."

His grin widened at a perceived agreeable alternative. "Then I may kiss your cheek?" he asked hopefully.

"No, you may not!" She shook her head in disbelief. "Sheesh! What's with the men over here?"

For the first time in a while, Stefano spoke up. "Perhaps most are simply overpowered by your beauty and charm and cannot help themselves."

Prickling at Stefano's tone, Racine crossed her arms over her chest. She rocked back on her heels. "Well, I notice you didn't do that!"

Stefano's responding shrug was like a slap in the face.

Twisting her head, Racine glared at Sly, who quietly giggled with pleasure. However, a few seconds later, Racine's intensity forced Sly's laughter to cease, and now uncomfortable, Sly moved closer to Paulo, who in turn watched the scene in awkward muteness.

Racine's sights zeroed in on Stefano once more.

"You," she growled, only to be cut short by George.

"Stefano!" his father said in admonishment, shaking his head with authority. "Once again, I must ask you to apologize."

After first nodding stiffly to his father, Stefano bowed

toward no one in particular inside the room. "My sincere apologies."

Sincere? Andra thought. *You sure can throw that word around a lot!*

Everyone jumped when, as if on cue, with a clatter of rattling utensils and cart wheels, Helena crossed into the room, her solid arms pushing before her a white-linen-tablecloth-covered cart filled with silver platters holding various edible delicacies as well as assorted coffee, teas, and other beverages.

"Dinner is on time, Mr. Georigios," she said, stopping to clean her hands with her apron. Smiling, she kept her English words slow, enunciating them carefully. "Will you be ready for the eating then?"

Delayed in his reaction to her question, George took a moment to break his reproachful stare from Stefano. He then shook his head as if to clear it. "I apologize, Helena." With a strained smile, he nodded at her. "Yes, I thank you. We will be ready."

It seemed to take Helena a moment to absorb the emotionally charged atmosphere. Her ready smile slowly disappeared, transforming into a hesitant frown. Nodding with awkward uncertainty, she turned and disappeared from the room as quickly as her wide girth could carry her.

Andra stifled a frustrated sigh at the turn of events.

Great. Now we've managed to frighten poor Helena to the point she probably doesn't want to show her face again. She couldn't help but let out a drawn-out breath. *It's gonna be another unbearable night. And my family's here, so I won't be able to lock myself inside the bedroom.*

As if he'd heard her dismal thoughts, Jayson ducked his head. "Doc," he whispered, "I predict this is going to be some dinner. You'll be there, right?"

The smile she gave Jayson camouflaged her misery. In her peripheral vision, Andra covertly observed Stefano pour himself another full glass of brandy, which pretty much confirmed her forecast.

It wasn't a good start.

28

Knowing more people roamed the house, Andra didn't feel the need to lock the bedroom door. She felt safe in assuming an impromptu visit from either Stefano or Sly had dropped from probable to zero.

So when the door swung inward, although not finished dressing, she remained perfectly calm.

Jayson slipped into the room.

As usual, his virile good looks took her breath away, leaving her paralyzed and speechless.

How do I find the strength to leave this man?

He grinned at her, pivoted, and shut the door.

Still unwavering in her decision to separate from him, she'd come to the conclusion that the last time they had made wonderful, all-consuming love would be their last time.

The click of the bedroom door locking sounded loud. She froze, clearing her throat. "Hey, buddy, what are you doing?"

Andra's eyes darted about, trying to focus on anything other than his hand resting dangerously upon the doorknob, and her sights ultimately landed on a chair supporting a pile of unfolded clothes.

Jayson faced her, his carefree smile turning dangerously seductive. "With so many people walking about the villa, I wanted to make sure we had a little privacy." With graceful stealth, he approached her. "I wouldn't want anyone walking in on us."

His chuckle caused goose bumps to spider across Andra's flesh.

She quickly finished zipping her dress. "Well, I guess so. It'll be a little awkward—them bursting in on you while you're changing for dinner." She attempted a laugh; however, it came out jittery and high pitched. "And speaking of clothes, I'll fold those clothes and put them away while you change."

"You're deliciously tantalizing, Doc," he said, as if she hadn't said a word. Deliberately, his eyes roamed her body. "Like sweet dark chocolate—tasty, delectable, good enough to eat."

Andra's eyes widened at the simile. She shook her head. "Nope, we don't have time to fool around." At his approach, she moved in reverse, her legs ultimately bumping against the mattress. "Stop playing, Jay, and get dressed for dinner. Your in-laws are waiting."

He laughed. With a firm finger, he pushed her shoulder, forcing her to land on her back across the bed. "We're married, remember?" he asked. Bending, he captured one leg to slide his palm along her calf toward her foot, where he leisurely took off one high heel and then the other. "I believe Al wouldn't object to her son-in-law pleasuring his wife, right?"

He draped himself over her, forcing her body deeper into the mattress. Ravenously, his lips latched on to her neck; he then used them as a human suction cup, pulling her flesh inside his mouth.

"Stop it," Andra moaned. She wanted to push him away but couldn't find the strength. "Jayson, we don't have time for this."

"So now it's Jayson, is it?" he mumbled, his full mouth chewing her delicate skin.

"Yes."

Andra raised weakened fingers to separate herself from his lips but found to both her frustration and delight that Jayson impeded her effort by grasping her wrists. He stretched them upward, pinning them above her head.

She turned away from his mouth, unwittingly exposing more flesh for his suction pleasure. She murmured in undiluted ecstasy as the pressure immediately increased.

"Like I said, you taste like sweet dark chocolate," he whispered against her neck. "And I'm a starving man."

When he finally released her wrists, they somehow stayed in place without his assistance.

She arched her spine as Jayson's mouth made a moist trail along her skin. It traveled south to the cleft of her breasts. His tongue, wet and smooth, plunged deep between the divided mounds displayed above her bodice's scooped neckline while his sliding palms moved along her sides to stop at each breast.

His large hands wrapped around them, and as if testing two melons, he firmly squeezed.

"Hmm, your breasts are getting fuller, baby." He pushed them together, causing the fleshy crests to bubble up below her chin. "As far as I'm concerned, I like it a lot."

"I believe I'm coming upon that time of the month," she said, her voice breathless. "So I wouldn't go for it if I were you."

Andra closed her eyes as her husband's body slid farther south. His lips took time to generously kiss each breast point and then her flat belly, only to finally hover above the hem of her flared skirt. Looking up at her with sultry eyes, Jayson smiled. "I'll chance it."

"I don't understand. Why am I such a priority now?" she asked, moving her head from side to side. "You've basically ignored me since we got here."

Jayson answered by leisurely lifting her hem. He paused to push aside her protesting hands and then glided his warm palms along her outer thighs until they completely disappeared under her skirt. Andra felt a tug on her panties, and without being asked, she lifted her bottom to assist in their removal.

The swoosh of lacy material sailing through the air to land somewhere across the room was barely noticeable. As Jayson bunched her skirt to her belly, Andra willingly drew her dangling legs upon the bed and bent them at the knees. She opened them wide at his sigh of pleasure.

"You always have been, and will always be, my first priority, Doc," he said. Chuckling softly, he pressed gentle lips against her inner thigh, only to do the same to its twin. "Just a taste, baby. A small snack before dinner."

Forgetting her pledged celibacy with her husband, she returned her hands, palms up, above her head. Arching her back, she lustfully inhaled the moment her husband's eager mouth claimed her womanly core.

A knock sounded.

"Hey, Andra?" Racine's muffled voice penetrated the locked door. "You decent?"

Both heads jerked up. Quickly, Jayson repositioned Andra's skirt over her thighs just as she let out a loud exhalation.

"Race, hold on a minute!" she called out. "I'm coming!" Sitting up, she stole a glance at Jayson, who remained on his knees before her, his face grinning from ear to ear. "What's so funny?" she asked him.

He wagged one eyebrow. "I'm coming?"

Her face drew a blank until she realized what he meant. Embarrassed, Andra gently kicked him with her big toe. "Climb outta that gutter you crawled into," she whispered. "You're so nasty!"

"What?" he asked her, rubbing her covered thigh. "You said it, not me!"

"Oh, just go get dressed!"

Jayson rose, brushing off the knees of his charcoal-gray pants. "Don't need to. I'm wearing this to dinner."

He threw her a flirtatious wink before heading for the door. Upon his arrival, he again looked her way, his dark eyes matching almost perfectly his black button-down shirt, waiting for Andra to rise off the bed.

Signaling to him that she wasn't quite ready to let Racine in, she scanned the room for her discarded underwear. She located them hanging partially off the chair that held the clothes she intended to fold. Spinning to retrieve them, she stopped short when her husband shook his head.

"Keep them off. I might want a quick snack later."

Feeling decadently exposed without panties underneath her dress, she mutely received the kiss he blew.

With enthusiastic vigor, he flung open the door. "Well, hello,

Sis—gorgeous as ever." Before Racine could respond, Jayson threw Andra a playful look. "You *coming?*" Suggestively, he wiggled an eyebrow again, and Andra giggled.

Racine released an impatient sigh. "I don't know what that's all about, but"—she pushed Jayson across the threshold and out into the hall—"we'll be right there. I just want a minute with my sister. See you downstairs." She shut the door in his face.

"Racine, you were rude!"

Her little sister swatted the air. "Oh, he loves it, and you know it." She strolled over to Andra, hugged her, and then plopped onto the bed recently dented by Andra's frame. She patted the mattress beside her. "Come on. Let's talk! How've you been?"

Sighing in both exasperation and love, Andra sat next to her. She immediately stretched out on her side and propped herself up on one elbow, causing Racine to duplicate her position. They faced each other in close sisterly proximity.

Andra winced when Racine got right to the point.

"So what's up with you and Miss Prima Donna? I can see you don't like her," she said. Her volume dropped, her pitch suddenly low and confidential. "I'm with ya. I'm pretty sure I know what's up, but I don't wanna jump the gun. You tell me."

"I'm not sure I understand your meaning," Andra said, sniffing.

Flopping onto her back, Racine laughed hysterically. She then swiped at merry tears. "Now I *know* something's up! Whenever you get that proper uppity tone in your voice, you're trying to cover up!"

Andra clicked her tongue at her sister's on-target assessment and flopped onto her back as well. She gazed upward as sparkling speckles of spackled white ceiling stared down on them from up high. "Well, okay," she admitted. "Sly's been a thorn in my side since I've been here. She's always hanging around, not to mention she's young and beautiful."

Racine propped herself up on both elbows to stare down at Andra. "What? That girl? Beautiful? Please!" Racine snorted.

"She's got nothing on you, Sis, not with those buck teeth and her extra-wide forehead."

Andra gaped at her sister. "You're kidding, right? She's probably the most gorgeous, perfect woman I've met in person." Andra laughed at her sister's dubious expression. "Present company excluded." She paused to swat Racine's arm. "Come on—admit it."

Dubiousness made way for reluctant concession. "Okay, I guess she's cute, and I may have exaggerated a bit concerning her flaws—which she does have." Racine made sure to interject the last bit. Her voice lowered reflectively. "But maybe you're exaggerating her looks in the opposite direction. She's not all that either. Nobody's perfect."

As Andra pondered her words, Racine maneuvered her body into a sitting position, turned directly toward Andra, and sat cross-legged. Leaning forward, she rested her palms on bent knees. Her eyes delved deep to study Andra's. "You've got a kinda twitchy look about you, like you're ready to jet." At Andra's startled expression, Racine reached over and patted her arm. "You can't hide anything from me. Like I said, Sis, I've known you too long."

Swiftly, Andra sat up, the hasty motion causing the room to sway. Recovering quickly before Racine had time to make a big deal of it, she carefully mirrored her sister's cross-legged position, making sure to discreetly keep her pantie-less situation under wraps.

She waited for the room to stop dipping before she felt steady enough to speak. "Okay, but you can't tell Mama. I don't want her to worry." At Racine's consensual nod, Andra continued. "True, I was seriously contemplating flying home. Things have been, well, not so good due to Jayson's family business and all."

Racine's brow lifted. "The 'and all' is probably the most frustrating, I imagine."

Sly's face, although not quite as perfect now, floated inside Andra's head, and by the sour expression on Racine's face, she figured the same face had insinuated itself into her mind as well.

Racine stretched forth to tap Andra's kneecap, causing Sly's daydream image to evaporate into nothingness. Intently, Andra focused on her baby sister's lips, which were in serious motion.

"Hey, you being an upstanding doctor and all, I'm cool with the fact that you don't want to get your hands dirty. Just say the word, and I'll kick her butt all across this Grecian countryside for you. When the dust clears, they'll never find the body."

Andra looked off into space, her mind wrapping itself around her newest daydream fueled by Racine's words. A few blissful moments raced by before she shook her head. "No. Actually, I thought about kicking her butt myself, but it wouldn't be right." She sighed and threw her sister a small, hopeful glance. "Would it?"

Racine shrugged in noncommittal silence. Then, as if a lightbulb had blinked on inside her brain, she frowned. "So, Andra, you were ready to jet outta here, only to have us show up. Don't tell me we stopped you from going home?" At Andra's uneasy silence, Racine hit the heel of one palm against her forehead. "I told Mama to hold off on coming over here! But you know how determined she can be."

Her words trailed off into innocent nothingness, causing Andra to stare at her in mute astonishment. Finally, neither could keep a straight face, and they both tumbled onto the mattress, holding their sides and laughing with abandon.

All too quickly, another knock sounded at the door. Muffled broken English quelled their laughter.

"Dr. Andra ? Dr. Andra's sister? Mr. Jayson asks you for dinner," Helena's muffled voice said from the other side. "It is ready, please."

"I'm not going," Racine said, blinking once.

Unfolding her legs, Andra swung them off the bed and stood up. Daintily, she smoothed her skirt, attempting to coax Racine off the bed with no luck. Finally, she had to physically pull the stubborn girl to her feet.

"You are going," she whispered to Racine. She then called

out at the closed door, "Thanks, Helena! We'll be right down, okay?"

"Nai, Dr. Andra."

Racine's jaw dropped. Facing Andra, she pointed at the closed door. "Did she just tell you no?"

Andra stifled a giggle, slapping Racine on the arm. "Shh!" She waited until she heard Helena's subdued steps retreat down the hall. "No, you big dope! *Nai* means 'yes' in Greek."

Before Racine could get out a snappy comeback, Andra held up a hand. "We're going to be on our best behavior, right, Racine?" When she didn't answer, Andra placed determined fists on her hips. "You were the one who wanted to come over here uninvited. This is the outcome you get with that decision, so deal with it!"

With another nonchalant shrug, Racine lifted her chin a notch to stare down the length of her nose at Andra. "Fancy schmancy!" her younger sibling said mockingly in an aristocratic tone. "They've sent a servant to announce dinner." Her face twisted into a devilish grin. "Maybe I should speak to the old girl in private about liberating her from the big, bad Massah!"

Abruptly, Racine walked toward the door with an exaggerated, old-timey slave gait, the song "We Shall Overcome" dripping from poked-out lips.

Scooping up her shoes, Andra raced over to Racine and caught her by the arm. "Don't you dare say anything to her! You hear me? Helena loves it here. She's not the one with the problem. You are!" Andra's expression was both firm and entreating. "Please be good. For me?"

Racine stopped, her expression serious before a slow grin transformed it. "Okay. For you."

"Thanks, kid." Smiling as well, Andra wrapped her arm around Racine and hugged her. "I'm so glad you're here."

Racine reciprocated with a quick squeeze. Gently yet firmly, she extracted herself from Andra's embrace to continue her trek toward the door. "I'm glad I'm here too," she said. Abruptly, she stopped short and turned, staring at Andra's bare feet. "Okay, so tell me—what were you two doing before I knocked?"

After glancing over at her discarded lacy black underwear dangling precariously off the chair in the far corner, Andra made a face of pure innocence. "Well, Jayson was getting ready to have a snack," she said, slipping on her shoes. Moving past Racine, she headed for the closed door. "But once you interrupted him, he decided to forgo it—for later."

Racine pretended to puke and rolled her eyes. "Andra, guess what. If this is your attempt at a porn reference, you can just keep it to yourself."

Flinging open the bedroom door, this time it was Andra who smiled devilishly.

29

Dinner with the Theonopilus Clan, Andra mused silently. The title would make for a good reality TV show.

Directly across from her mother, Andra watched as Al draped her napkin across her lap and leaned toward George, her soft laughter drifting across the table at something he whispered in her ear. Leaving them to their private moment, she glanced around the rest of the table at the seating arrangement.

To her right sat Jayson and then Racine, and to Racine's right sat Stefano. Her eyes immediately bounced off his melancholy face to his right, where Sly sat looking as if she had squatter's rights. Next to her were Paulo, then Al, and then George.

She didn't know whom to feel the sorriest for: Racine or Stefano. Both projected looks akin to angry displeasure. However, in the end, Andra decided she felt worse for Racine. She remembered her first uncomfortable night at the villa, when she'd had the misfortune of sitting next to Stefano and across from Sly.

Jayson came in a close second for her sympathy. He struggled to maintain a one-sided conversation with a grumpy Racine, who sat mutely beside him. It was almost too painful to watch.

Andra coughed. "Excuse me, George."

Turning away from Al, he smiled graciously. "Yes, my dear?"

Andra shifted in her seat. "Uh, Papa George, would you be offended if I switched places with Jayson?"

George and Al took a moment to glance at the opposite end of the dining table, both unaware of a possible emotionally explosive situation brewing down that way.

He leaned her way, his mature hand patting hers. "As much as I would like to be selfish and dine between two beautiful women, I understand, my dear." His voice rose. "Jayson, my son, would you mind switching places with your lovely wife, as much as it grieves me to ask you to do so?" George smiled. "I have an important matter to discuss with you."

Simultaneously, Jayson and Racine looked relieved. As he rose, Sly quickly spoke up. "But, Papa George, now it won't be a boy-girl-boy-girl seating arrangement."

The others stared at her, their expressions ranging from "Really?" to "So what?" to "What's it to you?" to "Does it matter?"

George politely cleared his throat from the table's head. "It will be fine, my dear." He nodded toward Jayson. "Son?"

"Yes, Papa."

Somber, Jayson stepped behind Andra, planted a kiss on her cheek, and gallantly pulled out her chair. She quickly scanned the table, mentally calculating everyone's reaction to the current events.

George, Al, and Paulo had positive reactions. Sly's was negative. Racine looked relieved. Stefano was unreadable.

As Andra finished switching seats with Jayson, Racine sighed, causing Andra to reach out and squeeze her baby sister's hand. "So how you doing over here?" she whispered.

"How do you think?" Racine said, although not as angrily as she could have. "I can't imagine how you endured this all by yourself. I've half a mind to stay in my room for future dinners."

Secretly, Andra agreed with her; however, she couldn't bring herself to tell Racine she'd already done as much, nor would she allow her sister to follow suit. It would make her whole family look like antisocial recluses.

She exhaled in relief when Helena entered the dining

room, pushing before her several dinner courses. The dishes' aromas combined to burst forth in delicious eclecticism. She moved around the table, carefully placing hot dishes around various floral decorations at the table's center.

Smiling up at the servant as she placed a platter of dessert pastries a few inches from her plate, Andra experienced her mouth water just as her stomach filled with gastric bubbles. Swallowing hard to push down a tide of rising bile, she nudged Racine's arm. "Hey, I hope you're not serious about being scarce for dinner," she said. She shook her head. "You don't want to appear rude, especially since you're a guest here. It wouldn't look right."

Her face a mask, Racine fidgeted with her silverware, repositioning the eating utensils at an exact distance from each other and her plate. After she made sure they were dimensionally correct, her frown deepened. "I guess so. It's just that it threw me to have to sit next to Boris and across from Natasha."

Andra stifled a giggle at Racine's reference to the villainous husband and wife team from the *Rocky and Bullwinkle* TV reruns they'd watched as children. Her eyes quickly bounced from Sly, who listened in on their conversation yet pretended not to, moving to Stefano who stared moodily at his brandy and ice.

For a brief moment, a small slice of her pity went to Stefano, who appeared as if he didn't have an ally in the world.

"Stefano's not so bad. He's just profoundly deep is all," Andra whispered. She took a deep breath. "It's got to be tough running his family's business, you know? Like madcap stressful."

From across the table, Sly daintily cleared her throat. "So, Racine, how are you acclimating to Grecian life?" she asked. "Very different from your own, yes?"

Warily, the sisters stared across the table.

"It's okay." First taking a quick peek at Andra, Racine displayed an amicable smile while addressing Sly. "I thank you for asking."

Seemingly taken aback at the decreased hostility, Sly

examined her empty plate. She glanced up again, her eyes now sparkling with the unknown; they traveled back across the table, this time landing directly on Andra.

"It's nice to see you at dinner again, Yatros," she said. At Racine's surprised expression, Sly laughed. "You see, Yatros Andra has not been to dinner since her arrival the first night. She has been—how do you say?—holed up in her room all this time."

And you would definitely know, wouldn't you? Andra fumed.

Feeling like an adolescent who'd just been tattled on, Andra lowered her head to study her elegant dinnerware. Her body went slack and then stiffened under Racine's quiet wrath.

"Andra, what's she talking about?" Racine hissed, turning to Andra. "And what's with this Yatros?"

"*Yatros* means 'doctor,'" Sly said, interjecting happily.

Racine eight-balled the Grecian with a searing glare. "If that's what it means, why didn't you just say *doctor* in the first place?"

At Sly's answering shrug, Racine's hardened expression screamed, "I'm not in the mood, so why don't you mind your own business?"

She turned back to Andra.

"Tell me something," she said tightly, "why would you tell me I can't stay in my room during dinner, when you—"

"We have not given the doctor a reason to come to dinner, have we not, Sly?"

Surprised, Andra lifted her head to gawk at her brother-in-law.

Her face now indignant, Sly stared as well. "I do not know what you mean, Stefano!"

Ignoring her, his eyes shifted toward Andra, their dark orbs landing somewhere above her face. "Papa, Jayson—speaking of business," he blurted out.

Both George's and Jayson's heads jerked to look down at the other end of the table.

"We were, Son?" their father asked, his face blissfully

ignorant of the tension that swirled at the other end. Smiling, he turned to Jayson. "Were we speaking business?"

"I don't recall hearing the word *business*." Jayson looked directly across the table. "Did you, Paulo?"

Paulo, in the midst of piecing off a thick section of Greek bread, hastily looked up. "Nor did I," he said. With a nervous laugh, he concentrated hard on the task of drizzling heated olive oil over the warm bread. His eyes flickered toward Stefano. "But I am willing to listen to all strategies and plans, if needed."

Stefano motioned for Paulo to send the bread his way. After receiving the platter, he first offered it to Racine, who hesitated before reaching out to tear off a small section for herself. After helping himself to a piece, Stefano next extended the plate Sly's way. Her face showed her displeasure at not being offered the bread first. She shook her head.

Stefano returned the platter to Racine to pass the bread on to Andra.

"What about the business, Son?" George asked.

"The investor will be here tomorrow."

A hush settled over the dinner table at the word *investor*; it generated a perceptible uneasiness, as if a ghost had suddenly manifested inside the dining area.

Jayson broke the silence. "What is this person's name, Stefano? What time will he arrive tomorrow?"

"His name is Harlan Grainger from Texas. And the meeting is for ten o'clock in the morning."

Jayson said the name once and paused, his face a mask of concentration. He repeated it a second time. "Where have I heard that name before?"

Stefano's lips pinched as if he'd just sucked on a sour ball. "I do not know," he said. "However, I do understand he compares himself to a farm animal. I am not completely sure what to make of him at the moment."

Jayson's face cleared. He nudged Andra with his elbow. "Harlan Orlando Grainger!"

"Yes," Stefano said, his tone not quite hiding his disgust.

He then studied Jayson, lifting a quizzical eyebrow. "How did you come to know the gentleman's name?"

Jayson laughed. "Andra and I met him on our flight over. Man, it's a coincidence he turned out to be our potential investor. What are the odds?" Bewildered, Jayson grinned, grabbing Andra's hand. "He was a character, wasn't he, Doc?"

"Yep," she said, squeezing back. "A character right out of a soap opera."

Smiling, Andra scanned the table to include everyone in the conversation, only to stop at Paulo. Whipping into doctor mode, she took in his ashen appearance and the way his hand trembled while lifting his wineglass to his lips. "Paulo, are you all right? Do you need me to give you a once-over?"

As the entire table eyed Paulo curiously, he laughed uneasily. "I've never had a doctor as beautiful as you give me the once-over before—but I will pass today." He slowly rose from the table, rubbing his stomach. "I believe I may have eaten something earlier that does not agree with me. Pardon me if I return home and rest." As he pushed in his chair, his eyes darted Stefano's way. "You do not require me at this investor meeting tomorrow, do you?"

Lifting his brandy-filled glass to his lips, he stared over its rim. "No," he said. "Why should we?"

"Good!" Paulo said, the word sounding as loud as a lit firecracker. Fidgeting with the back of his chair, he smiled self-consciously and cleared his throat. "That is, I will come by in the afternoon—after the meeting has concluded."

Sly too stood, throwing her linen napkin onto her empty plate. "I will go with my brother." Her stormy eyes bounced between Andra and Stefano. "Suddenly, I am not so hungry."

"Good night, you two," Racine sang out sweetly. Her smile widened at Sly's toss of her hair. "It's been fun!"

George and Jayson rose from their chairs, also bidding them good night.

Once the two had disappeared beyond the dining room's threshold, Racine exhaled. She leaned toward Andra. "I don't know about anyone else," she whispered, "but if you ask me, the atmosphere just got a little less heavy."

Before deciding to rebuke her sister, Andra took a quick consensus of the table, only to reluctantly admit Racine was right. Everyone's mood suddenly appeared relaxed since the pair had vacated the vicinity. Even Stefano's stony demeanor had softened somewhat.

George laughed in delight at something Al said before extending to her a vegetable dish, patiently holding it out for her to serve herself. Upon returning the platter to the table, he looked back to his eldest son. "Son," he said, waiting for Stefano's nod. "About this Mr. Grainger. We should have a meeting right after dinner. I want to make absolutely sure I understand all there is to know beforehand."

To Andra's left, Jayson carefully forked freshly sautéed garlic-and-olive-oil pasta onto his plate. "Fine by me, Papa. But if you don't mind, not too late. I want to have a snack before turning in this evening," he said, and Andra kicked Jayson under the table. Grinning, he covertly massaged his bruised ankle with his other foot. "You know, so I can be fresh for our meeting in the morning."

"That is a good idea, Son." George turned to Al. "Would you also care for a snack before retiring, my dear?"

Again, Andra kicked Jayson's shin; she then gritted her teeth when Racine kicked her at the same time.

"Thank you, my friend. I would love a snack before turning in for the evening." Al produced a wistful look. "I used to indulge when my husband was alive. After his passing, my appetite kinda died with him. I loved Raymond very much." She took a deep breath and smiled at her host. "Yet now look at me, sitting here in Greece, talking about having a snack with you, George."

Racine snickered. "Boy, you and Jayson have started something," she whispered to Andra, her voice filled with satanic glee. "You're both going to hell over snacks."

"Why not we all have a snack?" Stefano said, his tone part joking and part sarcastic.

"No, thank you," Racine said, disgusted.

"What, Racine—you don't like eating snacks?" Jayson asked innocently.

"Don't get her started." Andra kicked his shin once more for good measure. She smiled smugly at his painful grunt. "That's what you get, buddy."

Silence fell, and the only sounds were clicking glassware and clattering silverware against platters.

George cut into his grilled goat, speared it, and placed a piece in his mouth. Thoughtfully, he chewed in silence. Then he said, "Stefano?"

"Yes, Papa?"

"We have not agreed upon anything with this Mr. Grainger, correct?"

"Correct."

"Good. Depending upon the type of businessman he may be, we do not want to agree upon anything right away."

"But he's flown all the way from Texas," Jayson said.

"And it was his decision to do so. He appears to have enough money for such adventures." Stefano's eyes bounced toward Andra and back to his plate. He toyed with his bread. "No, we have not committed ourselves to anything yet. It is not too late to dissolve the plan."

Racine delivered a kick lighter than before, letting Andra know she'd observed Stefano's brief glance her way.

Ignoring her, Andra good-naturedly nudged her husband in the ribs. "Hey, buddy, you gonna pass the pasta this way, or what?"

"I can't wait to see Mr. Grainger's face once he realizes it's my family's business he wants to invest in." Jayson turned to Andra and winked, handing her the porcelain platter. "This is going to be some meeting!"

As she dished up the steaming pasta, her mind wandered back to Paulo's nauseated pallor previous to his and Sly's exodus. Like Paulo, she experienced a touch of queasiness. The brother and sister's abrupt exit didn't sit well with her, nor did the investor meeting the next morning. Neither did the whole freakin' situation.

Andra couldn't put her finger on why.

30

Throwing open the double doors to the formal sitting room, Stefano preceded the others, only to stand off to the side, allowing George, Jayson, and Harlan Orlando Grainger to pass on through into the area lit by the midmorning sun.

Just outside the door, Helena moved closer to Stefano. "Is there anything you need?" she asked in rapid Greek. Smiling, she wiped her brow. "I will have to start lunch for the family soon."

"One moment. I will ask."

After waiting until the men settled into their chairs, he cleared his throat. "Helena has asked if anyone would care for anything. A drink? Maybe hors d'oeuvres? She will create whatever you wish."

George and Jayson shook their heads.

Hog, who sat on the matching couch across from them, grinned broadly. "Well now, that's mighty hospitable of you, partner," he said, his voice near booming. "Maybe I'll take a drink later. But for now, I'd rather my tank run on empty to keep my mind focused on business."

Nodding, Stefano graced the servant woman with a gentle smile. "Thank you, Helena—we are all fine for the moment."

"I'll be in the kitchen if you need me."

After closing the door on her retreating back, he strolled toward the couch to sit a few feet from their visitor. Covertly, he studied the tall older Texan, who'd settled at the other end of the long white settee as if he owned the place.

"Let us proceed," George said.

Hog laughed. He leaned forward. "I like a straight shooter—someone who comes out guns a-blazing and wants to get to the point. Those are the kinda folks you can do proper business with."

George shifted forward, mirroring Hog's posture. "Mr. Grainger, we have not decided whether we will do business," he said. Eyeing Hog, George slowly sat back. "However, I wish to thank you for traveling such a great distance to discuss the possibility."

"Shoot, think nothing of it. I do stuff like this all the time." Hog's grin lengthened as his focus shifted across the low coffee table to Jayson. "Well now, it's nice to see you again, youngster. It's a small world, us meeting on the plane coming over, isn't it?"

Jayson returned the Texan's smile. "It sure is, Mr. Grainger."

"Ah-ah!"

"I mean Hog."

"There you go," Hog said, missing Stefano's disgust at the nickname. He pressed on. "So, young'un, how's the doctor wife these days?"

"Still absolutely beautiful, if you recall," Jayson said proudly. "And we're still over the top in love."

"Good, good!" Hog exclaimed, once again bobbing his head. "Now, remember, love can just about conquer anything."

"Could we conduct our business?" Stefano asked, trying yet failing to mask his irritation at the direction the conversation had taken. "Please."

Hog turned his way, lifting one brushy eyebrow. "What? You don't care for your sister-in-law, young Theonopilus?"

"Why would you say such a thing, Mr. Grainger?"

Hog shrugged. However, Stefano didn't quite buy the gesture's displayed nonchalance. "I don't know. Maybe your tone. Your demeanor," he said agreeably.

"Jayson's wife has nothing whatsoever to do with this meeting," Stefano said. "Let us just stick to the business at hand."

"I see."

"And what is it you see, Mr. Grainger?"

"Oh, nothing. Nothing at all." The Texan grinned. "And please, do call me Hog."

"I prefer not, Mr. Grainger," Stefano said, his voice tight.

Hog shrugged again. "Suit yourself." Casually, his eyes wandered back to Jayson. "Never minding your brother, I wouldn't mind seeing your little filly again to say hello."

"I can arrange it," Jayson said. He quickly rose from his seat, his relieved expression akin to that of a prison parolee. "If you'll excuse me, I'll go bring her in after you three have finished your meeting."

Hog studied Jayson with a curious eye. "Don't you want to get in on our talk, son?" he asked.

"I'm here for show. It's my father and brother who have the final say if this venture's to happen."

"But aren't you part owner here as well?"

"Technically, yes," Jayson said. "But they actually run the business, so you're talking to the right people. Me? I'm going into ministry soon."

"I see."

"And what do you see this time, Mr. Grainger?" Stefano asked, feeling the tic above his left eye materialize.

Hog lifted a palm toward Stefano. "Now, don't get your panties in a wad, young man. I'm just making friendly chitchat. That's all."

The tic ceased as Stefano's brow rose in reproach. "Your colorful euphemisms are not needed—or wanted—in this meeting, Mr. Grainger. Please kindly keep the conversation professional, if you don't mind."

"Yes, my son is right. If we can get on with our business," George said.

"As you wish," Hog said gruffly. "My apologies for offending."

The room grew silent until Jayson, who shifted on awkward feet, softly padded across the floor as if leaving a wake.

"I'll leave you gentlemen to it," he said in hushed tones. He gently closed the doors behind him.

"Now, that's a mighty fine lad you've got there Mr. Theonopilus," Hog said, his eyes cutting toward Stefano. "Yessir, Jayson's a mighty fine boy."

"Thank you," George said. "Now, Mr. Grainger, please continue."

Hog coughed once to clear his throat. "All righty then. My research on your family business reveals you've been having some difficulties over the years increasing, or even maintaining, your olive crops. Me, being a businessman of some means, figured I could help out by offering my services and resources to you—get your family's business up and running to its previous glory days."

"Other than a shareholder's profit, what, may I ask, would you get from this proposed investment venture?" Stefano asked.

"Well now, let's see—there's the actual investing aspect. As I told Jayson on the plane ... By the way, it's such a coincidence I happened to be sitting behind him and his bewitching wife on the flight over. Don't ya think?" Smiling, he paused to gaze at the others, as if waiting for their confirmation. When none came, Hog chuckled clumsily and continued. "I'm looking to jump outta my cattle box into different business ventures. You know, expand my financial portfolio."

"Why have you chosen Athens?" George asked. "Why us?"

"Actually, a few years back, I purchased a small villa some twenty miles north of here. My wife, Lillian, bless her soul, loved it whenever we vacationed there. We had planned to move over here permanently once I retired. Alas, she passed away before it happened. Lillian was a lovely, vibrant, highly intelligent woman."

George's eyes turned sad. "Yes, I understand your loss, for I too lost my wife some years ago."

Hog wiped away a real or imaginary tear—from his angle, Stefano was unable to tell. "Yes. Andra kinda puts me to mind of my Lillian," Hog said.

"Oh," George said with a wistful smile. "Was your wife African American as well?"

The Texan's expression turned reflective. "No, my Lillian was a beautiful, fiery Spaniard. That was my name for her: Beauty. Her sexy Spanish ways could set a man's blood to boil!" His face quickly took on a hardened quality. "I loved

Beauty deeply, and she was mine, until she was taken away from me too soon."

Hog's words seemed to push George into his own private world of agony; his eyes misted from memories no one else could see.

The room grew quiet. When Hog cleared his throat for the second time, his pain sounded genuine. "Well now, it's a small world, each losing the loves of our lives right before we truly began to live."

"I am sorry for both your and my father's loss, Mr. Grainger," Stefano said. "However, we are at a business meeting. No disrespect, sir, but please continue with your reasons for investing in our olive business."

"Right again, boy." Hog sniffed once more for good measure, his expression melancholy as he smiled. "Women tend to get you off track, don't they?" At Stefano's noncommittal stare, he continued. "Anyway, the wave of the future is natural, organic, and such, so I figured I'd invest in said wave. Olive oil, particularly virgin olive oil, is extremely healthy and in high demand, especially in the States, and can be used for anything from consumption to skin care—even hair care. Your daughter-in-law, Mr. Theonopilus, can attest to that. Hair care, especially olive-oil-infused products per se, are very big with her people. An extremely huge market."

George looked surprised at the information but nodded anyway.

Hog returned the nod and continued. "Within the past few years, demands within the business sector, as well as from the individual consumer, have skyrocketed. Investing in your company just makes good sense."

Stefano glanced over at his father, who gave him a quick nod to signal he would ask the next question.

"Yet you will be investing money into a company you yourself have admitted is struggling. Why do it?" George shrugged. "Why not simply invest in a company more financially stable? Is this not how good business works?"

Hog's head bobbed. "You have an excellent point, Mr. Theonopilus. Most people play it safe and invest in stable ventures with little or no risk involved. But I'm not most people. I haven't gotten where I am by playing it safe. Sometimes you have to go with what looks unstable and stabilize it. I find that kinda risk's more challenging and usually more profitable if it works out."

"And what if it does not work out?" Stefano said.

"Well now, young fella, that'll be like succumbing to defeat, and I'm not one for givin' up easily." Hog's smile was confident. "Besides, I've got plenty of money left to go on to the next venture. And there's the profit-and-loss column on my income tax for such deficits if they occur."

At the word *succumbing*, Stefano rose and made his way to the bar. As he fixed himself a drink, he decided to stay where he was instead of returning to sit next to Hog. Lifting his brandy and ice, he paused in contemplation before taking a small sip. Swallowing slowly, he lowered his glass and gazed into it. "You appear to have it all figured out, Mr. Grainger."

Hog laughed. Following Stefano's lead, he stood and crossed the room to stand with him at the bar. Grinning good-naturedly, he clapped a hearty hand on Stefano's shoulder, but he immediately retracted it when Stefano glared at it. "Sorry, son—didn't mean to invade your personal space. I'll have that drink now, if you don't mind. Scotch and soda over rocks, please."

Hog waited until he had his drink in hand before continuing. "Well, young Theonopilus, I didn't come to be as successful as I am now without learning a thing or two before jumping into anything businesswise, including marriage."

Stefano attempted to suppress a grimace at the word *marriage*, yet by the way their inquisitive visitor studied him, he knew he hadn't succeeded.

The knock at the study's door came abruptly; a second later, Jayson and Andra entered.

Stefano turned his back to Grainger and watched them step into the room. Completely dismissing his younger brother, Stefano felt his breath catch at the sight of Andra, who was dressed in fitted blue jeans, a white sleeveless tunic, and white athletic running shoes. Her attire, demure by the day's standard, draped her shapely body to perfection. Her thick brown hair fell in fat ringlets about her arresting face, and extra-large silver hoop earrings peaked out beyond the naturally curly strands.

Desperate to hold back his imagination, it ran amok anyway; Stefano's mind envisioned her clothing falling away to ultimately leave Andra magnificently naked and sensually vulnerable.

"Well now, isn't she stunning?" Hog said to no one in particular.

Once again, Stefano was aware the Texan carefully studied him. Unnerved, he reigned in his lust concerning his sister-in-law and quickly rerouted his thoughts to the section of his brain that continuously worked on sending her back to America.

"Are we too early?" Jayson said, holding Andra's hand.

"No," Stefano said, walking away from the bar and their visitor. This time, he chose to sit on the couch next to his father. "We have concluded the meeting. Please come in."

Alone at the bar, Hog stood uncertainly with his drink in hand; he then plastered a smile on his face and made his way over to Andra. Reaching out, he enveloped her much smaller hand in an enthusiastic handshake. "Well, hello, Doctor! It's a pleasure running upon you again." His grin was infectious. "Your husband's right—you're still as fine a-lookin' filly as ever." Releasing his grasp, Hog swept his hand toward the waiting empty couch. "After you, my lovely lady."

Andra giggled self-consciously. "Thank you, Hog. It's nice to see you again too."

She strolled ahead of Jayson and Hog to sit in the middle section of the couch. A second later, he and Jayson lowered themselves to the left and right of her, respectively.

Under silver-colored eyebrows, Hog's blue orbs bounced from one man to the next. Brusquely, he cleared his throat. "Are we done here? I wasn't sure."

"I believe so," George said, nodding. "We need time to consider your proposition."

"I can draw up some numbers for you to ponder," he said hopefully.

Stefano kept his eyes focused on the silver-haired Texan, wanting to remain silent, but thought it necessary to add to the conversation, if only to put it to an end. "No, you've given us all the information we need for now, Mr. Grainger."

"All righty, fair enough." Hog put away his scotch in one quick swallow and briefly lifted the drained glass. "Good liquor. Well, I've got other things that need attending to. I'll be in Athens another week or two. Driving to my villa to see what's what over there." When he received no answer, Hog turned toward Andra, who sat quietly studying her hands in her lap. "So, Doctor, how are these fellows treating you here? Is it what you expected?"

Andra flinched. Momentarily, she lifted her head to stare at Hog. "Very well, sir." Her eyes shifted across the coffee table to look at George's smiling face, next Stefano's stoic one, only to return to Hog. "It's a lot to take in, but I'm adjusting."

"Well, I was telling your father-in-law how much you remind me of my wife, Beauty. Either one of you can set a room ablaze just entering it."

Andra's smile was shy. "Thank you—you're much too generous with your compliments."

"I have to say it's true, lil' lady."

Unable to keep his own eyes off her, Stefano observed Andra fidget under Grainger's heavy-handed praise until he realized the older man again watched him. He swiftly shifted his gaze to his brandy. When the older businessman finally stood on cowboy-boot feet, Stefano couldn't help but exhale with inaudible relief.

"Well, I must be off," Hog said.

The other men rose in unison.

George circled the coffee table to shake Hog's hand. "I apologize for not asking you earlier, but would you care to stay for lunch, Mr. Grainger?"

"Yes, please stay," Jayson and Andra said, joining in.

"I thank you three kindly. I would, but I've another meeting to attend," he said, and when Stefano stared at him with blatant curiosity, Hog laughed nervously. "Somewhat impromptu." He bent to place his empty glass on the coffee table and turned to face Andra, grabbing her hand again in a gentle handshake. "Good to see you, darlin'. I'm sure we'll meet again real soon." He grinned widely, but the smile dimmed once he faced the others. "Good morning, gentlemen. I'll just find my own way out."

His tall frame strolled from the room. The sitting area remained quiet as Hog's boot-clad feet stomped their way across the tile foyer floor and out the front door.

Stefano never had been so glad to witness a person leave.

"Tell me your thoughts," George said, returning to his seat.

"I cannot be sure, Papa." Stefano made his way back to the bar to refresh his drink. His eyes left the pouring liquor to touch upon Andra's face. "When it comes to this Mr. Hog, there is—how do you Americans say?—more than meets the eye."

"Close enough," Andra said. Her tone then turned defensive. "However, I like him. He's nice."

Jayson raised his hand. "I agree, Stefano. He may come off as a little rough around the edges, but I believe he's a good fellow. Yes, I'm with Andra; he's very nice."

Looking off into space, Stefano sipped on his brandy before speaking. "Nice, Jayson? Nice is what draws a person in—right before the knife is inserted in one's back." He turned and faced the room. "In my opinion, I believe we must tread lightly and wisely when dealing with Mr. Grainger. His outward appearance displays a harmless and almost capricious demeanor, but ..." He paused, not wanting to say too much.

George crossed over to the bar to stand next to Stefano and helped himself to a brandy too. "I have to agree with you, Son. There is a possibility this man might be hiding his true intentions."

Jayson and Andra still sat side by side across the room. Jayson smiled and then nodded when Andra whispered into his ear. Agile, she rose to her feet.

"Well, I believe I'll take my leave," she said to everyone. "I'm going to explore the grounds for the first time and afterward head upstairs for a short nap."

"Nothing is wrong, I hope," George said, his mature features softening with worry.

Smiling, Andra shook her head at him. "Nope, I'm probably still recovering from jet and room lag. The exercise will do me good." She strolled across the room, stopping inside the door's threshold. "If my opinion counts for anything, I'm still with Jayson concerning Hog."

Stefano tried not to appear too conspicuous in watching her body as it moved with panther-like grace across the sitting room's floor, yet he couldn't help but outwardly study her form as she stood by the door, magnificent in her unique beauty, while she waited for a reply from anyone willing to supply it.

Mute, he could only nod, while his father spoke out.

"Thank you, my dear. We will keep your opinion in mind," George replied indulgently. "However, I fear between the four of us, we are divided when it comes to Mr. Harlan Grainger."

Stefano watched her nod and then leave, closing the doors. The room magically transformed, becoming duller and dimmer—practically lifeless. He glanced over at his father, who sipped on his brandy as he too observed Andra's exit. Once she had disappeared from sight, the elder's countenance deflated a notch.

"Yes." George spoke quietly, his voice weary. "A house divided."

And a house divided usually falls, Stefano's mind gloomily retorted.

31

"Good morning, Dr. Andra's sister."

Racine sighed as Sly entered the villa's breakfast area through the back entrance. "Why are you always here?" she asked, lowering her fork. She placed it on the table exactly one inch to the right of her half-eaten plate of scrambled eggs. "Don't you have a home to go to?"

"Maybe I can ask the same when it comes to you, Dr. Andra's sister."

Although she preferred her Christian name not trip off the silly woman's tongue, Racine also didn't want to be continuously referred to as Dr. Andra's sister, or, in other words, the Inconsequential Sister with No Name.

She figured Sly knew it too—that was why she continued to do it.

"The name's Racine, as you well know." She took the white porcelain creamer from the table's center and poured thick cream into her black coffee. After dumping heaps of sugar in, she stirred the concoction thoroughly while keeping an eye on her unwanted guest. "I'm here visiting, which means I know I'm a visitor, can say I'm a visitor, and will be leaving at some point as a visitor." Racine tasted her coffee and blanched. She added more cream and sugar. "Can you say—and do—the same?"

Sly laughed heartily. "You are so funny! I believe I like you."

"No, thank you." Looking away, Racine tasted her coffee again and decided it was a lost cause. She took a long swallow anyway. "What'd you want?" In her peripheral vision, she watched Sly approach the table and sit in a chair to her right. Being deliberate, she made a conscious effort not to put more distance between them by shifting her chair in the opposite direction, especially since she knew it would throw off the balance of the other chairs.

"Oh," Sly said, her expression and voice wistful, "I came by for girl talk."

After retrieving a clean coffee cup from the centered rack, with a dainty hand Sly helped herself to coffee. Racine shook her head, marveling that the idiot reached for neither cream nor sugar but elected to drink the thick concoction black.

The girl was not to be trusted.

"Okay, so talk."

Elbows on the table, Sly used both hands to bring the cup to her lips. She sipped the strong brew slowly and prettily, as if she reveled in Racine's attention. Then, lowering her drink halfway, she eyed Racine and giggled. "You know, you and I are not so different." When Racine opened her mouth to dispute that statement, Sly presented a raised palm. "No, we are not. Listen, we are around the same age, we are two attractive women, and we both do not like the situation between J. J. and Dr. Andra."

Racine's eyes narrowed as Sly casually took another sip. "What are you talking about, Ms. Thang?"

Sly set her cup on its saucer with a firm clink. "Also, we are both highly intelligent women." She smiled at Racine. "I believe you can understand my meaning."

Attempting to gather her thoughts to return a witty yet biting reply comprised of feigned ignorance, Racine lifted the morning paper in order to buy some time, only to be stupefied once she realized the blasted thing was written in Greek. She rattled the paper, pretending to read it anyway. "I don't know; you evidently assume you're more intelligent than the next person," she said, turning a page. "I guess you're gonna have to spell it out for a dummy like me."

Sly leaned forward. She glanced at the newspaper and then studied Racine's face. "Would you like me to read to you?"

Racine slammed the paper onto the table, glaring with

satisfaction when Sly jumped. "I asked you earlier—what do you want?"

Her motions deliberate, Sly looked over each shoulder, first at the exterior and then at the interior entrance to the breakfast room. Satisfied that both were empty, her emerald eyes returned to gaze into Racine's flashing ones. "Where is Dr. Andra and J. J.?"

Racine smirked. "Andra and Jayson?" She picked up the newspaper again, casually licked her finger, and turned a page. "They're probably upstairs humping their brains out." At Sly's confused expression, she smirked. "I thought you were so intelligent. It means making love, okay?"

At the other's dubious countenance, Racine shook her head. "What do you care where they're at? Why're you so worried about Jayson anyway?"

Sly sat back to fiddle with her cup handle. "I do not want them to unexpectedly interrupt us while we have our little girl talk."

Giddy with the knowledge that she knew information Sly didn't, Racine bombed her inquisitive visitor with the Theonopilus family's current affairs. "Mr. George and the boys are, right this moment, taking a meeting with someone in the sitting room. Andra and my mother are probably upstairs in their rooms."

"Okay, good."

Trying not to show she was intrigued, Racine ceased pretending to read the newspaper and, with extreme care, took her time to fold it neatly—fold and then smooth, fold and then smooth. Gently, she placed it next to her plate. Putting on her poker face, she stared at her unwelcome guest. "This will be my third and last time asking. What do you want?"

"First, you must promise me"—Sly paused to once more look behind her—"what we speak now is between you and I."

Biting her tongue, Racine nodded succinctly.

"I believe you are not fond of the marriage between your sister and J. J."

"You're repeating yourself," she said. She rolled her eyes only to narrow them. "Where do you get off thinking you know anything about me?" Racine went on to mock Sly's accent. "Besides, I like J. J."

Sly dipped her eyes. "I know. I like Dr. Andra as well, but—"

"But what? Spit it out!"

"Well, I do not believe they are to make a good match. I sense you believe the same."

Looking away, Racine straightened her knife, making sure there was equal distance between it, her fork, and the plate. "So what? It's their life." Her eyes lifted to glare at Sly. "It should be their call—so none-ya."

Sly's brow crinkled. "None-ya?"

"None of your business."

Sly smiled, nodding slowly. "Yes, I agree. Maybe it should be none-ya." She pouted prettily. "But they may not understand how much their marriage is affecting both sides of the family."

"Which you're a part of—the other side of the family, I mean?"

Sly had the nerve to blush. "Well, yes. I and Paulo were little children with Stefano and J. J."

Rolling her eyes at Sly, Racine shook her head with disdain. "I believe you're jealous of my sister."

"I do not know what you say," Sly said, quickly looking away. "I am not."

"Yes, you are." Racine scanned the other's defensive posture above the table and nodded once. "I can read you like a cheap novel."

At the answering silence, Racine shifted forward, allowing her breasts to rest upon the tabletop, knowing her globe-like twins were displayed to their full advantage. With satisfaction, she reveled in the envious glance Sly gave them.

"Where are your parents?" Racine asked, drawing Sly's attention back to her face. "Why don't they come over here as often as you do?"

Sly's jaw swiftly drooped with sadness. "I and Paulo are orphans since we were children. We stay with our grandmother, who is quite old and cannot get around like us."

Remembering her deceased father, Racine sat back. "Sorry," she mumbled. She grew silent, only to flash a knowing smile. "Wait! So that's it. You've always had designs on Jayson and this grand villa—and Andra beat you to it by ball-and-chaining him first, right?"

"What?" Sly giggled, shaking her head. "No. Being very serious, J. J. is like a brother to me. I have no designs on him, as you say."

Racine's forehead crinkled. "Okay, so what's this about? Why do you want them to split?" At Sly's reticent silence, Racine slowly rose. "If you can't spill everything, you can just count me out."

Sly reached out a hand to stop Racine. "Okay, okay!" Sneaking another peak about her, she let out an exhausted sigh. "It is not me; I could care less who J. J. marries. Dr. Andra's as good as anyone he could have picked."

"But?"

Sly's face was miserable. "But Stefano doesn't believe so." At Racine's stunned silence, Sly rushed on. "He wants J. J. to stay and help him run the business, but he wants Dr. Andra to go. Stefano asked for my help. I feel I have no choice but to do what I am told."

Racine sat for a moment to study the girl. "You love Stefano." Initially, she had thought to form the thought into a question, but she knew she didn't have to. It was written all over the other's face.

Pondering Sly's silent misery, which appeared far above the regular unrequited puppy-dog crush, Racine recalled the quick glance Stefano had thrown Andra's way at the dinner table. Abruptly, another unbelievable revelation struck her.

"But Stefano's in love with Andra. It's the reason you're all gung ho to help him out, right? This has nothing to do with Jayson at all; it's about getting Andra outta Stefano's orbit—to clear it for you."

Her table companion's continued silence answered for her.

Anger rising, Racine shook her head. "So all this time, big man on campus was acting as if he couldn't stand my sister, running around here acting as if he's better than my entire family, only to be in love with Andra? Why, he's nothing but a hypocritical, racist son of a—"

As Racine's voice grew louder, Sly shushed her with a desperate whisper. "Please! It is nothing like that. He is nothing like that!" At Racine's outraged look, Sly attempted a placating smile. "Stefano is kind and thoughtful and extremely smart."

"Stop!" Abruptly, Racine presented her palm. "I'll help you."

"You will?" Sly asked, appearing breathless at the rapid turnabout in Racine's stance. "Why?"

Racine rose to loom over Sly. "Why? This was my fear all along. It's why I tried to make my sister see reason in not marrying Jayson. I want to get Andra away from you and this whole dang-blasted family! This situation has way too much drama and intrigue. So stupid!"

After shoving her chair in at just the right angle, Racine headed for the door, leaving Sly to sit at the table alone. "We'll be in touch, Ms. Thang."

Sly stood to watch her retreat. "All right, but where are you going?"

"If you must know, I'm going to my room." Racine stopped to let out an impatient snort. "Right now, I've had my fill of you. You stink to high heaven of drama. Drama, drama, drama!"

Racine shoved past the swinging door. Crossing the circular foyer to head for the main staircase, she threw a sour glance at the closed doors to the formal sitting room, where, on the other side, she could only assume the business meeting was still going strong.

For the hundredth time, she shook her head at the mind-boggling intrigue Andra and Jayson's marriage continued to stir up.

Can't wait to drag Andra back home where she belongs and leave all this stupid drama behind!

Still, as Racine took the stairs two at a time to the second level, she couldn't silence the accusing voice inside her head that screamed maybe she was the biggest drama queen of them all.

3 2

Leaving the Theonopilus men behind closed doors, Andra let out a sigh, her spirit lifting the moment she stepped into the large foyer.

As much as she loved Jayson and adored his father, George, she still couldn't get a handle on what to make of Stefano. She understood a subtle change had occurred within him concerning her, something imperceptible to the naked eye. When it came to respecting one another, they had both risen to a higher emotional level. She was unable to pinpoint how or when it had happened, but it had.

Now she needed to figure out what to do with it.

However, the unexpected shift in their relationship brought both relief and confusion. She was relieved that they'd established a shaky truce; she still remained confused concerning how he'd stare at her with a hunger-driven intensity only to have those same eyes ration out the same measure of disgust.

"Don't worry about it," she mumbled. She made her way toward the kitchen and the back door, which led out to the lush, rolling green acres beyond. "Andra, why don't you and your nonsense just take a hike?"

Andra broke out in a smile over her unintentional pun. Humming a carefree tune, she reached the kitchen's swinging door only to abruptly stop. She remained still at muffled voices drifting to her from the other side. Wanting to hear better, she gently palmed the door and pushed it open a crack.

They were female voices.

Turning her head, she placed an ear to the opening. At once, she identified the voices and smiled ruefully. Her smile morphed into the urge to chuckle out loud as the kitchen conversation progressed, and she was forced to slap a hand over her mouth. Her body shook with silent mirth at Sly's salutation of "Good morning, Dr. Andra's sister" and Racine's biting response of "Why are you always here?"

It was a question Andra constantly asked herself concerning the girl.

An unexpected weariness overtook her. She didn't care why Sly was at the villa again; she just knew she didn't want to endure the pesky interloper while in her present good mood.

Stepping back, she eased the swinging panel in place. On silent feet, she retraced her steps, this time heading for the main entrance. Her eyes once again touched upon the closed doors to the sitting room, and her feet sped up to reach the front door in record time.

Andra quickly stepped out into the glorious sunlight to release a grateful sigh.

She didn't feel too guilty about leaving Racine with Sly; she knew her sibling could hold her own with the likes of that female Athenian. Truthfully, she should feel sorry for Sly. Her baby sister was like the runaway train in *Unstoppable*. It was best to simply get off the tracks and let someone strong, such as Denzel, take care of stopping it.

Andra paused to breathe in unrestricted fresh air while trying to decide which direction to head. During the process of making up her mind, she suddenly glanced upward. A bird soared at a safe distance as its cheerful chirping called out a hello. Using her hand to shield her eyes from the brilliance of the sun, she strolled as she watched it circle above, her lips smiling in a return hello.

She marveled at the bird's effortless flight and kept her eyes on it until it reached the end of the villa. The bird flapped once, tucked one wing, and sharply turned the corner to disappear from sight.

Intrigued, Andra decided to follow.

By the time she rounded the villa, the soaring bird had

vanished, as she'd known it would. Still, she made her way along the lengthy wall. Thanks to many years of nature's handicraft, the stone was exquisitely decorated with bright green climbing ivy arrayed with tiny colorful flowers.

Her thoughts wistful at not having explored its outer splendor sooner, she walked along the cobblestone path, savoring her surroundings. Once she reached the back of the villa, which led to acres and acres of land, she stared in awe. She knew those vast grounds eventually spilled into an even greater portion of land that supported the Theonopilus family's olive groves.

Her eyes, ears, and nose took in the beauty of God's creation—and for the first time, Andra understood Jayson's reluctance to abandon the splendor of his childhood home for a second time.

She shook her head in wonder. "Why would you leave this place, Jay? Will seeing all this again stop you from returning to Florida?"

Stefano, his image darkly handsome, entered her head.

Nope, not today. Her feet picked up speed, attempting to outrun her imagination. After a minute, she forced herself not to break into an actual sprint and slowed down to take in the surrounding beauty.

After some time, she stopped to brush aside wind-blown hair; glancing back at the enormous villa, she wanted to gauge just how far she'd come. Its height and width now appeared much smaller; mentally, she calculated her distance to be more than a mile or so away.

Time paced itself with her progress as she hiked over level grass until the ground abruptly became a hilly incline. Halfway up, she stooped to pick a white-and-blue lily. Shoving the stem of the flower behind her ear, Andra closed her eyes, allowing the darkness to mentally erase her simple blouse, blue jeans, and tennis shoes, replacing them with a one-shoulder gossamer gown.

In her mind, the gown billowed about her body, the sensation unlocking an inner wildness. Capriciously, she spread her arms wide, pretending to be kin to her friend the soaring bird. Like it, her spirit embraced the wind as sunlit breezes lifted her body higher and higher toward the heavens.

She imagined she possessed the same freedom the ancient goddesses of old embodied within their godlike state.

Like Aphrodite?

The unexpected question jolted her from her daydream, shifting her thoughts immediately to Stefano. Standing in the open field, she felt exposed, as if he watched her. She again looked toward the villa and the tiny window that she knew was part of Stefano's office. Feeling naked, she wrapped her arms about her body to reassure it; even if he stared out it, she was too far away for him to truly see her.

Embarrassed at the volatile direction her wayward mind had taken her, she cleared it of all goddesses—and the man who still believed in them.

She trekked on.

Ten minutes later, Andra stopped to shield her eyes. In the distance to her right, she viewed tiny workers moving among the olive groves, their voices projecting diminutive foreign words that conveyed no meaning for her. As she watched them, the carefree spirit that had deserted her earlier unexpectedly returned, and like an old friend, she gladly welcomed it back.

Soon enough, the rising temperature shook her from her reverie.

Lazily, she scanned the area until her sights landed on a quaint little stone cottage. At first glance, it appeared to be abandoned, but upon closer inspection, she knew it to be storage for the grove's smaller gardening equipment. Standing motionless, she debated whether or not to head for it.

Soon perspiration dotted her forehead, and its watery appearance decided for her. She quickly made her way toward the tall structure and the cool promise of shade behind it.

Her breathing heavier, Andra allowed her thoughts to stray toward Jayson and their marriage. As usual, her heart skipped a beat the instant his handsome face and perfect body materialized into mental view. She ached for him and loved him beyond reason, yet at the same time, her heart grew heavy at knowing she would soon leave him behind once she headed back to America.

With a bittersweet feeling, she pondered their airplane ride over and what Hog had said about love.

Maybe sometimes love wasn't enough.

A burning behind her eyes painfully blinded her.

"Stop it, you dunce!" she firmly told herself. "Don't you dare cry."

Determined not to stain the beauty around her with despondent tears, she blinked rapidly until her eyes cleared.

Andra finally reached the toolshed and rounded its corner, grateful to step into the building's shade. At once, an extreme weariness washed over her, and she backed against the bumpy chill of the large, irregular-shaped stones, allowing gravity to pull her to the ground. Sighing with ecstasy, she undid her top buttons, allowing delicious, zesty breezes to caress her heated skin.

Closing her eyes, she reclined against the stone wall and relaxed, her mind embracing no other thoughts but the soft summer wind, the smell from sweet green grass, and the unwinding of her exhausted body.

Andra woke with a start, her sleep-filled eyes darting upward to encounter a looming darkness. Her heart beating wildly, she opened her mouth to scream, only to have the shadow stoop and swiftly cover it.

The figure placed a vertical finger against pale lips in a silent command.

"I'm sorry. I did not mean to frighten you," Stefano said. Rising slowly, he removed his palm from her lips only to extend it. "I meant no harm."

Seconds passed as Andra stared at the proffered hand. He stood there like an eternal Greek statue, ready and willing to outwait her. An indeterminate amount of time passed before she finally placed her palm in his.

Easily, Stefano pulled her to her feet and toward him, their bodies now separated by mere inches.

His warm grip wrapped her in comfortable warmth, giving the illusion their hands had been created to fit perfectly inside one another. The familiarity stunned Andra. Emitting a small gasp, she jerked free and took a wobbly step in reverse.

"What are you doing here? Where's Jayson?"

Stefano moved closer. "I believe he is at the villa, looking for you."

Andra's eyes widened. "Did you tell him where I was?" At his silence, she frowned. "You didn't tell him, did you? Wait a second. How did you know I was here?"

His shadowed eyes skimmed her body, their mood reflective, until they came to a rest upon her partially open blouse. Not wanting to bring any more attention to her exposed skin, she fought the urge to refasten her buttons under his watchful stare.

Why am I always in some state of undress when it comes to encountering this man?

An eon later, his eyes lifted. "I studied you from my window. I knew you would perhaps end here. Everyone does at one time or another."

Stefano's voice drew her in with its electric baritone. Fascinated, she watched his mouth.

"I decided to seek you out."

"I don't understand. What do you want from me?" she asked. When he licked his lips, Andra forced her gaze from the glistening result. "I believe you know your brother wouldn't like this at all. If you've noticed, I don't go out of my way to bother *you*."

Silently, Stefano's eyes watched her mouth only to look to her left. His hand lifted to capture the blue-and-white lily, pulling it with sensual ease from her hair. He brought it to his nose and breathed deeply.

She stood gaping at the hand that clutched the fragile flower with amazing gentleness. In a flash, her mind cruelly dished up a memory of the two of them inside her bedroom, where that same hand had crushed her semi-naked body against his. Abruptly, she grew angry with Stefano—and herself—when she wished to be the lily he now held.

Painfully, she swallowed. "Why can't you just leave me alone?"

Andra held her breath and watched as he inserted the plant's stem into his shirt pocket, the flower looking like a simple wedding boutonniere.

His hands were now free.

Stefano moved closer. "As I stated to you in the library, I want nothing except to speak with you alone. I informed you then we would continue this conversation at a later time. Now is the time."

He was close enough for her to smell his perspiration mingled with aftershave. The combination mingled with the lily's fragrance, and she refused to inhale too deeply the arresting blend. Resolved, she placed a trembling hand against his chest in order to push him away. Instead, it lay there like a limp dishrag.

"Please back up," she whispered. "I can't ..."

Think. Speak. Breathe.

"Can't what?" Stefano asked. He moved closer, forcing her other hand to join its mate in holding him at bay. "Maybe you can't understand why it is imperative you leave my brother and return to the States?"

Energy left her body in a slow leak. She said nothing, glad he'd offered an alternative answer to the truth.

Stefano captured a curly lock of her hair. In an unhurried manner, he wrapped it around one finger. "Must I spell it out for you, my lovely one?"

Andra swallowed nervously. She fought an automatic response to rub her cheek against his unnervingly close hand. "Yes," she managed to say. "You may have to."

He delayed a reply to reach inside his pocket and pull out a black handkerchief. Turning slightly, he coughed twice into it, and then, without looking at it, he returned it to its hiding place.

At once, her mind replayed Stefano's coughing fit when he'd almost kissed her inside the bedroom, its bloody result leaving her to soak her white bathrobe before Jayson returned that afternoon.

"What's wrong with you, Stefano?" she asked. "Are you sick? I'm only asking because back in the bedroom, you coughed up some blood."

Stefano paused to release the strand of hair twirled about his finger. Then, lowering his hand to the curve of her neck, he allowed his thumb to delicately trace her jawline. "I bit my tongue earlier in the day." His eyes locked with hers, causing a violent tingle to run along Andra's spine. "Would you like to examine me, Doctor? Make sure I am well?"

The distant echo of men's laughter, tweeting birds busily flitting from tree to bush, and their own mingled breathing were abruptly interrupted by someone clearing her throat.

Both heads jerked simultaneously at the sound. Sly stood at the building's edge, watching them with her arms folded. Seeing her, Stefano calmly stepped away from Andra.

"I am sorry. I didn't mean to interrupt. I was taking a hike," Sly said. Her green eyes cooked with fiery intensity as they bounced between Stefano and Andra. "Please, do not mind me."

"Did I not tell you everyone ends here?" he said ruefully.

Panicked, Andra slipped past Stefano to move closer to the incensed girl. "Sly, there's nothing to interrupt. Believe me." Her heart was determined to hammer its way through her chest at the ensuing silence that suddenly poured from the two. Andra's eyes shifted from Sly to appeal to her mute brother-in-law. "Right, Stefano?"

"I must return to the house," he said, his tone all business. He walked away from Andra and past Sly, motioning to the latter with his head. "Would you care to walk back with me, Sylvia? There are things we need to discuss."

Pausing behind his retreating back, Sly scowled, scrutinizing Andra's undone buttons, which brazenly revealed her glistening brown skin. After throwing her a hateful "I've got you now" look, Sly turned and ran after Stefano.

Alone once again, Andra took a shaky breath and leaned against the toolshed for support. She wasn't sure whether she was more bothered by the possibility of Sly squealing to Jayson about finding her and Stefano in a compromising position or by the fact that Stefano hadn't bothered to ask if she wanted to walk back to the villa with him too.

33

The knocking came in rapid, nervous taps.

Hog took his time crossing the hotel room floor, wanting the person on the other side of the door to feel more anxious and off balance with each passing second. It always gave him an edge.

By the time he opened the door to Paulo's sickly expression, he couldn't help but chuckle with delight. "Well, well, well! If it isn't my partner in crime! Come on in!"

Paulo tucked his shoulder and slipped past Hog, his evasive maneuver effectively dodging the pounding his back would've received in welcome. "Good afternoon, sir."

Closing the door, Hog turned to his young visitor. "You know, son, I wouldn't mind it at all if you called me Hog." At Paulo's reluctant expression, Hog moved toward his hotel suite's sitting room. "Suit yourself. You Greeks are a little too formal for me."

Paulo nervously glanced around the elegant suite as he trailed behind Hog. "Mr. Grainger, I am sorry, but I do not believe I can assist you with your takeover." He quickly took the seat Hog motioned to. "It's ..." Paulo's misery forced his remaining words into nothingness.

From his chair, Hog studied the young Greek, now summing up Paulo's extreme apprehension as a possible liability. For the first time, he grew worried. Tuning into his business sixth sense, he realized the anxiety Paulo displayed could yank him beyond any manipulation he had planned.

Hog coughed assuredly. "Well now, son, I'm not asking you

to do anything illegal." He curled the fingers on one hand to nonchalantly study his nails. "I'm just asking you to stay close by and report what's happening. That's all."

The sigh Paulo uttered sounded like that of a cornered animal. Unsteadily, he stood and ambled over to the sliding glass door that overlooked the balcony. His back to Hog, he stared through the pane into opulent blue skies. When he finally spoke, his voice grew wistful, as if he wished he could take flight beyond the horizon he beheld. "Myself, it seems wrong. I am their friend. Their family."

Choosing not to speak until he recalculated his thoughts, Hog rose and crossed over to the minibar. He took his time fixing a scotch on the rocks. "Well, Paulo, there's nothing underhanded going on here. I can assure you. As I told you before, I'm trying to help out your family."

"Yes, but you're attempting to take away their business."

"Maybe I was initially. But once I sat down and talked with the Theonopilus clan, I've decided to modify my plans."

Paulo pivoted toward Hog, his expression hopeful. "In what way, may I ask?"

"I'll still initially invest the money and take over the company; however, once I get things planted on solid ground again, I'll turn it back over to them and move on."

"You will?" he asked, his face breaking out into a relieved smile. However, just as quickly, it disappeared. Paulo's eyes narrowed. "Why?"

Noting the other's squinty suspicion, Hog lifted a palm. "Now, listen. I've met them personally; they're more than a paper deal to negotiate. They're real people—honest, hardworking, decent family men." He took a sip of scotch. "But unfortunately, they're a proud and arrogant group of boys, especially that Stefano fella. Might not take too kindly to someone like me bailing them out—me not being family and all, such as yourself."

Hog considered his young patsy before continuing. "So, I've decided not to tell them what I'm planning until I'm able to return the business back to them fully running, operational, and profitable."

"Well, if this is your plan," Paulo said, his voice soft with hope.

Hog nodded. "Yep, you've got my word on it, son." He produced a smile he hoped projected sincerity. "Good people shouldn't have to lose things that are extremely precious to them. It's never right—I should know."

Exhaling, Paulo returned to his seat. He sat on its edge like a schoolboy sitting before a school's headmaster. "That is very kind, Mr. Grainger! If all goes well and everything is returned to normal, I believe Papa George and the boys should be grateful for such assistance."

Tension flowed from Hog's body at Paulo's pleased tone. Smiling broadly, he refreshed his drink and returned to his chair. "Glad I'm able to get you to see it my way." He paused, purposely drawing Paulo's undivided attention. "Did anyone discuss our meeting with you?"

Paulo shook his head. "Stefano informed me I was not needed; therefore, no information will be imparted to me. And I must agree with him."

Hog nodded. "Fair enough. But I still want to gain access to their weaknesses." At Paulo's returned concern, Hog pitched him another palm. "And strengths. Make sure this thing goes the way we want it to." Subliminally, Hog threw in the word *we* for Paulo's sake. "Unfortunately, my meeting with them this morning didn't go as I'd hoped. As I said, there's a prideful, stubborn streak a mile wide over there. From what I can tell, they might be leaning toward pulling outta the deal."

Hog took another nip from his drink and said, "Ahhh," before he smiled at Paulo. "But during the meeting, I learned a piece of information that's most interesting. I believe I've stumbled upon a weakness of young Stefano's."

"You have?" Paulo lifted a curious eyebrow. "Yes?"

"Andra."

Paulo's expression went from curious to confused; however, after another second passed, his face gave way to a benevolent smile. "No, no—you are mistaken. You must mean Jayson's weakness. Dr. Andra is his wife."

Hog grinned. "I understand that, son. Remember—I told

you I met those two young'uns on the flight over." He held up a hand for emphasis. "Dr. Andra, as you call her, is the youngest one's weakness—that's a given. But she represents a greater weakness for the eldest. Mark my words: that boy's in love with his sister-in-law."

Paulo shook his head. "It cannot be," he said, his voice adamant. "I have it from my sister, Sly, that Stefano actually despises Dr. Andra."

Chuckling, Hog drained his scotch and set the empty glass on the coffee table between them. "Your sister's in denial—either that, or there's something in it for her believing such a thing. Any direction you come at it, she's wrong."

At Paulo's insistent head shaking, Hog impatiently scrambled to his feet. He headed for the suite's exit, knowing Paulo didn't have a choice but to follow. "I've been in business far too long not to detect things—these subtle carryings-on. Just keep your head up and your eyes and ears open," he said over his shoulder. "Since I've pointed it out, you'll spot it sure enough for yourself."

Hog arrived at the door and opened it wide.

Paulo hesitated to cross the threshold; instead, he stared out into the hallway, his body language uncertain. "But what if I do see it? What am I to do with such information?"

Hog placed a large hand on his visitor, gracing him with a firm pat on the back. Hog then gave him a friendly shove out the door. "That's what I'm paying you for, son." He grinned at Paulo, tipping an invisible Stetson his way. "You figure it out. You've got my number. Call me."

The door closed abruptly in Paulo's frustrated face.

34

Insistent knocking sounded.

Sighing, Andra slowly pulled the damp washcloth from her forehead and swung lethargic limbs off the bed. She sat up. Gripping the mattress edge with both hands, she willed the room to stop spinning long enough for her to stand.

More knocking produced a throbbing inside her head.

"Coming! Just a minute."

Attempting to get her bearings, she glanced about the room. The cloak of darkness threw off her senses, and she was unable to pinpoint the time. The balcony curtains were closed tightly; she'd made sure of that prior to succumbing to a nap.

After crossing to them, she averted her eyes as she flung aside the curtains and opened both doors wide to allow the late-afternoon sun to pour in. Stumbling toward the bedroom door, Andra squinted at the nightstand clock, noting it was 3:50 p.m.

Knocking, louder than before, erupted again.

"Andra?" Racine called from the other side. "You in there? What's taking so long?"

"Okay, okay! Wait a sec!"

Andra forewent putting on her robe and moved toward the door wearing only her light gray T-shirt and panties. She'd barely disengaged the lock and cracked the door before Racine pushed through.

"I didn't think you were ever going to let me in!" Racine made her way over to the rumpled bed and fell upon it. "Where were you earlier? I looked all over for you."

You wouldn't want to know, she thought as the toolshed, Stefano, and Sly popped into her head. "I went for a walk." Wearily, she closed the bedroom door and turned to face her sister. She flinched at Racine's "Wow!"

"A walk, eh? Well, it didn't do you much good, did it? Man, you look a mess!"

"Thanks," she said, moving toward the bathroom. She left the door ajar while she took care of business. "And I was asleep, hence the mess!"

"Girl, the way you're looking, the word *mess* should be thrown out the window as an understatement," Racine called out. She grew quiet, the sound of her voice replaced by vague shifting noises, leading Andra to believe Racine was probably straightening something in the next room. "So where's my gorgeous, albeit naive, brother-in-law? I thought you two would be in here knocking glorious boots together."

"Don't be crude—it isn't pretty on you," Andra said. With an unsteady hand, she tore off toilet paper and wiped herself. "George told me Jay's gone to the village to speak with a priest at his family's church. He won't be back until later this evening."

"A priest?" Racine asked. "Has Jayson gone to ask for an annulment, I hope?"

Not bothering to answer, Andra flushed the toilet, washed her hands, and, as an afterthought, splashed water on her face. She straightened to review the damage in the sink's mirror. Not surprised, she took in puffy eyes, their whites sporting spidery blood vessels that made it appear as if she'd been awake forever. As far as her body was concerned, it seemed as if she had.

Her exhaustion was so great that she wanted to eject her sister from the room, return to bed, and extend her nap for a week. Instead, she rushed back to the toilet and threw up.

The bathroom door exploded inward, the force of it banging the panel against the bathroom wall. Frantic, Racine sprinted to her side. "Sis, what's going on?" she asked. She reached out to rub along Andra's curved spine. "What's wrong with you?"

Unable to answer right away, Andra remained bent over

the toilet until her frame produced nothing more than residual dry heaves. Sluggishly, she straightened and returned to the sink. After rinsing her mouth thoroughly with tap water, she snatched a face towel from the wall rack and wiped her ashen face. "Oh, nothing seven months won't cure," she finally said. Not bothering to rehang the towel, she let it drop directly into the sink. "Give or take a month."

Racine took a step back, her mouth wide open in horrified surprise. Andra couldn't decide whether her sister's reaction was from her baby news or the fact that she hadn't hung up her facecloth.

"You mean you're ..." Racine's words trailed off as she moved toward the discarded towel.

So both. "Pregnant," Andra said, finishing for her. Not bothering to linger for a response, she turned from Racine's towel folding and headed for the bed.

"How could this happen?" Racine said, entering the bedroom seconds later.

Andra stopped her crawl onto the mattress to look over her shoulder and throw her sister a "Really?" look.

Chuckling mirthlessly, Racine caught up with her. Gently, she helped Andra get under the covers and neatly tucked her in. She quickly circled the bed and sat on Jayson's side. "Okay, so I know how it happened," she said. "But tell me. With everyone passing out birth control pills like they're candy and condoms like they're chewing gum—and for goodness sake, you're a doctor—how could you allow this to happen?"

Again, Andra blinked at Racine.

"Stop with the looks, Andra!" After kicking her sandals from her feet, Racine swung her long legs up and sat cross-legged. "Jayson's a babe and all, and if I was married to him, I probably wouldn't be able to keep my hands off him either. Maybe. Still."

Andra closed her eyes and exhaled. She knew Racine was right; they had been careless in their lovemaking and their attempt to naturally prevent a pregnancy from happening. Yet the odds always had been stacked against them from the start. Jayson, being a future minister, didn't believe in man-made contraceptives.

Now the inevitable had finally happened.

Involuntarily, her mind flashed with racy images of their many lovemaking sessions together and varied erotic positions. Her respiration accelerated at the memories.

Once she actually thought about it, she was surprised she hadn't gotten pregnant much sooner. *Like maybe our first night together.*

She jumped at the nudge to her side.

"So what are you gonna do?" Racine asked, poking her again for good measure. "Have you told Jayson? You gonna tell Mama anytime soon?"

Feeling bombarded with too many questions, Andra reached over to the nightstand and retrieved her damp cloth. Its previous coolness had downgraded to an uncomfortable ickiness, but she didn't care as she replaced the compress over her eyes. All she wanted was relief.

Andra cautiously shook her head. "I don't know what I'm going to do."

Racine shifted, her next words coming forth softly yet clearly. "Have you thought about, you know, getting rid of it?"

Andra remained calm beneath her towel; she'd already prepared herself for the question she'd known someone would eventually ask. "No! Never in a million years." She placed her hand tenderly atop her flat tummy. "There's a living, breathing human being growing inside me. He or she is a person created by me and the man I love. No way."

"Get off your soapbox, Mother Earth—I hear ya." Racine paused reflectively. "However, there are those who, once they find out, might not agree with you."

Stefano's face quickly came and went inside Andra's head. "I know. Listen, Racine." She lifted a corner of the sodden rag to peek out at her sister with one puffy eye. "No one but you know about this. I'm counting on you to keep your trap shut until I can at least tell my husband."

Racine laughed, this time a little more carefree. "Trust me, I won't have to say a word. If Mom gets a peek at you right now, she'll guess." The room grew quiet as both contemplated the situation. Racine nudged her again. "So what are you gonna do now? Is it still your plan to cut and run?"

Andra winced at the word *run*, for it sounded even more cowardly when it slipped from someone else's tongue other than her own. She snatched the rag from her face. "No, I will not! Jay's my husband, and I love him." It was a struggle to sit up, but with Racine's help, she managed it. Out of breath, she rested her spine against the headboard. "I'm not going to let him go—especially now."

Abruptly, Racine's expression darkened. "Why him, Andra?" she asked, her eyes glistening with unshed tears. "Why did you have to choose a white man?"

Andra paused to truly consider the question, knowing deep down Racine didn't have anything against Jayson per se, just the idea of him. "What is it that makes someone fall for one person and not another?" Within the quiet pause, Andra shrugged philosophically. "I fell in love with my husband not because he was black or white, rich or poor, handsome or ugly. I fell in love with him because he's Jayson."

Racine remained quiet, glaring down at her hands in her lap.

"I love Jayson because he gets me. He makes me laugh." Again, she paused in an attempt to go deeper. "Who he is makes me want and need to be a better person. And I know I am with him. I think that's the greatest gift anyone can give another."

Andra braced herself, believing she would have to further champion her reasons for marrying someone outside their race. Instead, she was shocked to witness Racine's nod.

"Okay. I hear ya." Brushing away a fallen tear, Racine leaned against the headboard. "You know, at first, I believed you had made a terrible mistake, mixing your Kool-Aid flavors and everything." She held up a stiff palm at Andra's wide-eyed expression. "And the jury's still out on that! But I do have to admire your guts for taking a stand for what you want, and I can see how much you care for Jayson. So."

At her pause, Andra nudged Racine. "So, *what*?"

Her sister's shrug was careless. "I guess you have my blessing."

Despite her nausea, Andra produced a lopsided grin. "Finally! I'm so glad!" She rolled her eyes upward. "I couldn't have gone on with this sham of a marriage without it!"

They both giggled until Racine abruptly sobered again.

"What?" Andra asked.

"Now here lands a fly in your ointment." Racine paused, poker-faced, until Andra nudged her again. "I had a talk with your little friend Ms. Thang—or, more accurately, she had a talk with me. She asked for my help in breaking you and Jayson up."

Her nausea forgotten, Andra leaned forward. "What! That little bit—"

"Whoa, watch your language, Miss Prim and Proper. Let's just slow your roll—I'm not going to do it."

"You not going through with it is not the point," she said, huffing in anger. "Who made Sly the universe's queen goddess, giving her permission to come between—"

"She didn't invent this little scheme by herself," Racine said quietly, interrupting. "In fact, it was Stefano's idea. He recruited her."

Andra blinked at building tears, and for a second, she didn't understand their sudden appearance. At once, understanding rushed upon her: the tears were a product of her mounting hurt against Stefano.

"How could he do that to Jay and me?" she whispered.

"Easy. He wants you gone. He wants us all gone." Racine rotated toward Andra. "But now it's up to you."

Not wanting Racine to decipher the meaning behind her accumulating tears, she kept her eyes lowered. "What do you mean me?"

Racine let out an impatient sigh, as if she dealt with an imbecilic child. "Come on, Sis. You've so elegantly declared you're not gonna throw Jayson away—and the baby has tightened that resolve. You've got to make up your mind."

Not knowing how to defend herself, Andra kept quiet.

She sensed rather than saw Racine shake her head in admonishment.

"You're gonna lose Jayson if you don't fight for him. Stop being such a scaredy-cat."

Racine's harsh words pushed Andra to lift her eyes. "You're right—I have been living in fear." Drying her tears, Andra directly met her sister's gaze. "But so have you."

"Whatever. We're not talking about me." Guilt radiated from Racine's orbs as she looked away and batted the air as if to deflect Andra's boomerang truth. "Come on, Andra. You know as well as I do it's always up to us women to do the right thing. Men can't. They'll hurt you and abandon you."

A tight silence hung in the air, replacing further words Racine chose not to say.

Andra covered Racine's fist and gently squeezed. "Hey, sweet pea. Have you ever considered that whether or not Daddy was alive, what happened to you might've still happened?"

Racine reclined her head against the headboard, closing her eyes. Her fist coiled tighter. "I've considered that every day since it happened." She opened her big brown eyes, which shone brightly with tears. "I try hard not to blame Daddy and to stop asking him why he wasn't there to protect me, knowing he can't hear me."

Andra drew her near and rocked, softly humming a made-up tune.

After a good while, Racine pushed her away. "Stop, Andra," Racine said, sniffling. "I'm not a baby."

"I know. It's just that I love you."

"And you can keep that to yourself." Her expression slipping in its sternness, Racine stood and slid her feet into her perfectly aligned sandals. "Save the emotional crap for your brother-in-law. Heaven knows he needs it—him and that sourpuss of his."

"He called me Aphrodite once."

Racine twisted to stare at her. "Who? Stefano?" At her nod, Racine's expression turned thoughtful. "Hey, isn't she the goddess of sex or love or something?"

Embarrassed that she'd let that piece of information slip, Andra could only nod again.

"Why would he call you—" An indignant hand on her hip, Racine stopped. "Okay then, Aphrodite. Stand!"

From nowhere, Andra's brain downloaded her favorite Janet Jackson video featuring the song "Love Will Never Do (Without You)." Her smile wistful, she pictured Janet's playful romp on a beach with a fair-skinned actor hired to portray her lover, who, coincidentally, looked startlingly similar to Jayson in color and build. The black-and-white pair were simpatico in their beauty as the upbeat melody swirled around them, their bodies laughing, hugging, and touching and their outlooks determinedly free.

The lyrics to the beautiful melody communicated an us-against-the-world attitude; no matter what people said or thought about their eclectic relationship, they would weather the storm called prejudice and stay together.

"You're playing that Janet Jackson video in your head, aren't you?"

Andra gaped at Racine. "Race, how did you know?"

Displaying a mysterious smile, Racine leaned across the bed and placed a finger under Andra's chin, closing her mouth. "What else would you be thinking of? I guess you gotta do what you gotta do to keep hope alive."

At Andra's silence, Racine straightened Jayson's side of the bed; once done, she stepped back, hands on hips, to survey her efforts. "Well, if you don't want Mom knowing anything about the baby, I'd better head her off at the pass. If she comes in here and sees you, man, the jig's up!"

Her long legs propelled her toward the door; however, halfway there, she stopped to bestow a grin on Andra. "Still, you won't have to worry about Jayson knowing you're pregnant; men are totally oblivious to anything outside their own pleasure zones. Catch ya later."

Andra frowned as she watched Racine disappear beyond the closed door.

Although she believed Racine's last statement was mostly due to residual feelings from the aftermath of her rape, Andra had to admit there was truth to it. Lately, Jayson couldn't see beyond what was happening outside himself, his family, and the business.

Determined to shut off unpleasant thoughts, Andra yawned loudly as she nestled inside her covers. She closed her eyes only to pop them open again when the door cracked open.

Racine poked her head inside the room. "You know, I can't wait to see Stefano's and Sly's faces when they finally get wind of"—she peeked over her shoulder in a covert fashion before continuing in a whisper—"the baby."

Her giggles were cut off by the closing door.

Wide awake, Andra decided to ignore her exhaustion and slid off the bed. With her hands on her hips, she searched for her jeans, only to discover they were not on the floor, where she'd kicked out of them, but folded neatly atop her dresser.

Racine. "That girl's got issues," she muttered.

Purposefully, Andra jammed her legs into them while Stefano's brooding face and Sly's smirking expression emerged inside her brain.

She didn't know exactly what she was going to do about them, but she knew she had to do something.

35

Andra shifted on anxious feet.

She stared at the closed door, her uncertainty rooting her to the spot. Wiping sweaty palms on her pants, she realized what she was doing and uttered a small groan. Disgusted, she assessed the water damage to her jeans, only to sigh in relief upon realizing there was none.

Inhaling deeply, Andra lifted a fist and knocked softly, hoping no one answered.

"Come in."

Her exhalation came out in one nervous puff. *Blast it.*

Throwing back her shoulders, Andra twisted the knob. The office door swung open, and she paused within its threshold. Her eyes immediately traveled to Stefano, who sat at his desk with his back to her.

In the background, classical music flowed from the small CD player on his desk. Rimsky-Korsakov's "Flight of the Bumblebee" softly played.

Stefano swiveled in her direction, and his face registered surprise; the emotion was replaced a second later by a pensive watchfulness.

He rose and gave a slight nod. "Please, come in."

Andra hesitated. Silently, she debated whether to shut the door for privacy or leave it open for propriety. She decided to take a chance and opted for the privacy. "We must talk," she said, closing the door. His eyes deliberated on her mouth. Nervous, she nodded as if he'd denied her. "Yes, we do."

Stefano politely swept his hand toward an empty chair.

Moving past him, Andra felt an energy surge like an electric current flow from him to mix with her own. Her brain painfully reminded her that his eyes watched her every step, causing her stride to feel stilted, as if she walked on mechanical legs.

Doubting she would be able to sit down gracefully once she reached the designated chair, she instead chose to stand and study a family portrait hanging above the chair.

Andra scrutinized it, taking in first her husband's adolescent smile and then Papa George's proud patriarchal expression, only to move on to the lovely woman she knew to be their mother and wife. Lastly, her gaze landed upon the face of a twenty-something Stefano.

Her eyes lingered on a face youthful in beauty. Yet his outer attractiveness wasn't the sole reason she stared at his image. A lightness in spirit poured from his arresting features; his aura projected an irresistible happiness he now lacked at his current age.

Music from Mozart's *Symphony No. 40* jolted Andra from her mesmerized reverie. She cleared her throat, shifting her focus to the solitary female in the picture. "Your mother," she said, pointing at the older woman's likeness. She tilted her head to study her deceased mother-in-law's expression. "She was extremely beautiful."

Stefano strolled over to stand next to Andra, his face passive as he too stared at the wall photo. "Yes, she was," he said. He lifted his hand as if to touch the portrait, but midway, he let it drop. "She was fairly young when she left us."

Surprised, Andra turned to him. "Left you? I'm sorry. I understood she died."

After pivoting, he returned to stand at his desk and said, "She did."

Once Stefano left her side, Andra experienced a weakening in her body, as if his nearness had somehow sapped her strength and took it with him. Grateful for the space between them, she gripped the armrests behind her and, with trembling hands, lowered herself into the chair.

"Well, yes, my father left us too when he was quite young."

She waded through her uneasiness, wanting to say anything to move beyond the moment. "I'm sorry for your loss."

"I am sorry for your loss as well." Stefano sat. From a small distance, his eyes briefly caressed his mother's image. "You remind me of her."

Andra lifted an eyebrow. "Huh?" She rotated her head and glanced up at the photo again, taking extra note of his mother's pale beauty. "I'm sorry, but I don't see it."

"It is not so much physical; it's more spiritual. Something intangible." He coughed self-consciously. Turning his back to her, he focused on shuffling papers. "What, may I ask, would you like to discuss with me?"

To Andra's relief and terror, the moment of confrontation had finally arrived. She licked her dry lips. Withdrawing what little resources she had left in her courage bank account, she straightened to stare at the nape of his neck, noting the razor-sharp perfection of his neatly trimmed hairline. "Yes, I know how busy you are, so I'll get right to the point." At Stefano's continued shuffling, Andra mutely dared him to face her. "I know what you're doing, Stefano. It won't work."

Stefano's hands paused; still, he refused to face her. "And what might that be, Doctor?"

She sighed angrily. "You know what! You're trying to destroy your brother's marriage, using Sly as part of your arsenal. Like I said, it won't work."

"Are you not a part of the marriage?"

Andra blinked with confusion. "Yes, I am. Why?"

"You eliminated yourself just now when you spoke." He continued his shuffling. "Perhaps you have already counted yourself out?"

"No, I haven't!" Andra jumped up. "Look, Stefano, what Jay and I have is real. Nothing you or anybody else does can change that. I love him."

As his chair slowly turned, Andra steeled herself for his indignant wrath. To her surprise, his face showed only regret.

Her eyes rose with him to involuntarily run the length of his tall, slender frame. They locked on him as he paced before her.

"When my mother passed away, my father did not adjust to the change very well. Slowly, he withdrew from life, leaving Jayson and myself behind." He ceased pacing to look at her. "You must understand he didn't mean to abandon us in such a way—yet he did."

At her silence, Stefano resumed pacing and ultimately walked back to her. Again, he gazed at his family's photo, seemingly lost in the past, a man who had forgotten she stood beside him in the present.

When he spoke again, his voice had a faraway quality to it. "I returned from college to help with the family business." His expression a void, he lingered on the photo until his eyes focused on Andra standing there. His face cleared, and he smiled faintly, only to move away. "You see, I took on the responsibility of stepping into my father's shoes—not only for the business but for Jayson as well."

A subtle change came over Stefano; he appeared to deflate as though air had been let out of his spirit. Lowering into his chair, he studied his tightly clenched fists. "Do my responsibilities extend to depriving my brother of his happiness?" He opened one hand and considered its open palm, as if searching for an answer there. He shook his head. "I thought I was doing what was best for Jayson—for the family. To everyone's detriment, I sometimes allow the burden I carry to hinder my good judgment." Stefano's head lifted. He stared straight into her eyes as his glittered like black diamonds. "I regret my actions."

The CD track changed; the poignant music from Tchaikovsky's "None but the Lonely Heart" softly filled the room.

Her brother-in-law's vulnerability drew her in, pushing aside the nervousness she'd initially felt upon entering. Silently, it pulled her across the room to him. As she stood over him, a small flash of blue and white caught her attention, and her eyes traveled across his mahogany desk to meet it.

Sitting upon his desk was the lily he'd earlier withdrawn from her hair, cradled almost reverently inside a small crystal vase.

Seeing the flower twisted something inside her. Andra knew her discovery was of great significance, but she refused to identify what that great significance could be. She simply told herself it was just a flower in a vase.

Compelled by an unknown force, Andra lifted a palm and placed it on his cheek. His olive skin was cool, and she felt the prickly stubble of new growth beard.

I regret my actions.

She understood he hadn't out and out apologized for what he'd done, yet in many ways, he had. He hadn't fully admitted the extent of what he'd done, yet he did. Continuing to learn about Stefano the man, Andra was willing to accept what little he had said at its truest value.

"Thank you," she said.

His eyes lowered from her lips to roam her swollen breasts. She chose not to be offended; she knew it was the way a man was created.

"If only," he said, his voice low and wistful.

A strong inner compulsion made her want to lean over, touch his face to hers, and whisper, "If only what?"

Yet something even greater stopped her: her love for Jayson.

His abrupt rising startled her into stepping back. She braced herself as he extended his arm.

"I hope we are on good standing," he said, staring into her eyes.

To Andra, his proffered hand appeared both benign and dangerous; it promised freedom, yet could be her captor. Her own hand itched to take it, if only to again experience the sensation of his skin against hers—yet she was afraid.

Ambiguously, his hand hung suspended in air.

Exhaling, Andra hesitated a few more seconds before sliding her hand into his.

Stefano didn't immediately complete the handshake; he simply held on, waiting for her response.

"Yes, we're good," she finally said.

Their grip and their stare stretched on longer. Separate sounds—soft classical music, the quiet ticking of the antique wall clock, birds tweeting beyond the windowpane—vaguely filtered into Andra's brain. As they stood, their frames frozen, she had the notion that any moment, Stefano would pull her into his embrace and—

Stefano stirred, as if awakening from a trance. "As much as I am compelled to do so, I will not seek you out again. This is my promise."

When he finally released her hand, it throbbed as if seared by a hot iron.

"I must return to my responsibilities." He presented his back to her upon returning to his chair and swiveling toward his desk. However, he didn't immediately start working but gazed at the small vase holding the blue-and-white lily. "I hope the remainder of your day will be pleasant."

"Thank you." Not knowing exactly why, she felt her spirit dip at his abrupt dismissal. "Yours as well."

Slightly confused at his—as well as her own—attitude, she quietly headed for the door.

"Andra?" he said.

She turned expectantly, her spirits suddenly lifting at hearing him say her name for the first time. "Yes, Stefano?"

At his pause, the air crackled with unspoken thoughts straining to be said. She longed to see his face and gauge his reaction to the words he would speak, yet he kept his back to her.

"Andra, I, uh ..."

She refused to breathe, waiting for words that had the ability to either uplift or crush. When they finally came, they did neither.

"I will not be at dinner tonight, so I will say my good night now," he said.

She knew he couldn't see it, but Andra nodded anyway. Quickly slipping from the room, she closed the door behind her, cutting off the haunting melody of Liszt's "Hungarian Rhapsody."

36

Sly looked beyond her busy hands immersed in dishwashing bubbles to glare out the picturesque kitchen window.

From time to time, she'd squint against the window's framing of the afternoon sun, its brightness hindering her from seeing into the distance for long. Although she knew it was irrational to be upset with the sun for obstructing her view, her wrath rose at it exponentially.

Behind her, Sly heard the creaking of her grandmother's rocker, its rhythmic sound spilling forth from the alcove's corner.

"Be sure to wash them well, my sweet princess, as I know you can," she said in ancient Greek. Her antique hands moved quickly and precisely as her nimble fingers knitted a blue woolen afghan shawl. "Make sure to sweep and mop the floors."

"Yes, Yaya," Sly said absentmindedly, keeping her back to the old woman. "I will."

She continued searching the landscape until she finally spotted Paulo's slow gait cross the field. Her body relaxed at his appearance. In her haste to speak with him, she felt as if time slowed drastically; it seemed it took him forever to reach the back door. However, she knew in real time, it took less than ten minutes.

"Where have you been? I have waited so long for you!" she said foregoing a greeting. She slowly pivoted as he walked by. "Where do you go at times?"

Paulo's expression resigned, he moved in exhaustion as

he crossed over to their grandmother and placed a small kiss on her cheek. He then plopped down in a chair at the small breakfast table.

"I was out doing business." He paused to glare at her. "And stop talking to me as if I am younger than you. I am the eldest."

Sly turned away and resumed washing dishes in silence. She chose not to bully him into getting her way, as she usually did, but instead decided to let him believe he was in full control of everything. She recognized her brother was upset, and when he was in his present frame of mind, if not handled delicately, Paulo could become as stubborn as a bull.

"I'm sorry." She continued sloshing soapy water. "You are right."

"What are you two saying?" their grandmother asked, her faded green eyes staring at them with intense curiosity, while never missing a beat with her knitting. "You know I cannot understand the English."

Simultaneously, Sly and Paulo sighed at the known revelation.

"Nothing at all, Yaya," Paulo said to her. "We were speaking hello to one another."

Their grandmother stopped rocking. "Is not 'hello' in the English *hi*?" At Paulo's reluctant nod, she pushed the chair into motion again. "I did not hear such a word."

Her back to her brother and grandmother, despite her foul mood, Sly couldn't help but smile. She loved her grandmother greatly, especially when she said unexpectedly funny things.

"True, Yaya," Paulo said with a small smile in his voice. "However, there are many ways to say hello in English."

The ancient one tutted. "I do not understand why you must speak it here. I know nothing."

Sly pivoted, facing them, her soapy hands dripping water onto the floor. "Yaya, maybe you should learn, as we have. It is always good to speak other languages, especially the American language."

Their grandmother tutted again and returned to her knitting, her actions silently giving them permission to go ahead and speak English, although she was not happy about it.

Sly picked up a dry dish towel and wiped her hands on it. She studied Paulo's pensive face. "What's wrong, big brother? You can tell me."

Paulo paused for a long time, appearing as if he would refuse to speak. Eventually, he broke the silence with a long sigh. "I was at a meeting with a Texas businessman."

Sly stopped drying her hands. "You mean the investor Stefano has been talking about?"

A startled expression lit up Paulo's face. He slowly shook his head. "I do not understand how you know everything." At her silence, he continued. "Yes, with him."

She placed balled fists on her hips. "And the family knows nothing about this, I can assume."

Once again, Paulo shook his head in amazement at her correct reasoning. He stared at his folded hands, which rested atop the table. "No."

Mutely, Sly gazed at Paulo's bent head. Throwing her towel over one shoulder, she sat across from him, her curiosity pushing aside her initial anger at his perceived duplicity. "What was this meeting about?"

Again, Paulo looked ready to shut down.

Sly reached over and laid a gentle hand upon his. She squeezed. "Come now, Brother. We are family; I will always be there for you in everything you do."

Sly's reassuring touch seemed to give him strength. Eventually, he pushed forth another sigh and said, "The Texan, Mr. Grainger, wants me to assist him in taking over Papa Georigios' olive business."

Surprised, Sly snatched her hand away. Slumping in her chair, she stared at him incredulously. "Why would you even consider such a thing? What, may I ask, is in it for him?"

"Nothing. He simply wants to buy out the company, make it profitable again, and then return it to the family once it is stable economically."

"I do not understand, Paulo," she said. "Are you sure that

is all he wants?" At his hesitant nod, Sly frowned. "How can you be sure?"

"What?" The old one dropped her knitting into her lap, the lines in her face deepening. "What are you talking about now?"

"Again, nothing, Yaya—just discussing the price of food," Sly said, switching to Greek. She tried not to blink guiltily at the lie. "It is getting so expensive."

"Pish! The price of food has—and always will—go up. No need to worry about what is."

Sly acknowledged the older woman's misplaced wisdom and attempted a neutral expression for her sake. "Yes, Yaya."

The old woman shook her head and revisited her knitting; for show, Sly plastered a smile on her face and lowered her tone to neutral. She directed her attention back to Paulo. "Tell me, what exactly does this Mr. Grainger expect you to do?"

"Find out their weaknesses and report to him." Miserably, Paulo shrugged. "He states he has already figured out one major weakness concerning both Stefano and J. J." Slowly, Paulo's dark brown eyes left his hands to rise and stare at Sly. "He stated you were wrong."

Sly was taken aback. "What does he mean I was wrong? About what?"

"Stefano," he quickly replied. "You told me Stefano hated Dr. Andra."

She shifted angrily in her chair, her mind returning to Stefano and Andra standing so close inside the shade behind the tool building. Agitated, she leaned forward. "I do not understand, my brother. What does that have to do with Stefano and J. J.'s weaknesses?"

After another pause, Paulo let out a heavy sigh. "He said that both J. J. and Stefano are in love with Dr. Andra. She is their weakness."

Sly slammed back against her seat, her abdominal muscles twisting painfully in the process. A queasy feeling washed over her at Paulo's words; she knew immediately her nausea was due not to this truth but to the fact that someone else recognized Stefano's obsession with the beautiful black doctor.

Not wanting to address whether she – or the nosy Mr. Grainger – was right or wrong, she sat forward. "What does he want you to do if he already knows this?"

Paulo bobbed his stooped shoulders. "I do not know. He instructed me to keep my eyes and ears open just the same."

Pondering, Sly looked off into space. Her sharp manicured nails tapped loudly against the tabletop.

"Stop that," her grandmother said, never ceasing her rocking. "It is unladylike and annoying."

"Yes, Yaya," she automatically replied. Watching Paulo, she slid her hand across the surface to grab his. "What are you getting for your assistance to this man? Can he be trusted to return the company back to the family intact?"

Her brother covered their grasped hands with his free one, holding tightly. "I am so torn. I truly do not know." He shook his head desperately. "I need to believe Mr. Grainger will do what he says he will do. Jayson and the family need this badly in order to financially survive."

Sly exhaled impatiently. "You did not answer my other question. What will *you* get from this?"

She watched Paulo rise from the table, walk over to the sink, and begin washing dishes. Both she and her grandmother looked on in shock.

"What is it?" their grandmother said, her ancient bones attempting to rise from her rocker. "What is wrong, my son?"

By the time Paulo turned to face them, his face wore a placating smile, one Sly knew was for their grandmother's sake alone.

"Yaya, I am helping Sly out, as I should have for a long time now." He ran over and helped her back into her rocker, lowering his face to hers. He gently kissed her forehead. "Do not worry."

She took a moment to stare at him with ancient, loving eyes. "I do not worry. As the man of the house, I will leave it up to you." She smiled at him and resumed knitting.

Returning to the sink, he waited until Sly joined him. Silently, they worked side by side until all the dishes were washed, rinsed, dried, and put away.

"Tell me," Sly said when the last utensil was stored.

"He has offered to pay me for my services." At Sly's stunned expression, he shook his head firmly. "I too must provide for this family. The economy has deeply hurt us as well. And although they are hurting somewhat, the Theonopiluses will always have more than we do." Paulo placed a gentle arm about Sly's shoulders. "Besides, based on what Mr. Grainger said about Dr. Andra being their weakness, it does not appear as if you will ever marry into their family—through Jayson or Stefano—as our own family had someday hoped."

At once, Stefano and Andra's encounter behind the tool house filled Sly's head. Feeling her blood bubble toward its boiling point, she wanted to cry, scream, stomp, and violently throw things, as she had when she was much younger.

"As the Americans say on their TV reality shows, don't bet on it!" She angrily shook off Paulo's arm. "I wish Dr. Andra had never come here!"

The volume of her voice rose, causing their grandmother to glance up. This time, the older woman shrugged and resumed her knitting in silence, allowing them to handle their disagreement by themselves.

"Paulo, I want you to do it," she said, throwing her towel down on the countertop. "You help Mr. Grainger."

At Yaya's disapproving glance, she hurriedly retrieved the discarded rag and then neatly folded it and placed it on the towel rack to dry. "And I will help you."

37

"**G**ood morning, my beautiful ladies!"

Sitting around the table, Andra and Al smiled as George entered the spacious breakfast area, his face lit up like the morning sun.

"Good morning, Papa George," Andra said, reaching for the sweet bread with the hope it would alleviate her morning sickness. "I pray you slept well."

"Ah, George," Al said, daintily dabbing the corners of her mouth. "Good morning."

Racine snorted. Lifting scrambled eggs from her plate, she paused. "Man, I tell you—it's really disturbing how you Greek men are extremely comfortable throwing around compliments all the time." Stuffing the eggs in, she talked around them. "It's a wonder your women even know if or when you guys are telling the truth."

George laughed. He sat at the breakfast table and politely reached for a cup and saucer, helping himself to a generous amount of Greek coffee. The pouring liquid infused the air with a robust, pungent aroma. "That may be true, my dear. But in this case, no one could ever refute my observations concerning the women at this table."

Andra and Al laughed as Racine good-naturedly rolled her eyes and said, "Whatever, Papa George! It's seven o'clock in the morning—far too early for so much sugar."

Delighted, Andra locked eyes with her mother, and they shared a secret smile at Racine's inserting Papa into George's name. Observing his ecstatic expression, she determined the title was not lost upon her father-in-law either.

"Sweets for the sweet, my little one," he said. At Racine's second eye roll, his grin encompassed the entire table. "So, my dears, what have you planned for today?"

After trading indecisive looks between themselves, the women looked at him.

"I don't know," Al said slowly. "Maybe peruse the grounds? Andra remarked on how charming the landscape is."

Sipping his coffee, George sputtered abruptly, only to set his cup down with a firm hand. Dubious, Andra peered into her own untouched thick brew. After she glanced back at George, whose face wore a mock traumatized expression, she relaxed, knowing his reaction had nothing to do with the drinkability of his morning beverage.

"No, no, no! I must show my beautiful family Athens." George tore off a section of sweet bread and carefully buttered it. He then considered the occupants at the table. "It would honor me to be your tour guide for the day. I will even drive you myself. What is your answer, my sweet ones?"

Andra took a moment to examine George. His skin glowed with health and vitality; it appeared tight upon his full face. Since her arrival, his whole countenance had miraculously blossomed and gained strength from the inside out.

Al clapped with delight. "I'd love to!" Her eyes circled the table expectantly. "Girls?"

"Count me in!" Excited, Andra turned to her left. "Race, what about you?"

Her little sister shrugged indifferently.

"You know you want to!" Andra pushed her, causing Racine's body to sway to one side. Andra pointed at Racine's white teeth peeking through her stern lips. "Baby sis, I see the smile you're trying to hide."

Racine pushed her back. "Okay, okay—leave me alone! I'm in." Springing from her chair, Racine scanned her comfortable clothing consisting of tee-shirt and sweatpants. "But I gotta change! Give me thirty minutes."

As if anticipating her departure, Helena quickly shuffled

into the room, the scent of sugar, spices, and dough trailing behind her, and expeditiously headed for Racine's breakfast dishes.

Passing her, Racine patted the servant on the arm. "Thanks, Helena! I owe you one!" she called out, disappearing through the swinging door.

Multi-tasking, Helena smiled as she pushed in Racine's chair. She shook her head good-naturedly as meaty hands collected dishes while she muttered softly in Greek—most likely concerning the today's youth and their over-exuberance.

Waiting for the servant to disappear through the other door leading to an area designed exclusively for cooking meals and washing dishes, Al grinned across the table at Andra. "Did you see that? Racine didn't bother to push in her chair at just the right angle." Al smiled her approval. "That's a good sign."

"A very good sign," Andra agreed, cautiously tasting her coffee.

"Would you not mind if I made a comment?" George asked. He waited for their nods. "I noticed at dinner how she is most precise with everything she does."

Andra shifted uncomfortably, now staring down at her coffee for an altogether different reason.

Al nodded, speaking solemnly. "Yes, it's Racine's way of coping with life." She sighed. "In what she believes is an out-of-control world, she would like to control at least a small part of hers."

Within the next few quiet seconds, Andra's apprehension blossomed as she tried to decipher George's thoughtful look.

He finally nodded. "Yes, I understand all too well," he said sadly.

Al reached out and gently placed a hand over his. "You do? How do you understand?"

Setting down his bread, he patted the hand that covered his. "My wife, Cecil, had the same affliction." Then, as if suddenly realizing what he'd just said, George chuckled wistfully. "Well, I guess at the beginning the marriage, I believed it was an affliction." He sighed. "Yet at the end of her life, I determined it was an endearment."

One lone tear slid unnoticed along his cheek, causing Andra to switch chairs and sit next to him opposite her mother. Her hand topped theirs. "I'm so sorry, Papa George."

"Me too," said Al.

As if emerging from an unfathomable emotional depth, George shook his head, inhaled deeply, and let out a cleansing breath. "Thank you, my dears." As he wiped the stray tear from existence, his face suddenly brightened. "But it was an old lifetime ago. And now I have the new to brighten my days." His glowing eyes swung from Andra to Al and back again. "I suggest, my lovely ladies, you duplicate Racine's actions and get ready. I will bring the car around in thirty minutes."

Not bothering to wait for a reply, George stood. Taking his uneaten bread with him, he turned and disappeared beyond the swinging door.

Her mother waited until the door stopped swinging completely before speaking. "He's a good man, Andra."

Still gazing at the empty space her father-in-law had vanished through, she smiled in agreement. *And I have a younger version I hope and pray will always be mine.*

"*Kalimera*, family!"

Andra's smile vanished. Her warm feeling disintegrated, replaced with the sensation of cold water splashing her face. Bristling, she stared at the woman who entered the kitchen through the villa's back door as if she owned the place.

Andra carefully replaced her cup on its saucer as Sly stopped beside the chair George had recently vacated.

"*Kalimera* means 'Good morning,' Dr. Andra and her mother."

Involuntarily, Andra scanned Sly's well-dressed frame, taking in her white button-down shirt, white shorts, and strappy, low-heeled white sandals. Although the ensemble would've been simple on most, it was far from mundane on Sly. Her tan skin and shapely body caused ordinary, nondescript clothing to morph into a powerful fashion statement.

Andra grunted her hello. At feeling her mother's curious

stare, she swiftly put on a pleasant face, the action producing strained lips that were ready to crack under the weight of her fake smile.

Al's inquisitive stare returned to the newcomer. "Kalimera, Sly. And how are you today?"

Tossing her thick hair over her shoulders, Sly pulled out a chair and sat. Andra resisted the urge to do a Racine-like eye roll; she instead retrieved her cup and, as dignified as the queen mother herself, sipped her coffee.

"I am good, Dr. Andra's mother."

"Please call me Al," her mother said pleasantly. To Andra's distress, Al immediately rose. "George is taking us girls into town to do some sightseeing and maybe some shopping. You care to come, Sly?"

Abruptly, Andra recalled yesterday's toolshed encounter and the hateful stare Sly had thrown her way right before turning to run behind Stefano. She held her breath. *Say no, say no, say no.*

"I would love to, Ms. Al," the girl replied. She cut sparkling green eyes toward Andra's crestfallen face before returning them to the older woman. "However, I must get back home. My brother, Paulo, and I have things to discuss this morning."

Relieved, Andra exhaled, only to realize she had done so prematurely.

"But would you not mind, Miss Al, if I spoke with Dr. Andra privately?"

Her mother paused for a moment to glance at Andra, telepathically asking if she would be all right.

Reluctantly, Andra nodded.

"Okay, baby girl, but don't be too long," Al warned. She hesitated, her eyes bouncing between them. "George said thirty minutes. We don't want to reward his kindness by keeping him waiting."

"Yes, Mama."

"It will not be long, Ms. Al."

Again, her mother paused. She revisited Sly's amicable face. "Good morning, Sly. I hope to see you again soon."

Don't worry—you will, Andra thought, watching the Grecian nod. *You can count on it.*

Al turned and disappeared through the swinging door.

Once the swaying panel came to a standstill, Sly faced Andra, displaying a smile neither hot nor cold, just neutral. "I like your mother because she is extremely kind. You are very lucky."

At Andra's "Thank you," she continued in a more deliberate tone. "So did you enjoy your walk yesterday?"

Putting herself on guard, Andra remained mute.

"Yes, I am pretty sure it was educational for you." Sly moved aside an empty plate on the table before her and leaned forward. "I will not tell Jayson what I saw yesterday."

Andra stiffened. "Don't be silly. You didn't see anything. There's nothing to tell."

Sly threw Andra a "Suit yourself" look. "Whatever," she said, smiling in a catlike manner. "Anyway, on our way back to the villa, Stefano instructed me nothing happened too."

Andra's eyes widened in surprise as mind-numbing relief flooded her body. "He did?"

Sly's laugh was petty. "No. But as you would say, does it really matter?"

Balling her fists so as not to reach out and strangle the girl, Andra rose from her chair, and her feet propelled her toward the kitchen door. Upon reaching it, she came to a stop, rotating at Sly's next words.

"As I said, I will not tell J. J. this time." Carelessly, she lifted toned, tan arms. "But the next time, who knows?"

Andra stared at her nemesis for a spell until she could speak in a normal tone. She then produced a sympathetic smile. "Wow. It must be killing you."

"Signomi?"

"Sly, I could excuse you all day long, but it wouldn't do any good, would it?" Her lips curling farther, Andra allowed one dimple to show. "Yep. It simply kills you to know you don't have the same effect on Stefano as I do." She shook her head. "You know what? I'm feeling kinda sorry for you right now, little girl."

Even as her words rolled forth, Andra knew she shouldn't have said them, realizing her jab could have possible repercussions and create trouble for her marriage due to retaliatory backlash from Sly. However, the fury on the other's face made any potential trouble worth it.

"Chalk one up for me, right?" Andra let out a delicious giggle at the answering silence. "Signomi—I gotta go now."

When it appeared as if the girl were about ready to throw the heavy ceramic sugar bowl at her head, believing her work was done, Andra pushed past the kitchen door.

She suddenly felt victorious.

38

Sitting at the kitchen table, Paulo pulled his cell from his back pocket. Upon reading the incoming number, he grimaced.

Acid-tasting bile rose in his throat, forcing him to swallow hard. With each ring, he felt more and more ensnared—like a trapped animal. He didn't want to answer; instead, he wanted to pitch the phone in the trash and purchase a brand-new one—one with an unlisted number.

Gritting his teeth, he clicked in the caller. "Yassas?" he said.

The answering boisterous chuckle set Paulo's teeth on edge. "I take it *yassas* means 'hello,' correct?" At Paulo's nonresponse, Hog laughed it off. "So, youngster, how're things hangin'?"

Not quite understanding the older man's lingo, and not wanting to, Paulo decided to forgo inane pleasantries with the Texan. "Yes, Mr. Grainger, how can I assist you?"

At the other end came a pause. Paulo stifled a heavy sigh, hoping the caller wasn't hesitating just to insist he use the name Hog. He exhaled in relief when instead, the Texan's voice became as brusque as his.

"I'm checking in. Got anything good for me concerning our little project?"

Claustrophobic helplessness closed in on Paulo, as it always did whenever he talked to the man. He compared himself to an insect caught on a spider's web— where the ensnared bug knew if it tried to shake itself loose from the web's stickiness, the vibrations would alert the arachnid of its presence, thereby ensuring the insect's demise. Yet the insect always attempted to wiggle itself free anyhow, only to be cocooned and eventually eaten alive.

Paulo shuddered. He wanted badly to break all ties with this annoying, dangerous foreigner, but he sensed his wiggle for freedom could possibly lead to unspeakable consequences. "No, I have yet to find out anything—" Paulo broke off as Sly burst through the kitchen's back door.

"I hate her," she ranted, violently pulling the screen door shut with a loud *wham*. She stomped over to the sink to grip its edge as her stormy eyes glared through the curtained window that faced the Theonopilus villa. "I wish she had never come here!"

On the other end, Paulo heard Hog's voice increase in volume.

"What's going on over there? Who's that—your sister? What's she saying?"

Paulo wanted to shout into the mouthpiece, "This could not be any of your business!" Instead, he politely said, "Hold, please."

Pushing the mute button on his cell, Paulo lowered the phone to glare at his sister. "What are you ranting about now?"

Sly pivoted on angry feet, placing her back to the window and the bright, sunny day beyond it, her face in contrast, bestowing Paulo with a black thundercloud expression. "Now Dr. Andra has got Papa Georigios wrapped around her finger too! He's taking them into the village for sightseeing and shopping!"

In exasperation, Paulo sighed. "So?"

"So?" she yelled back. Her wild eyes searched the area as if looking for an object to throw, only to return to his gaze in defeated tears. "I was not asked to go!"

Paulo took a moment to stare at the phone in his hand. He couldn't decide whether he preferred to deal with the dangerously manipulative Hog or the equally distressing temper tantrum produced by Sly.

Family comes first, he thought.

"Sly, I am sure you exaggerate," he said. "Knowing you, I believe someone asked you along, but in your stubbornness, you said no. Correct?"

Her nonresponse answered the question. Impatiently, he waved his cell at her, indicating he didn't have time for her bratty foolishness. "Why do you not just go back over there and ride with them? I'm sure no one will kick you from the car if you choose to go."

To his frustration, fat tears popped free from Sly's eyes to descend past pinched cheeks.

"It's too late—they are most likely gone by now!"

With a teary toss of her head, she stormed from the room. Paulo believed she made a noisy path for her bedroom in order to lock herself inside.

He sighed heavily. His acid reflux churning, he toggled the mute button. "Please excuse, Mr. Grainger. Where were we?"

"I was asking if that was your sister. What's she all riled up about?"

Before answering, Paulo paused to count to five, knowing his quest to remain calm with the pushy older man was quickly failing. "She's upset because Papa Georigios is taking Dr. Andra and her family into the village square for sightseeing."

Hog's chuckle grated against his ear. "I believe your li'l' sister's jealousy is showing for the doctor, you know?" At Paulo's noncommittal silence, Hog coughed delicately. "So when's the sightseeing trip supposed to happen?"

Paulo assumed Hog wanted to keep him on the line with small talk because he hoped to covertly get information from him. He could stomach it no more. "My sister said they recently left." Trying to hold back the impatience in his voice, he took a deep breath and released it. "Mr. Grainger, about my helping you. I feel now is not the time for any takeover. The family will most certainly not allow it."

"Well, maybe, maybe not," Hog said. "But if we—"

Pulling the phone away, Paulo stared at it in disbelief. Shaking his head, he returned it to his ear. "Mr. Grainger," Paulo said, cutting off Hog's current string of words, "there are things requiring my attention here, so I must go now. Goodbye."

"Well, okay then. Goodb—"

Paulo hurriedly ended the call. Taking a moment to massage his midsection, he quickly rose from the table in search of bicarbonate soda, which he hoped would appease his churning stomach.

39

George's automobile sailed smoothly along the divided highway, which displayed Athens's breathtaking scenic coastline on one side, while on the other side, a tall ridge blocked their view for more than a mile. Skillfully, he made his way toward a bend in the road.

He cleared his throat. "Ladies, behold!"

The Audi took the curve with ease, clearing the ridge completely. At once, a magnificent view of the Aegean Sea appeared. White foaming waves rolled over a dazzling azure-colored sea, meeting seamlessly with blue skies. As the women gaped, they murmured in unison as floating clouds magically parted to display the grandeur of a distant snowcapped mountain.

"Simply incredible," Al said from the front seat. She turned to George, whose face beamed with pride for his country. "Thank you so much for this, sir!"

"You are most welcome," he said. Briefly glancing over his shoulder, he pointed eastward toward a distant mountain. "My dears, Mount Olympus, the Greek home to the Olympian gods Zeus, Hera, Poseidon, Apollo, Hermes, and Aphrodite, to name a few."

Grinning, Racine turned to her backseat companion, who looked uncomfortable. "Aphrodite, you say?"

At Andra's poke in her side, Racine stuck out her tongue. She then shifted to stare at the rearview mirror, which framed George's merry eyes. "Do tell."

His face, bright with innocence, radiated pure joy at

Racine's request for more information. "Ah yes, Racine—Aphrodite! I am enchanted with her."

"So is Stefano," Racine muttered for Andra's ears only. She bit her lip at the twisting pinch applied directly to her arm.

"And her legend," George continued, his words unbroken. "She is the goddess of love, desire, and sex and is legendary for her beauty. Our folklore states any mortal man who looked upon her beauty fell madly in love with her—only to be lured to his demise."

Racine snickered, while Andra simply gazed out her window.

"Why to his demise, George?" Al asked with all innocence.

"Well, some say since she is a goddess and therefore unobtainable for mere mortals, men go mad due to the unfulfilled desire Aphrodite evokes within them."

"Fascinating," Racine said, looking over at Andra's averted head.

"You know, I've always wanted to climb a mountain," Andra said hastily.

"Since when?" Racine said.

Andra ignored her, staring past the front seat and out the windshield. "Anyhow, that beautiful mountain looks as good as any to try."

"And somehow most appropriate," Racine quipped. She lowered her voice. "Aphrodite."

Andra hit Racine hard on the arm, forcing her to gladly return the favor.

Their mother turned to stare, her face exhibiting both puzzlement and consternation at the commotion in the backseat. Plastering an innocent expression on her face, Racine plied her mother with a sweet smile and quickly stared out her window at the passing scenery.

Thirty minutes later, they arrived at the village square. The area was a fascinating mix of both old- and new-world charm, and as George maneuvered the car into an impossibly small parking space, Al ducked to stare through his window. She exclaimed with delight, "Andra, look over there! Freshwater sponges!" As soon as the car came to a complete stop, she jumped out and slammed her door. "I've got to get me some to take home. Race you guys!"

Andra quickly exited the backseat and, with less force than her mother, shut her door. "Be right there, Mom!" she called over the car's roof. Smiling, she bent to peer into the backseat. "Hey, brat, you coming?"

Racine shook her head. "Naw, I'm not into that kinda stuff." Glancing to her left, she looked beyond the window to the bustling cobblestone across the street. She pointed. "I'll be over there, browsing some clothes. You guys meet me when you're through. Then we can hang."

With a single click of her tongue, Andra straightened to capture George's eyes as he too exited the car. "Would you like to join us?"

He graced Andra with a smile. A moment later, his eyes lowered to lock with Racine's. "If you and your mother do not mind, I believe I will hang with Racine."

Startled at hearing slang come from lips that usually spoke words in a carefully modulated accent, Racine and Andra burst out laughing. Their gaiety caused George's smile to broaden.

"What is it? I say it correctly, yes?"

Andra nodded, still chuckling. "Yes, you did. Perfect!" She took a moment to search the busy village square. "Okay, I've spotted Mama over by those sponges. Wow, those things are huge!" She shook her head and laughed delightedly. "Anyway, as soon as I can pull her away, we'll come find you guys."

"Sure, you two knock yourselves out." Racine rolled her eyes George's way, causing him to chuckle. *We're in Greece, and they're perusing sponges? Really?* Shaking her head at his amused expression, she pulled her purse onto her lap and quickly rummaged through it to make sure she'd remembered to bring money. She then jumped in surprise when her car door opened to reveal an amicable George holding it wide for her.

At her hesitation, he stretched forth his hand. "Your mother and sister did not give me a chance to be polite—to celebrate them as women." His hand motioned for her to take it. "I would like to do this for you. Come."

Exhaling loudly, Racine placed her hand in his and allowed his strength to pull her from the backseat. "Thank you," she muttered, embarrassed, although she didn't quite know why. Rotating her head, she perused the bustling square to take the focus off herself. "Jeez, this place is packed! Okay, lead on, Papa George. I just hope you know where you're going."

"I will try not to get us lost—however, it might be difficult, especially since I have lived here my lifetime." Laughing with Racine, he too scanned the crowded pavilion. "Well, since you have given me the privilege to decide, let us partake in refreshments before we do actual shopping."

Lightly touching the small of her back, George guided Racine across the congested street teeming with natives and tourists alike; they dodged everything from small cars to mopeds to bicycles, only to head for a small, rickety shack-like structure. Varieties of hanging spices, various appetizing colorful fruits, and other strange oddities hung from different vantage points about the tiny restaurant. Hastily, he pointed toward a vacant table on the sidewalk out front. Constructed from a rotund upside-down fish barrel, a heavy circular plank of aged wood served as the tabletop. Four small wooden chairs surrounded it.

Three similar table-and-chair sets were positioned in tight proximity beside the empty table. Those tables and chairs were occupied.

A bit reluctant to sit at a table that, by American standards, would have been clearly deemed an unstable health hazard, a virtual lawsuit waiting to happen, Racine felt her breath rush from her lungs as the sprightly older man pushed her into one chair only to quickly slide into the seat across from her.

"Good! We were able to get a seat."

Really? Is this a good thing?

Soon after, she watched George gesture at two men who meant to take away their table's empty chairs, spitting out quick-fire Greek to stop them. Once he'd gotten his point across, he granted the departing men a nod of thanks and then turned a victorious smile Racine's way.

"They were about to take Al's and Andra's seats." He shook his head in mock grievance. "We cannot have that."

Racine chuckled, shaking her head with him. "No, we cannot, Papa George. They'd skin us alive!"

"Georigios!"

They both turned toward the deep, melodic voice. A person Racine assumed was the shack's owner swooped in with boisterous salutations. Amid Greek hugs and two-cheek kisses, Racine was introduced to Clio, a medium-built, handsome Greek with extremely dark, weather-beaten skin and silver-and-black hair. She decided not to guess the older man's age—to her, all Athenians projected an agelessness most other people didn't.

It wouldn't have been worth her trouble to guess.

For a brief period, Racine listened to George and Clio converse in animated Greek as the two men played catch-up concerning who knows what. Content yet bored, she broke from their lively foreign banter to peruse the surrounding area, hoping to spot her family; however, she couldn't see past the impossible crowds. Bewildered, she shook her head at how so many people could move so quickly from one bartering stand to the next without crashing into each other. Each person's bulky tote bags swung almost wildly, and small pushcarts zoomed in and out with efficient economy, yet as impossible as it seemed, they managed to avoid major collisions.

For Racine, time became a contradiction, as it passed by both leisurely and rapidly, until she found her curiosity about the surrounding alien culture gradually turn to concern. She bit her bottom lip, worrying that her mother and Andra had gotten lost in all the crowds and were unable to find her and George.

Finally clapping George on the back in friendly parting, Clio disappeared into the restaurant. As her table companion returned his attention, Racine endeavored to submerge her uneasiness.

"There," he said with a voice pleasantly carefree. "I have ordered us refreshments until Al and Andra find us."

Smiling noncommittally, Racine continued her casual search between the tiny gaps the crowds allotted as wave after wave of strolling people flowed by.

"You think they're okay?" she finally asked.

George took a moment to survey the area. "I'm sure they are fine." He paused to study Racine's expression before he decidedly rose. "Yet I can see you are worried. If you feel we should search—"

Racine shook her head. She reached over and tugged on George's sleeve, coaxing him back in his seat. "You're right. Sometimes I get a little nutsy over things. I'm sure they're fine."

They sat quietly for a time, both scanning the crowds. The uneasy tension was interrupted when the owner of the restaurant returned.

"Here we are!" Clio exclaimed in broken, heavily accented English. "Two glasses of ouzo and some meze."

With a flourish only a well-seasoned Greek could have accomplished, he rested on their table an extremely used round serving platter that held two goblets and a shot glass filled with wine. A small saucer displaying appetizing sliced ripe tomatoes, black olives, soft white feta and goat cheese, and crackers accompanied their drinks.

After sliding their drinks and food onto the table, Clio plucked the smaller glass from his serving platter and lifted it in a toast, first to Racine and then to George. "*Stin iyia sas!*" Quickly, he tossed back his head, guzzling the drink in one gulp. Grinning broadly, he smacked his lips and winked, only to tuck the serving tray under one arm and once again head for the shack.

Incredulous, Racine stared after the shopkeeper's retreating frame until he disappeared inside. With her mouth agape, she turned to George. "I just want to know—does he do that with every customer?" she asked. "Because if he does, he'll be hammered by closing time!"

George laughed delightedly. "No, my dear, he does it only

for the people who are special." He duplicated Clio's action by lifting his ouzo to her. "This is for you, my special one, to your health!"

Up to the challenge, she lifted her glass high. "*Stin iyia sas!*" she said, her face warming under his pride-filled expression. "To your health!"

Tentatively, Racine sipped her wine. Although she wasn't much on drinking alcohol, the ouzo had a mild, not-too-unpleasant taste. She took another sip. Once she witnessed George put his drink down to study his hands, concern made her set hers down too. "What's on your mind, Papa George?"

He opened his mouth as if to speak but didn't. Closing his lips, he hesitated again. A second later, he nodded. "Yes, I would speak to you about a personal matter."

"Okay," she said slowly. "Shoot."

"You remind me so much of Cecilia, my wife," he said, his manner forlorn. "I loved her very much. After much time passing, I still do."

"Yep, I can see that."

"Yes, well, I would like to tell you about my Cecil—how we met and how we loved."

Racine produced a vague nod. "Okay."

George cleared his throat only to taste his wine again. Carefully placing the glass back on the worn tabletop, which probably had seen much festive—and sorrowful—activity, he stared into her eyes. "Ours was an arranged marriage. We had not met one another prior to our engagement."

Racine's brows lifted. "Yikes—what a bummer!" She shook her head at the foreign concept. "Didn't it make you angry, being fixed up without having a say?"

He gave a solemn nod. "I must admit I had rebellion in my young heart because I could not choose my own bride. However, I also knew it was my duty to my parents to do so. In obedience, I remained silent."

"Wow!"

"But you see, the moment I met my Cecil, I immediately fell in love with her."

A tiny smile broke across Racine's face. She bobbed her head. "So that's good, right?"

George paused to contemplate the question. He then sighed. "Yes and no. My dilemma surfaced when her feelings did not match mine."

Racine's mouth formed a circle. "I can't believe that. It's not possible!" she said indignantly. She searched his distinguished face, which was still quite handsome even at his present age. "Was she blind?"

Shaking his head at someone else who suddenly came up to claim the empty chairs, George chuckled wistfully. "Thank you, my dear girl. No, she was not blind—simply in love with another. She too did not agree with her parents concerning our match."

It was still early in the day, and a slightly intoxicated man looked out of place in the sunlit square as he weaved his way between tables. During his stumbling trek, he accidentally bumped into George's chair, causing Racine to jump nervously. After blurting out a slurred "Excuse me," he continued his unsteady quest toward the entrance to the small restaurant.

On edge, Racine watched the drunk's progress until he finally disappeared inside. Quaking inside, she attempted to dismiss the inebriated man and focused on her table companion again. "So what happened?"

George, who had also watched the drunken patron, appeared reluctant to reengage the conversation. Uncharacteristically, he gulped his wine down; directly, his body straightened, as if the purple liquid had fortified him. Still, his face showed reluctance upon his resting his glass on the table.

He sighed. "I created in my mind to court her and make her understand I could love her as much as the other man. Yet daily, her heart grew cold toward me. And I am ashamed to say I became desperate in my desire for her."

Tensing, Racine remained quiet, not wanting to predict the direction his story headed.

"My desire overcame my logic, until one day ..." He stopped.

"Go on," Racine said. His reluctance to speak helped her form a conclusion to his story. "You raped her."

In the wake of her building anger toward George, she was also surprised to feel conflicting pity for him when, across from her, his eyes promptly filled with tears.

"As much as I loathe to tell you this, yes, I did." Nervously, he fidgeted with his glass stem. "My love was strong, and my will was weak. I now know I violated her to force her into marriage with me."

Without warning, a manic rage swirled inside her, abruptly manufacturing blinding tears of her own. She sensed more than saw him extend his palm toward her. Angrily, she snatched her trembling hands out of his reach and balled them in her lap.

"How could you do that to her?" she hissed. "To any woman?"

As if burned, George retracted his arm, his face guilty. He hung his head. "I do not truly understand myself, but my desire for her was strong and my male pride even stronger, which made me believe I had the right." He looked up with solemn eyes. "Over time, I had to face what was true. If I had truly loved her, truly respected her, I would not have behaved in such a manner."

From an emotionally great distance, Racine stared at the older Grecian who sat across from her. She hardened herself against the buried anguish in his voice and the overwhelming genuine repentance of his confession.

Suddenly, she stared at him in veiled curiosity; she believed his soul-cleansing confession went beyond what he'd done to Cecilia and his need for forgiveness from her—he was extending his apology to Racine as well.

Why?

Intrigued despite herself, Racine sighed heavily. "Go on. What happened next with you and Cecil?"

He nodded, as if they'd gotten far away from the story, and he was glad to get back on track. "Ah, she agreed to marry me. Once I took her for my wife and brought her home, I believed I could convince her of my love. But no, she drew further away.

The more I showed her love, the more she appeared to be an imprisoned bird slowly dying in a cage called marriage."

Not knowing what to do, Racine moved her wineglass an inch to her right; however, her action threw off the appetizer platter, which she had to shift to the left and up in order to properly center it on the table.

At the unexpected silence from George, she glanced over to witness him staring mutely at her precision work with a look of melancholy spreading across his face. Her cheeks grew warm at being caught trying to make her environment symmetrically perfect.

"It started small—the behavior," he said, as if there'd never been a break in his words. "First, it was her clothing, shoes, jewelry, and perfume bottles. The items had to be in perfect alignment, in a precise place. Next came her table setting, chairs, pictures—everything. They all had to be perfectly arranged. I witness this particular behavior in you."

"Don't try to psychoanalyze me," she interjected calmly, deliberately forcing herself not to scream the words at him. She rose on unsteady feet, now desperate to locate her mother and Andra. "You don't know me."

George reached out and gently grabbed Racine's hand. "Please do not run away. Please sit." He waited until she reluctantly returned to her seat before he continued. "I am telling you this to let you know men can be ruthless, hurtful, and blind. Blind to the truth that everything we want, we cannot have—or through our selfishness and cruelty, we can destroy something as lovely and fragile as a woman's spirit with one greedy act."

As if caught in a tumultuous cyclonic eye, anger and shame whirled inside Racine, driving her to cover her face with her hands. Yet she refused to let any man see her cry.

I will not cry.

"Whatever happened to you, my dear, sweet Racine, whoever harmed you in the past was wrong, as I was wrong. We were wrong. And I am here now to apologize—not only for what I did to my Cecil but also for what he did to you. I am so sorry. Please forgive us."

Inside her open palms, Racine allowed the building tears to flow freely, wishing desperately they could finally cleanse her tormented soul. Blindly, she let in a variety of street noises—blasting horns, tooting scooters, passing laughter, clamoring people hustling by. They were such life-giving sounds. However, George remained still, and for some reason, his silence comforted her even more than the surrounding clamor.

She wept and wept until she could weep no more. Finally, she pulled her hands away and, with tearstained eyes, looked up.

George was there with a tentative smile on his face. It said he would wait patiently for her, however long it took for her decision to live again.

Wiping her eyes and nose with her hand, she returned his smile when he extended an embroidered linen handkerchief her way.

"I guess I can predict the ending to your story," she said, her voice wavering with residual tears. She grabbed the handkerchief and blew hard. "Evidently, it worked out between you and Cecilia. You have two gorgeous sons to prove it."

He smiled gently. "Would you like to know how I won her?"

Mopping her face with the cloth's cleaner side, Racine mutely bobbed.

"I first had to let her go and release her to return home to her parents. I needed her to come to me willingly. Yet I never stopped courting her, and I did so gently, consistently." His expression turned wistful. "Six months later, she returned to me. I refused to force my love upon her, as I had before, but desired to cherish her like the delicate treasure she was."

At the next table, two men laughed joyously, and although Racine knew they weren't laughing at her, she still recoiled at the sound. Lowering the sodden cloth, she found herself twisting it into knots. "You know, at least for Cecilia, it was only one man involved—you. And even though you were wrong to rape her, you actually tried to make things right by marrying her afterward." Sighing wearily, Racine paused in an attempt to gather her hurricane-like thoughts so she could express them correctly. "With me, it was three men— three sick, twisted drunk bastards who violated me in every possible way while others watched and did nothing. I was a virgin too. So much for saving myself for that special guy."

"Racine, you are still special—a priceless treasure, my little one." He covered her hand, not caring about the residual snot and tears that lingered on her skin. He squeezed reassuringly. "Were you able to prosecute those men?"

"Yes, what little good it did." She snorted ruefully. "They were all out within a year for good behavior. College frat boys. White college frat boys."

Across the table, George's face distorted with misery. "Once again, I must extend apologies, my dear. No woman deserves what happened to you." Angry, he raised his fists and rotated them, contemplating them with stormy eyes. "If I could, I would kill each one with these hands."

Racine sniffled loudly, only to then surprise herself.

She laughed.

"Put them away before you hurt somebody. Those punks ain't worth going to jail over." She reached over to briefly cover his fists. "But thank you, Papa George."

Sitting back in his chair, his expression suddenly turned reflective. "You are extremely close with your sister."

She couldn't help but smile at his change of direction in subject as well as his instinctively knowing to form his words, not as a question, but as a declaration. "Yeah, Andra's always been there for me, sorta a second father and mother. She and Mama were in there tough after what happened." Not knowing what to do with her hands, she folded and refolded the sodden handkerchief. "Although Mama was really great, it was Andra who got me over the hump."

Through glittery tears, she stared at George's wavering image. "I tell you, under her sweet-doctor exterior beats the heart of a fierce gangsta! She actually went looking for those guys while I was in the hospital. But fortunately, they had already been arrested and jailed, so she couldn't get to them. All kinds of bad things could've happened if she had come across those creeps." Swiping again at her damp eyes, Racine smiled proudly. "What I mean is, it's fortunate for those white boys she couldn't get to them. Andra don't play."

They both laughed.

"So she's—how you say?—a fierce gangsta." George shook his head. "I cannot perceive it."

Racine looked off into the crowd but didn't see the people. "Yeah, back in the day, Andra used to get into fights. There was a girl who kept picking on Andra. Sis got so mad she knocked the bully out. I mean cold. Put the girl in the hospital overnight." Racine read George's astonishment and laughed apologetically. "The school administration agreed it was all self-defense. She's actually more restrained since then."

"Why do you believe she was so angry?" George asked.

"I don't know. A number of things. It could've been my father dying so young and abandoning us. Or the fact that certain girls were jealous of her looks and brains and would pick on her regularly."

"Why would they treat your sister in such a horrible fashion?"

Racine shook her head. "Who knows? Maybe they were trying to prove something to themselves—that they were just as good looking and just as smart as Andra." Reflectively, she chewed her bottom lip. "After what happened with her classmate—you know, the one she knocked out—it scared her. She told me one day that was the reason she wanted to become a doctor. To channel her anger into something good."

George nodded, impressed. His face quickly sobered to allow a few silent seconds to tick by. "There is something I must say, Racine." George's smile was apologetic yet firm. "Your father did not abandon you. He simply died—there is a big difference you should try to understand."

She ducked her head, uncomfortable in her embarrassment at the quick psychological analysis. "Yeah, sure. I know you're right."

"And not all white men are evil."

When she said nothing, George cleared his throat. "May I ask what do you want to do with your life, my dear?"

"Well," she whispered, hating the tremble in her voice, "I don't know. It's as if my trying so hard to forget what happened blocks me from moving forward. Andra's right. I'm afraid of everything. Beyond her and my mother, I don't see a future."

She buried her face in her open palms again, hearing the silence between them grow into a deafening roar. She then felt a gentle tug on her hands, which were instantly engulfed within George's. Embarrassed, Racine looked across the table.

"My darling girl, you must live the life you were meant to live. That can only come with an open heart."

Racine couldn't stop a snort from slipping out and he shook his head.

"No, we all must find a way to love beyond the damages life sometimes inflicts upon us. It takes courage." He added a fatherly wink. "As your young people speak, I double dare you to live life to its fullest. *Entáxei?*"

"Entáxei," she said, the Greek word for *okay* slipping clumsily off her tongue. "I'll try."

As he squeezed her trembling hand, his eyes implored her. "Listen to me. You do not have to go back to America and remember. You can stay here under my protection. You and Andra can be the daughters my Cecilia could not give me. I understand you two are grown women. But girls still need a papa at any age."

"My papa's dead," Racine said defiantly.

George nodded once. "Yes. But I am not."

Suddenly, Racine's eyes blurred.

At witnessing her tears, George presented her with a hopeful smile. "The family would love for you and your family to live at the villa indefinitely."

His words caused Racine's face to fall. She snorted. "For real?" she asked. "Are you sure about that?"

"Yes," he said eagerly.

"Even Stefano?" she asked disdainfully.

At the mention of his son's name, George sighed. "Yes, I know. Stefano does have his problems. I do not want to make excuses for him—"

"So don't, Papa George."

"Please give him some time. If given the chance, I believe he would come to love you like family, Racine."

"You mean the way he loves Andra?"

"What?" he asked, his face confused. "What do you mean?"

Racine jerked her eyes away from George's upon hearing her name and glanced around. Immediately, she spotted her mother's wild approach. Al was rushing toward them in a frenzy, weaving in and out and knocking aside people who stepped into her path, her face the epitome of panic.

Racine and George jumped to their feet. George's sodden handkerchief floated to the ground forgotten as Racine ran into Al's embrace.

"What is it, Mama? What's wrong?"

"Please! You two must help me find her!"

"Who?" Racine searched beyond her mother's trembling frame. "Mama, where's Andra?"

"I don't know," Al sobbed. She released Racine to next fall into George's open arms. "She was walking toward an open van that was maybe selling—oh, I don't know! Something! I turned around when someone tapped me on the shoulder and asked me to purchase something. And then." She sobbed raggedly, causing a hiccup to erupt when she attempted to catch her breath. "When I turned back around, the next thing I knew, both she and the van were gone!"

40

The main study was quietly subdued as Jayson entered it. His eyes scanned the area and stopped at his far right. Stefano, the lone occupant in the room, was already at the bar. His mouth grim, Jayson glanced at his wristwatch. "Ten thirty in the morning. That's a record even for you, big brother."

Stefano's straight posture didn't change as he lifted ice tongs with slightly unsteady hands.

"How long have you been at it this morning, Stefano?"

"Long enough," he replied, his voice emotionless.

Silence followed. The trivial sound of ice dropping into a brandy glass was immediately followed by pouring liquor. Both men remained mute until Stefano resealed the brandy container.

With a full glass in hand, he finally turned to Jayson, a sardonic expression layered his pale, drawn face. "You should try it sometime, Priest."

He ignored the sarcastic religious reference, and despite his ever-present suppressed anger for his older brother, alarm filtered inside Jayson's brain at Stefano's appearance. Precipitously, he took in the ashen pallor of his brother's skin; Stefano's sunken eyes displayed dark circles that could've easily been smudged with black coal.

He didn't know why he hadn't noticed before. Jayson took a step closer to his brother. "Hey, man, what's wrong with you? You don't look so hot."

Stefano paused to pull a long swig from his glass before he stared directly at Jayson. His faced produced a smirk.

"You have been in America too long." He turned to refresh his brandy, pouring an even greater amount than before. "You speak like they do."

Jayson quickly covered the distance separating them. Reaching out to grab Stefano's upper arm, he forced him to turn around. Brandy droplets splashed in an outward arc and landed upon the floor as well as on his and Stefano's clothes. He didn't care. "When you say *they*, do you mean my wife and her family?"

Stefano pulled away from Jayson's grip and uttered a blunt, careless chuckle. The sound chilled Jayson to the bone. "If you wish," Stefano muttered.

Irritated beyond reason, Jayson violently combed his fingers through his hair. The strands on his crown bristled when he observed Stefano watch the gesture only to laugh with a slightly inebriated unsteadiness.

"Little brother, you are going to go—"

"Bald! Yeah, yeah, I know!" Jayson said. "I've heard it before, Stefano. What I'd like to know is what you've got against Andra and her family."

Slightly unsteady, Stefano strolled around him to head for a single-backed settee across the way, which, coincidently, faced the bar. He lowered himself into the chair and reclined, crossing his legs in the process. His shrug was careless. "I have nothing against them in particular," Stefano said. After placing his glass on the table next to his chair, he folded his hands across his lap. "However, they do not belong here. This is not their world."

"And I guess you're the judge, prosecutor, and jury as to who can fit in whose world, right?"

Stefano lingered in his silence.

Jayson stalked over to Stefano and attempted a threatening stance as he loomed over his older brother's chair. His ire cranked to the next level when Stefano's demeanor showed no intimidation but instead remained cool inside his slightly intoxicated air.

Wanting to come across as both adamant and defiant, Jayson shook his fist in his brother's face. "Stefano, you're wrong. Andra belongs in whatever world I'm in. And that goes for Al and Racine too."

"Very touching, little brother." Stefano's lips curled in a benign manner. "Along with being a holy man, you can be a poet as well. A priest and a poet. You are full of many talents."

"And you're just full of it!"

"My, my, what is all the shouting? Are we interrupting a business meeting?"

Jayson whipped around at the female voice and saw Sly and Paulo enter the study. Not quite understanding why, he grew furious at their appearance. "Look, you two, now is not the right time for a visit."

At his words, Paulo appeared ready to back from the room. Sly glanced at him and stopped his retreat with a firm hand. Although her smile appeared sweet, her eyes were glassy and hard once they returned to Jayson.

"Visit? I thought we were family?" Her green eyes sliced the air, moving between Stefano and Jayson. "Or has someone changed your sentiments?"

"Oh, for the love ..." Jayson trailed off, combing his fingers through his already disheveled hair. He attempted a calmer voice. "Why don't you come back later? The ladies are not here to visit with."

"I know," Sly replied. She made her way to a chair on the far side of the room, away from the brothers. Ladylike, she took a seat. "Papa Georigios has taken them into town, and they probably won't be back until this evening."

"Okay, so why are you here?"

"Yes," Stefano interjected darkly. "Why are you here?"

Sly's demeanor changed from outward rejection at Jayson's words to downright lividness at Stefano's. After uncrossing her legs, she slowly rose. "So this is how it is to be, yes? After growing up with you." Her remaining words tapered off uncertainly. However, a moment later, she jammed her fists into her hips and stomped one petite foot. "Maybe I am here to impart some important details about two certain people."

Paulo arrived at Sly's side, seizing her arm. "Sly, let us go," he said. When she snatched her arm away from his grasp, he grabbed her again, this time pulling her toward the exit. "Be quiet! What is happening here is not our affair."

Yanking free, Sly took a couple steps forward beyond his reach. "Ha! Affair is right!" Folding her arms, she tossed her head so that her perfectly combed locks fell in perfect disarray over her shoulders. "Jayson needs to know the truth about his precious Dr. Andra and big brother, Stefano!"

Jayson's stomach churned at her unspoken accusations. "What are you talking about, Sly?" he asked quietly, his lips so pinched he could barely push his words through. He saw the Trojan-horse thing fly out the window. "What nonsense are you going on about now?"

"Nonsense, yes? Was it nonsense when I came upon Stefano and Andra behind the toolshed in the north field, standing so close there was no room to breathe? Is it nonsense I came upon them just as they were about to kiss?"

Momentarily, Jayson stood paralyzed in place, his mind force-feeding him images of Andra locked sensually inside Stefano's embrace. A thick crimson fog soon rolled in, slowly at first and then gradually picking up momentum, to cover each mental picture one at a time until all he could envision was red.

Paulo pushed past Sly's rigid form. When he arrived before Jayson, his head moved from side to side in an attempt to lock eyes with him. "Listen, J. J., let us all stay calm. We are distraught over this investor, this Mr. Hog person, and he has put everyone on edge. We need to—"

Suddenly, Stefano rose, his unwavering stare glued to Paulo's face. "How did you know Harlan Grainger went by the disgusting name Hog? No one here told you such information."

At Stefano's dark displeasure, Paulo backed away from Jayson, looking around as if ready to ditch Sly and head for the nearest exit all by himself. "No, I am sure you or Jayson mentioned his horrible nickname at one time."

His watery gaze glued upon Paulo, Stefano shook his head. "No, my dear friend, I would have certainly remembered."

Jayson's fist connected hard with Stefano's nose, sending his tall frame crashing backward into the chair he'd recently vacated. He appeared stunned as he used shaky fingers to touch his nose. He pulled his hand back slowly, his watery eyes coming in contact with the ruby-red stains that coated the first three digits. At first, he studied them as if unable to decipher what he witnessed, and then a mental clarity seemed to dry his dark eyes.

His demeanor turned sober, and one eyebrow shot up as he gave Jayson a dismal smile.

Jayson growled in return, stabbing his finger at the air toward Stefano. "Now's not the time for a subject change, big brother."

Rubbing his bruised knuckles, Jayson observed with grim satisfaction the thin bloody trickle that slid from Stefano's nostril to stop at his pale upper lips. When he chose to speak again, his throat felt on fire due to his attempt to hold back building tears. "I want to make this clear: Andra is my wife, I love her, and I don't ever want you near her again. If you do go near her, I swear on our mother's grave I will kill you—do you understand me, Stefano? I will kill you dead."

Stefano chuckled, the sound mixing with a grunt-like noise as he hoisted his body to sit straighter. Silent, he removed a handkerchief from his pants pocket and compressed it against his bloody nose. No one in the room moved as he blew loudly into it to. After pulling it away, he took a moment to study the sullied cloth, his eyes seemingly searching for a profound answer to an unspoken question within the bloodstains. He neatly folded it and returned it to his pocket. "You are too late, my little brother," he said softly, sniffing once. "I am already dying. God has already done the job for you."

Taken aback, Jayson felt as if Stefano had physically punched him. "What are you talking about?"

An urgent knock at the door sounded, followed by the unexpected, strange phenomenon of Helena rushing into the room before waiting for permission to do so, her round face flushed and covered in monster-sized tears.

"Mr. Jayson, Mr. Stefano, something terrible has happened!" she cried. "Adonis has just told me Dr. Andra is gone!"

His anger at Stefano completely forgotten, Jayson rushed over to the agitated servant and firmly grabbed her upper arms. "Slow down, Helena," he said, gently shaking her. "What do you mean Andra's gone? Isn't she with the family? When did you speak with Adonis?"

Adonis was her great-nephew who sometimes worked as a custodian for the police department.

Her head shook from side to side, as if she wanted to deny the words that spilled from her own mouth. "You do not understand," she said, her voice breaking between each Grecian word. "He called me just now to say someone has taken Dr. Andra. Your papa and Dr. Andra's family are at the *astynomia* right now."

"They're at the police station?" he asked. He looked about the room in a daze, seeing no one. "Someone's got Andra?"

"Come—we will take my car," Stefano said, jumping to his feet. He shuffled Jayson toward the foyer just as the landline rang. "Hurry."

"It must be the astynomia." Helena's voice rose as they rushed out the door. "I will tell them you are on your way!"

Jayson mentally switched to autopilot, trying to hold it together, refusing to be incapacitated by his panic. He knew Doc needed him calm and rational. Everything was forced from his brain—Stefano's betrayal and declaration of his impending death, as well as Sly's stupid jealousy.

He cleared his mind of everything except how he would get Andra back.

41

Upon entering the study, Stefano quietly strolled over to the bar, stared at the brandy bottle, and decided to forgo his routine drinking ritual.

Instead, he turned toward the others who occupied the room: Papa, who sat on one couch, flanked by a distraught Al and Racine, his arms tenderly cradling them both; Sly and Paulo, who, to his surprise, appeared extremely shaken over Andra's kidnapping; and Jayson, who looked as if he would suffer an emotional breakdown at any moment.

The room was quiet and subdued except for occasional sniffling from Al and Racine.

Feeling the need to occupy his hand, Stefano selected a brandy glass that sat atop the polished wooden counter. He hesitated and then proceeded to pour cool water into it. He sipped on it as his mind wandered back to his and Jayson's arrival at the police station.

Naturally, the police could provide little assistance—due to no fault of their own but to the limited information Andra's mother had contributed about a generic beat-up white van. Countless white vans traveled along the countryside and within the city limits daily—so many, in fact, that any number of people could be brought in for questioning. For now, protocol dictated that the police conduct a formal investigation at the crime scene and interview anyone who might have witnessed the kidnapping.

According to his father, it was highly unlikely any

information would be forthcoming, given the crowds that were out and about during their excursion.

As for the family, the officer assigned to their case had advised them to go home and sit by the telephone to wait for a possible ransom call.

A second later, Jayson had come unglued and had to be physically carried from the police station.

Stefano stared into his glass, wishing it contained something with more of a kick to it. Yet he knew what he needed more than his usual brandy were two aspirin to accompany his water. His brain, and the section of his nose Jayson had soundly connected with, still throbbed.

Ruefully, he reasoned that he'd deserved the punch. Stefano gingerly touched his bruised nose and sighed.

In addition to the pain in his head, Stefano's stomach continued its rolling queasiness, which had started the moment Helena had burst into the room with the news that Andra had been kidnapped. Strangely, the moment she'd spoken those horrible words, he'd somehow believed it was his fault that the situation had manifested—yet he couldn't discern how it was his fault, so he found it difficult to go about finding a resolution to it.

For now, the only thing to do was wait for the kidnappers to call.

In deep meditation, Stefano paced before the liquor bar. He recognized that each passing second drew Andra closer to her demise. It was a known fact that statistically, things seldom ended well for kidnapped victims.

Whether or not the abductor was paid, death was usually the outcome.

He stopped walking and shivered. He couldn't imagine what the little life he had left to live would be like if anything happened to her.

For an indeterminate length of time, no one in the study moved or said a word; the only sound came from the steady ticking of the antique grandfather clock.

A sudden knock on the door sounded off like an unexpected

gunshot, causing Stefano to jump along with the others. George found his voice to call out, "Come in!"

Helena, her face swollen from recent tears, quietly entered, holding a small package covered in thick brown butcher paper tied with a thin white string. Boldly scrawled across the package were the words "For Jason Theonopilus' eyes only."

On heavy feet, she moved toward him. "Mr. Jayson," she said, switching to broken English after glancing at Racine and Al, "this come from boy. He says it for you."

Jayson stared at the package, his body motionless, as if what Helena handed him were a bomb ready to explode. After a moment's hesitation, he reached out and took it.

Staring intently at the wrapped box, Stefano moved toward Jayson. "Helena, did you recognize who delivered it?"

She nodded. "Mr. Stefano, it was local boy who deliver packages. He told me he not know where it comes from."

After looking around at the room's quiet occupants, the older woman quickly left.

Everyone watched her retreat; then, like magnets, their eyes revisited the package.

"Maybe you shouldn't open it," Racine said, rising to her feet. "Maybe we should wait for the police."

"No!" Jayson shouted. He glanced at her hurt expression and said softly, "I'm sorry, Racine. I can't wait—I need to open it now."

"There's something," Stefano said. He pointed to the handwriting across the package's top. "They've misspelled your name. It's spelled J-a-s-o-n."

His fingers in the midst of pulling at the string to untie the box, Jayson gave Stefano a "So what?" glare that quelled him into silence.

Everyone made his or her way from different areas of the room to stand around Jayson. No one made a sound as he pushed aside the thin string and wrapping, revealing a three-by-four-inch black velvet box.

"That's an expensive container," Stefano said, mostly to himself. He shook his head. "Why?"

Pursing his lips at Stefano's words, Jayson lifted the lid.

After reaching inside with trembling fingers, he pulled back his fist and rotated it. It opened to reveal an expensive set of wedding rings: an enormous solitaire and a thick wedding band with smaller inlaid diamonds. The rings sparkled almost menacingly.

The women gasped at the expensive discovery.

Jayson's eyes closed against the rings. Breathing deeply, he enclosed them inside his balled fist and placed it against his chest.

Racine cleared her throat with an angry, raspy sound. "Jayson, get a grip!" Her hand stretched toward the open box. "There's something else inside. What is it?"

At Racine's wrath, Jayson's mental fog seemed to lift. He reached back into the box and extracted a folded white slip.

"What does it say?" Al asked. "Please tell us."

Nodding, Jayson dropped Andra's rings into his shirt pocket. A hush came over the room as his lips moved, but no words came forth. After he finished reading, he slumped in his chair.

"What?" Stefano snatched the paper from his limp hands and read it. He suppressed a gasp as his eyes rose in disbelief. "They want fifty million dollars for her return." He scanned the remaining message. "They have provided a telephone number to get in touch with them. It also instructs us not to contact the police if we wish to see Andra again."

"Fifty million dollars," Al whispered as if punched in the gut. Looking upward, her eyes spilled anguished tears. "My sweet Lord Jesus, please help my baby girl."

Despite his throbbing nose, Stefano's face wrinkled in concentration, the transformation drawing his father's worried glance.

"What is it, Son?"

"This does not make much sense, Papa." Scanning the note again, he shook his head. "If these people are looking to receive money, why did they return jewelry as valuable as her rings? Why not keep those as well and sell them on the black market if this is about money?"

"What?" Straightening, Jayson reached up and snatched the note from Stefano's hand. "Who cares?"

"Yeah, who cares?" Racine echoed. She looked around the room in desperation. "They still want fifty million dollars, and we don't have fifty million dollars. Do you guys?"

His expression once again dejected, Jayson stared at the box in his lap. George shook his head.

"What are we gonna do?" Al asked, her eyes now spilling large tears. "This is my baby."

"I don't know, but we must figure something out," Stefano said.

"What do you mean *we* must figure something out?" Fists clenched, Racine stepped toward him. "This should be exactly what you wanted. You wanted my sister outta the picture—now you've got your wish!"

"Racine, please!" Al said. She grabbed her daughter, rocking her inside a tight embrace. "Hush. You're distraught and making things worse. You don't know what you're saying!"

Racine sniffled. "I do know! Stefano enlisted Ms. Thang over there to come between Andra and Jayson—and send us all packing home!"

The same stunned expression that lit Al's face simultaneously appeared upon George's. His eyes turned to Sly, who immediately hung her head, before swinging to Stefano. "Could this be true, Son?"

Before Stefano could answer, Racine leaped from her mother's embrace. "Yes, it's true, Papa George! Now Andra's been kidnapped—and I'm afraid for her and the baby."

"What!" Jayson and Al exclaimed together.

After tossing the empty box aside, Jayson gripped the arms of his chair and used them to rise on unsteady feet. "Andra's pregnant?"

Returning to her mother's arms, Racine nodded.

"Andra, my Andra," Al chanted softly. "My grandchild."

With her skirt rustling about her legs, Sly boldly stepped forward. "Who is the father?" she asked, her glittery gaze swinging from Stefano to Jayson and back again. "Is it yours, Stefano?"

Shame immediately engulfed Stefano, and his posture stiffened as he quickly pictured his naked body joined with Andra's, only to wish Sly's accusation were somehow true.

Everybody inside the room was still. However, their indignation gave way to surprise when they heard a sound like a whip cracking the air when Paulo slapped Sly.

"That is enough, you brat!" he said, firmly taking hold of her upper arms and shaking vigorously. "I want you to apologize immediately."

"No, Paulo, you don't understand." Sobbing, she shook her head, her black hair falling haphazardly over her face. "I will not apologize!"

"Yes! Yes, you will," he demanded, shaking her harder. "I said apologize!"

At Sly's continued crying, Racine moved toward them, her hands curled into threatening claws. "Here. Let me do it," she snarled. "I'll make her apologize!"

"Excuse me," Helena said breathlessly as she reentered the room. "Mr. Grainger waits in hall."

At the servant's rapid entrance, Racine stopped to give Sly a scathing 'You'd better be glad Helena just saved you' look.

A few feet away, Jayson shook his head. "Helena," he said. Slowly, his eyes returned to the box on the small, round table. "We can't see him now."

With a flurry of noise, Hog burst into the room, his tall, stocky frame moving with jovial ease. "Howdy, all! I know it's pretty rude to barge in on you folks like this, but—"

The Texan stopped abruptly, a frown replacing his previous smile. Looking around the room, he coughed nervously into his fist. "Heck, I'm so sorry! I didn't mean to barge in on a family situation." His worried glance circled the room again. "Is there anything I can do to help?"

George shook his head. "No, but thank you. This is a family matter, and we prefer to keep it—"

Racine pushed past George and Al, rushing up to Hog. "No, maybe he can help us," she said. Her shorter, shapelier frame stopped before his tall, beefy one, her desperation radiating through glittery brown eyes. "You're rich, right?"

At his hesitant nod, she grabbed his arm tightly. "My sister's been kidnapped, and they want fifty million dollars to return her. Please! Can you lend it to us?"

"Kidnapped!" Hog gaped. "When did this happen?"

"Today!"

Stefano stepped forward and placed a restraining hand on her arm. "Racine, maybe we should—"

Startled, he felt her violently shake off his touch. He suppressed a wince when she turned resentful eyes his way.

"I don't care what you have to say. Besides, what's it to you? You wanted her gone anyway!" Racine yanked a backward thumb toward Hog. "If he has the means to get Andra back, so be it!" She threw Hog a desperate look. "Please help us!"

Hog took off his tall Stetson and scratched at his head. "Well, little lady, fifty million is a hefty bit of change."

At his words, Racine's frame seemed to deflate, and a frantic sob broke free from her trembling lips. "If you don't help us, I don't know who can."

"Well," Hog said. Shifting from one foot to the other, he again scratched his head. "Are you all even sure someone's got the doctor?"

"Yes," Jayson said eagerly. "They've returned her—"

"Jayson!" Stefano interjected, only to soften his tone. "I believe we must be discreet in all information concerning your wife's abduction."

Jayson's desperate eyes circled the room, his stare nonverbally asking the other men to weigh in. Both George and Paulo gave their silent agreement. Nodding pathetically, he returned to Hog. "Yes, we're positive someone's kidnapped her."

"Well, young man," Hog said, his voice wavering, "I don't know."

"Please," Racine begged as tears and snot mingled, running freely. "Please, we have no one—you're our only hope."

At Racine's heightened anguish, Hog's large frame straightened; his light blue orbs once again circled the room, landing first on Jayson, next on George, and lastly on Stefano. "The pretty lil' lady's right. If you need money for the doctor's safe return, I'd be honored to give it to you."

Racine stopped crying long enough for her to throw herself at Hog and embrace him. His beefy arms went about her, hesitant at first and then squeezing tightly.

"Thank you, thank you, thank you!" she cried, her tears wetting the front of his cowboy-style shirt. "Thank you!"

Jayson and Al too gathered around Hog to express their relieved gratitude. However, along with Sly, Paulo, and George, Stefano hung back.

"I do not understand," George said, having to speak above the boisterous chatter surrounding Hog. "We are exceedingly grateful for your generosity, but why are you, a stranger to this family, willing to give us so much money?"

"Yes, I must concur with my father," Stefano said, attempting not to frown outright.

His face aglow amid the surrounding trio's hero worship, Hog seemed reluctant to break free from the crowd. Through wary eyes, Stefano watched the Texan stranger move toward him, his expression now sober.

"Ever since my wife's passing, I haven't much joy except buying an occasional small company or investing money. At this point in my life, I've got more money than anyone can shake a stick at—and no one to leave it to." Hog chuckled mirthlessly. "Me being by myself, I wouldn't be able to spend it all if I lived ten lifetimes. I might as well do something worthwhile with it before I go home to be with my Beauty."

Hog ducked his head, rotating his hat within both hands. When he glanced up again, his eyes glistened with unshed tears. "I've taken a liking to your sister-in-law and all—like I said, she reminds me of my Beauty. If my paltry money can save her life, well then, this would be the best investment I could ever sink it into."

"Amen," Jayson said through a watery smile. "We want to thank—"

"But how will we be able to pay back so much money?" Stefano said, deliberately ignoring another of Jayson's scathing glares. "You have intimately researched our family business. You must understand we cannot possibly repay you such a large amount anytime soon, if at all."

"Yes," George said, moving to stand beside Stefano. "What is it you want in return?"

Hog shifted on his feet, his beefy hands once again rotating his Stetson. He coughed uncomfortably. "Never you mind that, Mr. Theonopilus. We can always talk about these things later—after the doctor's return."

Stefano shook his head, still ignoring Jayson. "I believe we must talk about this now—before we contact the kidnappers."

With a jerky motion, Jayson combed angrily through his hair; he lowered his hand, drawing Stefano's attention by silently patting the pocket in which Andra's rings lay hidden. "Must we?" Jayson said. "Remember—this is my wife we're talking about!"

Stefano took a moment to recall the rings—how they looked and how they'd sparkled before Jayson tucked them away prior to the annoying Texan's arrival. He wanted to step into his brother's shoes concerning his anguish over Andra. Although he felt a similar anguish, he also knew he carried a heavy responsibility for the entire Theonopilus family as a whole—one he was not ready to relinquish quickly.

"Mr. Grainger?" Stefano finally said, closely watching Hog. "Again, what is it you want?"

"All right, young Theonopilus," Hog said slowly. He pivoted and walked away from the group, distancing himself. The lines in his forehead deepened within his silence. A few seconds passed before he faced Stefano directly. "Okay. I'll take seventy percent stock in your company as collateral."

Paulo gasped, stumbling backward to cover his mouth in surprise. Sly stopped sniffling long enough to stare at Hog with reddened eyes. Al and Racine glanced around the room in naive expectancy, while Stefano and George stared at him in disbelief.

Hog's expression turned sheepish. "My proposal would give you three ten percent each as owners. Hopefully what I propose seems fair to you all."

Jayson rushed forward, grabbed Hog's hand, and pumped it. "It's a deal!"

At Stefano's objection, Jayson turned on him. "Yes! He can

have my share—I'll give it all away. I don't care. I just want my wife and baby back."

The Texan's eyes widened as a small smile lit his face. "Your lil' woman's pregnant?" Hog placed a large hand on Jayson's shoulder—whether in congratulations or sympathy, the action was undecipherable. "Surely we must get your doctor back, by all means."

Jayson turned tearful eyes to Stefano and George, who remained silent.

Hog's arm dropped to his side as he turned to face Stefano. "Seventy percent—that's my offer. I'll leave it with you." The Texan pulled out a business card and handed it to Jayson. "I meant to give this to you the last time I was here. My cell's on it. Don't wait too long to contact me. Things like this should be handled ASAP."

Hog grabbed Jayson's hand and shook it in commiserating consolation. "If not handled swiftly and just right, this here kidnapping could quickly go south, if you know what I mean." His pale blue eyes circled the group. "My condolences."

After putting his hat on, he silently tipped it and left the room, the sound of fading cowboy boots echoing across the outer foyer.

The whole house vibrated as the front door slammed shut, and the sound caused Jayson to face Stefano and George, his expression livid. "We're doing this, right? For Andra and my baby."

Wearily, Stefano glanced over at his father, and the older man's eyes confirmed what needed to be done. Stefano nodded. "I believe we have no choice," he said.

Jayson's frame sagged with instant relief at Stefano's words. He then sprinted toward the study's door. "Hog's probably still outside!" he called over his shoulder. "I'm going to catch him before he pulls off—get the ball rolling for the money."

Stefano flinched upon hearing the front door open and slam shut for a second time. The sound was like a metaphor for the Theonopilus family's future—it had become a closed door.

42

Sneezing, Hog ambled through his comfortable-sized villa to one-handedly pull dusty sheets from the sparse furnishings contained within the home. He allowed the dirty coverings to billow to the floor next to their corresponding pieces of furniture in an unheeded fashion, until he entered the last room, the kitchen. As he regarded the lonely area, his face and posture grew grim.

Resting his hands on his hips, he let out an elongated sigh.

To his own ears, the noise sounded like that of a wounded animal. He knew if he allowed it to go on any longer, it would turn into a broken sob—and now was not the time to fall apart, especially when things were finally going his way.

Determined, he clamped his mouth shut, cutting off the sound. Instead of self-pity, he opened himself up to his inner rage. *Now, anger—that's an emotion a fella can get a lot done with.*

Allowing his eyes to adjust to the room's dimness, he scanned the dusty kitchen countertops, antique-looking refrigerator and stove, and dull ceramic tile floors. Eventually, he would hire people from the village to do a major cleaning overhaul of the entire estate and maybe even have them perform some much-needed repairs. When he'd first arrived, he'd spoken with a few local villagers about securing their services for future work. However, he didn't want to bring them onboard just yet.

The timing wasn't right.

In the meantime, he would have to do any necessary cleaning and repairing himself.

After his precious Beauty had been snatched from him years before, he'd taken up the gauntlet life handed him and chosen to cook and clean for himself. He didn't mind doing domestic work. It kept his brain busy and focused during bleak times back at his Texas ranch. It stopped him from dwelling too hard on her.

Needing to clear his head of unwanted memories, Hog shook it. He reminded himself of the present task at hand.

Glancing to his left, he headed for the kitchen table and the woolen blanket neatly folded there. He grabbed it and tucked its scratchy thickness underneath one arm.

Although it was early afternoon, the kitchen was dim; yet despite the gloom, he was unwilling to throw open all the shutters to let the sunlight in. Instead, he would settle for one open window to provide him light.

Switching on the flashlight he carried, he headed for the door leading to the cellar. Upon disengaging the lock, he carefully opened it. Peering deep into an area even dimmer than the kitchen, he flashed his wide beam to and fro, making sure he wouldn't encounter hanging spiders and cobwebs on the way to the lower level.

Although he had earlier thoroughly cleaned the villa's cellar, he knew spiders were efficient little dickens that could hang homes as quickly as a person could knock 'em down. To his relief, the stairwell was clear of arachnid activity.

The circular beam bobbed as he descended the rickety stairs. When he reached the bottom, he noted the temperature had dropped, as if he currently ran an air conditioner down there.

Automatically, he glanced left at the room dedicated to the storage of fine wines.

Beyond its threshold, he shined his light at shelves displaying empty round holes. When Beauty had been alive, they had spent long, carefree hours talking about traveling the world to bring home various vintage bottles of expensive chardonnay, cabernet, Dom Pérignon, and various chateau brands upon retiring to the Grecian villa for good.

Smiling, Hog wiped his eyes. Her beautiful laughter echoed inside his head as she told him she wanted to celebrate life and having each other—with a strong drink.

His smile disappeared.

Those empty black holes were reminders she hadn't lived long enough to fill them, and he realized that like those vacant slots, his life was empty and black.

Stifling another anguished sob, Hog pointed his beam to the right. The illumination revealed a heavy wood-and-steel door locked from his side. With his free hand, he searched inside his pocket for its key and then inserted it and turned it clockwise. With satisfaction, he heard the inner mechanism disengage with a heavy clunk. Returning the key to his pocket, he grunted as he tugged the door open with one hand.

As the door slowly creaked open, the unoiled hinges sounded especially loud in the cellar, creating an eerie echo.

Gingerly, he stepped inside the room. He switched off his flashlight and placed it on a small table by the door, sliding it next to a desk lamp that provided limited lighting.

"Hello, darlin'. I brought you a blanket. I know how cold it can get down here."

Hog strolled over to a narrow single-sized bed with a headboard and footboard made of solid brass. He stopped to admire the woman who lay there on her back with her hands extended upward, tied to the headboard, and her feet secured to its footboard. Her clothed body was toned and firm yet voluptuous, especially her breasts. Her nipples were taut and hard due to the low temperature inside the room.

He wouldn't have minded reaching out.

Sighing wistfully, Hog shook his head. If his Beauty was alive, she wouldn't be pleased with him doing such a thing. Besides, this was strictly business—no monkey business allowed.

Well, at least not at the present time.

He would first have to consult with Beauty's spirit about

the situation to see if she'd eventually allow him free reign to be a man.

He flicked the blanket open and carefully covered the woman's body to the waist. His eyes remained glued to her uncovered torso, studying her enticing bumps and curves. He loathed to cover up such magnificence.

Despite Beauty's memory, it was still tempting to cop a feel of silky brown skin. He sighed again, this time with lustful frustration.

"It's been a long time since I've been with someone of quality," Hog whispered to her, finally sliding the wool blanket up her body to completely hide it from his view. Delicately, he tucked the blanket into the cot and then straightened, placing his hands on his hips. "Darlin', like I told your husband, you can set a man's blood to boiling."

Andra's brown eyes enlarged at his words, her mouth moving erratically in an attempt to speak beneath the black masking tape that sealed it shut.

Hog laughed good-naturedly. "Don't worry, Doctor. I won't take advantage just yet—my Beauty wouldn't like it if I didn't at least get her approval first."

His gaze perused her body; he liked the way her shapely outline called to him beneath the blanket. His hands itched to remove it, but he fought the impulse.

Hog's eyes then crashed with Andra's confused ones. "I know you don't understand what's happenin' right now, Doctor, but you will—very soon. All I can tell you is this: everything's going as planned." He rubbed a rough palm across his dry lips as he skimmed her body again. "When I come back with your supper a little later, I'll let you loose to do your business. Maybe we can even talk about the two of us getting together—after I confer with my Beauty, of course."

He stared hard at the blanket and smiled. "But I'm pretty sure I can predict what she's gonna say."

43

Stefano paced the floor of the study, stopping every now and again to glance at Jayson.

On the telephone with Hog's lawyer, his younger brother wore an expression that was all business as he handled the matters of expediting the deposit of Hog's loan into their bank account and finalizing the subsequent contractual agreement transferring 70 percent of the Theonopilus company's holdings into Hog's hands.

With every second, Stefano grew more and more agitated; his intuition told him that with each action they took, they were heading down the wrong path.

Everything about the situation was erroneous. His apprehension had started with the returned wedding rings.

Again, Stefano ceased pacing to study Jayson. He hung up to next dial the number disclosed in the kidnapper's note. His expression now was comprised of restrained anger, and he shifted jerkily in his chair as he spoke to the unknown person.

Stefano chose not to listen to the conversation and moved farther away to allow his brother some privacy; he wanted to give him space to be a man and deal with the grueling situation as he saw fit.

Finding himself at a safer distance, Stefano resumed his pacing. *Why would anyone return valuable jewelry if the whole purpose for taking Andra was money? And why did they choose Andra? Why not kidnap Papa, Jayson, or me? Taking Andra appeared too ... Too what?*

An instant later, the word abruptly dropped inside his brain: *personal.*

It was as if whoever had taken her somehow wanted to make a statement with her rings.

Yet what statement?

He ceased pacing once he realized Jayson had stopped talking. "So?" Stefano, followed by his father, arrived before Jayson as he hung up. "Is it done?"

"Yes," Jayson replied, his response curt. He cut his eyes sharply at them before looking away. "No thanks to you."

Ignoring his brother's anger, Stefano shoved his hands into his pockets. "Did you recognize the voice on the other end?"

"The voice was altered by a synthesizer or something, so no, I did not recognize it."

Their father moved closer to Jayson, placing a tender hand on his head. "Son, please do not think we were refusing to rescue Andra."

Jayson abruptly stood, forcing George's hand to fall away. "I've got to call our bank to finalize everything. And if you don't mind, I'd much rather handle it alone. I'll be in my room." Not waiting for a response, he stalked out.

George sighed heavily. "Did we handle this one correctly?" he asked no one in particular.

Despite not being personally addressed, Stefano answered. "Maybe, but perhaps not." He walked toward the bar, finally giving in to his desire for a drink. He sighed as he dropped ice cubes into his glass. "This whole thing feels wrong, Papa."

Saying nothing, George quickly lowered his eyes to his polished shoes; still, Stefano managed to catch twin feelings of hurt and dismay within them.

"Stefano, is it true what Racine said?" George asked, intentionally speaking in Greek so his words wouldn't be deciphered. "Did you attempt to undermine Jayson and Andra's marriage? Tell me my son would not do such a terrible thing."

Stefano stilled, unable to tell whether his hand shook from his illness or the fact that he had to tell his father the truth. He positioned the brandy decanter over his glass and poured the liquor carefully and slowly, attempting to delay the inevitability of watching the shame deepen within his father's eyes at his reply.

His own mortification now clear, he turned around with his drink in hand, knowing he had to face not only George but also himself. "Yes, Papa. It is true."

At his father's tearing eyes, he experienced a twisting inside his gut.

"Why, Stefano?" George said.

Stefano wavered between lying to spare his father even more disappointment or hurting the older man more by telling the truth. In the end, he knew there was only one answer. His existence was winding down fast; it dictated he couldn't compromise the integrity inherited from his papa by trying to justify any underhandedness on his part.

"The truth is, I was ignorant and prejudiced." He paused and then added more softly, "And extremely selfish. It was I who somehow lost my *philotimo*."

At George's continued silence, Stefano shook his head in misery. "My father, I'm sorry for my actions. I feel I may have set off this chain of events concerning Andra and her kidnapping."

George reached out and gently squeezed Stefano's shoulder. Despite the light touch, Stefano still suffered a terrible weight beneath it. "Son, I'm quite relieved by your change of heart. And I'm extremely proud of you as well. It takes a great man to acknowledge when he is wrong and an even greater man to make a change for the better because of it. Your philotimo— your worthiness—is intact."

"Thank you, Papa," he said gruffly, his father's hand feeling not quite as heavy.

Glancing at the brandy in Stefano's hand, George appeared ready to pour himself one, only to change his mind. He instead studied Stefano's troubled expression. "Son, tell me—why do you believe your actions may have caused the situation we now find ourselves in?"

Frustrated, Stefano wiped his brow. "I truly do not know, Papa. Yet something continues to bother me."

"Yes?" George said. "What is it?"

Unconsciously, Stefano switched back to English. "The rings," he said, his voice rising in concern. "Why did they not keep them to sell? Those rings are worth a lot of money."

"Maybe it's because they are Andra's—plain and simple," Racine spat from across the room. She ignored her mother's signal to be still. "Those rings are unique to my sister and identify her as the person who's been kidnapped."

Stefano bit back his response: *Yes, but why not cut off a finger to show they mean business and sell the jewelry on the black market? Or, less extreme, simply take a picture of her hand wearing the rings? Wouldn't that be what most hard-core, greed-driven kidnappers would've done?*

Instead, he said, "Yes, of course. You are probably right."

Immediately dismissing Racine's angry head toss, Stefano looked off into space; distracted, he swirled the brandy around inside his glass, trying to recall the other subject that had nagged him earlier.

Abruptly, his hand stopped. "Paulo!" he called out. He watched as Paulo broke from whispering to his sister and nervously glanced his way. "Paulo, I would like to meet with you."

"When?"

"Now." Stefano placed his untouched drink on the bar's countertop. "Come with me to the office."

"Is everything all right, son?" George asked, stopping short upon returning to the couch where Al and Racine sat. "Am I needed as well?"

Stefano smiled briefly and shook his head. "No, Papa, this only concerns Paulo and myself. Please stay with the ladies and come for me if anything new develops." Stefano turned and strolled from the room, leaving Paulo no choice but to follow.

The house was deathly quiet as the men walked across the foyer and to the right, their echoing footsteps the only sound as they trekked down the hall toward Stefano's office.

After asking Paulo to close the door, he motioned toward a single-backed chair. He then strolled over to his desk and casually leaned against it. "Please, make yourself comfortable." Stefano studied Paulo's nervousness as he lowered into his seat. His smile brief, he came right to the point. "How well are you familiar with Mr. Grainger?"

"Not well at all," Paulo said, studying his hands clasped atop his lap. "Only what you have told me."

"Is that so?" Stefano took a moment to cross his arms. "If you recall, I asked how you knew to call Mr. Grainger by the disgusting name Hog. Do you remember?"

Paulo's Adam's apple bobbed violently. "Yes, I do, but I do not recall how I knew, Stefano." He strived for nonchalance with a shrug but only came off as looking epileptic. "It was most certainly through yourself or Jayson."

Again, Stefano studied him. Paulo's eyes shifted evasively around the room, glancing everywhere Stefano wasn't. Although Paulo's darting eyes were too busy to witness it, Stefano shook his head.

"No. The first time the investor information was introduced was at the dinner table; prior to your leaving, neither I nor Jayson uttered that repulsive name." Propped against the desk, he took time to casually stretch out his legs and cross them. "Again, I will ask you—how did you come to know Mr. Grainger went by the name Hog?"

Unheeded, perspiration trickled down Paulo's temples. Faint ticking from the wall clock marked off each silent second; the lonely cry from a distant bird outside the window filtered in, accentuating the quietness within the room.

Looking on the verge of vomiting, Paulo finally flung his arms in the air. "All right. I met him prior to his meeting you for the first time."

"Oh?" Stefano asked, trying to maintain his calm. "Why, might I ask?"

At Paulo's hesitation, with deliberate slowness, Stefano pushed off the desk and strolled over to him. The younger man's frame seemed to shrink as Stefano's towered over him.

Patiently, Stefano sighed. "You might as well explain this to me, Paulo." At the other's prolonged muteness, he performed a one-shoulder shrug. "I believe at this point, as the Americans would say, you do not have much of a leg to stand on."

Timidly, Paulo glanced up at him and then back to his twitching hands. "Yes, I ... Well, I ..." He exhaled loudly. "Mr. Grainger paid me to keep an eye on you and the business. He wanted to learn of your strengths and your weaknesses."

"Like a spy, correct?" At Paulo's weak nod, Stefano nodded too. "Did he say why he wished to obtain this knowledge about me?"

Paulo glanced down at his hands again. "He wants to help you with your business—take it over and make it profitable again." At Stefano's sharp inhalation, he rushed on. "He informed me when all is well with the company, he plans to return it to your family."

Stefano's right eyebrow lifted. "Again, I must ask why. Why would he, a complete stranger, wish to help our family business become profitable by taking it over, only to generously return it back to us? Why did he not simply come directly to us with this plan?" He paused. "What is in it for him—and for you?"

Paulo shrugged tiredly. "I do not know; I believe he is simply a kind man who would like nothing more than to help you and the family." A few seconds passed before he was able to lift his head with a degree of courage. "He said his reason for not approaching you directly is due to your arrogance of not wishing assistance from outsiders."

"I see. And now we have simply handed our business over to him." Stefano made an attempt to display a neutral expression. "How much is he paying you?"

"I, uh ..."

"How much, Paulo?"

His previous limited courage now failed him. Paulo's lids once again lowered. "One hundred thousand dollars." Paulo flinched at Stefano's small exclamation, his slender frame bowing in shame. "He has already given me half the money, and he was to give me the remainder after the takeover was complete."

"My," Stefano said slowly, "what a small sum to sell out your family for. How great the desire for this Mr. Grainger to take over our business, it is a wonder you did not try to get more."

Suddenly unable to stomach the sight of Paulo, Stefano spun on his heel and returned to his desk, keeping his face averted. He bristled when Paulo's next words pelted him from behind.

"Family?" Paulo snorted. "Sly and I are only family when it's convenient for you."

Stefano's mind handed him one word: *touché.*

Behind him, Paulo let out a pitiful sigh. "I'm sorry, Stefano—please forgive me for such unkind words. Your family has been nothing but generous to Sly, Yaya, and myself."

"Forgiven." Not wanting Paulo to see how truly angry he still was, Stefano retained his averted stance. Desiring to do anything with his hands, he stacked loose papers on his desk. "So I assume you have reported to Mr. Grainger any weaknesses?"

From behind, Stefano sensed Paulo shake his head.

"But." Paulo paused. "It was he who told me of your weakness."

Stiffening, Stefano stopped shuffling. "I am at a loss. How could he possibly have knowledge of my weaknesses? I am barely acquainted with the man." Stefano paused to slide the stapler across the desk to its proper place—next to the vase holding Andra's blue-and-white lily. "I'm curious. What did he say was my weakness?"

Paulo coughed nervously. From the direction his voice traveled, Stefano could tell Paulo finally had found the courage to stare directly at his spine.

"Dr. Andra."

Abruptly, Stefano's gaze landed on the small crystal vase. Not wanting Paulo to witness his hands trembling, Stefano shoved them into his pockets. He reluctantly broke free from the flower to stare out the office window. "Signomi? What did you say?"

"He said," Paulo said, enunciating more clearly, "you were in love with Dr. Andra. He was very insistent about it."

Within their renewed silence, Paulo stirred. "Is it true, Stefano? Are you in love with your brother's wife?"

Stefano's tongue felt glued to the roof of his mouth; he labored to loosen the appendage and make it work properly.

"That is all, Paulo," he finally said, his tone deliberate. "Return to the others. I will be there shortly."

Listlessly, Paulo rose from his chair and moved across the room toward the door. Halfway there, he paused. "No, I must leave and take a drive. Clear my head." His sigh was heavy, borderline fearful. "I am sorry, my friend. I meant to cause no trouble to you and the family. In the beginning, I believed I was doing the right thing for all involved—my family and yours—but now I've come to realize I was misguided."

At Stefano's nod, he quietly left the room.

His body extremely weary, Stefano dropped into his chair. Placing his elbows on the desk, he lowered his face into open palms and rested. He sat there for a brief moment, inhaling and exhaling deeply in an attempt to gather his physical and emotional strength. He knew his debilitating internal organs were telling him that due to this added stress, his time was dwindling fast.

His breathing erratic, Stefano reached out to turn on his computer. Accessing Google search, he clicked on the advanced feature, and in the search-criteria boxes, he typed "Harlan Orlando Grainger, Texas businessman" and, after deliberating some more, also typed "breaking news."

Believing the computer would ultimately display information he knew he didn't really want to find out about but had to discover anyway, Stefano paused with his finger over the Enter key.

Taking a final glance at Andra's flower, he exhaled forcefully and then firmly pressed the key.

44

From her recent recurring dream, Andra woke with a violent start, dazed.

Her senses suddenly cleared, and she realized she'd just leaped from an unconscious nightmare to a waking one. The wrongness of her current state overwhelmed her to the point she couldn't speak or move.

Dismayed, she realized she physically couldn't anyway.

Her body stiff from lying in one position for so long, she tugged at the rope that bound her wrists above her head, alternately using her numb feet to kick at the second set that tied down her ankles.

The room she occupied was dimly lit and cold. Waves of aloneness washed over her, making her believe no one else existed on the entire planet except her. Trying to work out the kink in her neck, she slowly turned her head to the right, only to shrink back against her confining ropes once Hog's image came into view.

Motionless, he sat next to her prison bed, studying her with fathomless blue eyes.

He smiled pleasantly. "Ah, you're up, lil' lady. I was wondering how long you'd be out. I can imagine you must be starving." He jerked his head to the right, indicating a wooden shelf. "Brought you some grub to nibble on."

Andra closed her eyes against the wrapped sandwiches, the six-pack of bottled water, and his deceptively thoughtful manner, only to become aware of a dull ache in her lower abdomen. Panicking, she telepathically shifted her misery at him.

"Ah," he said, catching on right away. "Listen up; I imagine you need to use the facilities." He waited for her nod. "That's fine. I'm not a barbarian; I don't want to see you wet yourself. So here's what we're gonna do. We're gonna untie these here ropes so you can take care of your business, okay?"

Andra's response came out in a muffled jumble.

He gave her what could've been the Texas evil eye. "But I'm warning you: I don't want any trouble outta you. It won't go well if you cause trouble."

Figuring his implied threat was enough and needed no further explanation, Hog stood and moved to the foot of the bed. After throwing aside her blanket, he carefully untied her ropes.

"Now, I trust you won't give me trouble, right, Doctor? I'm stronger than you, enough to overpower you—like I did in the village square." The pressure at her ankles abated as he finished undoing her binding. "And if I have to hog-tie you again, well, let's just say your bed will also be your toilet from that point on. Got it?"

Andra nodded.

"Good girl," he said. After tossing the rope across the room by the cellar door, he next moved to her bound wrists. "Besides, if you tried to escape and somehow made it outta this cellar, you wouldn't have the foggiest notion where you are. You'll never find your way back to those Theonopiluses. I guarantee it."

After both scratchy ropes were gone, Hog stepped back. Rising slowly, she threw her tingling legs over the cot's side, each hand alternatingly massaging its opposite wrist. The masking tape across her mouth was the last to go; after peeling it off, she rotated her jaw.

"Where is the—"

Hog pointed across the room to where an antique chamber pot sat.

"No," she croaked in disbelief. She blinked at him. "No way. You've got to be kidding."

Hog chuckled. "It's either that or the bed, lil' lady. Take your pick."

Her bladder felt ready to explode. Wavering, Andra stood on wobbly legs, giving them a few seconds to steady. She then glared at Hog. "May I get a little privacy at least?"

"Sure," he said, grinning mischievously. He turned his back on her. "But you'd better make it quick. I'm liable to peek after a minute."

Wanting to choke the life out of him with her tingling hands, Andra hurried to the chamber pot. With trembling fingers, she pulled down her jeans, and her bottom barely touched the pot's rim before her urine gushed forth like a rushing stream.

"Man, you really had to go, didn't you? There should be some toilet paper behind you," he said once her stream slowed. "Be quick about it. I'm about ready to turn around."

Andra wiped herself, and trying not to grimace with disgust, she dropped the soiled tissue into the pot.

Crossing her arms, she studied her captor's back, knowing he knew she watched him. "Why am I here, Hog?" she finally asked. "What's this all about?"

Facing her, he gave her an agreeable wink. "I thought you'd never ask."

Andra's gastric juices rolled at his lighthearted performance. She scowled. "Then tell me." She watched his face turn stubborn. "Look, I know whatever's happening here has to do with Jayson and his family. What is it you want with me?"

She shivered as his eyes scanned her body, starting with her mussed hair and moving down to her scuffed tennis shoes only to return to her face.

He grinned mischievously.

"Don't even think about it," she warned. Although she was petrified, she kept her voice even. "You don't want rape added to the charge of kidnapping."

She reversed at his approach, cautiously moving around the urine pot to its other side. With nowhere to go, she pressed her spine against the cellar wall.

Hog's looming presence stopped mere inches away. "Rape? Not my style. Beauty wouldn't like it," he said. Hog reached out to lightly finger the button at the center of her blouse, directly between her breasts. "But seduction—now, that's a different story."

Recoiling, she slapped his hand away. Her loud, erratic breathing amplified to mingle with his lustful breaths, the sounds overlapping within the silence.

Hog broke the spell when he sighed longingly. "I promise you—I won't hurt the young'un baking inside you," he said. "At least I'll try not to."

Andra gasped. "How do you know about my pregnancy?"

Hog grinned. His curled lips seemed to support a malevolent darkness within him, giving her the impression he was a satanic spirit who supernaturally knew everything about her.

To Andra's relief, he abruptly spun on his heel and returned to the bed. Gathering the rope that lay on the mattress, he looped it over and over again around one hand. He took his time doing so, every once in a while glancing her way.

"You know, from time to time, I reflect on you and young Theonopilus holed up inside the airplane restroom, doin' your business." He made another loop slowly and carefully. "As I recall, you two were in there for quite a stretch before the flight attendant came and fetched you out. Mm hm. Confined in such a tiny space, you know?"

Andra remained silent, unable to respond to someone as crazy as she now knew him to be.

"Yessiree, I sat in my seat, trying to imagine what your young fella was doing to you inside that bathroom." Hog shook his head. His smile was vague, and his eyes were glassy, as if he currently relived the moment inside his head. He finished the last loop, grasping the coiled rope in one large hand, looking as though he were ready to lasso a bull. "Well, my sexy filly, I've got all the time in the world with you to figure it out. And figure it out I will." He chuckled softly. "You might not like it at first and might even fight against me initially, but in time, I'll wear you down with seduction. It's an art, you know. If my wife, Beauty, was alive, she'd tell you how skillful I am in that department."

Andra's cheeks flamed when his eyes lowered to her swollen breasts heavy with her pregnancy. She angrily shook her head. "It's not going to happen."

He gave her a look as if she were naive. "Oh, it's gonna happen between us." After strolling over to the door, Hog bent to retrieve the rope he'd removed from her feet. Still holding the first set, he looped it around the other at a much faster speed. "Now, your question as to the reason why you're here— well, that's between me and your in-laws."

Holding back her desperation, Andra stepped away from the wall to narrow the distance between her and her kidnapper. "Hold on. I have a right to know," she said. "What are your plans for me?"

"Well, Doctor, I guess I could say an eye for an eye." Hog winked again, yet this time the gesture had a hardened edge to it. "A life for a life. Or should I say, a wife for a wife?"

She took a step back from his sinister words, needing the wall against her spine to provide her some small comfort. For the first time, Andra studied the room and its contents, which were lit only by the small reading lamp near the door.

"Now, Doctor, try not to ponder too hard about yonder window or even those cellar doors over there." He pointed at both. "The window's too high to reach. And the cellar doors, like the window, are padded shut from the outside."

He walked a few feet toward the exit, only to stop and point at an enormous clay jar tucked in the far corner. "Oh yeah, and try not to mess with that. I trapped a gigantic black snake outside and placed it in there." Andra's frightened gasp caused Hog to chuckle. "If you don't bother it, it won't bother you. You'll be just fine as long as you keep the lid tight on it and let it be. I'll get rid of it soon enough."

Andra warily eyed the container, now wishing for company so she wouldn't be alone with the snake. She choked back a plea to ask Hog to stay once he made it to the door.

"Eat and get you some rest," he suggested. "We can discuss your situation when I return."

The door creaked shut. As an afterthought, she ran over to it just as it closed her in. She pounded furiously but stopped once she heard the key turn from the other side.

45

Racine observed the men leave the formal sitting area one by one.

First, Jayson removed himself to handle the bank situation, his body stiff with worry, anger, and some other emotion she couldn't quite identify. Next to go was the high-and-mighty Stefano, who practically summoned Paulo to follow. Papa George hung around for approximately thirty minutes before he decided to head for Stefano's office to find out what was going on.

Now only she, her mother, and something that could've crawled out of her worst nightmare—Sly—remained.

Intentionally ignoring the latter, Racine focused on her mother's curled body upon the long sofa, her sleep induced by the Theonopilus family doctor, who'd come earlier and prescribed sedatives to help calm her nerves. At his insistence she take one too, Racine had shooed him away.

To her relief, he'd left the villa without forcing lobotomy meds down her throat.

Racine dismissed Sly's first motion as she stood beside the sitting room's closed door. Yet as the foreign girl's beckoning grew in its urgency, Racine sighed violently, the sound causing her mother to stir restlessly.

Twisting on the couch, Racine glared Sly's way. "What?" she mouthed.

"Come over here," she mouthed back.

Her next exhalation muted, Racine stalked over to the door. "What do you want?" she hissed.

Sly gingerly reached out and touched her arm. "First, I would like to apologize for what I said about Yatros Andra and the baby." She gave Racine a faltering smile. "I believe it is Jayson's child."

"Who gives a care?" she asked, brushing aside Sly's hand. "Seriously, dude, you've got issues. You're definitely in need of some help."

Charmingly, Sly waved away her recommendation for psychiatric assistance. "I meant no harm to Yatros Andra."

Racine stepped back to cross her arms. "Do you understand *Yatros* Andra could wipe the floor with your bony butt if she really wanted to?" Racine raised a sardonic eyebrow at Sly's disbelieving stare. "Don't let that goody-two-shoes 'I'm a doctor who values life' exterior fool you. I don't know how she kept her hands to herself when it comes to you. Believe me, dude—you got off lucky."

Sly swayed uneasily. "Okay, okay," she said, flapping her hand as if waving off Racine's words. "Look, you and I need to stick together. I want to help."

Warily, Racine eyed her. "Help?" Racine lifted her hand to count off her fingers. "Number one, why would you want to help? Number two, why would I trust you enough to want your help? And number three, what do you think you can do to help?"

To her amazement, Sly's emerald eyes filled with unshed tears. "Yes, I have been a brat," she said with a sniffle. "And I too want to apologize for being so. I see how much Jayson loves Dr. Andra—truly loves her. I do want to help."

Racine forced herself to stay put when Sly moved closer.

"But, Racine, if we put our heads together, we as women should be able to come up with something." Taking the time to brush aside a small tear, she managed to shrug prettily. "As you know, we are the smarter sex."

Racine had to admit she had a point. "Okay, so what's your plan?"

At Sly's glancing about them, Racine grabbed her arm and vigorously shook it. "Would you cut the melodrama?" she whispered harshly. "You know we're the only people here!"

Sly's giggle was infectious, and Racine nearly chuckled along with her. However, she needed to remain steadfast in her resolve to stay serious for Andra's sake. She waited impatiently.

"You are right," Sly said. To Racine's annoyance, she paused to again glance over her shoulder. "What we should do is go to Stefano's office and listen at the door. Listen in on what they are saying. I can assure you they have information they are not telling us."

Frowning, Racine jammed her fists against her hips. "You know what, Sherlock? You need to lay off those American detective TV shows. Evidentially, you're spending too much time watching them."

"No, I am serious! I know Grecian men; they will tell us nothing because we are women." Sly tapped her shiny glossed lips, her face suddenly brightening. "We must stand outside the door and gather intel—see what we can do to assist Yatros Andra. She needs us!"

Racine shook her head in disbelief. "Gather intel? Are you serious?"

Sly smiled.

"So you're telling me, Ms. Thang, you want this to be like a Cagney and Lacey situation?"

"Yes, yes! I have seen reruns of this female police show! They are, what you say, badass broads!" Sly giggled. "Remember the show where one curled at the heels of the bad man, and the other pushed him in the chest? Remember how the bad guy flipped backward and cracked his head?"

"No."

Thoughtfully, Sly brushed stray hair from her forehead. "Well, maybe it wasn't this Cagney and Lacey. Maybe it was—"

"Please, just shut up." Racine sighed. Although she was trying hard not to, she found herself not disliking the Grecian beauty as much as she had before. *What a time to start going soft!* "Okay, Lacey." Grabbing Sly's hand, Racine opened the door and pulled her through. "Let's go snooping."

46

Under Hog's heavy hand, the hotel door swung open.

"Well, hello, young man," he said, giving his visitor a somber look. "I was glad you rang me up. How's it going over at the Theonopilus place? Any word concerning the kidnapping?"

Paulo stepped inside. Facing Hog, he remained silent until the door shut. "No word yet," he said, his expression unreadable. "But then, you are aware of this Mr. Grainger, correct?"

The tone in the younger man's voice unsettled Hog, but he pulled from deep within to produce a sad expression. Shaking his head, he led the way to the private sitting area.

"Such a god-awful thing, what's happening to those nice people." He stopped at the bar to fix a scotch and water but didn't bother to ask if Paulo wanted one. His drink made, he casually turned to his guest. "I'm just glad I was able to help in some way."

Mute, Paulo stared, as if sizing Hog up.

"Money isn't everything, son," he continued wistfully. "Now, if a person has pure love, joy, and happiness, that's priceless."

His manner stiff, Paul approached Hog and stopped a few feet away. "Please," he said, his lips pulling into a frown. "As you Americans say, can we cut the crap?"

Momentarily startled into silence, Hog slapped his knee only to burst out laughing. "Well done, son! Good one." Still chuckling, he walked around Paulo to settle onto his usual couch. When Paulo refused to take a seat for himself, Hog lifted one eyebrow. "So tell me—what crap am I supposed to be cutting, son?"

Paulo uttered a small cry. He pivoted and sat in a chair closest to the bar—and the farthest away from Hog. "This concerns Dr. Andra."

"Okay," Hog said slowly. He studied the agitated younger man. "I don't know what else to tell you other than I've already made the transfer for the ransom money into their account. I now own a seventy percent share in their company. Meaning you'll get the rest of the hundred grand I promised ya."

"Why?" The underlying green of Paulo's skin gave the impression he would upchuck at any moment. "Why are you doing this? Why do you need so much of their family business?"

Impatiently, Hog shrugged. "A personal matter." At Paulo's irritated silence, Hog leaned forward, placing his drink on the coffee table. "Besides, I don't understand why you're so worked up, youngster. If they got back Dr. Andra's wedding rings, they'll most likely get her back. Every movie I've ever watched can attest to that."

Paulo's eyes widened. "How could you possibly know Dr. Andra's wedding rings were returned? You were not there when the ransom note was delivered."

Standing, Hog coughed uneasily. "Now, look here, son—"

Paulo leaped from his chair. "I am not your son," he said, his dark eyes narrowing. "And I am not a naive youngster. Where is she, Mr. Grainger? Where have you taken Dr. Andra?"

Hog felt a gastric churning inside his gut at Paulo's correct assumption. Just as quickly, his nervousness turned to regret, and for a moment, he watched Paulo's expression vacillate between anger and expectancy. He had grown kinda fond of the handsome, albeit highly nervous, youngster. At one time, he had even pondered that Paulo could've been the son he and Beauty never had.

"Well, Mr. Grainger?" Paulo demanded. "Where is she?"

His immediate thought was to say, "Call me Hog," yet he thought better of it. "Paulo, I still don't believe you're seeing the bigger picture." At the other's raised eyebrow, Hog spoke slower. "It's actually quite ingenious, if you think about it. Not only do I get a majority holding in the Theonopilus enterprise, but I'm getting it for free. Don't you get it?"

A measure of bewilderment swept across Paulo's face.

"You see, because the money I'm lending them for the ransom will come back to me for the doctor's return."

Paulo was speechless, and his eyes bulged.

His frame shaking with suppressed mirth, Hog presented his palm. "And here's the best part: the high-and-mighty Theonopilus clan will have to pay me back the money I've already gotten from them through the kidnapping. So technically, in the end, they'll be paying me twice for their family business!" Again, Hog slapped his knee in delight, laughing harder. A second later, he straightened to wipe away a merry tear and glanced over at Paulo. "You've got to admit this scenario is irony at its very best!"

Across the room, Paulo gaped as if staring at a monster so hideous he couldn't fully comprehend what he envisioned. Stupefied, he shook his head. "Why are you doing this to them?"

Hog immediately turned serious, his face flushed, the volcanic pounding of his heart burning like molten lava inside his chest. "That family took from me a most valuable possession, something I can never get back—and I mean to have my justice."

Paulo backed up, covering his mouth.

Hog silently chided himself for his outburst and turned his emotional burner on simmer. Attempting an amicable smile, he moved toward Paulo, who in turn retreated until he hit the wall behind his chair.

"Paulo, I can make you a rich man," Hog said calmly. "How's ten million American dollars to start with? I'll give it to you as a gift for you and your family—so you can financially support them the way I believe, you being the man, want to."

Paulo stared at him, neither accepting nor denying his proposition.

Hog tried again. "Lookee here," he said. "You can even run their business for me. I'll put you in charge and give you a hefty salary on top of the ten million dollars. Then you and your family would be the ones on top—and those Theonopiluses will have to work for you! Doesn't that sound like heaven? It would be as if the universe had suddenly righted, allowing opportunity and fortune to tilt in your direction. You can make that happen."

Hog held on to the comforting fact that once he acquired the olive oil business, he planned to run it into the ground, totally destroying it. Subsequently, there'd be nothing left for Paulo to oversee and manage anyway.

"What d'ya say, son? Wanna get rich?"

Hog noted a small speck of interest within Paulo's eyes. As the younger contemplated the offer in silence, Hog extended his arm.

Paulo considered the hand before him but did not take it.

"Come on," Hog said impatiently, wriggling it for Paulo to take hold. "Make up your mind! Do we have a deal, young man?"

At the word *man*, Paulo's frame straightened. "I will make this deal with you on one condition," he said, his voice strong with determination. "You must take me to Dr. Andra. If she is unhurt and well, only then can I determine you are sincere."

Hog smiled graciously. "Done." He grabbed Paulo's hand and shook hard, only to abruptly abort the handshake. "Let's go."

Hog led the way out of the hotel room to descend the stairs toward the side entrance to the hotel. Heading for the building's rear, he rounded three huge trash bins, making his way to a parking lot behind the structure. Moments later, he stopped before a dilapidated white van with a wooden two-by-four block shoved underneath the front tire. After unlocking the side door, he tugged on it with some difficulty until it finally slid open.

Paulo stopped a few feet away. His neck craning, he stared at the van from a distance, attempting to peer into the dark cargo area.

Hog swept his hand toward the opening. "The doctor's in here, bound and gagged toward the back." At Paulo's indignant sputter, Hog patted the air. "Calm down. Listen, I tossed her in there because frankly, I didn't know what else to do with her. She's not hurt; she's on a pallet, sleeping. I kinda gave her a sedative to knock her out." He stepped back to lean against the passenger-side door. "Come on. Take a peek for yourself."

Paulo moved cautiously, his approach slowing to a stop once he reached the van. He took an elongated moment to eye Hog to his right before he leaned in.

Paulo paused to adjust to the dimness inside, only to withdraw his head. "I do not see h—"

Hog brought the heavy two-by-four high and crashed it down on Paulo's skull. His swift glance around coincided with Paulo's body as it pitched forward, his upper torso landing squarely inside the vehicle. Grunting, he hoisted the younger man's long legs off the ground and shoved, forcing his limp frame deeper inside the van. Grabbing the handle to the door, Hog yanked hard. The door slid a fraction and then stopped.

Mumbling under his breath, he tried again, and the door moved an inch only to stick again. He cursed.

"Signomi, *kirios*—may I be of assistance?"

Hog whipped around to see an employee from the hotel's restaurant staring at him curiously with one hand holding a garbage bag and the other lifting the heavy lid of the trash bin.

Placing a Texas grin on his face, Hog casually moved in front of the van's opening. Briefly peering over his shoulder, his eyes slid back to the busboy's face. "What does 'Signomi, kirios' mean, boy?"

The other scanned the area around him, as if searching for a hidden camera that recorded him for a practical joke. When he found none, he cleared his throat uncertainly. "It means 'Excuse me, sir or mister.'"

Hog nodded agreeably. "Well, partner, I thank you real kindly for your offering. But this is a matter I can handle. Alone."

Watching the Grecian's expression turn wary, Hog again glanced over his shoulder into the van's darkness. He could haul away two bodies as well as one. His grin for the employee widened. "However, if you want to help, be my guest."

The younger man stood motionless to study Hog. Soon his expression transformed from somewhat curious to downright fearful. Keeping an eye on Hog, the man quickly dumped his trash. The bin's lid fell in place with a loud bang. "Signomi, kirios. I am wanted back now." He spun on his heel and disappeared around the hotel corner.

"Wise choice, son," Hog said to the empty space the Grecian had left behind.

Returning to his task, he yanked and pulled until the van's sliding door finally crashed closed. Wiping his brow, he glanced around, making sure he was still alone. He was.

Whistling a peppy tune, Hog bounded around the automobile and climbed into the driver's seat. When he fired up the ignition, the old van spurted as if ready to die out, but after a few stomps on the gas pedal, it roared with renewed life.

His gruff voice broke forth in a made-up song as he exited the back parking lot. He proceeded south along the main country road toward his villa and Paulo's Dr. Andra.

47

Stefano woke with a start, mumbling the name Hog. Stiffly, he raised his head off the mahogany office desk. Using one hand, he massaged a kink in his neck. With the other, he wiped away a string of drool that dangled from his open mouth. He sat up.

Why am I sitting here? What was I doing?

As he blinked away the last of his impromptu nap, his vision came into sharp focus; his eyes immediately skimmed his computer screen, which displayed a news headline from the previous year: "Texan Billionaire to Bail Out Floundering Electronics Firm."

Harlan Orlando Grainger.

He sighed irritably, knowing his sickly body had forced a shutdown due to his frustration at not finding any significant internet story on the man who called himself Hog.

Brooding at his failure, Stefano heard a small noise from behind. Startled, he swung his chair around.

His face haggard looking, Jayson sat watching him. His sunken eyes were bloodshot from either exhaustion or crying, or both, and his usually smiling lips were compressed into a thin, straight line. "I want to talk to you," he said, his voice flat and broken.

Bracing himself for his younger brother's well-deserved tongue-lashing, Stefano stiffened. However, his brow lifted in surprise at Jayson's words.

"First, I would like to apologize for being angry with you during this situation with Andra's kidnapping." He sucked in his breath and let it go in one long exhalation. "After spending time alone, I realized I had only looked at this from my—and Andra's—perspective. You and Papa were trying to see the situation from everyone's perspective." Jayson's eyes lowered. "I wanted to say I'm sorry for being so selfish."

Stefano shifted uncomfortably in his chair, not sure if it was his brother's responsibility to do the apologizing. Their silence dragged on until Jayson finally looked up; only then did Stefano shake his head.

"No, Jayson, I am the sorry one. It was within your right to say and do what you did. This is your wife's safety we are dealing with—no one else's."

"Yes, she is my wife," Jayson said. His tone was not angry, just tired. "And I love her, Stefano. More than you could ever know. Andra's my life—I can't give her up for anyone, especially those kidnappers—not even for you."

Stefano shut his eyes against the pain that spilled from Jayson's, knowing he'd been instrumental in putting it there. "You are right, little brother; I had no right to tamper with your marriage." He opened his eyes, unashamed they were now moist. "But this vow I give to you: I will do whatever it takes to help return Andra safely to your arms again."

Jayson's smile was humorless. "Now who's the poet?"

"Not me, little brother—I will leave such frivolity to you."

"Stefano?"

"Yes, Jayson?"

"Besides the hue of her skin—her beautiful brown skin—what have you got against my Doc?"

Startled at the insightful question, Stefano searched his mind for a reasonable answer—and found none.

At Stefano's silence, Jayson produced a wistful smile, as if pitying him. "All you can see is color. However, what I see is a beautiful, intelligent, loving woman made up of bone and blood vessels and organs, just the same as you and me. The only difference is that her epidermis happens to be darker than ours."

"Epidermis?"

"Skin, big brother." Jayson laughed wearily. "You see, I've

learned a few medical terms from my exceptionally smart wife."

They stared at one another until Jayson broke the connection to study his hands lying uselessly in his lap. "Are you in love with Andra?"

Glad Jayson hadn't the courage to gaze directly at him when asking his question, Stefano was able to answer with some resolve. "No," he said, yet even in his own ears, the word rang out falsely.

The two existed through an uncomfortable silence before Stefano finally coughed. "Have you heard back from the kidnappers?"

Jayson shook his bowed head. "Not a word. I don't know whether it's a good or bad sign at this point."

"It could be either way," Stefano said, hoping to comfort him. He dug emotionally deeper, trying to compose encouraging words that didn't come off sounding trite. "Jayson, do not give in to despair. Cling to your faith, knowing God will allow this situation to come out perfectly in the end."

Jayson looked up, his face appearing both reassured and distressed. "I'll try. But there are moments when, well, it's hard." Despite his doubt, Jayson appeared grateful for Stefano's encouragement. His eyes studied Stefano for a spell. "You might have missed your calling; maybe you should've been a priest yourself."

"Yes, maybe," he said quietly. "Actually, the priesthood was a profession our mother wanted for me. She must have had the ability to foresee my future and predict I would never marry and thought the priesthood would better suit me." Stefano shook his head and smiled sadly. "However, I'm too far gone to engage in such a profound occupation."

"If you say so, big brother. Don't have a myocardial infarction."

Feeling like Racine, Stefano rolled his eyes. "A what?"

"Heart attack."

"Now you're just showing off, little brother."

His smile brief, Jayson stared at the big glass window beyond Stefano, his mind lost in unknown thoughts.

Momentarily, he shook his head as if awakening from a dream. "Next subject."

"Yes, Jayson?"

"Why didn't you tell me sooner that you were dying?"

Stefano stiffened. It was his turn to look away. "I wanted to badly. That was one reason I asked you to return—to inform you of my condition, as well as to have you step in and help Papa run the business." As he fidgeted with the crease in his pants, his mind automatically went to Andra. "But once you returned, the right moment never presented itself."

"Are you sure you're going to die?" Jayson asked, his expression shifting between ire and worry. "What is it you have?"

"Yes, I'm sure." Stefano shrugged carelessly. "I visited three different specialists, and they all ultimately came to the same diagnosis. It's a rare, aggressive form of leukemia, and at any moment, it could elevate into its last malignant stage."

A desperate hush filled the air until Jayson's hesitant voice broke it. "Have you told Papa?"

Looking off, Stefano shook his head.

Jayson's voice rose dramatically. "Well, are you going to tell him? He has a right to know—a right to prepare for your passing."

"Yes." Stefano focused on Jayson's younger eyes, which were so much like his. "I agree. However, I want to wait until this is all over and allow you to get your wife back before I choose to throw more grief onto the fire. Are we agreed?"

Saying nothing, Jayson stood, causing Stefano to mirror him. They stared at one another. Simultaneously, they moved to meet midpoint across the floor. Automatically, their arms wrapped in a brotherly hug; clinging together, their bodies swayed inside their embrace as a nonverbal agreement passed between them.

"I have always been proud of you, my little brother."

"Ditto, my big brother."

Embarrassed, they broke apart to return to their chairs.

Jayson gave a short laugh. "Stefano, remember your first

real girlfriend, Chloe? I had the meanest crush on her. I hated that you wouldn't allow me to tag along on your dates."

Stefano nodded. "Yes, I remember," he said. "Even at ten years old, you were such a bothersome little brat, trying to sabotage us whenever Chloe and I were together. You and I have always been so much alike, our tastes so similar."

"And we still are," Jayson said. "More alike now than ever before."

The room grew silent again. Stefano instinctively knew both he and Jayson shared the same mental image of a beautiful doctor named Andra.

Jayson stirred. "Papa said you made a comment earlier about the return of Andra's rings. It somehow appeared to you as personal."

Stefano grunted.

"How?" Jayson asked.

The mystical feeling of an elusive revelation again tickled Stefano's brain's perimeter; his frustration mounted when he couldn't catch hold of it. Stefano sighed. "I don't know."

The ensuing quiet was broken when Stefano cleared his throat. Avoiding the blue-and-white lily wilting inside its crystal vase, his eyes returned to the computer screen to reexamine the displayed frozen headline. He didn't bother to glance over his shoulder when Jayson strolled over to stare at it too.

If he speculated why Stefano had conducted a Google search on Hog, Jayson chose not to ask. Instead, he let go a reflective sigh. "It's so funny about love. Even someone like Hog can't get over his grief when it comes to his wife."

As he stared at the computer screen, Stefano's defeated thoughts crowded out Jayson's words. Yet once the words eventually filtered in, he mentally waded through his brain fog in order to catch their slippery significance.

His head jerked over his shoulder to stare at Jayson. "Wait one moment. What did you just say?"

"You know, even Hog has feelings despite what you might think of him."

"My sons, is everything alright?" George said, filling the

doorway. "What are you two doing in here? Is there anything I should know?"

Agitated with a mystical sense he was about to obtain knowledge of extreme importance, Stefano swiveled in his chair to face his father. "Papa, tell me everything you can concerning that consumer's death years ago."

Jayson's incredulous stare volleyed between Stefano and George. "The death of what consumer?" he demanded. His expression turned confused as he stared at his father. "Papa?"

George stood rooted at the open door, his face grief-stricken. He shook his head. "Stefano, I confided in you about such matters only because you had taken over the business for me—nothing more!" He stumbled over the threshold to an empty chair. "I do not want to discuss such a tragic moment, especially now."

Stefano stood, and together with Jayson, crossed over to where their father sat. He placed a tender hand on the older man's shoulder. "Papa, I sympathize with your not wanting to dwell on such things, but something tells me this is important." He stooped to stare directly into his father's eyes. "Tell us all you know."

George passed a palsied hand across his forehead. "I don't know the specifics. I chose not to know. I allowed the lawyers to handle it quietly and discreetly." Neither brother spoke as they waited out their father's distressed silence. Finally, the older man sighed. "It was around the time you were away at college, a few years before your mother's"—he swallowed hard—"death. A consumer had a lethal reaction to a batch of our olive oil and, from what I understand, died after ingesting it."

Slowly, Stefano rose to his full height. "No other deaths were involved?"

George quickly shook his head. "No, but I couldn't take any chances. I decided to recall all product that year, as well as the next two years—just to be sure there was no possibility of further consumer contamination."

Stefano stared at his father. A metamorphic change came

over the elder right before his eyes, his frame deflating into bowed despair.

That had to be the year the business started its downward slide.

His father's next words confirmed as much. "I wanted to close the business for good, but I couldn't." His eyes glistened with sorrow as he faced Stefano and Jayson. "I needed to leave this company behind for my sons, just as my father left it to me—despite what had happened."

As George sobbed quietly, his shoulders heaved, causing Jayson to place a gentle arm over them in comfort.

"Papa!" Stefano said, the urgency in his voice regaining George's tearful attention. "Can you recall details of the case? Any particulars at all?"

"I only know it was a female consumer."

Stefano sucked in a quick breath, feeling as if someone had blindsided him with a gut punch. Swiftly, he headed for his computer again. "Jayson, help me," he said over his shoulder, feeling his adrenaline kick in. He returned to his seat and quickly cleared the previous internet article to replace it with the Google search page. After clicking on the "I'm Feeling Lucky" link, he poised his fingers to type. "Mr. Hog's wife name—what was it?"

Jayson's feet quickly brought him to Stefano's side. "Why are you asking? What has Hog got to do with what happened back then or even Andra's kidnapping now?"

Then Jayson's face dimly lit from within, as if he were on the verge of understanding an epic revelation yet couldn't quite grasp it. His voice came forth hoarsely as he pushed past his barricade of unasked questions to answer Stefano. "He called her Beauty—which I believe is a nickname." Jayson's brow wrinkled and then smoothed. "That's all I remember."

"He mentioned another name during the meeting," Stefano said, his own brow furrowing. "I believe it was Lillian."

"Yes," George said wearily. "Yes, you're right, Son. Lillian."

Stefano typed in "Lillian Grainger" and pressed Enter. A story concerning someone named Lillian Grainger, who was nineteen years old at the time of the 1940 census, pulled up.

After clearing the search box, he entered new data: "Harlan and Lillian Grainger." No results were found. Determined, he next typed in "Harlan" and "Beauty Grainger" with a space between. More than a thousand articles mentioning Hog's name popped up, yet the first few links he perused never displayed the name Beauty. Overwhelmed by the fact that he didn't have the mental strength to sift through each one, he sighed in tired defeat.

"Type the terms *Harlan Orlando Grainger, wife,* and *death* into each field," Jayson said over Stefano's shoulder.

After following his instructions, Stefano pressed Enter.

Billionaire Mogul's Wife Dead at Forty-Seven

September 5. Sophia de Vega Grainger, wife of billionaire Texan oil mogul Harlan Grainger, was found dead yesterday at their ranch in Galveston, her death apparently caused by a rare allergic reaction to a batch of contaminated olive oil purchased overseas in Athens, Greece.

The grief-stricken spouse was unavailable for comment. A spokesperson for Mr. Grainger requested that the media respect his wishes for privacy during this difficult time.

"He gave us a fake name for his wife," Stefano said, unsurprised, his voice a flat monotone. "Her name is Sophia."

"But ..." Jayson stuttered after reading the news story, his remaining words trailing off.

His younger son's confused words caused George to bolt from his seat and hurry to the desk to stand next to Stefano's chair. "What?" Upon quickly scanning the article, he grabbed a handful of his shirt. "No. Oh no!"

Stefano's mind skipped backward, his memory's eye skimming over the kidnapper's scrawl across the brown paper wrapped around the ransom box and the way the unknown writer had misspelled Jayson's name; the person had unwittingly scribbled the Americanized version, Jason.

Rapidly, his memory tumbled forward to the previous conversation he'd had with Paulo, when Paulo had revealed Hog knew Stefano's weakness: Andra.

"Harlan Orlando Grainger—our own Mr. Hog—is the person who has Andra," he said grimly. His hands balled into tight fists, painfully cutting off circulation inside his clenched palms. "This I am sure of."

48

Sitting on the bed, Andra flung the scratchy blanket from her shoulders and jumped to her feet the moment she heard the lock disengage from the other side. The heavy panel slowly opened. Grimacing, she observed Hog stick his thick silvery mane inside the room.

"You decent?" Not bothering to wait for her answer, he glanced across the room to swiftly zero in on Andra. His pale blue eyes raked her body with a lewd scan before he pulled the door wider. "Good."

His tall, stocky body filled the doorway, dashing her hope of possibly darting past him. Momentarily, he grinned, as if reading her thoughts. "Don't even think about it, Doctor," he said with a playful wag of his finger. He glanced over at the large container in the corner. "I might have to go over and let your friend crawl out so the two of you can get better acquainted. Would you like that?"

"No."

Hog smiled winningly. "I thought not. So how are you this afternoon?"

She merely blinked at him.

"That's okay. I like a woman who's silent, barefoot, and pregnant." He glanced at her scuffed white tennis shoes and chuckled. "Well, two outta three ain't bad, my beautiful filly." He paused and then abruptly pointed a finger upward, as if he'd just had a lightbulb moment. "Ah, here's a thought. I believe I'll call you Beauty for short. I'm pretty sure my first Beauty wouldn't mind if you replace her, especially since she's long gone. In fact, she'd probably want me to, seeing as how she's always desired my happiness."

At Andra's silence, Hog glanced over to the prepackaged food and six-pack of bottled water he'd left earlier; only two bottles were empty, and the wrapped sandwiches remained untouched. His face displayed his annoyance. "You know, you should eat to keep up your strength for me and the little one inside ya. You're gonna need it."

Instantly, Andra wished she had eaten just so she could vomit his food all over him.

Ignoring the daggers in her eyes, he casually leaned against the doorpost, his orbs again scraping her frame until she felt as if she'd already been raped.

"You know something else? I've never made love to an expectant mother before. You see, my first Beauty couldn't have children, so I never had the pleasure with her. It'll be my first time, and I'm sure I'll enjoy it immensely. From what I understand, you will too." He held up a palm as if she'd disagreed. "Listen, I've heard tell the woman's erotic zones are heightened and way off the charts during pregnancy. It's a known fact there's nothing like makin' love to a woman with child."

She stared in disbelief at his lined forehead. "You're amazing, you loony tune."

At his "Thank you," she scowled. "You've sucked in so much useless, idiotic facts inside that ten-gallon vacuum cleaner of yours that it's a miracle your head hasn't exploded yet."

To her dismay, Hog grinned pleasantly. "Well, darlin', I try to keep current." He wiggled one eyebrow. "Afterward, I can cross that off my bucket list of things I've always wanted to do. Right, Beauty?"

She grew nauseated at his words, her mind stalling at the memory of the airplane restroom, where Jayson had said practically the same thing concerning his own bucket list. She glared at the man before her. "My name is Mrs. Jayson Theonopilus."

"Aw, come on, Beauty—don't be like that." He winked saucily. "You'll get used to me. Watch and see."

She couldn't help but gape at him in bewilderment. During med school, she had studied about people who outwardly functioned normally in society, and maybe even displayed extraordinary brilliance when it came to business, yet possessed a mentally imbalanced, psychotic nature. Evidently, she was looking at such a case study.

"I'd rather crawl in there with the snake," she spat. "Mister, you're a disgusting piece of trash and as batty as they come. You need help!"

Casually, Hog deflected her venom. "We'll see. In the meantime ..." He pivoted within the doorframe and bent over. His voice came out in puffs as he lifted a heavy object off the floor and threw it over one shoulder. "I brought you a visitor."

Andra sucked in an abrupt breath as she witnessed Hog carry an unconscious Paulo into the room like a sack of weighty potatoes. Blood dripped from an open wound on Paulo's head, landing in small splatters upon the concrete floor at Hog's cowboy-boot-encased feet.

49

Standing off to the right outside the Theonopilus family's office door, Racine gasped.

At the sound, Sly slapped a hard palm over Racine's lips while placing a vertical finger against her own to silently shush her. Shaking her head, her long, flowing locks swinging about her shoulders, she mouthed, "Be quiet."

Racine pushed aside the girl's hand and violently mouthed, "Okay."

Motioning for Sly to follow, Racine swiftly led the way back to the closed sitting room door, behind which Al still slept. Quietly, she peeked inside, and upon hearing the even breathing of her mother, she pulled back and closed the door.

Whipping around, Racine faced Sly, her blazing eyes barely noticing the beautiful setting of the spacious round foyer. "They just said that son of a bitch Grainger has Andra," Racine whispered. "It doesn't make sense. He was the one who gave us the money for her return. What reason would he have to kidnap her?"

At Sly's nervous silence, Racine grabbed her upper arm and shook hard. "You know what? Spill what you know—or I'll beat the crap outta you right here and now!"

"Okay, okay," Sly whined, wrenching free from Racine's grip. Soothingly, she rubbed her arm. "I will tell you all."

Whispering slowly, Sly recounted her conversations with Paulo concerning his dealings with Hog.

Racine clenched both fists. "You knew this and didn't say—" She quickly closed her mouth when she heard a noise.

Helena quickly waddled into the area from the direction of the kitchen; the older woman's face was a mask of frightened concern, her expression a question mark. Due to her abrupt appearance, Racine's imagination fed her an image of the older servant listening through a crack in the swinging kitchen door.

Stopping before them, the older woman wrung her hands. "Ms. Sly, Ms. Racine," she said slowly in English, "is something I can do?"

Racine produced a gentle, dismissive smile. "No, Helena, but thank—"

"No wait!" Sly said, cutting Racine off. "Maybe you can." Sly sashayed over to Helena and draped an arm across her rounded shoulders, pulling the servant close. "Maybe you've heard gossip among the others in town," she said softly and persuasively. "Yes, about a Texas American having a villa somewhere around here for some time?"

Intrigued, Racine moved closer to the two.

At first, Helena's expression was blank, but when Sly repeated her question in Greek, the older woman's face broke out in a smile. She gestured back at Sly and spoke rapidly. At a break in her words, the servant woman spread her meaty arms wide. She then went on to disclose more information.

Racine said insistently, "What's she saying?" but Sly urgently waved her to be quiet. Racine squashed the overwhelming desire to belt her one.

More foreign words slipped excitedly from Helena's mouth.

"Do you know where this villa is located?" Sly asked, beaming at the servant as if they had all the time in the world.

Helena, her smile eager, reciprocated in broken English. "On outskirts of Athens—one hour travel."

At Sly's prompting to find out the exact directions as best as she could, Helena waddled off to do her bidding. Grinning, Sly turned to face a severely agitated Racine.

"You'd better tell me all Helena said."

Sly chuckled, gleefully pulling Racine into a friendly hug. Racine waited in stiff irritation for the embrace to end, and when it did, she peevishly pushed away the Grecian, who proceeded to clap with glee. "So tell me, airhead!"

"Helena says someone in the village knows where the man's villa is located. You see, there are villagers who are waiting to repair and clean it. It is to pay big"—Sly imitated Helena by stretching her arms wide—"when it happens."

Sly took a moment to glance around surreptitiously, causing Racine's fist to rise. Sensing she was a prime candidate for physical harm, Sly quickly returned her green eyes to Racine. "Helena's friend Mara has a son and daughter who are waiting for a start date. I told her to call her friend for directions."

Her face brightening, Racine sighed in relief. "Okay, good. Now we can tell the men and make them check it out."

Sly's eyes widened as she shook her head. "No, no, no! We must not tell them."

Racine stopped in midstride. "And why not? We can't handle this alone."

"Oh, can't we, Detective Cagney? If we give them this information, they will make us stay home!" Stubbornly, Sly crossed her arms. "And what if this intel is wrong? Then the whole family would be disappointed for nothing." She shook her head again. "No, we must find out if Mr. Hog has Yatros on our own."

Racine stared at her cohort, trying to figure out if what she suggested was ludicrous or the most ingenious thing she'd spit out of her mouth to date. Andra's face—bloody, distorted, and completely still—flashed before her eyes.

"Okay, Detective Lacey," she said. "So what if Hog has people at his villa to help him? You know, like guards or hired guns? How are we to maneuver past them?"

Sly once again shook her head, staring sadly at Racine as if she were imbecilic. "I do not believe it is possible." At Racine's attempt to interrupt her, Sly produced an upraised palm. "First, this is not Mr. Hog's native country; I do not feel he would take the chance in hiring someone here to help him kidnap anyone, only to chance the same someone informing on him. We Greeks are loyal to one another. I believe he is too clever for that."

"Okay," Racine said begrudgingly. "Go on."

"Second," Sly continued, "if he had brought others with him for the kidnapping, the whole village would be alerted to more than one American traveling together—as with the case of you and your mother. The village knew of your arrival before Dr. Andra did."

Racine sighed. She hated when Sly exposed her smarts without warning.

Sly smiled charmingly. "We must go check the place out. If we see suspicious activity, we will return and alert the family." Calmly, she performed a quick lift of her shoulders. "And if we find zilch, well, at least we did not cause alarm for nothing."

Zilch? "Seriously, dude, you've got to stop watching so much TV." To Racine's annoyance, Sly tapped a strappy-sandaled foot while she waited patiently for a response. In the end, Racine let out a noisy exhalation. "Okay, Sherlock, I'm in."

"Sherlock Holmes." Sly beamed. "He is also my favorite!"

"Good gracious," Racine muttered.

As if on cue, Helena pushed past the swinging kitchen door with a folded note grasped inside her hand. She eagerly waved it at the two huddled women.

"I have got the goods," she said in fragmented English. Smiling, she shoved the paper at Sly, who snatched it. "You are good to go!"

Again, Racine rolled her eyes toward the ceiling.

Evidently, Sly was not the only Grecian woman disturbingly hooked on American detective programs.

50

"**N**o!" Andra called out.

She raced across the floor when Hog moved to dump Paulo's body in a corner of the cellar. Her eyes tearing, she gently cradled Paulo's head as it swung upside down from Hog's shoulder. "Please lay him on the cot. Gently."

"But if I put him there, where are you gonna sleep?"

"What do you care?" she said, glaring at him. "Just do it, please."

Shrugging his free shoulder, Hog meandered to the narrow cot and unceremoniously dropped Paulo onto it. "Okay, suit yourself," he said, straightening. "Although I highly doubt he's gonna last through the night."

Andra swiftly covered Paulo with her blanket, her hands economically tucking it tightly about his limp body to prevent him from going into shock. "Not if I can help it!" she said over her shoulder. "Remember, you nut job, I am a doctor."

"Oh yeah, I keep forgettin'." He chuckled. "You know, my other Beauty was smart too. I believe intellectual women make the best lovers. The mental wheels are always turning, if you know what I mean."

Unfortunately, she did. As usual, the older Texan's inane chatter managed to steer toward the gutter.

Bending over Paulo, she noted his ashen pallor and closed eyes. Opening each lid, she peeked inside, finding his pupils were not yet fixed and dilated, which signified he hadn't lapsed into a coma. However, listening to his breathing, she didn't like the way it came out in shallow puffs. Gently, she turned his head to take in his dark hair turned even darker by the blood that leaked from an open gash.

Her blood pressure rose, pushing her anger to extreme boiling levels at the man who'd caused the wound. Breathing deeply, she closed her eyes and took a moment to say a brief prayer to stabilize both Paulo's condition and her rage.

She opened her eyes, focusing on her new patient. "I need some bandages, gauze, towels, alcohol—anything you can give me to stop the bleeding and cleanse his wound." She slowly moved his head to the other side to assess the damage from that angle. "And bring me some hand sanitizer and more bottled water."

Hog shook his head. "No can do, Beauty. You have to make do with what's available to you down here."

She rose to her full height, glaring at him with hate-filled eyes. "Why?"

Glancing at Paulo's pale face, Hog placed large hands on his hips. "Like I told ya, he probably won't last the night." His eyes moved to her chest only to rise and meet hers. "Besides, it will give ya something to do with your time until we—"

Automatically, her hand balled into a fist, and she wanted to ram it into his leering face. Yet knowing she probably couldn't put enough force behind it to knock him out cold, she shook it at him. "You odious, egotistical, creepy, insane maniac!"

"I have to tell you—you're cute when you git all riled. Like a sexy lil' bobcat."

"I can't stand you, you evil son of a—"

Hog's hand swiped the air. "Now, Beauty, stop it! You're making me blush with such sweet talk." His chuckle turned devilish. "But I believe you can catch more flies with honey than you can with vinegar."

"Now you're comparing yourself to a fly?" she jeered. "Well, I wouldn't bother insulting it in the comparison. You are what flies hover around, you insufferable piece of garbage!"

Andra cringed at his loud, boisterous laugh.

"Woman, you crack me up!" He stopped to wipe away an imaginary tear. When he smiled again, however, the smile didn't quite reach his eyes. "You'd better be nice to me—for your sake as well as Paulo's. You understand?"

Standing next to Hog, Andra could feel the evilness radiating from the madman's soul, its darkness wanting to reach out and pull her essence inside him.

"I understand," she said, stepping to one side to put more space between them.

"Good girl. Like I said, I won't bring you anything medical— but I will acquiesce to your demand for more water as well as the hand sanitizer. Being a doctor, you most likely want germ-free hands." Hog turned to leave and stopped, his orbs again drawn to her body. "Maybe you can use your bra as a bandage. That way, there'll be less for me to remove when the time comes."

She shuddered. *Once again, the road straight to him and Sleazeville.*

At her silence, he clicked his tongue. "You're real smart, Beauty. You'll figure out a way to keep that youngster alive."

"Like you care," she muttered.

Hog's cowboy boots made a stomping noise as he headed for the door. "In a way, I do care—just like you—but for entirely different reasons. As a doctor, you'll be upholding your sworn oath to save a life." He reached the door and paused. "As for me, as long as you're keeping him alive, you have no cause to try to escape. If you try, you'll be forced to leave him behind."

At his abrupt pause, her mind envisioned different ways an unconscious Paulo could die by Hog's hands.

"And I wouldn't hesitate to finish him off. Of course, his death would then be on your head, wouldn't it, Beauty?"

"I hate you."

"I'll take your hate, Beauty. You wanna know why? Hate's just a step across the line to love. A thin line, in fact." He chuckled. "Believe me, it's only a matter of time before I can and will push your feelings over to love's glorious side."

Hog's unearthly grin sickened Andra, and she became even more nauseated.

"I guess there's no need to be locking you in anymore."

His eyes traveled the room, radiating false pity as they fell to Paulo's still frame. "You two wouldn't get far, would ya?"

Knowing her despicable captor was right, Andra chose not to debate on the matter; she instead addressed another issue. "When are you going to get rid of that snake?"

Hog chuckled again, appearing tickled pink at her fear. "In due time, my Beauty—when it suits me."

"But I haven't heard anything moving around inside." She gave him a suspicious look. "Maybe there's no snake at all. Maybe you're just trying to scare me."

Smiling brightly, Hog shrugged. "Well, if you think that's the case, go find out for yourself."

Shifting nervously, she scanned the snake's container only to swing fearful eyes back to the Texan-born human serpent.

"I thought so," he said, nodding once. "Like I said, I'll get it out soon enough. I've just got to take care of a few dangling participles."

Laughing at his own joke, Hog exited the door, leaving it ajar.

For the first time, Andra witnessed the door to her prison remain open. She listened to Hog's heavy footsteps cover ground beyond the cellar's room. Seconds later, she heard them clomp up the stairs.

Despite her captivity—and the big, fat black snake that served as her and Paulo's roommate—she sagged in relief at his disappearance into the shadowy area beyond. However, her body flinched at his abrupt yell from the top step, which made her feel as if he were still too close for comfort.

"Come upstairs anytime, and roam the villa. I've thrown open all the shutters to let the glorious sunlight in. This is your home now." Out of sight, a door creaked somewhere above. "Only be sure not to forget about your patient, Paulo— and stay inside for his sake."

Andra threw her arms about her, shivering more from the icy evilness of the deranged man who currently walked the floors above her than from the chilly air that circulated in the cellar room below him. Her eyes returned to the snake's lodging and then to an unconscious Paulo.

Determined, she lowered to her knees beside him, resting her elbows on the cot next to his head. Clasping her hands together, she closed her eyes tightly and prayed.

51

Stefano reached for the office desk phone with an urgency that caused his hand to tremble even more than before; however, at Jayson's restraint, his resolve turned into shock.

"No," Jayson said, pushing Stefano's hand off the receiver. "No."

"What do you mean no?" He swiveled in his chair to face his brother directly. "We must get this information concerning Grainger to the police."

Again, Jayson shook his head. "You read the ransom note. No police."

"But this is someone who refers to himself as a farm animal!"

Jayson nodded. "Exactly. This is a man who's lost what matters most to him—his Beauty. In my opinion, his actions appear as if even his money doesn't matter." Jayson turned away from Stefano to pace the floor. "Hog managed to fool Andra and me so completely from the start. We didn't see this coming. He's dangerous."

Stefano's body sagged. "Yes, of course—you are correct." He sighed loudly. "Little brother, what we are dealing with is someone who may have been driven insane by his grief."

George rose from his chair, his frame no longer stooped in despair but straight with determination. "No, my sons, this type of insanity has been with Mr. Hog long before his wife's tragedy. I believe her passing only brought it to life." He stared at one son and then the other. "So what are we to do?"

Abruptly, Stefano stood. He resumed pacing where Jayson

had left off. "We must go get Andra ourselves. No outside interference."

Both helplessness and fearlessness comprised Jayson's expression. "But how do we find out where Hog has taken Andra?"

Stefano stopped in his tracks. Out of the blue, Helena's image starring in different scenarios mentally materialized: eavesdropping, watching, and observing. She had the ability to obtain the latest news and dealings in and around the village, whether fact, fiction, or folklore.

"Helena," he blurted out. Immediately grabbing the phone, he dialed the kitchen's extension. Upon hearing her voice, he exhaled in relief. "Helena, meet us in the front foyer." He hung up. At the others' astonishment, he smiled grimly.

"Helena?" Jayson blurted out. "Helena is what you have to go on? What could she possibly know?"

"Yes, Son," George said, casting a worried glance at Stefano, as if afraid Hog's craziness had rubbed off on him. "I'm not quite sure how she could be of service to us."

"Helena's knowledge of activity within the village might give us a clue to Hog's whereabouts." He pushed by Jayson to head for the door. "It is the only option we have at this moment. Come!"

Swiftly, the men headed for the foyer, intersecting with Helena just as she burst through the swinging kitchen door, her hand holding high a piece of paper.

"Helena!" George called out. He stopped short when she rushed up to thrust her note at him.

"Here. You might need to use this information," she said, her voice hopeful.

George gently took the proffered paper and read the scrawled words with a confused air. He looked up. "Helena, what is this?"

"This is the address where the Texas American lives."

Having obtained information they needed but not yet asked for, the three men looked at one another before collectively returning their amazed gazes to Helena.

"You need this, right?" she asked.

"But I do not understand. How did you know to give this to us?" George asked, handing the note to Jayson. "How?"

Her face calm, she folded her ample arms across her belly. "I know."

Jayson turned away from her in impatience, dismissing her to focus on Stefano. "It doesn't matter. We've got to get moving and find Andra before—"

"Agreed." Stefano hurriedly addressed their father. "Please stay behind to watch over the ladies until we can investigate this."

"Yes, Son, I will. Be careful, both of you."

At Stefano's and Jayson's nods, Helena cleared her throat and jerked her head toward the closed door of the formal sitting room. "Ms. Sly and Ms. Racine are not there. Only Ms. Al," she said.

"What do you mean they're not there?" Jayson sped to the door and opened it, spying Al sleeping soundly on the couch. He whipped around. "Helena, where are Racine and Sly?"

She pointed to the piece of paper he held in his hand.

"Our Father in heaven," George muttered. His voice rose. "Helena, what time did they set out?"

"About half hour," she said, her body language growing more uneasy as each second passed. Her round eyes welled with tears. "Did I do something wrong, Mr. George?"

His expression showed he didn't know how to answer the question, so he simply shook his head.

"I don't get it," Jayson said to no one in particular. "How did they figure out to ask for this particular information?"

Stefano suspected the younger ladies had taken lessons from Helena's eavesdropping and gotten the information from outside his office.

"It does not matter," he said brusquely. "We need to stop them before they too fall into this madman's grasp."

Nodding, Jayson stepped forward to place a hand upon George's shoulder. "Papa, would you stay with Andra's mother and fill her in on what's happened?"

"Of course." Concern for Stefano and Jayson caused George's eyes to bounce worriedly between the two. "Again, be careful. I cannot afford to lose both my sons at this point in my life."

Stefano sensed Jayson's poignant stare and met it forthright, knowing his younger brother's thoughts deliberated on his impending death. "No, Papa, you will not lose us—not yet. I promise." Stefano broke Jayson's stare, and his misting eyes beheld his father's. "If we do not return within four hours, take Helena's information to the police anyway." He waited for George's nod. Then, to Jayson, he said, "Let's go."

Not unlike the famous crime-fighting duos admired from their childhood past, the brothers quickly exited the front door and made their way—not to Batman's Batmobile or Green Hornet's Black Beauty but to Stefano's powerful, sporty Jaguar.

52

Andra rolled Paulo onto his stomach. With extreme care, she positioned his head to one side so as not to cut off his air supply.

The faint moan he uttered was sweet music to her ears. It was a good sign because she knew he still hadn't fallen into a dangerous coma—or worse.

After first dousing her hands with the liquid sanitizer Hog had brought along with extra water, she bent and carefully moved aside a chunk of Paulo's matted hair. She examined his wound more closely. Although he had lost blood, she was relieved to find the gash was not as deep as she'd first thought. Biting her lower lip in absorbed concentration, she touched the open skin with delicate fingers, noting the blood flow had ebbed to a slow leak. Still, she would need to stop the flow completely before he eventually bled to death.

For the moment, that wasn't her main concern. What worried her was the possibility of internal hemorrhaging or irreparable damage to Paulo's fragile brain.

Straightening, she placed her hands on her hips and surveyed her surroundings. Upon inspecting the old cellar walls more closely, she noted a crumbling, dry claylike substance holding each layer of bricks together. She crossed over to one wall, ran a finger along a groove between two vertical rows, and then brought her dust-covered finger to eye level. Although she knew the crumbly material was unsanitary, she could use it to plug up Paulo's bleeding gash.

Andra made her way over to the door left ajar by Hog.

Cautiously, she poked her head out and listened. When she was assured Hog was nowhere in the lower-level vicinity, she pulled the door closed.

Quickly, she unbuttoned her blouse, stopping every once in a while to listen for any movement from upstairs. When she was sure she only heard silence, she removed her shirt. Using her teeth, she caught hold of the lower section of the garment and tore off a half inch all around the base. She paused as her mind replayed what Hog had suggested she do for a bandage.

Glancing over at her patient, determined, she reached behind her to unsnap her bra. Removing it, she hissed as her swollen breasts popped free to settle heavily unencumbered, their weight sending stinging sensations into both nipples. She forced herself to breathe deeply while her upper body got used to being unbound.

After a moment, she probed the cushiness of her sports brassiere, which was made from a heavy, absorbent fabric. "Jay, buddy," she whispered, smiling, "I'm glad I followed my first instinct this morning and threw this on instead of the slutty lacy bra you usually like." She sobered, speaking to her undies. "Find me, baby."

A thump overhead caused Andra to pause. Not hearing an accompanying approach of cowboy-boot footsteps, she quickly slipped on her torn top. It was then that Lady Andra spoke up.

You might as well be naked. Do you not think that peasant above is not going to notice the absence of your bra?

Yes, she knew he would take notice.

Determined to push aside thoughts concerning the perverted Texan, she focused on Paulo. After grabbing two waters, she used bottle number one to soak the torn blouse piece. Kneeling next to the cot, she proceeded to use the remaining water to rinse Paulo's wound while she dabbed at it with the saturated cloth. For several minutes, she cleansed the area as best as she could, and then she pressed the bloodied strip tightly against the broken skin to stop any fresh blood flow.

Groaning, Andra stood to massage her stiff knees, brushing off the dust on her jeans in the process. After hobbling over to the section of wall offering the most crumbling clay, she used her finger to painstakingly dig for granules until pieces filled her palm. Satisfied with the amount, she carefully poured water, a few drops at a time, onto the clay until it formed a thick Play-Doh-like substance.

Upon returning to Paulo, Andra dumped her clay onto the wet rag and then swabbed the open gash with liquid sanitizer. Next, using her thumb and finger, she pinched the wound shut with one hand while packing the clay mixture atop the closed wound with the other, until it was completely covered.

"How're you doing, buddy?" she asked her unconscious patient. "I'm almost done. Don't you worry; you're going to be okay. You hear me?"

Vaguely, she heard another distant thump overhead, but she chose to ignore it to focus on her task. She opened the second water and rinsed away the remaining blood and leftover plaster from the torn cloth. After wringing it out thoroughly, she folded it into a thick square bandage and covered the wound.

Andra placed one bra cup over the cloth. She worked economically, her hands steady as she wrapped the rest of the bra around his head and fastened the hook and eye together securely against his forehead.

Her task done and her fastidious focus broken, she once again noticed the cellar's chill. Retrieving the only chair in the room, she pulled it near the cot and sat down. Wrapping her arms about her, she watched Paulo like a dutiful sentry, realizing she wouldn't be able to fall asleep.

To take her mind off the brisk temperature, she occupied herself with something that would at least warm her spiritually.

"Lord," she prayed, "please touch Paulo's body for a complete recovery. I also pray for the safety and well-being of my and Jay's family." She paused. "Oh yeah, Lord, please help Jay find me."

Andra jerked awake at hearing a low moan. As she blinked, her vision came into focus. Paulo was lying on his stomach on the cot with one arm hanging off its side. To her relief, his eyes were open, yet they registered confusion. They searched the dimly lit room to ultimately land upon Andra's face.

"Well, hello there, Mr. Sleepyhead." Smiling gently, she rubbed her outer arms to warm them and then scooted her chair closer. She reached out to smooth the side of his face. "How do you feel?"

Paulo closed his eyes, as if blindly gauging his status. When his lids reopened, Andra read more disorientation within them. Deliberately, she held back a pity-filled sigh.

"Dr. Andra, my head hurts. I do not know where I am."

Andra bent closer, brushing his thick black hair away from his bra-covered forehead. "We're in Harlan Grainger's cellar. Can you remember anything prior to him bringing you here?"

Confusion and disbelief warred upon his face. Andra waited, knowing the disorienting amnesia would clear soon.

I hope.

"Yes," he groaned after a long moment. Attempting to push himself up with weak limbs, he grunted in frustration when he couldn't. "It was that terrible Mr. Hog. He told me he would bring me to you to make sure you were all right."

Andra straightened. "I see."

But she didn't. Many questions swirled inside her head concerning Paulo's relationship with her hated captor, yet she bit her lip to hold them back, knowing now wasn't the time for an interrogation.

She placed a restraining hand on his back when he again attempted to get up. "Paulo, don't move! Try to get some more rest."

Agitated, he stirred. "This Hog. Trying to take the family business." With much difficulty, he inhaled in order to continue. "Kidnapped you to make sure he would succeed."

"With Paulo's help, of course."

At the voice behind her, Andra jumped to her feet. She whipped around to witness Hog's presence fill the doorway.

Immediately, the Texan's blue eyes alighted upon Andra's breasts, whose unbound heaviness jiggled in her startled state.

Trying not to show fear, she stood her ground and endured his penetrating gaze. Still, she couldn't help but flinch when he licked dusty lips.

"Well, I'll be. Looks like you took my advice after all." His eyes still glued to her breasts, he slowly approached. "Beauty, your turnaround in obeying me was quicker than even I expected. It's gonna be so special when we finally come together; you're gonna enjoy—"

"Never," she said, interrupting. "I will never enjoy anything with you."

Paulo coughed in agitation. "You leave Dr. Andra alone, or I will ..."

The Texan stopped, looking amused. "Or you'll do what—with that bra tied around your head? Get real, son." His ancient blue eyes returned to Andra. "Besides, you're one of the reasons my Beauty's here with me today—so I guess I owe you that much."

Andra stood between Paulo and Hog, her stance protective. She glared at Hog. "What do you mean Paulo's responsible for me being here?" she demanded.

"Dr. Andra." Paulo coughed weakly. "I can explain."

"Don't bother, boy; she won't believe you." Hog chuckled. "You see, your friend here wanted money and power to get over on the Theonopilus clan."

"Please, Dr. Andra. It was nothing like how he—"

"And he needed me to help him do it," Hog said. He shook his head. "I guess living in the shadows of those Theonopilus young'uns all this time finally got to the boy."

"My family. Dr. Andra," Paulo said, tears running sideways over the bump of his nose to hit the mattress in tiny splashes, "I was stupid. I was trying to provide for my family."

"Enough!" Andra cried. She pivoted to kneel beside Paulo's bed, looking directly into his watery eyes. "It is okay, Paulo. I understand you're not to blame."

Hog grunted indignantly behind her. "Then who is to blame? Me?"

Andra leaped up on angry feet. "Yes, of course you!"

Agitated, she crossed her arms under her breasts to give them some support. "Who else could it be, you sick, perverted maniac?"

Hog locked in on her front again, his blue eyes ablaze with a lusty fire.

"Beauty, come with me," Hog said suddenly. At her wide-eyed hesitation, he glanced briefly at Paulo before returning his gaze to her. "Come with me upstairs if you want your patient to live. I've waited long enough."

His threat was unmistakable; she truly believed the older yet powerful Texan psycho wouldn't hesitate to carry out his plans to finish off Paulo.

"No, Dr. Andra, no," Paulo said, his weak voice determined. "I would rather die at his hands than allow him to touch you."

Looking over her shoulder at him, Andra shook her head. "But I prefer you don't, Paulo." Praying her expression conveyed her forgiveness for whatever part he'd played in her present situation, Andra smiled gently. "It's going to be okay. You hear me? Okay."

Paulo closed his eyes as if he couldn't bear to watch her sacrifice for him.

"It doesn't matter, does it?" Hog asked. The lust inside his orbs caused them to burn brightly. "Whether he lives or dies, whether you resist or comply, I'm still gonna have you."

"Curse you." Andra threw her captor a freezing glower. "Lead on, crazy Captain Bligh."

Hog chuckled. "Beauty, you've just bought your patient a little more time."

"No, Dr. Andra," Paulo whispered. His voice then grew stronger to spit out, "You are a pig, Mr. Hog!"

Ignoring Paulo's pun insult, Hog stepped to one side, sweeping an arm toward the cellar's open door. "You lead the way, Mrs. Christian," he said, his voice conveying his delight at her *Mutiny on the Bounty* reference.

Throwing her shoulders back, Andra walked past Hog, through the door, and into territory she had no knowledge of.

Cautiously, she made her way to the stairs which led to the upper level—and her unknown fate.

She felt her skin crawl when she not only heard, but also felt, Hog's evil presence close behind her.

53

With total abandon, Sly plowed her brand-new RAV4 through the wooded green hillsides of Greece.

Fearful for her life, Racine gripped the safety handle above. Her seat-belted body jerked with each jolt of Sly's speeding vehicle. The car sped along as if it were part of the wind that blew over the dirt country roads. Her mind shifted into a state of continuous prayer to God Almighty for their safe arrival at the appointed destination.

Yet she also prayed that if they did make, God would grant her enough restraint not to jump from the vehicle and quickly, without mercy, beat the driver to death with her bare hands.

A few times, the tires hit a prominent bump only to momentarily sail airborne before landing on all fours again. During one extremely hard bump, Racine gathered enough mettle to turn Sly's way. She couldn't help but marvel at the determined, ecstatically charged expression of the driver. Random strands of Sly's black hair whipped violently about her face inside the vehicle, while other tresses were sucked outside her window, billowing with curly abandon against the current.

Racine could almost imagine Sly sticking her head outside the open window at any moment to holler, "Yahoo!"

Yet she had to admit, despite the frightening excessive speed, she was glad to know they would get to Andra sooner— that was, if they survived the ride there.

"Hey, when did you get this car?" Racine yelled her way.

Her sights glued to the road, Sly laughed with delight.

"It was a present from my brother only yesterday!" she yelled back. Her glowing eyes shifted to Racine. "You like?"

Racine wanted to shrug in an "I couldn't care less" fashion, but she was too busy hanging on for dear life. "Sly, do you even know where you're going?" she asked even louder over the rushing wind and racing engine. "Do you have a clue?"

Unexpectedly, the utility vehicle lurched to one side and back again. Racine could only assume some woodland creature crossing the road at its own risk had been given a divine reprieve from being squashed to death beneath Sly's speeding tires.

"Yes, yes, Racine—I grew up around here."

Racine struggled not to imagine mangled human bodies and automobile parts intertwined, burning inside a fiery crash, and instead focused on Sly's animated profile. "What do you mean you grew up around here? I thought you lived next door to Jayson's family all your life?"

In horror, Racine watched Sly remove one hand from the steering wheel to brush aside a bothersome strand of hair that whipped across her eyes. A shriek formed at the base of her throat and she wanted to scream, "Keep both hands on the wheel, crazy!" However, Racine realized screaming hysterically at the driver might place them in graver danger, considering the speed at which they traveled.

Across the seat, Sly laughed with carefree abandonment. "No, silly! I have family around this area, but I have not seen them since my mother and father passed." To Racine's relief and then alarm, Sly placed both hands on the wheel only to take her sparkling green eyes off the road and dangerously grin her way. "Please, Racine, trust me. I know where to go."

Racine pointed to the road before them, causing Sly to laugh again. Smiling endearingly, she faced forward to resume her driving.

The women kept silent for the remaining miles, each in her private thoughts. Soon enough, Racine felt the vehicle's deceleration. Her heart pounding, she realized they were about to arrive at their destination. She sat straighter, rubbing her sweaty palms on her bare thighs.

At a narrow path ahead, Sly turned right and reduced her speed even more to travel through a dense, forest-like area.

"What are you doing?" Racine asked. Tense, she leaned forward to stare beyond the windshield gently lashed by the branches of green foliage. "Where are we?"

In silent concentration, Sly slowed to a crawl and maneuvered the automobile into a small clearing. Stopping, she threw the vehicle into park, and her foot pressed hard on the emergency brake. With a firm turn of her slender wrist, she cut off the engine.

Unbuckling herself, Sly twisted in her seat toward Racine. "We must conceal ourselves. We do not want this Mr. Hog to catch us sneaking on him."

Before Racine had a chance to answer, Sly opened her door and jumped out.

Now fuming, Racine mimicked her actions, slamming the door behind her. Quickly standing atop the running board on her side, she scowled across its roof at Sly. "Listen up, buddy! This is my sister we're here to rescue, so I'm in charge." She paused to intensify her glare. "You got that, Lacey?"

Sly hesitated, her face earnest as she contemplated Racine's words. "Yes, I understand. I am truly sorry."

Taken aback by her cohort's immediate contriteness, Racine was rendered speechless for a few seconds.

"So?" Sly said after the silence lengthened uncomfortably. "What do you want to do, Cagney?"

"Well, first, we need to erase this Cagney-and-Lacey thing," she said with a cough. After jumping to the ground, Racine circled the vehicle toward Sly. "Second, we need to stake out the place to see what's what."

Racine paused, searching the foreign land. "So, hmm, since you know this area, lead on."

Grinning broadly, Sly motioned to Racine.

The Grecian dove into the thick foliage, and after feeling a flash of uncertainty, Racine went after her. To her disconcertment, she ducked and dodged swinging branches, prickly bushes, and rough-edged boulders for more than a mile. Suddenly, Sly cleared the brush and abruptly stopped at an overlooking ridge.

Breathing hard, Racine pushed through the last of the bushes and nearly collided with Sly. Leaning over with her hands on her knees, she stole a breathless glance at her cohort.

"Why aren't you"—Racine coughed—"out of breath?"

"Pilates," she said simply.

Figures. "So what do you see?"

Shielding her eyes against the late-afternoon sun, Sly slowly scanned the expansive landscape. Suddenly, she gasped. "There!" She pointed toward the lower valley at a sprawling yet timeworn edifice. "See that villa over there?"

Straightening, Racine moved closer to Sly, her eyes traveling the length of the girl's arm to see a house; next to it was a partially hidden old white van parked alongside the north wall.

Overcoming her shortness of breath, Racine wanted to jump for joy. "It's the van Mom talked about! I know it is! Andra's in there—let's go!"

Racine moved forward, but Sly immediately grabbed her arm. Livid, Racine glanced at the smooth olive-colored hand that restrained her. "Get your grubby paws off me!"

"Racine, I am sure this Hog person has moved Dr. Andra from the van to inside his villa. I believe we must search there." Sly dropped the offending hand and raised one perfectly arched eyebrow. "We must proceed—how do you say?—stealthily."

Begrudgingly, Racine remained still, realizing her rashness at trying to get to Andra might end with them getting kidnapped as well—or worse.

Sly's next words agreed with her. "However, we do not want to get caught and be like Dr. Andra, do we?"

"No, we do not." Racine's focus returned to the villa, and she scanned the land surrounding it. All appeared quiet; the inactivity made the structure look like a deserted lover, but she didn't believe the deception for a second. She felt her sister's presence somewhere in the old house.

Diligently, her eyes circled to its back. Squinting, she stopped at the partial view of a door to a cellar built into the ground underneath. She would have bet money it was most likely secured with a thick, bulky padlock.

At least that's how most cellar doors are situated in every scary movie I'd ever seen featuring spooky, deserted-looking houses inhabited by deranged kidnappers.

She turned to Sly. "Toward the back, do you see a corner sticking out like it could be part of a cellar door? It could be a way to get inside the house undetected."

Sly narrowed her eyes to examine the nearly hidden exterior door. "I believe you're right. Let us go."

Once again leading the way, she crouched as she descended the slope before them; dirt, sticks, and small stones ricocheted behind her until she landed feet first at the bottom of the gorge. Hands on her hips, Sly turned to watch Racine make her way down courtesy of her backside. After neatly crashing to a stop, Racine jumped to her feet and took a moment to brush clinging dirt and twigs from her shorts.

Motioning to her left, Racine pointed out a small ravine that circled around the house alongside the van. Crouching, the two scurried along its path until they reached the rear of the decrepit automobile.

Slowly, Racine straightened and stretched her neck to take a cautionary peek inside the windows of the rear door. The dimly lit space, cluttered with dirty rags and discarded bottles was empty. Looking over her shoulder, she shook her head at Sly and carefully made her way to the front bumper. She glanced around it.

The view from that side of the house made the structure appear even more abandoned.

Racine motioned to the neglected backyard.

Nodding, Sly slid along the side of the van until she also reached the front bumper. Looking about, she kept her right arm tucked close and bent lower, running past Racine and over to the side of the house. Leaning against its side, she glanced back and, with her left hand, made an all-clear gesture.

Once she reached Sly's side, Racine paused and then nudged her cohort. "What if we get to the cellar doors and there's a padlock there? How are we gonna open it?" she whispered. At Sly's silent shrug, Racine thought for a moment. "You know what? I'm keeping my fingers crossed that if there is one, it's probably old and rusty like everything else on this place. We'll just have to find a way to break it open. Let's go."

Keeping low, they slid their bodies along the exterior of the house, ignoring the fact that the trendy garments they wore steadily accumulated more dirt and grime along the way.

The pseudo-detectives, fashion hogs in their own right, didn't notice.

54

Fascinated by Beauty's exquisite backside as she ascended the dimly lit shadows of the stairwell, Hog studied the feminine curve of her back, her impossibly small waist, and the muscular roundness that formed her buttocks. Before him, her toned legs climbed toward the lit landing of the villa's main floor, and it was all he could do not to reach out and hurry her moving parts along.

But he would be gentle. At least with her. The woman who walked before him was indeed a special female—just like his first Beauty—and he would treat her accordingly.

Those others from the past, the females he had to either pay for or lure to various hotel rooms, he soon found they were nothing special, just bodies to unleash lust, anger, or frustration upon. Only a few had produced tears as noses were broken, wrists were fractured, or lips were split due to his bloody rage.

To his initial surprise, some actually took pleasure in the thrashing he gave them. Those females were the ones he felt uncomfortable around. Taking a beating from him, only to like it—well, they couldn't be right in the head. He felt society had enough troubles without women like that running around loose, so out of concern for the rest of society, he disposed of them as often as he could.

Andra stumbled on a step. He reached out to steady her, only to have her angrily push his hands away.

He chose not to be offended by her refusal to accept his

chivalry. Unlike his first Beauty, not many modern women appreciated such things.

His current Beauty reached the top step and, with a slight hesitation, crossed over the threshold into the kitchen. Uncertain, she stopped to survey the unknown territory. Taking advantage of her indecisiveness, Hog finally gave in to his lust and drew her to his body.

She stiffened as he wrapped eager arms tight about her waist.

"I want you so badly," he whispered against her ear. Her body jerked within his embrace. "Your body's telling me you want me as well."

Ignoring her quiet sniffling, he kissed her thick hair, which was currently fixed into a long French braid. Deducing she must've plaited her hair after he'd left her in the cellar to attend to Paulo, Hog gently tugged it.

"This will never do. Before we hit the sheets, I want you to release your hair. Let it flow with wild abandon about your shoulders. You hear?"

She remained quiet, her frame rigid as he tenderly caressed her bare tummy exposed below her torn blouse.

"Ah, Beauty, I could fall in love with you," he said, inhaling her mussed hair, which smelled like mangoes—and dust. His hands traveled upward to stop beneath her breasts, his fingers lightly touching the smoothness of their round underside. "As a matter of fact, I'm just about there. How about you, my darlin'? Feelin' anything yet?"

Silence answered him.

Taking in her compliance, Hog believed it was a good sign that she in fact truly desired him, the man who could truly make her happy.

Unable to wait any longer, he pulled away to reach for her blouse's first button. Leisurely, he unfastened it. "I'm gonna take this nice and slow to allow you to savor our first time together." He kissed her earlobe and was only slightly offended when she jerked away. "Look, this has got to happen—you and me. Get used to it, Beauty."

Andra shook her head. "My name's Andra Theonopilus."

Her breathing took on an asthmatic sound when his fingers lowered to the next button. "No matter what you do to me, I'll never belong to you."

"Like I said before, we'll see. Just remember your patient below."

Chuckling softly, he went on to whisper the things he planned to do with her, watching with perverted interest how her bottom lip trembled and the hands at her sides clenched into tight fists. The power he wielded over her was intoxicating, surpassing the rush he'd always experienced after closing a major business deal.

His fingers moved to the next button, when she whipped around to face him. A slap as hard as a kick from a bucking bronco plastered his cheek, causing his head to lurch to one side. Rising anger at her violence against him rapidly turned to delight.

"The Good Book says to turn the other cheek. I'm willing." He grinned down at her, his deviant smile causing her defiant expression to turn into fear. "I'm glad you've got a lot of spunk, my Beauty. You and I are both gonna need it where we're going. Tit for tat is what I always say."

He grabbed her wrists as her fingernails went for his eyes. She let out a small yelp when he put a tight squeeze on them.

"Yessiree, that's exactly what I want."

Catching a flash of movement in his peripheral vision, Hog froze. His glance rapidly shifted toward the window above the kitchen sink, watchful, waiting. He couldn't tell what he'd seen—or if he'd actually seen anything at all—since it had happened so fast.

Dropping her hands, he stood before his Beauty, his mind undecided. He knew his tempestuous lust for the woman before him dulled his usually sharp senses, almost rendering him useless. Subsequently, his brain and body warred with one another. His aching body wanted to satisfy his volcanic desires with this woman, yet his brain pulsed with the desire to check outside in case something was wrong.

His Beauty gazed at him, her lovely dark face filled with confusion—and relief—at his paralyzed state.

His hands now clenching and unclenching at his sides, Hog attempted to gain control of his warring halves.

In a split second, Hog decided. "Come on," he said. Grabbing one wrist, he yanked Andra along.

55

"Can't this jalopy go any faster?"

Stefano glanced sideways at Jayson, taking in an agitated face created from hard angles. He chose to ignore his brother's ire and calmly returned his eyes to the road. He knew the speed the vehicle currently traveled was already twenty miles over the limit; he was determined not to risk their lives in order to appease his riding companion's need for speed. "Jalopy? This Jaguar, little brother, is the best money can buy."

At Jayson's exaggerated sigh, Stefano compensated his misery by increasing the car's speed a few more miles per hour. "Is this better?"

Jayson impatiently shrugged him off. "What good is this expensive car if it can't get us to Andra any faster?" Brooding, he exhaled even louder. "Could you go any slower?"

"We are making good time," Stefano assured him.

Jayson crossed his chest with rigid arms and stared straight ahead.

Uneasy, Stefano focused on the road, his gut alerting him that Jayson's agitation was not entirely about his urgent need to get to his wife. He waited out the silence until his gut was proven right.

"Stefano, you lied to me earlier."

He'd dreaded the arrival of Jayson's words, for he'd known they would eventually come. He exhaled in one long breath; however, he remained mute for the time being, allowing his younger brother the right to say his piece.

"And I was too much of a coward to refute your words. You lied to me, and I wanted to accept your lie." Jayson's face veered off to stare at the scenery that rushed by his window. "But now that we are going to her ..."

Stefano's hands gripped the steering wheel tighter in painful anticipation.

"You're in love with Andra."

Jayson's quiet words came forth as a declaration. Strangely enough, Stefano experienced relief. Technically, Jayson hadn't asked a question; therefore, technically, he did not have to supply an answer. Yet despite his reprieve, numerous versions of denials, rebuttals, and downright falsehoods rushed to fill his tongue. Stefano sifted through each one, trying to pick the right one to aid himself in feeling less guilty. He couldn't.

"Yes," he finally admitted.

An unseen hardness radiated from Jayson's side. His frame stiffened; an unavoidable silence filled the vehicle, as dense as granite and just as impenetrable. Yet Stefano knew that just as quickly as the wall around Jayson's heart had been erected, he had to hurry to tear it down.

"Jayson, I did not mean to," Stefano said. "It simply happened. Please forgive me."

At Jayson's continued silence, Stefano rushed on. "I must tell you that nothing happened between your wife and me. I swear it on our mother's grave."

Jayson's eyes were glassy hot as he turned toward him. "Don't bring our mother into this."

"She loves you."

"Who?" Jayson spat bitterly. "Our mother or Andra?"

"Both." Keeping his eyes on the road, Stefano suppressed a sigh. "Our mother did not want to leave us; she had to leave us. With my illness and what it has put me through, I finally came to this conclusion, and so must you."

Jayson sniffed hard. "I love my wife, but I used to be terrified to love her with everything I have to give."

"Why?"

Jayson's shrug was slight, barely noticeable. "Because I

was afraid she would somehow, in some way, be taken away from me."

"Like our mother."

Jayson's slow nod gave way to a look of determination. "That's how I used to feel about my Doc. But now ..."

"Yes?" Stefano prodded. "Go on."

"My fear of losing Andra is greater than my self-preservation instinct and my desire not to get hurt if something did happen to her. Like when I lost Mama." Jayson turned to stare directly at Stefano. "And just like with Mama, I have to compete with my love for Andra—with you."

Jayson's sudden weeping startled Stefano to the point he almost lost control of the car. The need to reach out to his sibling washed over him, yet at the moment, his touch might not be welcome. He kept his trembling hands on the wheel.

"Jayson, Mama loved you very much. You were always her favorite. Once she even apologized to me for loving you more than she could ever love me."

"What?" Jayson asked, his attention full upon Stefano. "Why?"

"She never wanted you to know this, but she had been raped by Papa before they were married. As a matter of fact, that's the reason she decided to be with him – because of me."

At Jayson's mute shock, Stefano stared straight ahead at the road.

"With you, it was different. By the time you came along, she loved Papa. You were born out of that love. With me, it was different for her, traumatic. I believe what you saw between Mama and myself was her attempt to over-compensate for the love she could easily give you, but was unable to truly give me."

"I-I didn't know. I'm sorry, Stefano."

He shook his head.

"No don't be. Mama and I made our peace with it a long time ago. I knew she loved me the best way she could. I am satisfied with that."

"But," Jayson said sadly, only to stop.

"Listen, I know you feel as if things were left unresolved

because of her death, but her dying was unavoidable and in the past—there is nothing you or I can do about it. But this is here and now." Stefano hesitated, attempting to express the right words. "About Andra. There is something you must understand: I cannot take from you what is not mine to possess. Andra loves you. She informed me as much—not only with her words but also with her actions." Stefano waited for a response that didn't, or couldn't, come. "We are going there to save Andra for you, not me. This you must continue to tell yourself, little brother."

Childlike, Jayson wiped his face with the back of his hand and once again stared out his window.

"The future exists for you and Andra. It waits for you, not me." Stefano decided to glance over at Jayson and was relieved to witness his younger brother's softened expression. "I want your happiness to go on beyond me."

Although it might have seemed manipulative, Stefano forced upon Jayson a gentle reminder of his impending death and the fact that although the present belonged to Stefano and Jayson, only one could lay claim to the future. "My love for you is eternal, Jayson."

To Stefano's relief, the atmosphere inside the vehicle liquefied into a pool of peace.

"Can't you drive any faster?" Jayson asked, his face not quite concealing a small, forgiving smile.

As a goodwill gesture, Stefano nodded. He pressed his foot on the gas pedal and floored it.

56

Cautiously, Racine and Sly moved along the side of the villa toward its back, not bothering to bend whenever they encountered boarded windows. Racine, who was taller than Sly by a few inches, felt a sharp tug on her shirt from behind, signaling her to duck when they came upon the last window, whose pane was unobstructed.

Racine berated her carelessness as she dropped beneath the sill but not before briefly spying through the dusty window a section of a dimly lit kitchen. Tightening her crouch, she sped up until she reached the corner of the house. Stopping short, she waited for Sly to reach her side.

Side by side, they each took a breath and peeked around the structure.

Racine exhaled sharply. As she'd somehow known it would be, the slanted cellar door was closed off tightly, the outer panel secured with a thick, rust-covered padlock.

Looking at Sly, she scowled. "Yep," she whispered. "This is a haunted-house Freddy Krueger nightmare waiting to happen! There's no way we can break that lock with our bare hands."

Grinning, Sly brought her right hand from behind her back, producing a long iron rod from an old-model tire jack. At Racine's surprised expression, Sly winked. "I found this underneath the van." She lifted it higher. "Pretty good for Cat Woman, huh?"

Impressed at the girl's ingenuity, Racine remembered where they were and the imminent danger they faced. She forced back a giggle. "Now we're doing Batman?" At Sly's carefree shrug, Racine critically scanned the area around them. All was quiet among the unkempt ankle-high weeds surrounding the villa. "Okay, let's move."

"Be sure to watch out for snakes," Sly warned.

Staying low despite the higher windows along the rear, on muted shoes, they cautiously waded through the remaining yards of grass until they reached the tilted cellar door. Once there, Racine took a moment to study the door, fingering the heavy padlock. She gestured at the steel ring the padlock was threaded through.

"We can't bang it open—it'll cause too much noise." She pointed at the space between the lock's hook and the ring on the door. "The lock's old and rusty. If we slip the tire rod inside the loop and apply pressure, maybe between us two, we can break this puppy open."

Nodding, Sly did what she was told, making sure the tip came out on the other side of the ring. Shifting it at an angle, Racine gripped the jack handle with both hands.

"Yes," Sly grunted within her accented whisper, her hands positioned right below Racine's. "The applied pressure should release the—"

"Well, well, well, what do we have here? A couple of fillies tryin' to break *into* my stables? This must be my lucky day."

Simultaneously, Racine and Sly straightened in surprise, allowing the rod to slip from their grasps. Noisily, it hit the cellar door, bounced off the splintered wood, and disappeared into the overgrown grass.

Sly whimpered.

Racine protectively stepped in front of Sly. Standing taller, she labored to contain the fear bubbling beneath her outward bravado, staring eye to eye with the man who called himself Hog.

He stood as a giant, his solid form formidable, while his eyes and grinning mug sported more than a touch of bemused insanity. Both arms were raised and positioned; he pointed their way something she'd only seen in old western movie reruns.

Staring into the double barrel of the biggest rifle she'd ever seen in real life, Racine exhaled, only to find herself tremble with fear.

57

Al awoke to experience a tiny headache upon her emergence from unconsciousness. Staring up at a high, vaulted ceiling, she had no idea where she was or why she napped while it was still daylight outside.

"Did you have a good sleep, my dear?"

At George's voice, she popped into a sitting position on the long couch and took in his familiar, kind face. However, a vague mental alarm went off at the tense way his body sat at the other end. Uncertainly, she smiled. Upon closer inspection, she noted worry lines about his eyes, and a flash of remembrance soon gave way to an avalanche of disturbing memories.

Her tentative smile dropped. "Yes, I did, thank you." Putting on a brave face, Al scanned the spacious area, noting it was empty except for them. "Where's everyone? Did we get word from the kidnappers concerning Andra's return?"

He shook his head. "I wish it was so," George said. He hesitated and glanced away. "We are still waiting."

She zeroed in on his reluctance to say more, her alarm heightening exponentially when he refused to look at her.

Swinging her feet to the floor, Al slid across the couch, stopping a body's width from George. "What is it? What are you not telling me?" At his miserable silence, she searched the vacant room again, trying to gather clues from its emptiness. When her inspection revealed nothing, her beseeching eyes returned to George. "Please?"

His profile sad, he sighed painfully and proceeded to slide

across the settee, erasing the small distance between them until their bodies touched. Fatigued, he placed an arm about her shoulders. "The boys believe Harlan Grainger has Andra."

Flabbergasted, Al stared at George, her throat initially clogged with surprise. Coughing once, she attempted to clear the illusory obstruction. "You mean that loud man who calls himself Hog?" At his silent nod, Al's voice rose. "The man you guys are considering doing business with, who also offered to give us the money to pay Andra's ransom?"

Silently, George nodded at all her questions.

Al's stomach rolled with a queasiness she hadn't experienced since she was pregnant with Racine. "Why? I don't understand."

"Neither do we completely." Once again, George hesitated, forcing Al to lean away from him and study his face as she waited for the next bomb to drop. He sighed. "But I believe it has to do with revenge on my family."

"Revenge? What—"

He cut her off and proceeded to tell her about Hog's wife, Beauty, and her death.

Al sat still, her body numb, paralyzed, the volume in her hearing lessening as if George's voice traveled a million miles away to recount the story of his family company's misfortune from long ago.

Time seemed to slow to a standstill once he finished his woeful tale. At her broken sob, time eventually resumed, allowing for an eternity of seconds to pass before he tucked her slumped body beneath his arm again.

He squeezed her shoulder blades as if to brace her for another impact. "There is more."

"More?" Al whispered. In a daze, she scanned the room again, a sense of clarity plowing its way through her mental fog. Suddenly alert, she pulled away. "Racine? Where's my baby?"

"She and Sly must have overheard us discussing Hog."

Al waited with bated, frightened breath.

"They went out alone to search for his villa and rescue Andra."

The wail that broke forth from her mouth burned her esophagus. Tears just as hot singed her cheeks, and she turned their wetness toward George, whose shirt immediately absorbed them.

"I am so sorry, Al," he murmured against her hair. "This is entirely my fault."

Tearfully, Al searched George's anguished eyes to see clearly the weight of the entire situation lodged there. "What if they both get killed? My only children, my baby girls—what if they die?"

Sadness draped George's face, its melancholy weight forcing a nod from him. "I too worry my sons will not come home, yet even if they do return safely, my Stefano will be taken from me anyway. He's dying—but has yet to tell me."

Al lifted her hand and placed its palm tenderly upon his cheek. Unchecked tears ran over her fingers and along her arm as he told her of his oldest son's impending death.

They held each other tightly, commiserating with one another over the uncertain plight concerning their grown children.

58

Kneeling beside Paulo's cot, Andra pressed the back of her hand against his forehead. It was feverish and slightly clammy.

Concern furling her brow, she lifted his eyelid and peered into his eye. Exhaling, she allowed the lid to fall into place once she realized his body had succumbed to sleep instead of a forced coma.

She stayed on her knees and watched him sleep. She had to admit her relief was only partially due to Paulo's stabilized condition—the greatest portion of it was due to the sexual reprieve she'd gotten from her disgusting kidnapper. She had no idea what had caused Hog's sudden turnabout and his command she return to the cellar, but he'd warned her that if she tried to escape while he was gone, her patient would end his life buried somewhere out there on the isolated acreage beyond the villa.

Her joints stiffening, she grunted as she rose to her feet, dusting off the knees of her dirty white jeans in the process.

Andra wasn't going anywhere.

She refused to kid herself. She instinctively knew Hog was going to kill Paulo anyway; he only prolonged the deed in order to keep her under control. Still, she had to play along with his madness to buy some time until she could figure out a way to overpower the huge Texan and somehow remove Paulo's unconscious body from the cellar.

For the millionth time, Andra's eyes circled the area until they landed on the large container in the corner.

Maybe I could throw the snake at him when he comes back. Even as she thought it, she shivered at having to handle the thing, poisonous or not. *Come on, Andra. You've handled grosser, bloodier things in the operating room.*

Slowly, she crossed the cellar floor. With every step, she stopped to listen. The container remained silent; not once had she heard so much as a slithering sound from it. Gathering more courage, she pressed forward again, not fully understanding her curiosity about it but knowing she had to see if a snake lay curled inside.

Her intuition told her the only snake at the villa was Hog.

Upon reaching the waist-high rounded ceramic pottery vessel, she paused to examine it. From the outside, it looked deceptively safe, even pretty almost. She took a breath and kicked its side, jumping back immediately. She strained to listen for a hiss, a thump, or the slimy rubbing of snakeskin as the reptile coiled in agitation, but she heard nothing.

Andra stepped to it again and kicked harder, this time drawing back a throbbing foot. Still, nothing sounded from within; however, this time, her foot's connection with the heavy container revealed that whatever lay dormant inside was too weighty to be a mere snake, no matter how large the reptile.

After giving the side one last kick, Andra firmly gripped the thick lid. Briefly closing her eyes in quick prayer, she lifted the top halfway at tortoise speed, ready to slam it down in case Hog had told the truth. When nothing jumped out at her, she removed the lid completely.

The heavy lid slipped through her nerveless fingers, falling to the ground. Andra placed a hand over her mouth to stop herself from screaming.

Stuffed inside the container was a woman. With a doctor's eye, she knew every joint on her frame had been broken in order to fit her body into the cramped hollow space; her neck cracked so that the back of her head touched her spine.

With blank eyes, she stared up at the ceiling.

Trembling with outrage and fear, Andra prayed the woman had been dead long before the breaking of her bones commenced, because if not, that particular manner of death would've been extremely tortuous.

The woman's vacant blue eyes ignored Andra, yet she had the strangest feeling that down inside the belly of that madman's villa, the corpse's broken neck would deliberately rotate until blank orbs stared directly at her.

Sapphire, minus her flight attendant uniform, looked out of place in her twisted, bloody street clothes.

Hog had made good on his word on the plane: he had proceeded to break Sapphire until she was broken for good.

~

Motionless, Andra listened.

Beyond the wooden cellar door that opened outward at an angle toward the back of the house, indistinct, muffled voices filtered in through the tiny spaces between the door's heavy planks. She strained to hear, yet she couldn't make out who was speaking or how many persons were on the other side. Heedless of the danger, she rushed forward, her feet stumbling over one another to get to the cement stairs that led to the padlocked door. Reaching them, she quickly bounded upward until she stood on the highest step possible.

Placing her lips near the seam between the two middle planks, she called out, "Hey! Hello? Anyone out there? Can you hear me?" She strained to listen for any response. When she heard none, she became desperate. "Please help me! Help!"

She pressed her ear against the splintered wood. She heard nothing. Frantic, she pounded the splintery surface until her hands stung from pieces of slivered wood embedded in her skin.

Breathing hard, she again took a moment to listen for a response. To her disappointment, only silence met her beyond the door. Pivoting on her heels, she descended the stairs. After staring at the wide container that doubled as a sarcophagus for Sapphire, she sat down on the last step and bowed her head.

After discovering the flight attendant's corpse, Andra now

knew for certain she and Paulo were both dead men walking. It was just a matter of time before they too found themselves in the same gruesome predicament, their limbs broken and their bodies stuffed inside clay containers—never to be heard from again.

Lifting her throbbing palms, she examined them through watery eyes. Using her chipped fingernails, she gently pulled splinters from her flesh. She worked quietly, sniffling once and then again, until she found herself hiccupping in an attempt to suppress her building tears. Finally, unable to hold them back any longer, she lowered her face to her bruised hands and wept.

"No need for crying, Beauty. I've brought you more company. Family, I believe."

Andra's head jerked around to take in the frightening yet wondrous vision of her baby sister, Racine, standing in the doorway in front of Hog. Right by her side was the annoying Sly.

"Racine!" She bolted from the stairs and immediately raced across the floor. "How? What are you doing here?"

"Andra!" Racine screamed. Their bodies crashed midway to frantically engulf each other in a gigantic hug. "We came to find you, Sis! Andra!"

"I'm right here, baby girl. I'm okay," she said, hugging her sister so tightly she thought Racine would break inside her arms. Through unshed tears of joy and fear, Andra glanced at a frightened Sly, who belatedly joined them. She reached out and pulled the girl into a one-armed hug. "Hey, Sly, I'm even glad to see you!"

Sly trembled within her embrace, and her voice held an air of shaky nonchalance. "Dr. Andra, still, your tone does not quite convey you are happy to see me."

"Why should she be?" Racine said, her voice rising. "When you—"

"Racine," Andra said. "Now's not the time."

"Yatros does not understand I am now sorry."

"Sorry?" Racine said, her voice raising. "If you hadn't—"

"Be still, all of you!" Hog roared. "Stop that caterwauling!"

Flinching, all three women turned toward their captor, their eyes widening at the shaking rifle Hog pointed their way.

His next words came out low and deliberate. "I wanna know how you two found this place. Is someone else trailing behind you?"

Briefly, Racine's and Sly's eyes touched in silent conference; seconds later, they turned back to Hog, shaking their heads.

He cocked the gun and pointed the long barrel at an object directly behind them. "Now, don't you be lying to me, or someone's gonna get shot."

Their eyes followed the sight on the gun, and Sly let out a scream once Hog's target was revealed. Shoving past Andra, she rushed to the side of her injured brother, who was lying face-down on the cot.

"Paulo!" she cried, falling on her knees next to his head. Paulo moaned in his sleep. Sobbing even louder, Sly jumped on agile feet and twirled. "What did you do to him, you animal?"

Hog smirked. "Nothing he probably didn't deserve. Now, tell me how you were able to find me—or I'll finish the job."

Sly screamed, frantically dropping to her knees and covering Paulo's head with her body.

Racine pulled away from Andra's embrace to step forward. "No one knows we're here," she told him. "We got the information from the housekeeper. We didn't tell her why we needed it."

Hog frowned. "Now I'm confused. How would you know to ask for it?"

Racine's face puckered with disgust. "It wasn't too hard for us women to figure out you were behind this entire mess. We asked Helena the right questions, and we got the right answers. That's all there is to it."

He studied her briefly, his expression calculating her words, mentally weighing and measuring them for the truth. A minute went by before he relaxed his grip on the gun and uncocked the trigger.

"I believe you, I guess. Those proud and haughty Theonopiluses wouldn't send girls to do their jobs if they knew about this." His eyes bounced to Sly, who still covered her unconscious brother like a shield. "Nevertheless, Beauty, I best decide what to do about these extra bodies before more interlopers show up. If these two"—he pointed the rifle at Racine and Sly—"could figure it out, others will too."

"What are you going to do?" Andra asked.

"I figure I could start with the young bird over there. His wing's already broken. Might as well put him outta his misery." At Sly's indignant cry, Hog used one hand to swipe the air. "Oh, park it into neutral, missy! Don't blame me for your brother's presence in my home or his injuries; his nosy nature is what nearly got him killed. You should be rightly glad my Beauty was here to nurse him. Without her, he would've been long gone."

"Beauty?" Annoyance, anger, and confusion caused Racine's eyes to bulge wildly as she stared at Andra. "Why does he keep calling you that? Are you supposed to be this Beauty?"

Mutely, Andra shook her head, only to have Hog contradict her.

"Yessir, your sister's my Beauty now. She's decided to stay with me."

Turning, Racine faced Hog directly. "Over my dead body."

"Okay." Hog raised his rifle's tip and pointed it at Racine's forehead.

Using more force than she intended, Andra shoved Racine out of the line of the gun, only to stand in her place. "If you kill her, you'd better kill me!" Ignoring Racine's yelp from the floor, Andra took a step toward him. "But you'd better make sure you finish me, because if there's one breath of life left in my body, I'm coming after you, Hog. Now, back off!"

The Texan lowered the gun and looked about the room. His gaze scanned over Racine, who now lay sprawled on the floor, staring at him with venomous eyes, to Sly, who was still on her knees, covering an unconscious Paulo. Then he looked back to Andra. He looked hurt. "Beauty, you don't understand."

"What?" she shrieked. "What don't I understand? That you're nuts?"

Hog's expression abruptly hardened yet still bore a trace of sadness. "You've got everything: a career, family, and a spouse who'd move the world for you. I've got nothing left. My life is nothing. Don't you see?"

Andra stood and watched her kidnapper, a man who should have been locked inside a loony bin, and felt an inexplicable, small twinge of sympathy for him. With one hard breath, she exhaled in frustration. "If your life's nothing, then change it. Only you have the power—the control—to do it."

As she spoke, Hog stared off into the distance at some point above Andra's head. After a few seconds of contemplation, he zeroed in on her again. His face now twisted in anger, he shook his head. "No, I've tried! I haven't had any control over my life since my first Beauty died." He took the time to carefully align the tip of his gun with each person in the room, beginning and ending with Andra. "As for you, you've got control over yours."

Unafraid, Andra stared into the twin barrels capable of ejecting shotgun shells at a velocity that would explode her head from her shoulders. She flung her hand toward him and the gun. "I have control? What kinda control do you think I have? As a black, I cannot control the world around me and the prejudices I have to endure at the hands of ignorant people I encounter on a daily basis."

"That's not me, Beauty," Hog said, his face now screwed up with hurt. "I love all women from every nationality; it don't matter. Just take a look at you and my first Beauty."

"Who cares?" Andra crossed her arms and scowled at Hog. "You wanna talk about unfair? Let's just throw being a woman into the mix, shall we? Now we're talking such things as sexual assault, sexual intimidation, and harassment, just to list a few, from darling little creeps such as yourself. Just ask the woman tucked securely in that sarcophagus over there."

"What?" Hog's eyebrows lifted, and then his eyes narrowed. "You peeked."

"What are you talking about?" Racine jumped up. She looked ready to head for the large container. "What's in there?"

Andra reached out and grabbed her sister's arm, shaking her head. She turned back to Hog. "No, when it comes to the outside world, I, being both black and a woman, am one of many who have no control over anything. But you know what? I somehow make it work and make it through, and somehow manage to do it without wreaking havoc on other people's lives!"

As Hog stared at her as if she were the crazy one, her small measure of sympathy for him vanished.

She lunged at him, shoving the gun's barrel aside. Using her jagged fingernails, she struck swiftly, gouging into Hog's eyeballs. Startled, he screamed, pointed the gun blindly, and pulled the trigger. She ducked just as the pellets blew over her head. Still in a tight end's position, she rushed forward to tackle him, and the shotgun flew from his hand. Enraged, she sat atop his barrel chest and proceeded to gouge deeper into his sockets until she felt brain.

At Sly's scream, she jumped from Hog's still chest and turned just in time to witness Racine on her back with blood everywhere and one half of her head blown off.

Andra wanted to throw up at the imagined goriness. Divesting her brain of the grisly daydream, she inhaled deeply. "I don't wreak havoc on others' lives. I try to do just the opposite—which is why I decided to become a doctor. To save lives, not destroy them."

Racine stirred behind her. The girl shrank back as Hog's eyes scanned her smudged white T-shirt and dusty jean shorts. Then she stood courageously taller. "Yeah, Mr. Hog, what have you done for mankind?" she said. "Other than, of course, sparing the world the pollution of your piggy offspring."

The cellar grew extraordinarily still as Hog studied Racine with venomous quietness.

"Lookee here, making sport of me and my first Beauty's inability to have children isn't very nice." Although his eyes appeared dead, his mouth curled into a civil grin. "Is it?"

Mute, Racine lowered her eyelids against Hog's burning rage.

"Well, young lady, I don't know what I've done for other

mankind, but I do know what I'm gonna do about this mankind," he said, pointing to his crotch. At Racine's "Oh, gross!" his smile tapered off sinisterly. "I believe I'll take you upstairs and teach you the finer points of being a woman—and all that entails."

Andra jabbed a finger his way. "Hog, I'm warning you. If you—"

The Texan swung the shotgun Racine's way, but he kept his eyes on Andra. "No! I'm warning you." He cocked the trigger once more and locked it. "If you take one step to stop me, I'll blow her head clean off."

Thinking of her vision of Racine lying in chucks of her own brain, Andra backed up a bit. "You wouldn't dare."

"Oh yes, I would. And I'd finish by killing the rest right before your eyes." He focused mainly on Racine, but his eyes darted to Andra every few seconds. "So what'll it be, Beauty? Me bronco-busting your sister upstairs or her brains splattered all over these walls?"

Andra's response lodged inside her throat. She threw a glimpse Racine's way, noting her sister's face contorted with both rage and fright at the threat of another rape.

Behind Andra, Sly rose to her feet.

"Okay, Hog, you win," Andra said, turning back to face his ire. She attempted a seductive, persuasive smile. "You can take me upstairs—you know, like you and I planned earlier. Leave my little sister outta this."

A strange glow radiated from Hog's orbs, creating instant terror for Andra at its unwelcome appearance.

"Nope, I want her now. She needs a good breakin' in. Believe you me, all the fellas who I'll allow to come after me will thank me." Staring at Racine, Hog methodically swung the shotgun to Andra's forehead. "What'll it be, my young filly—me and you upstairs, or would you prefer your sister's head?"

Silently, Sly moved forward to stand off to the side. The room grew tomb-like as Racine's face screwed up in contemplation of her fate with Hog. Finally coming to some type of conclusion, on slow feet, she walked toward him, stopping briefly to brush aside Andra's outstretched hand.

"Don't worry, Sis. I can handle it," she said, staring hard at Hog and his gun. "My virginity's already been taken by creeps like him. There's nothing else he can take from me."

"He could take your life. No, I won't let you," Andra said, stepping in front of her. "I'm going instead."

"No! You have to worry about the baby." Pushing Andra aside, Racine stepped up to Hog. "Don't worry about me. I'll eventually roll with the punches to put this mangy animal behind me. Right, Lacey?"

Mute, Sly paused and then nodded in fascination.

Hog's faded blue eyes roamed the length of Racine's fit physique. A sinister chuckle escaped his parted lips. "You don't mind if this mangy animal breaks a few bones in the process, do ya? Maybe a wrist?" At Andra's outraged cry, Hog snickered louder and continued. "Shoot, I'll go for a rib or two. Yessiree, I believe a tough girl like you could not only handle it, but will enjoy it as well."

More afraid for her little sister than she'd ever been in her life, Andra watched the rifle lift and rotate toward her when she stepped closer. "Please, Hog," she begged. "Please don't hurt her. I'll do anything."

"At the moment, all I want you to do is nothing." At her silence, his eyes filled with his insane version of pity. His voice softened a bit. "Okay, darlin', I'll try not to hurt her more than I have to—for you."

He lowered the rifle to allow Racine to pass him and head for the door. However, the moment she came into alignment with his burly chest, Racine performed a half spin toward him and shouted, "Lacey!"

Andra decided to enact her gory eye-gouging scenario despite the resulting carnage, but she stopped in surprise when suddenly, Sly dropped to the floor and performed a tuck and roll, quickly curling into a ball behind Hog's feet. A delayed second later, Racine shoved hard against the older man's chest.

The Texan's eyes swiftly bulged in surprise at his

unexpected balancing act. In an attempt to stay on his feet, he flailed his arms in an out-of-control fashion; his backward momentum caused the rifle to fly from his grasp and soar across the room. Acting on reflex, Andra lunged at Racine, bringing them both crashing to the ground just as the gun smashed against the wall, the impact causing a bullet in the chamber to discharge with a loud boom.

Hog's head hit the cellar floor, and his body jerked once only to lie still where he'd fallen.

Quickly, Sly scrambled away from the Texan's prone body, her bare legs obtaining further bruises as she crawled to where Andra and Racine lay sprawled. With trembling lips, she bestowed upon them a toothy grin. "Racine, I understood exactly what you wanted, yes?" She clapped twice. "What a team, us Cagney and Lacey, right?"

"I guess," Racine said, clumsily rising to her feet. Brushing herself off, she kept her face averted as Andra stared at the two with her mouth open.

"High five!" Sly exclaimed, lifting her right palm. When Racine didn't reciprocate, her lively expression turned concerned. "Can you not high-five? Please, I can teach you."

Andra let out a small, nervous laugh, causing Racine to push her. In exasperation, Racine turned to Sly. "Of course I can high-five, you idiot," she said. She jerked her head in the direction of an unconscious Hog. "The danger's not over yet, so could you please put that hand away?"

As if he somehow knew he was the focal point of their conversation, Hog made a small grunting noise.

"Yeah, save all that for later. We need to do something about him—now." Andra watched Hog clumsily lift his head and shake it, as if attempting to clear away mental cobwebs. Her sights quickly landed upon the rifle's severed butt. "Hold on."

Andra ran across the room, snatched the broken piece, and returned to where Hog lay. Stooping, she cracked him on the skull with it, the blunt force causing his head to drop to the dusty concrete floor again. For good measure, she brought it crashing down on his head once more.

"There," Andra said, throwing the butt away and brushing off her hands. She stared down at her victim. "That should do it."

Sighing heavily, she bent to pluck open the man's lids. Relieved that she hadn't killed him, she straightened with her hands on her hips and turned to see Racine stare at her with both admiration and reproof. "What?"

"Oh, nothing. It's just that you crack him over the head— twice, I might add—only to then follow up by making sure he's okay!" Racine laughed. "I should write a book about you called *Gangsta Doctor*. Should be a best seller."

"Yes!" Sly agreed.

"Or maybe a porn film: *Ms. Doc Holliday Does Med School*." Racine wagged one eyebrow. "A winner, huh?"

"Look," Andra said, grabbing Racine and Sly by the arm and dragging them away from the unconscious Hog. "I'm not proud of what I just did, but it had to be done. Nobody's going to die on my watch if I can help it, not even that scumbag over there."

"But it would've been in self-defense," Racine said, flashing an adorable smile. "You are who you are, Andra. You've got to learn to embrace the animal inside you instead of caging it inside those daydreams of yours."

Weary at the thought of even attempting a comeback or rational response, Andra looked around the room again. "Whatever. You guys help me find something to tie him with before he comes to."

"Maybe I can be of assistance."

Andra, Racine, and Sly whipped around to take in the tired-looking yet handsome man standing inside the cellar's doorway.

Stefano.

Involuntarily, Andra's stomach flipped at his magical appearance, and if the others had not been around, she believed she would've sprinted over to him and jumped into his arms.

"Stefano!" Sly did what Andra couldn't and raced across the floor, crashing into Stefano's chest. He automatically wrapped long arms about her clinging body. "My hero! I am so glad you came to rescue me!"

Andra's face grew warm as Stefano stared over Sly's head to gift her with an expression of relief—and some other emotion she never wanted to identify. "Where's Jayson?" she asked, breaking free from his eyes to look beyond Stefano and Sly. "Is he here too?"

Stefano's face produced a vague smile. "Of course he is," he said. He gently detangled himself from Sly's hug, which seemed to take some doing. He then glanced at the floor and a motionless Hog. "We chose to split up—he asked if I would go below while he searched the rooms above, believing he would find you first."

Abruptly, Stefano and Sly were shoved to the side.

"Doc! Baby, you're okay! Come here!"

Seeing Jayson, his arms stretched wide, Andra thought her face would crack from happiness. She ran to him, lunged into his open embrace, and lifted her face to receive his hungry kiss.

"Jay, I love you," she said into his mouth. "So much!"

"I thank God you're alive," he muttered, kissing her face and lips between words. "I love you."

"Okay, you guys, get a room later," Racine said, interrupting. She glanced over at an unconscious Paulo lying on the cot and pointed an impatient finger his way. "What's say we retrieve lover boy over there and get the hell outta here?"

"Yes," Stefano agreed. "Let us leave this place now. We contacted the authorities the moment we discovered Hog's white van parked outside."

Nodding, Jayson plastered Andra with another kiss. "Baby, I'm so glad you're all right," he said, wrapping one arm about Andra's waist and propelling her toward the door. He reached out to lift her hand to his mouth and placed a gentle kiss upon it. "I don't know what I would've done if anything had happened to you."

"You may still have to contemplate that, boy."

Jayson froze, forcing Andra to stop in her tracks with him. Everyone turned Hog's way, staring as he struggled to hoist himself into a sitting position. The room remained still, each person's expression one of disbelief as the older man reached inside his right cowboy boot and pulled out a .22-caliber pistol. He lifted the compact gun for all to see before pointing it with deadly precision at Andra.

Jayson yanked her behind him. "Why are you doing this, Hog?" Jayson said. "Why?"

"Well," he said matter-of-factly, "the sins of the father must be visited upon the sons." Hog stared at Stefano. "Especially one as self-righteous as you are."

Stefano cleared his throat. "You cannot shoot us all with your little gun, Mr. Grainger."

One-handed, Hog scooted backward on his tailbone until his spine pressed securely against the dusty cellar wall. "Maybe not," he said, tightening his hand on the gun. Glaring at Stefano, he used his other hand to soothe his bruised head. "But at least with my first shot, I can get your doctor."

"Why Andra?" Jayson asked. "Why target her?"

"Retribution—an eye for an eye. Your family took my Beauty, so I'll take yours." He laughed a short, mirthless laugh. His hard-edged stare moved slowly from Stefano to Jayson. "And the kicker is, by killing your wife, I'll hurt the both of you."

Sly made a strangled sound at his words.

"Oh, hush up, girl," Hog growled, deliberately ignoring her to glare at Stefano. "Everybody here knows about your lovesick plight over this one. Frankly, nobody cares."

Jayson took a step forward, causing Andra to desperately grab his arm.

"Jay, please don't."

"No, baby—it's going to be all right. I have to do this." After waiting for her silent acquiescence, he turned his dark eyes to Hog. "Do you remember when we first met? On the airplane coming over?"

Leveling the gun to align it with Jayson's heart, the older man reluctantly nodded.

"You said, 'The truth be told, sometimes love might not be

enough. But sometimes it is.' You then went on to say, 'I guess we'll just have to see.' Do you remember that?"

"I remember," Hog grunted. He crisply waved his gun. "Get to the point. Because no matter what you say, you don't need Beauty—I do."

Slowly, Jayson spread his arms. His posture might have displayed defeat in Hog's eyes, but what Andra saw in her husband's outstretched hands was resolve, not unlike Jesus Christ with his outstretched hands on the cross.

"No, you're wrong. The truth is, I love Andra so much; she's my very existence. I don't simply want her; I need her. I need her to complete me; I need her to survive. Knowing how much you loved your Beauty, I believe you must understand, sir."

Showing solidarity, Stefano left Sly to come alongside Jayson and place a hand upon his shoulder.

The Texan's eyes misted; his pale lips parted to push forth a painful sigh, as if doing so would somehow stop the tears from falling. His glassy orbs shifted to Andra. "Well, I guess love is enough in you two's case." The weapon in his hand faltered. Hog looked at it, his expression contemplative. "My Beauty would've never died if we'd just done what she wanted to do that year. She wanted to go to Spain to be with her family instead of traveling here to Greece. The whole thing was my fault. All my money—and I still couldn't protect her enough to keep her alive."

"You murdered Sapphire," Andra said in a whisper. "You've got to answer for that."

Hog's eyes alighted upon everyone in the room and finally stopped on her. "I've killed more than a dozen women since my Beauty's death; their bodies are scattered all over the world. I used my money to try them on for size, but none of them were worthy enough to take Beauty's place—that is, until I met you, doctor."

Andra, who dedicated her life to trying to save lives, angrily shook her head at the demented man whose purpose in life seemed to be in direct opposition to hers.

"You know, I thought we were gonna be together forever." Searching Andra's disgusted face, Hog sighed at what he witnessed there. His next chuckle sounded sad. "When I went to my lawyers to transfer the ransom money, I had them to name you as my estate's sole beneficiary."

The others remained silent as Hog coughed in embarrassment.

"I guess I won't be needing the money any longer." His faded blue eyes held Andra's, the melancholy within them overruling the previous madness shown there. "Use it wisely. You hear, Beau—I mean, Andra?"

They heard the faint sounds of police cars. Several vehicles skidded to a stop, followed by the sound of multiple car doors slamming.

"Gotta go to my Beauty." His glassy eyes glazed over to focus on Stefano. "But not before leaving a parting gift."

His lips tightening, Hog straightened the gun and pulled the trigger. The force of the bullet knocked Jayson off his feet, and he, along with Andra, crashed to the hard cement floor.

Then, just as quickly, Harlan Orlando Grainger shoved the pistol in his mouth and, before anyone else could move, blew a hole through the back of his throat.

5 9

With a club soda on the rocks in hand, Al shifted on her chair and let out a sigh. Glancing about the sitting room, her eyes took stock of everyone. She took in Racine, George, and Stefano. Helena's wide frame flitted about the room as she asked if anyone needed anything, her Greek-driven chatter infectiously bubbly.

Lastly, her sights landed on Andra sitting next to Jayson. His upper arm heavily bandaged, he kept it stationary inside a shoulder sling, where it would remain until his body healed.

The only ones unaccounted for were Paulo and Sly. Paulo was currently recuperating at the local village hospital, and Sly was at his bedside.

Al's gaze returned to a certain section in the room. Her girls were her main focus. *Women, actually*, she thought wistfully, correcting herself. Once in a while, she couldn't help but shake her head, marveling at their brave resilience despite what they'd both been through in their short lifetimes.

As she sipped her drink, her gaze stayed on Andra, whose head leaned against Jayson's good shoulder. Her beautiful face was all smiles, her body protectively wrapped inside her husband's one-armed embrace, their bodies fitting perfectly together. Every so often he'd whisper in her ear, and she would reach over to lovingly touch his cast, her voice laughing in shy delight.

Al's amusement grew when she shifted to Racine, who aggressively vied with Jayson for Andra's attention. Racine threatened to punch Jayson on his bandaged arm, while he, on the other hand, announced he would strangle her with his sling if she did. Her eyes misted over at their lively banter while she silently offered a prayer of motherly thanks to God for bringing them all home safely.

She placed her glass on the end table just as Racine imparted a few choice words to the snuggling couple before rising. Pausing to reassure the circling Helena she couldn't eat another bite, she then rolled her eyes at Al as she plopped down on the couch beside her.

"Man, I don't have time for all that lovey-dovey stuff—they can have it." Watching the lovebirds for a few second more, Racine dismissed them to smile ruefully at Al. Her expression immediately sobered. "You all right, Mama?"

Al patted her daughter's knee. "Right as rain." She laughed quietly at Racine's repeated eye roll concerning the old-fashioned saying and abruptly grew serious. "However, Race, I do want to talk to you about what you and Sly did. It was reckless and extremely dangerous."

Grinning, Racine deflected the rebuke. "You're right. But everything worked out, didn't it? I mean, all's good as long as we got Andra back."

Al smacked the knee she'd previously patted. "Sure, everything's okay now. But what if it hadn't worked out?" Al sniffed, attempting to hold back tears of both fear and relief. "What would I've done if I'd lost both of you? Don't ever do anything so foolish again, young lady."

Upon witnessing Al's falling tears, Racine nodded sincerely. "Sorry, Mama. I'll try to use my head next time." She glanced over at Jayson, who was in the process of placing a gentle kiss upon Andra's upturned face. "I'm just glad the bullet happened to hit Jayson in the shoulder and not somewhere more critical."

"Yes, thank the Lord," Al said. Pondering, she shook her head. "However, it's highly unlikely the bullet just happened to miss his vital organs."

Racine turned to stare at her. "What do you mean, Mama? You believe the Lord guided it?"

"Well, maybe," she said slowly. "But Mr. Grainger might've had something to do with it too."

"I don't follow you, Mom."

Al shrugged philosophically. "I don't know. The way you guys described the moment before the shooting, the proximity of Mr. Grainger to Jayson, the way he handled the gun—everything." Al glanced over at Jayson. "I believe if that man had wanted to shoot to kill, he would have."

"So why didn't he then?" Racine asked.

"Your guess is as good as mine," Al answered. "And we'll most likely never know why the man had a change of heart. Maybe he couldn't bring himself to actually kill Jayson but felt he had to at least wound him—force Jayson to carry around a wound for the rest of his life, probably like the one he was burdened with since his wife's passing."

"Hmm, you could be onto something," Racine replied, her expression thoughtful before turning angry. She shot a glaring look over her shoulder. "Still, I blame this whole thing on that slime-ball Hog—and him."

Twisting around in her seat, Al followed Racine's stare. Stefano and George stood at the bar, quietly engaged in a solemn conversation. She turned back to her daughter. "Who? Stefano?"

"Yes," Racine said, her focus steady. "Yes, him."

"Why in the world would you blame Stefano?" Al asked incredulously.

Racine's breathing grew rapid. "Mama, it's not fair how he's disrupted our family and—"

"Look who's talking about disruptions." Al cut in with a dismayed shake of her head. "That's like the pot calling the kettle black."

"Please stop with the antiquated sayings."

"Like I said, you're the last one to talk about disruptions."

"Okay, okay," Racine said, acquiescing with a huff. "Still, he's in love with Andra."

"Who wouldn't love Andra?" Al said quietly. "You?"

"Of course I do!" Racine said, desperation entering her tone. "How could you ask such a thing?"

"Okay, prove it." Al again shook her head. "Love does not rejoice about injustice but rejoices whenever the truth wins out."

Her daughter stared at her, dumbfounded.

"This time, it's not an antiquated saying, as you put it," Al said with a short nod. "It's from the Bible: First Corinthians 13:6. Read it sometime; you might learn something."

"But ..." Racine sputtered, her eyes darting back to Stefano.

"But nothing! And the truth is, Stefano's a good man, despite his faults," Al said, her voice low yet firm. Reaching out, she captured Racine's chin and forced her to look directly into her eyes. "His faults, his prejudices, are no less and no greater than yours."

Racine pulled her chin from her mother's grasp, hanging her head. "I know," she whispered. "But just look at him! Standing over there like he's—"

"Dying."

Racine's head jerked up. "Huh? What did you say?"

"He's dying, Racine." At Racine's expression of confusion, Al nodded. "George told me as much. So whatever you may feel about Stefano, his love for Andra, combined with yours, is what helped bring her safely home."

Simultaneously, both pairs of eyes returned to Stefano and George, who remained in deep conversation by the bar, their tall bodies close as they faced one another. All at once, George's kind face softened with grief; his lips moved with spoken words too soft to hear. He placed a tender hand upon Stefano's lean shoulder.

"How long does he have to live?" Racine asked, her eyes riveted on the men.

Watching them as well, Al let out a sigh. "I don't know. Andra informed me his illness looks to have gone into remission, and he appears to be holding his own. However, it could be a year, a few months, days, or anytime at all. It's anybody's guess at this point." Feeling Racine stir beside her, she immediately focused upon her child's abrupt rising. "Where are you going?" she asked.

Saying nothing, Racine strolled over to the huddled men, who glanced up with surprise at her appearance. She first presented George with a winning smile, only to transfer it to Stefano. "Care for a walk and talk, big brother?" she asked.

A faint smile appeared on Stefano's gaunt face. His hand trembled as he placed his glass of brandy and ice upon the bar counter. "Papa, I must leave you now," he said, his voice serious. His face produced a wisp of appreciation. "A beautiful woman awaits my attention."

An expression that displayed both happiness and sadness washed over George's face. He glanced Al's way, and she smiled at him. His eyes immediately returned to pass fondly between Stefano and Racine. "But of course, Son—I do not blame you."

Stefano held out his palm.

Hesitating at his gesture, Racine slowly placed her hand in his.

Leaning over, Stefano brought her cocoa-brown flesh to his lips and bestowed upon it a whisper of a kiss.

Shifting uncomfortably, Racine stared down at his bowed head. Then, her face broke out in a shy smile.

Pride bursting from every pore, Al watched as Stefano looped Racine's hand through his arm. In one accord, their bodies pivoted toward the open sitting room door. Suddenly, Stefano stopped in his tracks.

One eyebrow lifted, Racine tilted her head to stare at Stefano, her lovely face teasing him with a grin. "What's wrong, big brother? Having second thoughts?"

"No, I ..."

Looking on, Al stood uncertainly waiting for words that never left Stefano's open mouth.

She then gasped in horror when he pulled away from Racine and crumpled to the floor, his tall, lean body landing awkwardly, unmoving.

60

The hospital room was dark except for the small light above Stefano's bed.

Andra paused inside the threshold, holding the heavy door open with a steady hand. She peered across the private room's vastness at the patient, whose body lay motionless. Even from afar, she saw the paleness of his skin, its washed-out hue almost lifeless, the color especially noticeable against the white bedsheets surrounded by gleaming chrome handrails raised to an upright position.

His eyes were closed, and despite his sickly pallor, he appeared much younger than his years.

His face looked at peace.

Despite his repose, an inner alarm sounded as she gazed at his shut lids. She silently prayed they were closed due to him sleeping and not anything else.

Deciding she couldn't straddle the fence of Stefano's hospital room door forever, Andra stepped inside. Initially, she hadn't noticed the attending nurse who stood in the shadows off to one side, reading his vitals from various monitors. She stopped in her tracks when the woman turned her way and quickly advanced with nurse-driven determination.

"I'm sorry, miss," she said, her voice slow and heavy with her country's native accent, "but you must not be here. For family only."

"She is family, Amelia," Stefano said behind her, his voice weak and raspy. He coughed. "She's also a great doctor. Let her come to me."

Nurse Amelia froze momentarily to stare over her shoulder at her patient before her dark-as-night eyes swung back to Andra. Andra tried not to flinch as the nurse gave her body a thorough once-over, the woman's expression a blatant display of incredulous disdain.

"All right, Mr. Theonopilus," the nurse said, continuing to glare at Andra. Her voice lowered in warning. "But I will be right outside."

Bemused more than insulted, Andra observed the woman in white turn up her nose and, in a haughty manner, make a wide berth around her, the smell of antiseptic and liquid sanitizer trailing behind. Once she made it to the door, she yanked it open, paused to glower at Andra, and stalked out.

I guess she told me.

"Don't mind her—not everyone's as progressive in their tolerance as I."

Chuckling in amusement, Andra crossed over to Stefano's bed. With soft eyes, she regarded his pale face momentarily before lowering her head. She kissed him first somewhere above his right eyebrow only to shift lower to place her mouth in direct alignment with his. Their eyes held for a brief moment before she lightly touched her lips to his. Stefano's lips were dry and chapped—and exquisitely wonderful.

She pulled back slightly and shook her head. "You've got that right—no one's ever going to be as progressive as you."

Andra waited for his weak smile to appear before she straightened. "How're you feeling, Brother?" She took hold of his closest hand and gently squeezed. "Are you comfortable? Is there anything I can do for you?"

Stefano coughed again. Andra watched with concern as small projectiles of bloody spittle shot forth to sprinkle his dry lips. Quickly, she reached over to the side table, pulled free a couple of tissues, and carefully wiped away the spatters. After tossing the soiled tissue into the wastebasket, she applied sanitizer to her hands and then dipped her fingers into an ice container to retrieve a disc of ice.

He sighed, his cracked lips parting slightly, as she painted them with the frozen water.

"Better?" she asked, disposing of the rest.

"Yes." His tongue licked away the excess moisture before he spoke again. "And there is nothing else I need except your company."

Andra's stomach performed a flip-flop that was immediately replaced with a queasiness at the thought she'd never know this man beyond that deathbed. She tossed aside the thought and put on a brave face.

"You got it. My company's free, so at least it won't cost anything." She smiled and searched for a chair. Finding one, she pulled it close and sat down. "However, you my friend, would be considered a high-maintenance kind of guy."

Stefano attempted another smile; however, it came out like a grimace. "Only to you I am."

Andra blushed. His statement went deeper than mere words; it implied his feelings for her were more complex than for any woman he'd ever known. The rawness of his emotion twisted her heart, causing her to draw closer to his spirit than ever before.

Minutes passed before either one spoke.

"Where is everyone?" Stefano asked.

Looking off, she made a mental checklist of everyone's whereabouts. "Jayson went home to change clothes. Afterward, he's heading over to the church to discuss some things with the priest." She waited for any sign of distress at the hint of preparing for his funeral, yet Stefano's expression remained passive. "Papa George, Mama, and Racine are in the cafeteria, getting something to eat. Paulo and Sly are at your office, watching over things there."

Closing his eyes, Stefano remained quiet. Glancing at the heart monitor to make sure of a steady heartbeat, Andra decided to leave so he could get some rest.

"I heard," he said, forcing her to lower back into her seat. "That is, I understand you plan to use the money received from the Grainger estate to open a free clinic for the village?"

Arching her right eyebrow, she looked at him. "Tell me— why did you bother to ask a question when you already know it's true?" Smiling, she leaned forward to whisper in an exaggerated tone. "Who told you—our friend Sly?"

A smile of confirmation broke out across his face.

"That girl can't keep anything inside that huge trap of hers." Andra grinned at Stefano's attempt at laughter. "Anyway, of course I've instructed a lawyer to transfer your company's assets back into your family's hands."

Stefano's brief smile indicated he'd already known that information as well.

"And yes, it's true—I plan to liquidate the rest of Hog's estate and sink it into the village, specifically the church and the village's free clinic, where all that money can do some good."

His slight nod was difficult to perform. "That is most generous of you, Doctor."

She leaned forward to rest her chin on the bed's guardrail. "Well, I've heard I'm not the only generous one around these parts."

Andra chuckled at his raised brow, which questioned *her* source. "Yes, once again, our little human message center said you have willed both her and Paulo your share of the Theonopilus business to be split equally between them."

Stefano's paleness reddened when Andra studied him.

"You are amazingly generous, my brother," she said softly.

He waved her statement away with a weak, humble hand. "It was the right thing to do. Both are exceptionally smart, and they have been around the business long enough to help Papa run it if—" He stopped.

"If Jayson wants to follow his dream of being a full-time clergyman," Andra said, finishing for him. She sighed, knowing the sound was similar to that of a schoolgirl in mid-crush. "Thank you, Stefano—for him and me."

Stefano opened his mouth to say something only to commence coughing.

Alarmed as much at what he wanted to tell her as at his difficulty in breathing, she stood and reached for his frail hand. "Stefano, don't talk. Save it for later."

"I'm dying, Andra. Let me finally say what I feel." He

paused to catch another breath. "I must cleanse my soul of this so I may go to my mother not with a heart heavy with unspoken words, but a free one."

She braced herself and nodded.

Turning away, Stefano looked toward the ceiling only to close his eyes. "I hated you." He coughed weakly and cleared his throat. "At least I thought I hated you. But I came to realize I actually hated myself because of you."

Andra held her breath, wanting him to continue yet not wanting him to.

"Most of us are just angry people living on borrowed time. I was."

She thought his words deeply profound. Grief-stricken, she watched him suck in a shallow breath and slowly blow it out.

"You were so strange to me—and people tend to fear what they do not understand." He coughed again, the sound feeble. "Fear sometimes turns to hate simply because one refuses to understand. Yet sometimes that hatred masks an emotion even more powerful than itself." Stefano opened his eyes to gaze at her. "Come to me," he commanded.

As if in a trance, Andra rose next to his bed, her eyes gently beholding a person who'd come to mean a great deal to her. She paused, knowing what he wanted her to do without his saying a word. Lowering the bedside rail, she carefully climbed onto the bed and stretched out beside him on top of his covers.

His arm encircled her body.

Andra laid her head upon Stefano's shoulder and snuggled close. She allowed him to take her right hand in his left, and he entwined his long fingers with hers.

"This is much better; I wanted to feel you next to me as I cleanse my soul." He lifted their fused hands and rotated them; his brow remained smooth as he contemplated their combined light-and-dark oneness. Momentarily, he broke their connection to open her hand and place it against his chest. "Do you feel my heart? You did that for me—taught it how to beat again."

Andra nodded against the thinness of his shoulder blade, shifting the slight bulge of her tummy to a more comfortable position. He slowly lifted his head, but after some effort, he allowed it to flop against the white pillow again.

"So how is my nephew doing? Is he treating his mother well?"

Andra graced him with a motherly smile. "Oh, he—or she—is kicking up a storm, giving me grief whenever possible. You know, like his uncle Stefano used to do."

"Good. I pray he—or she—will at least resemble his uncle. His presence will help you to remember me."

"Don't worry, big brother—me forgetting you will never happen."

Silent minutes went by before she felt his chest lift slightly in a sigh.

"Do you know Aphrodite is the Greek goddess of love, and depending upon how a man views her, she could be either his salvation or his curse? You, my sweet Aphrodite, were both to me."

Knowing Stefano didn't want her to say anything, she used soft, unintelligible murmurs to let him know she listened.

"Jayson is my brother, and I love him deeply. I would never do anything to hurt him. Yet despite my love for him, I could not fight against the power you had over me—and my love for you."

Andra closed her eyes against the potent pull of his words. She too loved Jayson, her sweet and caring husband—more than she could ever love another man. Still, she also knew there was a force—an invisible link—that continued to draw her to Stefano and vice versa.

"There were so many times when your allure got the better of me—it nearly overshadowed my allegiance to Jayson. It created a desire within me for you. But I am glad you stood for your marriage and for my brother, Aphrodite, even though it was to my great loss."

She opened her eyes, experiencing a profound measure of respect for him. "Stefano, why?"

"Why?"

"Why do you love me?"

Letting go of her hand, he enclosed her body within the complete circle of his arms. "Because Jayson made me see past your dark skin to the beautiful woman you truly are underneath." He coughed once. "But again, I believe I already knew. I was afraid to see it for myself."

She nodded.

"In the beginning, I tried to destroy your marriage to Jayson out of my own selfish motives." He exhaled with difficulty, causing Andra to gently pat his chest. The comforting action caused him to continue. "I believed I was doing what was right for the family. In the end, I was forced to admit the reason I wanted the marriage to end was that I wanted you for myself."

The soft ticking of the clock on the wall and vague, distant hospital sounds beyond the closed door were the only sounds as Stefano labored to breathe.

"Lately, I asked myself if I had to do it all over again, could I have resisted you out of my love for Jayson?" His head shook. "No, God help me, nothing would have changed. My feelings for you would still be so, despite my love for my baby brother. It is better this way that I go." His smile was slight and regretful. "It's all about love." At her quizzical expression, he sighed. "Life. Life isn't just about living; it is about loving. I found that out almost too late."

Andra nodded.

"Jayson loves you. And you love Jayson."

"Yes."

Stefano's eyes glistened in the dim hospital light. "My leaving this earth is the only way out for me—for all of us."

Andra shivered at his confession, causing Stefano's embrace, although weak, to tighten.

"I once believed Jayson had lost his philotimo."

"Philotimo?"

"Honor, integrity, duty, sacrifice." Stefano sighed shakily. "But it appears it was I who lost it."

"Seems to me you managed to find it again." Andra smiled encouragingly at Stefano and replaced her head on his chest.

Her doctor's hearing took in the faint death rattle inside his lungs.

"Before you came into my life, I was afraid to die—afraid to take my last breath without knowing what it was like to truly love a woman and to be loved. I had a void inside me after my mother passed. I was afraid my emptiness would follow me to all eternity. Now ..." He sighed, his breath catching in silent contemplation.

"Now?" she said, somewhat breathless herself. Andra waited in a few seconds of silence before she gathered the courage to lift her head once more.

His handsome face, quiet in repose, had a wide-eyed expression of pure peace.

In the darkness of the room, within the dim circle of light, the heart monitor beeped once only to produce the elongated flat-line beep signifying he was no longer with her.

Tearing up, Andra smiled wistfully. She then lifted her hand to gently place her fingers over his open eyelids.

She closed them in eternal rest just as Jayson stepped into the room.

EPILOGUE

D usk crept like a secret lover over the back vineyards. Andra stood watching the evening sky's colorful display of parting magnificence from their upstairs bedroom's veranda. A breeze floated by, lightly kissing her face and gently lifting her thick, curly mane. Reaching out to grip the bedroom balcony's railing, she tilted her head. Closing her eyes, she allowed the breeze's feather-like coolness to wash over her and refresh her dark skin.

She wore the floor-length white tunic Sly had given her as a belated wedding gift. The frock transformed her into a totally feminine being. She pretended to be a Greek goddess living decadently, for she wore no underwear beneath the light, flowing material, which left one shoulder bare. The rest of the fabric draped across her breasts to gather at her other shoulder, where a round gold medallion securely fastened the one-sided tunic.

Another cool breeze swept across the balcony to meet her, and as if it brought him with it, Andra felt her husband's presence behind her. As usual, she shivered from a combination of love and lust for him.

"You can tell me, you know," Jayson said softly. She heard him shift uncertainly in the darkness. "You loved him, didn't you?"

Andra's grip on the balcony rail tightened. Not wanting to face him yet, she looked off into the rapidly diminishing sunlight on the horizon, attempting to hold back the various thoughts rushing at her from different parts of her brain.

She exhaled softly.

The purple, pink, and blue sky beyond the spacious porch shone vibrantly against her searching pupils, its beauty so intense she had to blink in order to take in the fading sight of the distant snowcapped mountain.

It was the mountain she'd planned on one day climbing, even if she could only make it a few miles upward.

Andra deliberated how to answer him. She knew a man's ego, once tampered with, could most times be damaged beyond repair, especially when it came to the idea of another man, even if said man was a brother—and a deceased one to boot.

Arranging her face into perfect placidity, Andra turned around. She floated as if on a cloud as she walked toward him, her long skirt flowing and parting on one side with each step. Upon entering his arms, she had never felt more alive in her life.

"You know I love you and that you're the only one for me, right?" Her face inches from his, she immediately tightened her embrace at his silence. "Right, Pastor?"

It was Jayson's turn to stare off at the darkening horizon, his expression troubled. "But Stefano—"

Andra lifted a hand and gently nudged his face back toward hers. "Stefano was your brother—and I loved him because of it." She managed to hold his gaze steady with hers, even though she knew they both wanted to turn away. "Yes, I must admit that in the beginning, it was rocky between your brother and me, but I believe he came to accept me for the person I am, not what he had perceived me to be. Thanks to you."

Breaking from his stare, Andra withdrew, pivoted, and retraced her steps back to the balcony, her eyes once again straining to see the distant mountain she one day hoped to conquer. She hesitated before continuing.

"And yes, with his new perception grew a fondness between us—one I hope honors you as much as it honored him."

"But you were there, lying beside him in his bed as he drew his last breath."

Hurt entwined his words, crushing them in its powerful grip.

Andra paused and softly exhaled. "He needed someone there with him, close, so he wouldn't feel alone. Other than the nurse, he was alone. I wanted to do that for him—for you." She glanced over her shoulder at him. "Would you have not wanted me—or anyone else—to do that for your beloved older brother?"

Jayson closed the distance between them. Slipping both arms around her waist, he possessively placed both hands over her growing baby bump. As he gently massaged her round tummy, Andra allowed her body to lean against his. She experienced the pressure of his chin as it rested atop the round medallion pin on her shoulder.

His sigh was great, as if he released a great heaviness from his soul.

"Yes, baby, of course I would," he said, turning her body inside his embrace. "You know, I have to say, what you and your family did for my family was a miracle. You guys brought us back to life—my father, Stefano, and me. I fear my brother had become a walking corpse before you entered his world. I'm glad you were able to resurrect him before he ..."

Tenderly, Andra placed a comforting palm against her husband's trembling cheek, hoping to convey a sense of peace and calm. It worked.

At first, he looked embarrassed, but then his face broke out in a brave smile. "Before he passed."

Andra pondered the family events that had taken place since Stefano's funeral. Upon Stefano's admittance to the hospital, he, George, and Jayson had agreed not to take on any investors. Instead, they'd taken out a simple-interest business loan through the bank to finance their olive grove infusion project, ensuring their company would always and forevermore remain within the family.

Although Papa George had refused any monies offered from Hog's estate, Andra had privately set aside a good-sized portion of it as collateral against the bank's loan just in case.

Her thoughts of family automatically ran toward Racine, who, at Papa George's insistence, had decided to stay in Athens and attend college there. She mentally shook her head as Racine's newly acquired best friend, Sly, popped inside her brain. After experiencing a short grieving period over Stefano's death, the Grecian beauty had decided to join Racine on her academic road to betterment.

The two, now like a pair of irregular peas in a pod, had even talked about getting a dorm room together.

Good luck with that.

Then there was Paulo. He'd recovered well from his head injury courtesy of Hog, but from time to time, he experienced spasms over one eye or in his hands. Despite his head injury, he was still as handsome and charming as ever, and he'd finally decided to settle down in matrimonial bliss, wisely choosing a healthy and vibrant girl from the village who viewed his eye spasms as "macho sexy," as she giggly put it.

Just then, Andra's thoughts turned to her mother. Currently, she and Papa George were on their way back to the States to sell Al's house and get her situated in order for her to return to Greece. Andra marveled at how much Mama and Papa George's friendship had grown—and where it might eventually lead. Knowing her mother, if George allowed Al to have her way—which, by the looks of it, he already had—they would do a lot of traveling.

The family's come a long way.

Coming back to the here and now, Andra heard the sound of soft flight. Drawing in a wondrous breath, she glanced upward in time to behold a striking white-winged dove sail gracefully overhead. The bird's silent ascent added to its beauty, and she parted her mouth in awe.

Jayson stirred behind her. She stiffened at his next words.

"You know, when I found out Stefano had called you Aphrodite, I didn't know if I could contain my jealousy," he said. He immediately soothed her tenseness by kissing the small of her neck. "Yet despite the fact that he said it, I have to admit he was right. You *are* Aphrodite—my own personal seductive, lovely temptress—and I'm blessed to have you for my wife."

Relieved, Andra grinned as he bent to whisper conspiratorially in her ear.

"And I would die a thousand deaths, go down with a thousand ships, just to keep you by my side, my beautiful Aphrodite."

"You know what your brother told me before he went to be with the Lord? He said life is for loving." Andra stood on her tiptoes to give Jayson a brief, tender kiss. "And I'll be darned if I'm not gonna do just that."

Stepping from Jayson's embrace, Andra captured his gaze as she lifted her graceful hands and unpinned her shoulder medallion. Her flowing white tunic parted to land in a quiet whisper at her feet. Against the moonlit backdrop, her breasts—swollen due to her nesting fetus—pushed forth hardened nipples in declaration of her love, lust, and craziness for him.

Her smile was both seductive and wicked, and her voice was low yet distinct. "Well, my handsome husband, can you hear my body's siren calling yours?"

Jayson froze as if he were a Greek sculpture from ancient days of old. Only his head and eyes moved; they followed her as she rounded his motionless form. Andra threw a saucy glance over her shoulder and disappeared inside the dark bedroom.

Only after the darkness swallowed her did he awaken from his lust-filled stupor to eagerly follow his goddess into the night.